PRAISE FOR

MISS BENSON'S BEETLE

"I fell in love with these characters—as unforgettable and unlikely a pair as Thelma and Louise. Their devotion to each other as they trek up and down mountains halfway around the world is a hysterical delight. This novel made me realize how hungry I am for stories about women loving each other into being their best selves. Many thanks to Rachel Joyce for writing one."

—ANN NAPOLITANO, *New York Times* bestselling author of *Dear Edward*

"A beautifully written, extraordinary quest in which two ordinary, overlooked women embark on an unlikely scientific expedition to the South Seas. A gripping tale of adventure and friendship, told from the subversive and often hilarious female view."

—HELEN SIMONSON, *New York Times* bestselling author of *Major Pettigrew's Last Stand*

"*Miss Benson's Beetle* is a pure joyride. Sweet, witty, poignant, filled with intrigue and unlikely friendship, it's a perfect escape. I loved it."

—LISA WINGATE, #1 *New York Times* bestselling author of *Before We Were Yours*

"For *Eleanor Oliphant* fans, *Miss Benson's Beetle* is pure gold—full of complex, memorable women, plot twists, and a deft balance of hilarity and emotion, it's a book you'll stay up late to finish."

—J. RYAN STRADAL, bestselling author of *The Lager Queen of Minnesota*

"Whatever you may look for in a novel—adventure, fully realized characters, humor, poignancy, a chance to learn something new—is all here in *Miss Benson's Beetle*. What's also here is the particular grace and humanity that Rachel Joyce brings to her work. She reminds us that we all are broken in one way or another, but that we are capable—oftentimes in unexpected ways—of helping to make ourselves and others whole. This beautifully written novel is an absolute delight."

—ELIZABETH BERG, *New York Times* bestselling author of *The Story of Arthur Truluv*

"So fast-paced and fun it'll make you remember why you loved reading in the first place. *Miss Benson's Beetle* has everything: adventure, mystery, and the greatest, most unlikely friendship, all rendered in some of the most beautiful, enchanting prose you'll ever read. It's full of humor, pathos, and insight, extolling the virtues of love, acceptance, and hard-won self-discovery—all that gleams about the human spirit. It'll capture you right at the beginning and hold you tight the whole way through. This book is a pure and serious joy."

—PAULA SAUNDERS, author of *The Distance Home*

"Exciting, moving and full of unexpected turns . . . [This is] Rachel Joyce's best novel yet."

—*The Times* (UK)

"A joy of a novel, with real insight into the lives of women, the value of friendship and the lasting effects of war."

—*The Guardian*

"Joyce's characters are so charmingly eccentric that they could have leapt straight from the pages of a Dickens novel. Enid is a comedic masterpiece, effervescent and brimming with life. This exhilarating story will scoop you up and carry you along to a dizzying crescendo. But it is also a story of an unlikely friendship and of women who refuse to be defined by the labels cast upon them. . . . Funny, wise, and utterly life-affirming."

"Rachel Joyce created an unforgettable character in Harold Fry and she's done it again with Margery Benson. . . . Hilarious."

"A hilarious jaunt into the wilderness of women's friendship and the triumph of outrageous dreams."

BY RACHEL JOYCE

Miss Benson's Beetle

The Music Shop

A Snow Garden and Other Stories

The Love Song of Miss Queenie Hennessy

Perfect

The Unlikely Pilgrimage of Harold Fry

MISS
BENSON'S
BEETLE

MISS BENSON'S BEETLE

A Novel

RACHEL JOYCE

THE DIAL PRESS
NEW YORK

2020 Dial Press Trade Paperback Edition

Published in the United States by The Dial Press, an imprint of Random House, a division of Penguin Random House LLC, New York.

Originally published in hardcover in the United Kingdom by Doubleday, an imprint of Transworld Publishers, a division of Penguin Random House UK, in 2020.

THE DIAL PRESS is a registered trademark and the colophon is a trademark of Penguin Random House LLC.

LIBRARY OF CONGRESS CATALOGING-IN-PUBLICATION DATA
Names: Joyce, Rachel, author.
Title: Miss Benson's beetle / Rachel Joyce.
Description: New York: Dial Press, [2020]
Identifiers: LCCN 2020006856 (print) | LCCN 2020006857 (ebook) |
ISBN 9780812996708 (paperback) | ISBN 9780812996715 (ebook)
Classification: LCC PR6110.O98 M57 2020 (print) |
LCC PR6110.O98 (ebook) | DDC 823/.92—dc23
LC record available at https://lccn.loc.gov/2020006856
LC ebook record available at https://lccn.loc.gov/2020006857

Printed in the United States of America on acid-free paper

randomhousebooks.com

2 4 6 8 9 7 5 3 1

Book design by Caroline Cunningham
Title-page and part-title ornament: border with palm
leaves: iStock/Andrea_Hill
Map by Neil Gower
Photograph on page 347 © Society of Antiquaries
of London (Kelmscott Manor)

This one is for you, Nell and Susan.

Seek and you will find. What is unsought will go undetected.

SOPHOCLES

Somehow, in the process of trying to deny that things are always changing, we lose our sense of the sacredness of life. We tend to forget that we are part of the natural scheme of things.

PEMA CHÖDRÖN

MISS
BENSON'S
BEETLE

1

The Golden Beetle
of New Caledonia, 1914

When Margery was ten, she fell in love with a beetle.

It was a bright summer's day, and all the windows of the rectory were open. She had an idea about sailing her wooden animals across the floor, two by two, but the set had belonged to her brothers once, and most of them were either colored in or broken. Some were even missing altogether. She was wondering if, under the circumstances, you could pair a three-legged camel and a bird with spots when her father came out of his study.

"Do you have a moment, old girl?" he said. "There's something I want to show you."

So she put down the camel and the bird, and she followed him. She would have stood on her head if he'd asked.

Her father went to his desk. He sat there, nodding and smiling. She could tell he didn't have a proper reason for calling her: he just wanted her to be with him for a while. Since her four brothers had left for war, he often called her. Or she'd find him loitering at the foot of the stairs, searching for something without seeming to know what it was. His eyes were the kindest in the world, and the bald top of his head gave him a naked look.

"I think I have something that might interest you, old girl," he said. "Nothing much, but maybe you will like it."

At this point he would normally produce something he'd found in the garden, but instead he opened a book called *Incredible Creatures*. It looked important, like the Bible or an encyclopedia, and there was a general smell of old things, but that could well have been him. Margery stood at his side, trying hard not to fidget.

The first page was a painted illustration of a man. He had a normal face and normal arms but, where his legs should have been, a green mermaid tail. She was amazed. The next picture was just as strange. A squirrel like one in the garden, but this had wings. And it went on, page after page, one incredible creature after another.

"Well, well, look," her father kept saying. "Well, now, goodness me. Look at this chap, Margery."

"Are they real?"

"They might be."

"Are they in a zoo?"

"Oh, no, dear heart. If these creatures live, they've not been found. There are people who believe they exist, but they haven't caught them yet so they can't prove it."

She had no idea what he was talking about. Until that moment she'd assumed everything in the world was already found. It had never occurred to her things might happen in reverse. That you could see a picture of something in a book—that you could as good as imagine it—and then go off and look.

Her father showed her the Himalayan yeti, the Loch Ness Monster, the Patagonian giant sloth. There was the Irish elk with antlers as big as wings. The South African quagga, which started as a zebra until it ran out of stripes and became a horse. The great auk, the lion-tailed monkey, the Queensland tiger. So many incredible extra creatures in the world, and nobody had found a single one of them.

"Do you think they're real?" she said.

Her father nodded. "I have begun to feel comforted," he said, "by the thought of all we do not know, which is nearly everything."

With that upside-down piece of wisdom, he turned another page. "Ah!"

He pointed at a speck. A beetle.

Well, how nothing this was. How small and ordinary. She couldn't see what it was doing in a book of *Incredible Creatures,* never mind whether it was not yet found. It was the sort of thing she would tread on and not notice.

He told her the head of a beetle was called the head, the middle was the thorax, and the bottom half was the abdomen. Beetles had two pairs of wings—did she know that? One delicate set that did the actual flying, and another hardened pair to protect the first. There were more kinds of beetle on God's Earth than any other species, and they were each unique in remarkable ways.

"It looks a bit plain," she said. Margery had heard her aunts call her plain. Not her brothers, though. They were as handsome as horses.

"Ah! But look!"

He turned to the next page, and her insides gave a lurch.

Here the beetle was again, magnified about twenty times. And she had been wrong. She had been so wrong, she could hardly believe her eyes. Close up, that small plain thing was not plain, not one bit. Oval in shape and gold all over, it was incandescent. Gold head, gold thorax, gold abdomen. Even its tiny legs were gold, as if Nature had taken a bit of jewelry and made an insect instead. It was infinitely more glorious than a man with a tail.

"The golden beetle of New Caledonia," said her father. "Imagine how it would be to find this one and bring it home."

Before she could ask more, there was a ring on the outside bell and he eased himself to his feet. He closed the door gently behind him, as if it had feelings, and left her alone with the beetle. She reached out her finger to touch it.

"All?" she heard him say from the hall. "What? All?"

Until now, Margery hadn't shared her father's love of insects—he was often in the garden with a sweep net, but it was more the sort of thing he would have done with her brothers. Yet, as her finger met the golden beetle, something happened: a spark seemed to fly out and her future opened. She went hot and cold. She would find the beetle. It was that simple. She would go to wherever New Caledonia was, and bring it home. She actually felt struck, as if the top of her head had been knocked off. Already she could see herself leading the way on a mule while an assistant carried her bags at the rear.

But when the Reverend Tobias Benson returned, he didn't seem to remember anything about the beetle, let alone Margery. He walked slowly to the desk and riffled through papers, picking them up and putting them down, as if none of them were the things they should have been. He lifted a paperweight, then a pen, and afterward he stowed the paperweight back where the pen had been, while the pen he seemed to have no clue about. It was possible he had completely forgotten what a pen was for. He just stared, while tears fell from his eyes like string.

"All of them?" he said. "What? All?"

He took something from the drawer and stepped through the French windows, and before Margery realized what had happened, he'd shot himself.

ADVENTURE!

2

What Are You Doing with My New Boots?

Miss Benson had begun to notice that a funny note was going around her classroom. It had started at the back and was now heading toward the middle.

The laughter had been quiet at first, but now it was all the more obvious for being stifled: one girl had hiccups and another was practically purple. But she didn't stop her lesson. She dealt with the note the way she always dealt with them, and that was by pretending it wasn't there. If anything, she spoke louder. The girls carried on, passing the note from one to the next, and she carried on telling them how to make a cake in wartime.

In fact, the Second World War was over—it had been over for five years—but rationing wasn't. Meat was rationed, butter was rationed; so were lard and margarine. Sugar was rationed. Tea was rationed. Cheese, coal, soap, sweets. All still rationed. The cuffs of her jacket were worn to thread, and her only pair of shoes was so old they squelched in rain. If she took them to be mended, she'd have no choice but to sit there in her stockings, waiting for them to be ready, so she just kept wearing them and they kept falling apart. Streets were lined with broken buildings—rooms with whole walls gone, sometimes a lightbulb left hanging or even a lavatory chain—

and gardens were still turned over to useful British vegetables. Old newspapers were piled in bomb sites. Men hung around on street corners in demob suits that had once belonged to someone else, while women queued for hours to get a fatty bit of bacon. You could go miles on the bus and not see a flower. Or blue sky. What she wouldn't give for blue sky—even that seemed rationed. People kept saying this was a new beginning, but every day was more of the same. Queues. Cold. Smog. Sometimes she felt she'd lived her entire life on scraps.

By now the note had reached the second row. Splutters. Titters. Much shaking of shoulders. She was explaining how to line a cake tin when someone nudged a girl in the front row, and the note was pushed into the hands of Wendy Thompson. Wendy was a sickly girl who had the constant look of someone expecting the worst—even if you were nice to her, she still looked terrified—so it came as a shock when she opened the note and honked. That was it. The girls were off, and this time they weren't even trying not to. If they carried on, the whole school would hear.

Margery put down her chalk. The laughter fell away, bit by bit, as they realized she was watching. It was sink or swim, she'd been told once. Don't try to be their friend. These girls are not your friends. There was an art teacher who'd given up after a week. "They hum," she'd wept in the staff room, "and when I ask who is humming, they look straight at me and say, 'No one is humming, Miss.' You have to be half dead to work here."

Margery stepped down from the wooden platform. She held out her hand. "Give me the note, please, Wendy."

Wendy sat with her head bowed, like a frightened rabbit. Girls in the back row exchanged a glance. Other than that, no one moved.

"I just want to know what is so funny, Wendy. Maybe we can all enjoy the joke."

At this point Margery had no intention of reading the note. She certainly had no intention of enjoying the joke. She was just going to open it, drop it into the bin, and after that she was going to clamber back onto the platform and finish her lesson. It was almost break time. There would be hot tea in the staff room, and a selection of biscuits.

"The note?" she said.

Wendy handed it over so slowly it would have been quicker to send it by post. "Oh, I wouldn't, Miss," she said quietly.

Margery took the paper. She opened it. Silence unspooled itself like ribbon.

What she had in her hand was not the usual. It wasn't a joke. It wasn't even a few words about how dull the lesson was. It was a sketch. It was a carefully executed cartoon sketch of a lumpy old woman, and this lumpy old woman was clearly Margery. The baggy suit was hers, and there was no mistaking the shoes. They were planks on the ends of two large legs—you could even see a toe poking out. Her nose the girls had done as a potato, while her hair was a mad bird's nest. The girls had also given her a mustache—and not a stylish mustache but a short, stubby one like Hitler's. At the top, someone had written, *"The Virgin Margery!"*

Margery's breathing reversed itself. There seemed not to be enough room for the mix of hurt and anger swelling inside her. She wanted to say, she actually wanted to shout, "How dare you? I am not this woman. I am not." But she couldn't. Instead she kept very still, hoping for one irrational moment that the whole business would go away and never come back, if she just stayed where she was, doing absolutely nothing. Then someone giggled. Another coughed.

"Who did this?" she said. In her distress, her voice came out oddly thin. It was difficult to shape air into those exact sounds.

No reply.

But she was in this now. She threatened the class with extra homework. She said they'd miss afternoon break. She even warned she'd fetch the deputy, and everyone was terrified of the woman. One of the few times she'd ever been seen to laugh was when Margery had once shut her own skirt in the door, and got stuck. ("I've never seen anything so hilarious," the deputy said afterward. "You looked like a bear in a trap.") None of it worked. The girls sat there, resolutely silent, eyes lowered, a bit pink in the face, as the bell went for afternoon break and outside the corridors began to swell, like a river, with feet and noise. And the fact they refused to apologize or name who was responsible—not even Wendy Thompson buckled—left Margery feeling even more alone, and even more absurd. She dropped the note into the bin but it was still there. It seemed to be part of the air itself.

"This lesson is over," she said, in what she hoped was a dignified tone. Then she picked up her handbag and left.

She was barely on the other side of the door when the laughter came. "Wendy, you champion!" the girls roared. Margery made her way past the physics lab and the history department, and she didn't even know where she was going anymore. She just had to breathe. Girls crowded her path, barking like gulls. All she could hear was laughter. She tried the exit to the playing field but it was locked, and she couldn't use the main door because that was for visitors only, strictly not to be used by staff. The assembly hall? No. It was filled with girls in vests and knickers, doing a wafty sort of dance with flags. She was beginning to fear she'd be stuck there forever. She passed the display of school trophies, bumped into a box of sports bibs, and almost went flying over a fire extinguisher. The staff room, she said to herself. I will be safe in the staff room.

Margery was a big woman. She knew that. And she'd let herself go over the years. She knew that, too. She'd been tall and thin when she was a girl, just like her brothers, and she also had their bright blue eyes. She'd even worn their hand-me-downs. It had been a source of pain—not so much the hand-me-downs, but definitely the height—and she'd learned to stoop at an early age. But being big, actually A Big Person, had only happened when her monthlies stopped. The weight piled on, the same as her mother, causing a pain in her hip that took her by surprise sometimes and made her limp. What she hadn't realized was that she'd become the school joke.

The staff room was too hot and smelled of gravy and old cardigans. No one said hello or smiled as she entered; they were mostly snoring. The deputy stood in the corner, a wry, spry woman in a pleated skirt, with a box of drawing pins in her hand as she checked the staff notice board. Margery couldn't get round the feeling that everyone knew about the sketch and that they, too, were laughing— even in their sleep. She poured a cup of not quite warm tea from the urn, took what was left of the biscuits, and made her way to a chair. Someone had left a pair of new lacrosse boots on the seat, so she put them on the floor and flumped down.

"Those boots are mine," called the deputy, not looking over.

Outside, the fog made smudges of the trees, sucking them to nothing; the grass was more brown than green. Twenty years she'd lost, doing this job, and she didn't even like cookery. She'd applied as a last resort. "Single women only," the advertisement had said. She thought again of the cartoon sketch. The care the girls had taken to poke fun at her terrible hair, her broken shoes, her threadbare old suit. It hurt. And the reason it hurt so much was that they were right. The girls were right. Even to herself, most of all to herself, Margery was a joke.

After school she would go home to her flat, which—despite her aunts' heavy furniture—was empty and cold. She would wait for the cage elevator that never came because people were always forgetting to close the door properly and, in the end, she would plod up the stairs to the fourth floor. She would make a meal with whatever she could find, she would wash up and put things away, then later take an aspirin and read herself to sleep, and no one would know. That was the truth—she could skip a few chapters, or eat everything in her flat in one sitting—and not only would no one notice, but it would make no difference to the world if they did. Weekends and school holidays were even worse. Whole days could pass with barely a word spoken to another human being. She spread out her chores, but there was a limit to how many times you could change a library book without beginning to look homeless. A picture came to her of a beetle in a killing jar, dying slowly.

Margery's hand reached to the floor. It put down the teacup and was round the deputy's lacrosse boots before her head knew anything about it. They were large and black. Solid, too. With thick ridges on the sole for extra grip. She got up.

"Miss Benson," called the deputy. "Excuse me? What are you doing with my new boots?"

It was a fair question, and Margery had no idea of the answer. Her body seemed to have taken charge. She walked past the deputy and the tea urn and the other members of staff—who, she knew even without turning round, had all stirred from sleep and were watching, bewildered, open-mouthed—and she left the staff room with the boots under one arm and her handbag under the other. She pushed her way through a crowd of girls, and found herself hurrying toward the main vestibule.

"Miss Benson?" she heard. "Miss Benson?"

But what was she doing now? It was bad enough to pick up someone else's boots and walk off, but her hands had decided to take things a whole stage further. As if to compensate for the deadliness she felt inside, they were grabbing items indiscriminately. A silver trophy, the bundle of sports bibs, even the fire extinguisher. She was in something terrible, and instead of saying sorry and putting it all back, she was making the whole business a thousand times worse. She passed the headmistress's study. The locked door to the playing field. She marched right into the main vestibule—which she knew—everybody knew—was strictly not to be used by staff and was hung with portraits of old headmistresses, all of whom were definitely virgins.

The deputy was on her trail and getting closer by the second. "Miss Benson? Miss Benson!"

It took three goes to open the main door, and she could barely keep hold of everything. The fire extinguisher, for instance, was far heavier than she'd expected. Like carting off a small child.

"Miss Benson. How dare you?"

Swinging back the door, she lumbered through in time to turn and glimpse the deputy's face, white and rigid, so close the woman could have grabbed Margery by the hair. She slammed the door. The deputy screamed. She had a terrible feeling she'd hurt the deputy's hand. She also had a feeling it would be good to accelerate, but her body had done enough already and wanted to lie down. Worse, there were more people on her heels. A few teachers, even a cluster of excited girls. She had no choice but to keep running. Her lungs were burning, her legs felt wonky, her hip was beginning to throb. As she staggered past the tennis courts, she found the world had begun to revolve. She ditched the fire extinguisher, netball trophy, and sports bibs, and got to the main gate. As the number seven rose smoothly over the brow of the hill, she hobbled toward the bus stop as fast as her great big legs would carry her, the boots clamped beneath her arm like an unwilling pet.

"Don't think you'll get away with this!" she heard. The bus stopped ahead of Margery. Freedom was in sight.

But just at the moment she should have launched herself to safety, shock set in and her body froze. Nothing would work. The conductor rang the bell, the bus began to roll away and would have left her behind, were it not for the quick thinking of two passengers who grabbed her by the lapels and yanked upward. Margery clung to the pole, unable to speak, barely able to see, as the bus carried her away from the school. She had never done a wrong thing in her life. She'd never stolen anything, apart from—once— a man's handkerchief. And yet her head was buzzing, her heart was kicking, and the hairs were standing up on the back of her neck. All she could think of was a place called New Caledonia.

The next morning, she placed an ad in *The Times*: "*Wanted. French-speaking assistant for expedition to other side of the world. All expenses paid.*"

3

A Really Stupid Woman

Something had happened to Margery the day her father showed her his book of incredible creatures. She didn't even know how to explain. It was like being given something to carry that she was never able to put down. One day, she had said to herself, I will find the golden beetle of New Caledonia and bring it home. And somehow also with this promise came another—far more oblique—that her father would be so happy and pleased that he, too, would come home. If not physically, then at least metaphorically.

But New Caledonia was a French archipelago in the South Pacific. Between Britain and New Caledonia, there were over ten thousand miles, and most of them sea. It would take five weeks by ship to Australia, another six hours on a flying boat; that was just getting there. The main island was long and thin: roughly 250 miles in length and only 25 wide, shaped like a rolling pin, with a mountain chain running from top to bottom. She would need to get to the far north and rent a bungalow as base camp. After that, there would be weeks of climbing. Cutting a path through rainforest, searching on hands and knees. Sleeping in a hammock, lugging her gear on her back, not to mention the bites and the heat. You might as well say you were off to the moon.

Years ago, Margery had collected things that reminded her of what she loved, and kept her true. A beetle necklace, a map of New Caledonia, an illustrated pocket guide to the islands by the Reverend Horace Blake. She'd made important discoveries about the beetle: its possible size, shape, and habitat. She'd made plans. But suddenly she'd stopped. Or, rather, life had. Life had stopped. And even though she occasionally found her eye caught by something that, at a distance, looked like a piece of gold and turned out to be trash, she had abandoned all hope of getting to New Caledonia. So this time she would do it. She would go in search of the beetle that had not yet been found—either before someone else went and found it first, or before she was too old to get onto a boat. Next year she would be forty-seven. And while that didn't make her old, it made her more old than young. Certainly too old to have a child. Her own mother had died at forty-six, while her brothers hadn't made it to their midtwenties. Already she felt her time was running out.

No one, of course, would think it was a good idea. Margery wasn't even a proper collector for a start. She knew how to kill a beetle and pin it, but she'd never worked in a museum. She didn't have a passport. She couldn't speak a word of French. And who would go all that way for a tiny insect that might not be there? Margery wrote to the Royal Entomological Society, asking if they would kindly fund her trip, and they kindly wrote back and said they wouldn't. Her doctor said an expedition to the other side of the world might kill her, while her bank manager warned she didn't have enough funds. Also, she was a lady.

"Thank you," said Margery. It was possibly the nicest thing anyone had said to her in years.

Four people replied to her ad: a widow, a retired teacher, a demobbed soldier, and a woman called Enid Pretty. Enid Pretty had spilled tea over her letter—it wasn't really a letter, more of a shopping list—while her spelling verged on distressing. Enid said she wanted to *"Liv life and see the worlb!"* After that she'd put carrots, and a few other things she needed, including powbered egg and string. Margery wrote to all of them except Enid Pretty, explaining briefly about the beetle and inviting them for tea at Lyons Corner House, where she would be dressed in brown and holding her pocket guide to New Caledonia. She suggested midafternoon in the hope she wouldn't have to fork out for a full meal, and Wednesday because it was cheaper midweek. She was on a tight budget.

There was also a letter from the school. The headmistress skipped lightly over the matter of the fire extinguisher and the sports bibs but requested the immediate return of the deputy's lacrosse boots. Now that Margery was in the business of taking other people's footwear, she was no longer required to teach domestic science.

The wildness Margery had felt that afternoon was gone, and all she felt now was wobbly panic. What had possessed her to steal a pair of boots? She hadn't just walked out of her job; she'd walked out and made it impossible to go back. As soon as she'd got home, she'd stuffed the boots beneath the mattress where she couldn't see them, but it isn't easy hiding something from yourself—ideally you need to be out of the room when you do it—and she could as easily forget the boots as her own two feet. She had spent several days barely daring to move. She thought, That's it. I'll get rid of them. I'll send them back on my way to Lyons. But the postmistress insisted on knowing what was inside the parcel, and Margery lost her nerve. Then, as she was walking away, the heavens opened and one of her old brown shoes split apart. In effect, she was wearing a flap on her foot. Oh, to hell with this, she thought.

She put on the boots.

New problem. Lyons Corner House was busier than she'd expected, even on a Wednesday afternoon. Every single woman in London had come out for tea, and they had all decided to wear brown. She had a table by the window, along with her guidebook and a list of questions, but her mouth was as dry as a flannel. She could barely speak.

"Miss Benson?"

She jumped. Her first applicant was already at her side. She hadn't even noticed him approach. He was tall, like her, but without an ounce of flesh on him, and his head was shaved so close she could see the white of his skin. His demob suit hung loose.

"Mr. Mundic," he said.

Margery had never been what people called a man's woman, but then again, she hadn't been much of a woman's woman, either. She put out her hand, only she paused, and Mundic ducked to sit so that—like a dance that had already gone wrong—by the time her hand reached him he was halfway to his chair and instead of greeting him like any normal person, she poked him rather forcefully in the ear.

"Do you like to travel, Mr. Mundic?" she asked, consulting a notebook for her first question.

He said he did. He'd been posted in Burma. Prisoner of war. He pulled out his passport.

It was shocking. The photograph was of a great big man in his late twenties with a beard and wavy hair, and the one opposite was more of a walking corpse. His eyes were too big for his face, and his bones seemed ready to burst out of him. He was nervous, too: he couldn't meet her eyes, his hands were shaking. In fact, his hands were the only part of him that seemed to belong to the man in the photograph. They were the size of paddles.

Politely, Margery steered the conversation to the beetle. She took out her map of New Caledonia, so old the folds were transparent. She pointed to the biggest of the islands—long and thin, the shape of a rolling pin. "Grande Terre," she said, speaking very clearly because something about Mr. Mundic suggested he was struggling to understand. She marked the northern tip of the island with a cross. "I believe the beetle will be here."

She hoped he might display some enthusiasm. Just a smile would have been nice. Instead, he rubbed his hands. "There will be snakes," he said.

Did Margery laugh? She didn't mean to. It came out by accident: she was as nervous as he was. But Mr. Mundic didn't laugh. He flashed a look of defiance at her and then dropped his gaze back to the table, where he kept twisting his fingers and pulling at them as if he wanted to take them off.

Margery explained you didn't get snakes in New Caledonia. And while they were on the subject of animals you didn't get, there were no crocodiles, poisonous spiders, or vultures. There were some quite big lizards and cockroaches, and a not-very-nice sea snake, but that was about it.

No one, she said, had ever caught a gold soft-winged flower beetle. Most people didn't believe they were real. There were gold scarabs, and carabids, but no collection contained a gold flower beetle. To find one would be really something. It would be small, about the size of a ladybug, but slimmer in shape. Lowering her voice, she leaned close. Since making up her mind to find it, she was convinced everyone else was looking, too, even those people currently enjoying tea and meat pies in Lyons Corner House. Besides, there were private collectors who would pay a small fortune for a beetle that had not yet been found.

She followed with her evidence. First, a letter from Charles Darwin to his friend Alfred Russel Wallace, in which he (Darwin!) mentioned a rumor about a beetle like a gilded raindrop. Then there was a missionary, who described in his journal a mountain with the shape of a blunt wisdom tooth where he'd come across a beetle so small and gold, he'd fallen to his knees and prayed. There had even been a near miss for an orchid collector searching at high altitude: he'd seen a flash of gold but couldn't get to his sweep net in time. All of them referred to the island Grande Terre in New Caledonia, but if the missionary was right, and the orchid collector was right, the beetle had to be in the north. Besides, collectors in the past had always stayed south, or on the coast, where the terrain was less dangerous and they felt safest.

As far as science was concerned, the beetle didn't yet exist because nothing existed until it had been presented to the Natural

History Museum, described, and given its Latin name. So she would need to bring home three pairs of specimens, correctly pinned, and if they were damaged in any way, they'd be useless. She would also need detailed drawings and notebooks. "I would like the beetle to be named after my father. Benson's Beetle. *Dicranolaius bensoni*," she said.

But Mr. Mundic didn't seem bothered by what anyone called it. He didn't seem that bothered about the beetle. He skipped right from the bit where she told him about the job to the bit where he accepted, without the vital bit in the middle where she made the offer. Yes, he would lead Margery's expedition. He would carry a gun to defend her from savages, and kill wild pig for her to cook on the campfire. He asked what date they would be leaving.

Margery swallowed. Mr. Mundic clearly had a screw loose. She reminded him she was looking for a beetle. This was 1950: there was no need for guns, and New Caledonia was not an island of savages. Fifty thousand American troops had been safely posted there during the war. As well as French cafés and shops, you could now find hamburger restaurants and milkshake bars. According to the Reverend Horace Blake—and she lifted her guidebook as if it were the Bible—the only things Margery needed were gifts like confectionary and zippers, and as for food, she'd be taking her own British supplies in packets and tins.

"Are you telling me I'm not man enough to lead this expedition?" Mr. Mundic slammed his fist on the table, narrowly missing the salt and pepper. "Are you saying you can do it without me?"

Suddenly he was on his feet. It was as though a switch had flicked inside him. She had no idea what she'd done. He was shouting, and little balls of spittle were shooting from his mouth. He was telling Margery she was a stupid woman. He was telling her she'd get lost in the rainforest and die in a hole.

Mr. Mundic grabbed his passport and left. Despite his height, he looked small, with his hair too short and his suit too big, his bony hands balled into fists; he was pushing past the waitresses in their little white hats and the diners politely waiting to be seated as if he hated every one of them.

He was a casualty of war, and Margery had no idea how to help.

Her second applicant, the widow, was early, which was good, and wanted only a glass of water—even better. But she thought Margery meant Caledonia, as in Scotland. No, said Margery. She meant New Caledonia, as in the Other Side of the World.

That was the end of the interview.

By now Margery was struggling to keep her nerve. Of her four original applicants, the first, Enid Pretty, had eliminated herself before she'd even started; Mr. Mundic needed help; the third had left after three minutes. She was beginning to think the expedition of her lifetime was already over when the retired teacher arrived. Miss Hamilton strode through the teahouse wearing a raincoat that could happily have doubled as a curtain, while her skirt was elasticated at the waist and a practical shade of gravy brown to hide all stains. She also had a beard—not a substantial one, but more than a few sprouty hairs. Margery liked her immediately. She waved to Miss Hamilton, and Miss Hamilton waved back.

Margery had barely told her about the beetle before Miss Hamilton whipped out a notebook and began her own set of questions, some of which she spoke in French. Was Margery interested in butterflies? (No. Only beetles. She hoped to bring home many specimens.) How long would the expedition take? (Five and a half months, including travel.) Had she rented a hut as base camp? (Not yet.) The interview was entirely upside-down. Nevertheless, Margery was thrilled. It was like meeting a new and improved version of herself, without the nerves and also in a foreign language. Only when Miss Hamilton asked about her job did Margery panic. She gave the name of the school and changed the subject. She even shoved her feet under her chair—not that Miss Hamilton would have known about the boots, but guilt is not logical.

"You don't need one of these blond hussies as your assistant," said Miss Hamilton, just as a blond hussy conveniently clip-clopped past the window. "What did any of those young women do for the war effort but lie on their backs with their legs open? Family?"

"I'm sorry?"

"What is your background?"

"I was brought up by two aunts."

"Siblings?"

"My four brothers were killed on the same day at Mons."

"Your parents?"

"Also gone."

Margery had to pause. The truth about her father was a crater with KEEP OUT! signs all round it. She never went close. Her mother's death had been different. Maybe because it came while she'd been dozing in her chair, and even though Margery had found her, it hadn't been a shock. Her mother alive and her mother deceased had looked comfortingly similar. As for her brothers, she'd lost them so long ago, she thought of herself as an only child. She was the last tin in the Benson factory. The end of the line.

Miss Hamilton said, "Two world wars have created a nation of single women. We must not hide our light under a bushel." She hitched her handbag over her arm, as if it had tried to escape before now and she wasn't taking any chances. "Goodbye, Miss Benson. What a marvelous adventure. Consider me in."

"You mean you want to come?"

"I wouldn't miss it for the world."

It would be a lie to say Margery skipped all the way home. She hadn't skipped since she was a child. Besides it was dark and raining—the smog was thick—and the lacrosse boots were rubbing at the heel. But as she walked/limped, everything she passed—the filthy broken buildings, pitted with shrapnel scars, the women queuing for food, the men in civvies that didn't fit—seemed precious, as if she'd already left it behind. Briefly she thought she heard footsteps, but when she turned there was no one: with smog, people came and went, like ink in water. She had spoken about the gold beetle with three strangers and, while it was true that two had left in a hurry, the beetle had become even more real in her mind and even more findable. Margery opened her handbag for her key and wondered what she'd done with her map, but there was no time to worry because an envelope lay beneath the door, from the headmistress.

> I regret to inform you that after your failure to return the stolen boots, the matter has been passed into the hands of the police.

Margery's stomach fell, as if she were in an elevator and someone had cut its suspension. She hid the letter under the bed and pulled out her suitcase.

4

Just Get Rid of It!

For years, Margery did not know what had happened to her father. After he walked through the French windows, she'd heard the gunshot and seen a spray of blood against the glass, and it had terrified her so much that she'd remained exactly where she was. Then came other sounds—a hundred birds, her mother's scream—and the rectory had seemed to fill with new voices. She didn't know anymore what was safe and what wasn't. All she could see was the red on the window, all she wanted was her father, until eventually someone thought to look for her and found her wedged beneath the bookcase. This person—she had never seen him before but, then again, he was lying at a sideways angle in order to coax her out—said her father had met with an accident and she would need to be a very good little girl, and not cause trouble or hide under any more furniture.

Over the next few weeks, everything disappeared from the rectory. Not just Cook and the housemaid, but even the contents. Margery watched as things that had made up her life to date—the table she had run into when she was four, the wardrobe where she had once hidden a whole afternoon, her brothers' cricket bats, her father's books—were loaded into carts and driven away. Then she and her mother left, too, her mother in dark crêpe, Margery wearing an old pair of trousers and a scratchy boater. One suitcase was all they had.

They took the train to her aunts' in London. Her mother sat wedged in the corner of the carriage, sinking toward sleep, while Margery counted every station and spoke the names out loud. Her mother was a big woman, but there was nothing soft about her. Nothing gave when you tried to hug her. If anything, it became more solid.

"I will never be happy again," she said, as if grief was something you put on, like a hat.

And Margery—who hadn't a clue what she was talking about—leaned joyfully out of the window and announced she could see the River Thames.

Aunt Hazel and Aunt Lorna were her father's twin sisters, and they were very religious. They wore black, even on a good day, and prayed before and after every meal, sometimes in the middle. They didn't make conversation as such but gave edifying pronouncements, like "We rejoice in our suffering, knowing that suffering produces endurance," and "We are never sent more than we can bear." The kind of thing other women stitched on samplers. They did all that spinsters of a certain class were allowed to do—dusting, of which they did an awful lot, counting the laundry but not actually washing it, and polishing silver until it shone like the sun. Everything else they left to the live-in maid, Barbara, a terrifying woman who wore her hair in a topknot and took all instruction as a personal affront. The aunts owned a mansion flat in Kensington with a hundred steps. As for the garden, there wasn't one: it was just a communal square.

After the suitcase had been brought in, Aunt Hazel poked up the fire and Aunt Lorna pulled the curtains, while her mother landed in a chair by the window, like a toy that had lost its stuffing. The parlor was filled with vast furniture that made no concession to the smallness of the room, so everyone was a bit cramped. Her aunts observed in horrified tones that Margery was big for a girl, and also dressed like a boy. Her mother yawned and explained the problem was that she kept growing. "May I play, please?" said Margery. Her aunts said she could play in the square so long as she didn't shout or bend the flowers. But when she asked, "Is my father coming soon?" all three women closed their eyes. For a moment Margery thought a prayer was coming on.

Then:

"Tea?" said Aunt Hazel.

"Ring for Barbara," said Aunt Lorna.

"I'm so tired," yawned her mother.

And that was how it went for the next few months. Margery roamed the square and tried her best not to shout or to bend flowers, but when she asked for news of her father or when she would go home—even if she asked about her brothers—her aunts rang the bell, her mother closed her eyes, as if overcome with a fairytale kind of tiredness that might last centuries, while Barbara crashed into the parlor, furious, bearing an overpacked tea tray. No one meant to hurt her. In fact, they meant the opposite—they meant to spare her from shame—but it was like passing through a bewitched land, a place without signposts or boundaries where everyone was asleep but her. Panic set in. She wet the bed. She cried over nothing. For a while, she spent her days checking that the men in bandages and wheelchairs outside were not her father. Finally, her brain made a decision: it was better not to keep things that clearly were not meant to be kept, and a hole opened. Everything from her life before the aunts disappeared. The war came to an end, and her brothers and father belonged to a part of her life that seemed incredibly far away, like looking at something distantly across a lake, so that even though she missed them, she didn't feel it. It didn't hurt. And, after all, there was nothing strange about an all-female household: a generation of men had been wiped out.

Life carried on. Her aunts replaced her brothers' hand-me-downs with plain frocks, and so long as Margery didn't run or make a noise, they failed to notice her. A school was found to which she seldom went, and when she did, she kept herself apart. Meanwhile, her mother continued to sit in one place and grow heavier, not just in her body but in her eyes and voice, and still no one said anything about her father. Margery forgot his book of incredible creatures.

Then, coming into the parlor one afternoon, she found four women balanced on the furniture. Even the maid, Barbara, was up there, and so was her mother—it was the most agile thing Margery had seen her do in years.

"Just get rid of it!" shrieked Barbara, sounding not like a maid. All four women pointed at the window.

Attached to the curtain like a little black brooch, Margery found a beetle. "Hello," she said. Feeling she had its confidence, she eased it into her hand and opened the window. She felt giant with the responsibility. She certainly wasn't afraid.

But when she tried to set the beetle free, it wouldn't move. Had she *killed* it? She gave the smallest shake of her arm—she even prayed—and, to her delight, its back suddenly lifted and split into two hard wings. Beneath them a second miraculous pair fanned out, as delicate as sweet wrappers, and began to pulse. I know this, she thought. I know about this. The beetle paused for a moment, as if to check everything was in good working order, then lifted upward, heading straight for the wall before swinging out its tiny legs and righting itself in the nick of time. It made such a busy noise and, for the first time, she felt she understood something about the perilous mechanics of flight. A beetle might be small, and on the chunky side, but its will to travel was spectacular. She began to laugh.

And when the beetle returned a few days later—or another that looked exactly the same—she caught it in her hands and took it to her room. She kept it hidden in a small box that she filled with leaves and other things it might like, including dirt and also water. She gave it a name, Tobias Benson, because that was her father's, and she drew so many pictures that she ran out of notebook. It lived for two weeks without anyone finding it, and the day it died, she cried so much her aunts thought she was coming down with something and said extra prayers.

But it marked the beginning of her passion for beetles. She went out looking all the time, and it was amazing, once you started, how easy they were to find. No matter what she was doing, beetles were always in her thoughts. She drew pictures, she made notes, she borrowed books from the library. She learned that within the beetle kingdom there were more than 170 families—including the carabids, weevils, scarabs, blister beetles, and stag—and that within each family there were thousands of variations. She learned their common names: dung beetle, June bug, cockchafer, green tortoise beetle, devil's coachhorse. She knew where they lived, what they fed on, where they laid their eggs, how to tell them apart. She kept her specimens in homemade houses and jars, and filled notebook after notebook with her drawings and descriptions.

Beetles she understood. It was people who had become strange.

5

A Small Crushing Feeling Somewhere Beneath the Rib Cage

"*bear miss denson, Is the jod still avaladle?*"

"*bear miss denson, bib you get my letters? I want to be your asisstent!*"

"*Milk, Epsom slats, caddage.*"

Over the next few days, three more barely decipherable letters came from Enid Pretty, though one was, strictly speaking, a shopping list and meant for the grocer.

There was no time to reply. There was barely time to think. Chance favors those who are prepared, and Margery had her own lists and budgets everywhere she looked. *Corned beef, stockings, ethanol, search permits.* Now that Miss Hamilton was her assistant, the expedition had gained a life of its own. Miss Hamilton wanted to be home in good time for the Festival of Britain the following May. If they left in three weeks' time, in mid-October, that would allow six for travel, three months' trekking, with a departure from New Caledonia in February. Three weeks was nothing. It was actually insane. It also meant being there for the hottest season, when the Reverend Horace Blake warned of cyclones. But she was in this now. She'd given up once before, and if she did so again, she knew that would be it. Her dream would be over.

Time to get a passport.

The young man behind the desk said it took a month to process an application and, in any case, hers was not valid. He was very thin, verging on spindly, and his lashes were so pale his eyes looked shaved. "But I only have three weeks," said Margery. "And what exactly is wrong with my application?"

"You haven't provided a photograph. And you can't describe your face like that."

"Why not?"

"You can describe your face as round. Or thin."

"That's it? That's the only way I can describe my face?"

She had been queuing at the passport office for two hours. She'd had to wait in front of a woman with a cold, whose germs were hopping all over the place. She had filled in her form correctly, and when it asked for a description of her face she'd written "Intelligent." If she hadn't provided a photograph, it was because she didn't have one.

"Any photograph will do," said the passport official, handing her a new application form, "so long as you're not wearing a hat. You must have an old photograph?"

But, no, Margery didn't. She didn't have a new one and she didn't have an old one, with or without the hat. As a young woman she had once cut her face out of all the photographs of herself that she could find—and now it had become habit. She didn't even know why she did it anymore. She just felt happier if she wasn't in them. But the woman with the cold was beginning to sound bronchial, the passport official was staring at Margery as if she were some kind of ancient fossil, and none of that made any difference to the fact she had no photograph. "Unless you would like to accept one without my head?"

The passport official said he wouldn't. The head, he said, was the whole point. He sent her in the direction of a special coin-operated photo booth.

Margery was an intelligent woman, as she'd put on her passport application, but the special coin-operated booth seemed to have come from another planet. The sign on the front advertised PHOTOS WHILE YOU WAIT!, raising the question of how you could possibly have your photo taken while you went off and did something else, but there was no time to take this up with the passport official because another person—Woman with Cold—had already come to have hers done, too. So Margery went inside the booth. She inserted her coins, she took off her hat, and was just bending forward to double-check the instructions when the flash went and missed her completely. She stepped out of the booth, queued again, then went back in and inserted more coins until she realized she didn't have enough. By the time she returned with a fresh supply, a couple were already in the booth, using her coins, and also the booth, for something livelier than a photograph. Afterward she felt a need to wipe the seat, just in a hygienic way, so that a tutting queue began to form and, in her distress, she made it too high. Consequently, her second strip of photos were of her head but only the lower half. She looked barely human. More coins, more queuing. Her third set would have been perfect were it not for a helpful stranger who thought Margery might be having difficulties and opened the curtain as the flash fired: even though there was a full portrait of Margery, there was also one of a dark-haired woman she had never met, looking surprised and terribly apologetic. By now it was midafternoon.

As she approached the passport official, he did his best to duck. ("I can still see you," said Margery.) Quickly he stamped her application and said it would have to do. He would mark it as urgent.

19 stockings (not in pairs)
1 gray skirt
1 gray cardigan

2 girdles
Illustrated Guide to Beetles of the World
Insects, Their Ways and Means of Living by Snodgrass
1 guide to rare orchids
1 brown frock (belt missing)
1 French dictionary
30 packets of oatmeal
1 pair of lacrosse boots
Pocket Guide to New Caledonia by the Reverend Horace Blake

Time was passing too fast. Her veins throbbed, her head spun, her jaw was a clamp. Write to L'Office Centrale de Permis in New Caledonia, write to the French embassy, write to the British consulate. Margery seemed to exist permanently above the surface of things. Buy supplies. Sort collecting equipment. Pack suitcase. Get vaccinations. And now that the stolen boots were in the hands of the police, Margery half expected to find a man in uniform, with a warrant for her arrest, every time she stepped outside.

Miss Hamilton wrote daily, full of new ideas and suggestions. *Wouldn't it be jolly to dress as men and hire mules?* Frankly, it wouldn't. Margery had a thing about mules: she had been bitten as a teenager, and would do anything to avoid their large yellow teeth. She also had less in the way of funding than she'd let on. She had never been a full-blown liar—Barbara once made her take a bite out of the soap when she swore she hadn't taken the sieve for beetle collecting—but the trust fund she had inherited from her aunts would barely cover the return voyage. She wrote again to the Royal Entomological Society, and once again they refused to help. The letter ended with a clear warning: *Do not on any account make an expedition into the remote northern regions of New Caledonia.* The same advice came from the Foreign Office.

Cash, cash, she needed more cash. Margery sold everything but the bare bones of her flat. Once again, she watched a cart drive away, loaded this time with the furniture that had belonged to her aunts. It would have appalled them, and it appalled her, too, but she had no choice. As the buyer pointed out, it was better than a smack in the eye with a wet fish. So many things, she thought, would be better than that that it was hard to see this as a helpful remark.

Margery visited the travel agent and paid for two tickets in a shared berth, tourist class, on RMS *Orion* from Tilbury to Brisbane, returning home on February 18. The agent showed her a pamphlet with brightly colored photographs of yellow deck chairs and a sea as blue as a swimming pool; spacious cabins with yellow flowers and yellow beds and yellow curtains at the porthole; though when she asked if she might keep the pamphlet, he said sadly not. She booked a twin room at the Marine Hotel in Brisbane, where they would spend two nights before catching the flying boat to Nouméa. She converted all that was left of her savings into traveler's checks; she had vaccinations against typhoid and yellow fever— for a few days her left arm was about as useful as a third leg—and began to collect supplies.

"Throughout New Caledonia," wrote the Reverend Horace Blake, *"toilet facilities are primitive. Take all precautions against possible infection."*

Where there had once been furniture, her flat was now crammed with towers of Izal lavatory paper, Chamberlain's colic and diarrhea remedy, James's powder for fever, water-purifying tablets, sulfuric acid, emetic tartar, talcum powder, Epsom salts, and lavender water, as well as two folded tarps, calico sheets, two mosquito nets, a pocketknife, Walkden's ink powder, strops and hones, needles, thread, tape, gauze-worsted stockings, four months' supply of Spam, condensed milk—basically, anything that came in a tin and that she could get without coupons—curry powder, powdered coffee, batteries, bandages, quinine, brushes, twine, blotting paper, notebooks, pencils, two hammocks, and a canvas tent. She sent off to Watkins and Doncaster for specialist collecting equipment— a sweep net, a pooter with two rubber tubes, specimen vials, killing jars, a supply of ethanol and naphthalene, trays, mothballs, cotton wool, paper, labels, and insect pins—but when she unpacked the box, the vials were smashed and she had to send them back.

Strange, though, to see these things after so many years. To hold a length of tube again. To place one end in her mouth and the other over an imaginary beetle, and suck quickly, the breath not too sharp, and not too soft, either, pulling the insect up the tube and depositing it safely in a specimen jar. It was as though her senses had secretly kept hold of a memory her mind had put away.

In terms of clothes, Margery packed an assortment of brown things, plus her best purple frock for special occasions. She tried to buy a safari helmet and was offered a sun hat. She asked about a plain jacket with pockets and flaps, and was told the style was available only for men. But supposing she needed to put things in her pockets? And keep them there with a flap? The assistant suggested a handbag. Handbags, he added, in case she really hadn't got the point, could be found on the ground floor between cosmetics and hosiery. In the end she gave up on the jacket and found a second-hand pith helmet that looked more like a cake tin than something a human being would put on her head. The supplies of food and camping gear would be sent ahead in a tea chest, while she would keep her precious collecting equipment in a special Gladstone bag.

With five days left, Margery delivered her tea chest to the shipping company. The next time she saw it she would be on the other side of the world. Impossible to imagine, like standing on her head. Waiting for her at home was another letter from Miss Hamilton.

"Dear Miss Benson . . ." The message was unusually short and Margery read slowly. Miss Hamilton wrote that she had been doing a little *"searching and investigating of my own!"* That sounded a happy thing and in no way prepared Margery for what came next. Following some communication with Margery's previous employers, Miss Hamilton regretted she was no longer able to accompany her on account of *"an unfortunate incident that is now in the hands of the police."* Margery felt a small crushing feeling somewhere beneath the rib cage. She had to reach for the console table—only

the table was no longer there and instead she stumbled into the wall.

It is easier for human beings to believe the worst things said about them than the kindest. Margery felt as if Miss Hamilton had found her way into her most shameful secrets and was now serving them jubilantly on a plate for the whole world to see. She couldn't stop shaking.

Could she go without an assistant? Of course she couldn't. She couldn't possibly manage all the equipment and, anyway, it wouldn't be safe. No use asking Mr. Mundic: he'd be deep-frying beetles before she so much as grabbed her sweep net. There was only one choice left, and admittedly it was scraping the barrel. With three days to go, Margery wrote to Enid Pretty and offered her the job. In terms of packing, she told her to travel light. A hat, boots, three plain frocks, plus one for special occasions. All bright colors, flowers, feathers, pom-poms, ribbons, et cetera, were in the worst possible taste and entirely to be avoided. She ended with an instruction to meet at nine beneath the clock at Fenchurch Street station where she would be easily recognized by her safari outfit. True to form, Enid Pretty's reply made absolutely no sense.

"bear miss denson. Please to acept! pink hat!"

Margery wrote to the shipping company, adding Enid Pretty's name to the passenger list. She had a pith helmet (√), boots (√). She had an assistant, who clearly had problems telling *b* from *d*, a passport—albeit one with a photo of a woman she'd never met in the background—as well as the Reverend Horace Blake's pocket guide, a full set of new collecting equipment, and enough lavatory paper to supply a small town. Yes, there had been a disappointment, but it was not the end of the story. This was just the beginning of a different adventure.

And finally she was doing it. She was on her way to New Caledonia.

6

A Bit of Fun

It started as a bit of fun. To put her in her place. Plus, he had a thing about teachers. He'd never forgotten the idiot who'd moved him to the class for retards. "I can read," he'd said.

And this teacher, he'd said, "Then show us, Mundic. Show the class you can read."

So he'd picked up the book, doing one word at a time, but the teacher was right, he couldn't do it. He couldn't get the words to stop jigging. The class laid into him after school. Retard, they called him, and they'd kept it up from that day on, ragging him and shouting *"Reee-taaaaard."*

So, yes, he didn't care for teachers.

After the interview, he'd waited for her outside Lyons. He'd wanted to spook her because it wasn't right, the way she'd laughed when he'd said there'd be snakes. What did she know? She was a woman. She needed him to lead her expedition. Five years he'd been back from Burma, and he still couldn't hold down a job. Either he'd get sick, or something would upset him, and he'd land in a fight. There were people queuing for food and people going on buses and people waiting to cross the road, and he couldn't remember, he couldn't remember anymore how to be ordinary like them because he had seen things in Burma none of those people had seen. Sometimes he couldn't even remember who he was. He kept his passport in his pocket just to remind himself. And there were times he'd be okay, but then he'd open a newspaper and find another story about a POW who'd hanged himself and that was it, he was back in Burma all over again. There were days he even had the same thought. All he wanted was to get away.

So he followed her as she left the Corner House—it wasn't difficult, with the fog and everything, and he liked hiding in doorways when she turned, having a laugh at her expense. After that he got curious. He wondered where a woman like her lived. He guessed a shabby terrace house. The last thing he expected was a fancy mansion block.

He went back the next day, even though it was so cold he'd had to stuff his hands into his pockets to keep warm. But it was a thing to do because there'd been days recently he couldn't even summon the energy to play a game of cards, or he'd start, and it was like a switch inside him had got stuck, and he wouldn't know how to stop. He was about to leave when she appeared at a window. He felt a bolt of adrenaline, like he hadn't known since the day the army had marched past and he'd signed up on the spot. So he counted the windows and he did it out loud because sometimes his thoughts got scrambled, and now he knew she lived on the fourth floor.

After that, it became his job, following her. He left the hostel every day like he was going to work. He got a notebook and he called it the Book of Miss Benson. He wrote facts he knew, such as her address, and he kept the book safe in his pocket, alongside his passport and her map.

He went through her rubbish and found out she liked tinned soup and biscuits. He found out she lived alone. He followed her to a travel agency, and as soon as she left, he went and spoke to the chap, and he said, "I fancy a cruise to the other side of the world," and the chap laughed and said what a coincidence, he'd just sold two last-minute tickets for the RMS *Orion*. Mundic said, "When's she going? When's she coming back?" That was his first mistake: he shouldn't have said that—it gave him away—and he started rubbing his hands because he was scared. But the travel agent didn't notice. He said, "Leaving Tilbury on October the nineteenth and returning home on the eighteenth." So Mundic wrote those details in his Book of Miss Benson. And the chap said, "Take a leaflet, why don't you, sir? If you're interested?" Mundic put that into his notebook as well.

The more he found out, the more powerful he felt. Sometimes he said to himself, "In five minutes Miss Benson will walk onto the street." And when she did, it was like he was so big nothing could hurt him ever again. Besides, she wasn't the kind to give in. It wasn't as easy to spook her as he'd thought, and he liked that. It kept him on his toes. When her collecting equipment arrived, he stopped the delivery chaps outside and said he would look after it. He broke a few things while they weren't looking. Little ones. Just so she'd know he was watching.

Three weeks of following her, and it was more than teaching her a lesson; it was like being a man again. And now she was going to leave. She was going to New Caledonia.

He didn't know what he would do without her.

7

Where Is Enid Pretty?

Fenchurch Street station, October 19, 1950. Nine o'clock on the dot. No sign of Enid Pretty. No sign of anyone beneath the station clock, except Margery in her pith helmet and boots, holding her insect net like an oversized lollipop, glancing left and right to check the path was clear of policemen.

The evening before, she couldn't eat. Despite the waste, she'd scraped her meal into the bin. The night had been even worse. She'd slept in fits and starts; the only dream she had played itself on a loop and was about her watch being broken. It would have been less exhausting if she'd sat up for hours, staring at the wall. Later, waiting outside for a cab in the morning, she had glanced up at her empty window and, just for a second, felt bereft. She was convinced she was seeing it for the last time. But she'd noticed someone on the other side of the road, and quickly moved on in case he thought she needed help.

The railway station was mayhem: crowds rushing, locomotives shunting and chugging, whistles sounding, doors slamming, pigeons flying to the rafters with a clatter of wings. And everywhere the soot, the smoke. Several people noticed Margery's helmet and slowed for a second look—she might as well have stuck a bowl of fruit on her head. Five minutes passed. Ten. Across the concourse, a short, thin woman, with hair like bright yellow candy floss, stood smoking nervously. Quarter past nine. The train was going to leave at half past.

But finally here was Enid Pretty. A neat woman with one suitcase and sensible brown shoes, hurrying toward the station clock as if her life depended on it. Margery waved her sweep net: "Miss Pretty! Miss Pretty!"

The woman caught sight of Margery and paled. "I'm sorry, I don't know who you are. My name's not Miss Pretty. Please leave me alone." She rushed past.

By now a small crowd had gathered, waiting for Margery to do something even more entertaining, like leap through a ring of fire, or produce a saw and cut herself in two. She had no idea where to look.

"Marge?" The woman with yellow hair noticed her for the first time. She pulled something from her pocket that turned out to be pink and stuffed it on top of her head. "Is that you?"

It seemed to Margery that everything paused. Even pigeons. Even the clock. The small crowd turned to look at the yellow-haired woman, now struggling to gather up not one, but three whacking great suitcases and a red valise, then turned for a good look at Margery in her pith helmet, as if there were a tight line running from one to the other that made no sense. Margery saw nothing but a wall of eyeballs, swinging left and right.

"Marge!" called the woman again. "It's me!"

Margery wondered if it was too late to pretend she was someone else. A woman who happened to be carrying an insect net on behalf of another person altogether. She shoved it inside her coat until a helpful man called, "Don't suppose you'll catch much in there."

Well, everyone thought that was hilarious.

Meanwhile, the short woman tottered across the concourse, her luggage so heavy she could only wave at Margery with her foot. Her hair was a stiff puff with the perky hat pinned on top: about as useful in terms of sun protection as a beer mat on her head. She wore a bright pink two-piece travel suit that accentuated her round bust and hips, tiny sandals with a pom-pom at the toe, and her nails were painted like juicy sweets. A blond bombshell, twenty-five if she was a day, and Margery was old enough to be, if not her mother, then at least her maiden aunt.

"What are you lot all staring at?" the woman said to the crowd, at which point it wisely stopped staring and moved on.

Being close, and also half Margery's size, she had to tilt her face upward to speak. She wore so much makeup that her face was orange. Her mouth, by contrast, was bright pink, her eyelashes thick and black. And then there was her hair, which was such a luminous shade of yellow you could have shut her in the dark and still found her. Only her eyes were natural: dark green with tiny gold flecks.

"Enid Pretty," she said merrily, as if announcing her arrival at a party. Margery was speechless. There was less chance of this woman blending into the background than there was of Margery winning a beauty pageant. The humiliation she had suffered while waiting and the terrible hurt that had been dealt her by Miss Hamilton, along with something else, something so old she couldn't even name it, all these things now regrouped themselves into a base longing to lash out at Enid and humiliate her, as if it was completely normal to wear safari helmets in railway stations and completely odd to go without them.

She pointed at Enid's tiny excuse of a hat. "What is that?"

"Beg pardon?"

"What are you *wearing*?"

Enid blinked. "Clothes and stuff," she said, all question mark.

"This isn't a cheap holiday to Butlin's. It's a field trip to the South Pacific. The post is no longer available."

She was turning to pick up her luggage when Enid grabbed Margery's elbow. She had shocking strength for someone so small and brightly colored. "Please," she hissed. "Don't do this to me, Marge."

The way she said it implied they had been friends for a long time and what Margery was about to do was the kind of thing she always did, and for once in her life she should try doing something better. Margery pulled herself free. She reached for her Gladstone bag.

But in her desperation to get away she made the move too fast, igniting a flash of pain right through her hip. Her body pitched forward and, for a terrible moment, she thought her leg was coming off. It hurt just to breathe. Enid bent close.

"Marge? Why aren't you moving? We need to hurry."

"It's nothing. Only my hip."

"Your hip?" Enid shouted, as if Margery was not only disabled for the moment but also deaf as a post.

"It gets stuck."

"Do you want me to whack it?"

"No. Please. Please do not whack my hip. I might fall over."

Enid cast a terrified look toward the platforms. "We've got to hurry, Marge. We can't miss our train." Then something seemed to click in her mind and she said, "Right. I'll sort this out. Wait."

Before Margery could object, Enid had gone again, legs moving like scissors—her pink skirt was no wider than a sleeve—but not with her abundant luggage: this she left behind. A paper boy bawled out the headlines: "Norman Skinner to hang for murder of call girl!" A flock of people surged forward to buy the latest edition. The story had been in the papers for weeks and still no one could get enough.

"Marge! Marge!"

Here came Enid, pursued by an enthusiastic young porter with a trolley. Swiftly he loaded Margery's equipment and suitcase, followed by Enid's luggage. "Oh, you are so clever, oh, you are so strong! How could we possibly manage without you?" she sang, though she snatched up the lightest one—the red valise—before he could get his hands on it.

"Your train leaves in five minutes," he said. "We're going to have to make a dash."

Dashing would have been a very good idea, except that Margery was stuck.

"Still?" said Enid.

What came next verged on assault. Enid sprang behind Margery, buckled her round the waist with the strength of a bear, and yanked upward. It was like being seared. But then—by some miracle—the pain was simply not there. It was as though a hole had opened all the way from Margery's head to her foot, and the pain had spat through the end of her toes.

"Better now?" said Enid, dusting off her gloves.

"I think so."

"We need to hurry. We have three minutes."

They made a ridiculous pair, as they chased the porter, like a brown ostrich coupled with a pink-hatted canary. Gulping for breath, Margery noticed the way men caught sight of Enid and stared, as she wiggled past at high velocity, clutching the handles of her valise with both hands as if it were a motor propelling her forward, either oblivious to attention or so used to it she took it as read that men would stop and watch. The guard was already raising his flag as they fled past the barrier and reached the train.

"Here you go, ladies," said the porter, swinging open the first door they came to. "Are you sure I can't take that suitcase?"

"No, ta," said Enid, taking it in one hand so that she could help Margery. ("Thank you, but I can manage," said Margery, hoisting herself upward with difficulty.)

The door was barely closed. The whistle went. The train pulled out.

"So, the thing is, you should have seen it. I said to him, I said, 'You don't think I'm going to buy that, do you? Because that hat, I said, that's not a hat! That's a helmet! I can't wear *that*!'"

Or: "I knew this woman, this is true, Marge, and when she died, she had a worm in her belly the size of a hosepipe!"

Margery had never been a talker: she always felt she came across better if she stuck to letters and cards. She'd had a correspondence once with another beetle enthusiast that had gone wrong only when they'd met for tea. "I thought you were a man," the woman

had said. ("But I'm called *Margery,*" said Margery.) After that she
didn't even want to talk beetles; she just crumbled her scone and
left. But Enid Pretty was Margery's polar opposite: now they were
safely on the train, she wouldn't shut up. It was as though she had
a button set to "on," and unless Margery found "off," Enid would
continue forever. Talk, talk, talk. Half the time there wasn't any
hint of a connection—she just leaped like a mad woman from one
subject to the next. She didn't even pause for periods. As well as
saying multiple times that she couldn't believe Margery was a real-
life explorer from the Natural History Museum—no time to correct her—and that they were going to the other side of the world,
Enid also covered safari hats, terrifying parasites, the weather, Mr.
Churchill, rationing, the weather again, and her own personal bi-
ography. Her mother and father—lovely people!—had both died
of Spanish flu when Enid was tiny—so sad!—and Enid had been
brought up by neighbors. Worse: she still couldn't get the hang of
Margery's name. She was calling her "Marge" as if she was a highly
processed alternative to butter. Then a woman squeezed past with
a toddler, and Enid changed tack all over again.

"Babies! Don't get me started on babies!"

"No," said Margery, not wanting to get her started on anything
at all.

Too late: Enid was already off.

"I love babies. Maybe it's cos I had no family. I had a twin but
she died at birth. My husband said that's the reason I talk so
much—"

"Excuse me. You're married?" The question burst from Margery
several moments later, but Enid was going so fast she appeared to
be speaking in tongues.

"Didn't I say that in my letter?"

"About a husband? No. You said nothing about that."

Enid stalled. She paled. She actually looked struck. "Well, it
doesn't matter. He's away."

"Where has he gone?"

"Beg pardon?"

"Has he gone away for work?"

To Margery's confusion, tears now filled Enid's eyes, making the gold flecks even fleckier. "That's right!" she said. "For work!"

After that she was off again, telling a horrific story about a dog she'd seen chained to a wall and eating its own paw. Nothing, it seemed, could happen to Enid without her needing to recount it in tortuously small detail to someone else. Outside, rain stuck to the window in beads that shattered and stippled. Beyond that, row after row of gloomy houses. Desolate allotments, where bits of underwear hung on lines, and privies were patched together. Margery had no idea how she would survive five weeks on a ship with Enid Pretty, let alone climb a mountain. By the time they reached Tilbury, she felt murderous. If she could have killed her, quietly and without anyone noticing, she would have.

A huge crowd crammed the departures hall. It was hard to believe they would all fit into Australia, let alone on the RMS *Orion*. The liner stood waiting out in the dock—the very opposite of the chaos inside: solid and massive, with a custard-yellow hull and a single funnel. Its porthole windows were lit like a city, even though it was broad daylight.

Enid threw a glance over her shoulder, as if checking for someone she knew. "So let me get this straight." She had to shout to be heard. "We're crossing the world to look for a beetle that isn't there?"

"No one has found it yet. They've only seen it."

"Isn't that the same thing?"

"No, Mrs. Pretty. A thing doesn't exist until it has been caught and presented to the Natural History Museum. Once the Natural History Museum has accepted the beetle, and read my descriptions and notes, and found that it is genuinely a new specimen, it will be given a name. And then it will exist."

"Even though we'll already have found it?"

"Yes."

"So we're going to find a beetle that isn't there?" They were back at the beginning. Fortunately, a customs official appeared and

Enid got distracted. "You do think he'll let us on the ship, don't you?"

Margery smiled. It wasn't that she had begun to like Enid. It was more that in that moment she had experienced the rare pleasure of liking herself. Crossing to the other side of the world to find a beetle suddenly seemed such a simple and beautiful thing.

"Of course. All you need is your passport, Mrs. Pretty."

But Enid went the color of cold porridge. "Beg pardon?" she said.

8

Getting There Is Half the Fun!

It was one thing almost to miss the train to Tilbury: it was on a whole new level almost to miss the liner to the other side of the world.

Margery did not intend to wait for Enid Pretty. She fully intended to board the ship without her: fortune, it seemed, had come to her aid. But as Enid was led off to a private interview room, Margery paused to explain to the customs official in a helpful way that she had only just met this woman and they weren't even friends. The customs official folded his arms and asked why they were traveling together if they didn't know one another.

Which was how Margery found herself being led off to her very own private interview room.

"Why are there two women in your photograph?" asked the customs official, checking her passport. The room was no bigger than a newspaper stand. Also, he was wall-eyed: she wanted to be polite but had no idea which one to look at. "Is the other woman the blonde?"

"No. She is not."

"She looks like her."

"She looks nothing like her. The woman in the photograph has brown hair. I'd never met her before. She just charged into the booth."

"Another woman you'd never met before? Is this a habit?"

He then asked if she would like to remove her watch, her hat, and her boots. Margery wisely interpreted that none of these were actually questions, but she had tied the laces in a double knot for safety reasons and it was difficult to get her feet out. "They're not even mine," she said, stalling for time.

"Oh?" he said. "Are they stolen?"

This, she realized afterward, was his idea of a joke, but not until she'd turned hot as fire and denied it so many times she sounded like Peter after the Last Supper.

Two policemen entered the room and, without even saying hello, began an inspection of her bag of collecting equipment. When they almost dropped the ethanol, she yelped, not because it was her only bottle but because, in a room that size, a smashed bottle of preserving fluid would be enough to floor all four of them. "You seem nervous," one said. Sweat prickled her hairline; her heart was running uphill. "Anyone would think I had done something wrong!" She laughed. "Anyone would think I had committed murder!" Only comedy had never been her strong point and she now sounded like a woman who had done both those things. "Next you'll be putting the noose round my neck!" At which point everyone stopped examining her killing jars, and point-blank stared, even the first customs official, though he had one eye on her head, the other on her feet.

Then from the next room she heard Enid's wild laugh. The door opened and yet another man squeezed into the room—sardines had more space in a tin—and began whispering something that made the others grin. "Your friend's a card," the new arrival said. She was about to remind them that Enid was not her friend but thought better of it. "Off you go," he said. They handed back the boots, her watch, and her helmet, and repacked her Gladstone bag with such care she could have wept. And that was the swift and miraculous end of Margery's first-ever police interview.

By the time the door to the adjoining room opened and Enid flew out, fixing her buttons, her cheeks like red dots, there was only time—yet again—to run. "Quick!" she shouted. "Follow me!"

"Again?" said Margery. The rushing, the crushing, surely they had already done that. Enid grabbed her suitcases as if they were the hands of children and pelted through the door. Outside, people crowded the jetty, waving balloons and shouting. They were hemmed in on every side—it was like pushing through a wall. There was a brass band, there was bunting, there was a woman sobbing her heart out and, to top it all, there was rain, the fine British kind that sticks to your skin like mist and soaks you in minutes.

"Don't you dare go without us!" shouted Enid. She seemed to be threatening the RMS *Orion* itself. But the deckhand was already stepping down with the chain to close the gangway; the foghorn sounded. Any moment now it would leave. "Stop that right now!" she yelled.

Margery plodded in Enid's wake. A vertical seam of pain ran the length of both legs and, no matter how hard she tried, she was unable to gain full access to her lungs. Her Gladstone bag was considerably heavier than her suitcase, and she swapped them from one hand to the other until she was unable to tell whether it was better to continue with the throbbing in her right arm or change to instant pain in the left.

"Wait! You wait!" bawled Enid, at the deckhand. Spotting them, he dropped the chain and ran down to help. She sprinted past.

"Not me, darlin'," she called over her shoulder. "Help the lady behind."

Despite the awful weather, the decks were packed. As the ship slid free, the band on the jetty struck up with a round of "Rule Britannia," and passengers hurled down hundreds of thousands of streamers that filled the dock in a giant web, while Enid whooped and blew kisses, though presumably not to anyone she knew. "Goodbye!" she shouted. "Goodbye, ol' Blighty!" After that, Margery stayed on deck, watching as everything she knew pulled away and lost shape, the docks, the coastline, fishing boats, until even Britain was a small gray hat on the horizon. She was doing it—she was finally doing the thing she'd dreamed about as a child, the thing she'd given up on in her twenties, and deep inside she felt a leap of excitement because it was finally happening and she could hardly believe it. It was so easy to find yourself doing the things in life you weren't passionate about, to stick with them even when you didn't want them and they hurt. But now the time for dreaming and wishing was over, and she was going. She was traveling to the other side of the world. It wasn't just the ship that had been unmoored. It was her entire sense of herself.

Enid fetched a handsome steward to help with their luggage. ("Oh, you are so kind!" she trilled. "Oh, you are so helpful! Thank you, sweetheart! I'll keep the red one!") He told them about the wonderful things they could do onboard. Not just the free dining and swimming, but all the extra clubs and activities. Getting there was half the fun. He pointed out the lines of yellow deck chairs, a whole arcade of shops, a hairdresser, a cinema, and even a ballroom, while Enid gasped and clucked, like a hen laying an egg. Yellow was the company color, he said. No other ship had a yellow funnel, like the RMS *Orion*'s.

"Matches my hair!" She laughed.

"So it does!" He laughed back.

She then told him everything she knew about the gold beetle, which was obviously not much, though that didn't put her off in any significant way. Marge was an explorer, she said, from the Natural History Museum. "I'm her assistant! We're going on the adventure of our lives!"

"I could show you some adventures!"

"Now now, sailor! Don't you be so saucy!"

And slowly they continued to tourist class, conversing entirely with exclamation marks, and bumping the luggage down so many stairs, they might as well have been descending to the bottom of the ocean. At last the steward stopped outside a cabin.

"This is it?" said Margery.

"Ooo! Ain't it lovely!" sang Enid.

So the space they were to share for five weeks was small. Really small. It would have been a squeeze for a single person, but for a big one and her excitable, nonstop-talking assistant it was less a cabin, more a cupboard. It looked nothing like the berth in the pamphlet. And after the cold outside it was also suffocatingly hot. Within seconds, Margery had to undo her coat, and she seriously regretted the wool vest.

A set of bunk beds took up one side, and on the other, a rack for clothes, as well as a tiny cupboard, a tiny washbasin, a yellow chair and a tiny desk, a mirror and wall light. Above, a ceiling fan moved slowly, not exactly cooling the air but rather dolloping it from one half of the cabin to the other. Lavatory and shower facilities were at the end of the corridor, as was the laundry room. A sudden jolt from the ship sent all three flying sideways, and Enid landed in the arms of the steward. "Ow!" she went, as if he had pinched her. "Hands off, sailor!"

"Ha-ha-ha!" laughed the steward. "I bet you know how to have fun!"

Once he'd gone, there was an awkwardness in the cabin, as if Enid had taken off something she shouldn't. Margery hung up her three frocks and made a pile of her books on the desk. She informed Enid she would take the bottom bunk, but Enid was so busy testing the lock on the door, she failed to reply and Margery had to say it all over again. "I have used the left-hand side of the cupboard," she continued, nudging her way past Enid's suitcases. They looked even bigger now that they were in the cabin, more like coffins for baby dinosaurs. "You can use the right. Clearly space is an issue in here."

"I think it's really nice," said Enid, apparently happy with security arrangements, vis-à-vis the door.

"This is going to be difficult. I suggest we establish some rules."

"Beg pardon?"

"This will be my half." Margery pointed at the left side of the cabin, which she had designated as her own. "That will be yours."

Technically this meant they had joint ownership of the cupboard and lamp in the middle and that Margery took the desk, while Enid got the mirror. "Obviously I will need to pass through your half of the cabin to reach the door. Another thing. My name is not Marge."

"It isn't?"

"No."

"I see. Is that an alias?"

"An alias? No, of course it isn't an alias. My name is Margery. Marge is a cheap butter substitute."

"Beg pardon?"

"People call me Miss Benson."

"Miss Benson?" Enid made a scowl face.

"Yes."

"Okay, Marge. Well, I'll just unpack, shall I?"

There was no time to argue because at this point Enid produced an abundance of small bottles and jars, and tossed them into the cupboard, without any order, and also on Margery's side. It hurt just to watch. Margery had no idea how one woman could need so much. She had packed only a jar of Pond's Cold Cream, and that could last a whole year. Then Enid began to empty her luggage. Another shock. There was not one single brown camouflage item anywhere. Everything she owned came in bright colors—skimpy frocks, a tiger-print bikini, a fur coat that seemed to shed hair even as she lifted it, flowery high-heeled slippers, more tiny hats, and a prawn-pink dressing gown. Clearly she'd rammed her entire life into her suitcases, and most of it was pretty patched and threadbare. The only one she failed to open was the red valise. Checking the lock, she shoved it beneath the chair. Then they changed for dinner at opposite ends of the cabin—which in effect rendered them side by side. Margery put on her best purple frock. Enid got into something abundantly flowery.

"Is your hair naturally curly?" Enid asked, pulling at her own as if she'd bought it from a shop.

"It is."

"You don't have to get a permanent?"

"I've never had a permanent. Would you like a hanger?"

"A what?"

"For your clothes?"

"I'll just leave them on the floor. You're so lucky with your hair. I have to do mine every week. Look how thin it is. And this color isn't natural."

"It isn't?"

Sarcasm was lost on Enid because she laughed. "Oh, no, Marge. This comes from a bottle. Want me to do your makeup?"

"May I remind you, Mrs. Pretty, that the purpose of this expedition is to find a beetle?"

"No harm having fun, though." Enid dabbed her face all over with orange powder and then sprayed herself in a scent that was so devastatingly powerful it made ethanol smell like a walk in the park.

"I assume your French is fluent?"

"Yup," said Enid. "Bon *shoor.*"

"And on the subject of the beetle—"

"Oh, yes?"

"You need to stop telling people I'm from the Natural History Museum."

"Why, Marge? You should be proud of your work."

No time to put her straight. The ship's bell sounded for dinner. Margery checked the ruffles were straight on her bodice and picked up her handbag. "Also, you need to stop talking about the beetle."

But Enid's attention was a dandelion clock. She had just spotted herself in the mirror and was now checking how she looked from an assortment of angles, mostly side-on. "Beg pardon?"

"We need it to keep it secret. There's a black market."

"In secrets?"

"In beetles, Enid. I'm talking about beetles."

Enid shook her head. "People are nice on this ship. Trust me, I've met some types in my life and these are not like that. Don't you worry, Marge. Your beetle's safe."

• • •

Margery wanted to question Enid about her passport over dinner, and practice some beginner's French, but she hadn't realized that tourist class meant sharing with other people. The dining room was low-ceilinged and vast, with shiny wooden paneling. It was lined with hundreds of tables that had bright yellow cloths and silver jugs of water; most seats were already taken, and the noise was deafening. At the sight of so many strangers, Margery seized up. She even wondered about going straight to bed. Meanwhile, Enid wiggled here, she wiggled there, greeting people as if she loved them dearly, until she found two free seats at a table of ten: "Over here, Marge! Over here!" There was no chance of a private conversation. Neither had Margery realized how much food would be served—after all the rationing, it was more than she'd eaten in years. She finished the oxtail soup, then the ham with pineapple, and when it came to trifle, she had to reach beneath her cardigan and loosen her zipper. Meanwhile, Enid spooned up every last scrap—she didn't once use a fork, and neither did she close her mouth; she was the worst eater Margery had ever met—and laughed ecstatically when the waiters offered seconds.

Margery had begun to wonder if her assistant was an entirely stable person. Despite the clear warning, she told everyone that Margery was from the Natural History Museum, so now they were all asking questions. They were even asking what other expeditions she'd been on. There was a newlywed couple immigrating to Australia on ten-pound tickets, a widower traveling the world, a missionary whose English was not so good, and two sisters on their way to Naples. All wanted to know what it was like to be a famous explorer.

The widower inquired if Enid had done any other job except insect work, but she was sketchy about her previous profession. She said she'd had a job in catering, but as for where she'd catered, Enid was vague. She was also vague when he asked how you went about collecting beetles.

"Oh, you just pick 'em up."

"With a net?"

"Or with a spoon. Or just your hands."

"You're not afraid?"

"Of a beetle? Not me."

"And is it valuable?"

"Yeah. Very. Well, it's gold, you see. Everyone wants to find it."

"Your husband must be sorry to see you go?"

"Beg pardon?"

"Your husband?"

Enid stared for a moment, like a stunned marsupial. "My husband is a solicitor," she said, which was nice to know, but not the answer to the question. Then she asked who had seen the film *Mrs. Miniver.* It was her favorite film in the whole wide world.

Margery was hinting it was time to retire when a man called Taylor joined their table. Taylor recognized Enid and Margery as the two hilarious women who had almost missed the boat. He was a short man with shoulders like structural beams and a solid mustache that looked as if it would fall off if he moved too fast. He said there was a ballroom next door with a proper band and he just wondered if anyone fancied a dance.

"No, thank you," said Margery.

"Now, wouldn't that be smashing?" said Enid, springing up like a jack-in-the-box.

Margery excused herself and said she would take an early night. It had been a long day, what with nearly missing two major forms of transport and enduring a quite traumatic police investigation.

It was a relief to be in the cabin. It was a relief to be alone. She would never call herself vain, but—despite her fears—it had been something to have all those people briefly treat her like an important person. It would be something, too, to come home with three pairs of specimens, male and female, correctly pinned. To present them to the Natural History Museum, along with all the other rare beetles she'd found. There might be an offer of a job. Her name in the newspapers . . .

Margery must have fallen into a deep sleep because when she woke she had no clue where she was. The bed was narrow, it was hard, and, now that she thought about it, it was going up and down. She was on the ship, she remembered. And the joy she felt was instantly replaced with panic as she realized someone else was in the cabin. Enid Pretty. The dreadful woman who couldn't stop talking. Light from the porthole cast a thin blue pallor; Enid was kneeling on the floor and had a suitcase wide open. Margery's skin went cold. Enid was going through her things.

She tried to tell herself it couldn't be possible but only because she didn't want to have to deal with what would come next.

"Mrs. Pretty?"

Enid slammed down the lid. "Marge? I thought you were asleep."

"What are you doing?"

"Nothing. It's fine."

Clearly this was a lie. It wasn't fine. Though Margery could see now that she'd been wrong. It wasn't her suitcase: it was the red valise Enid had been at such pains to hide. Not only that, but she'd been crying. Her eyes were black flowers.

"Have you lost something?"

"Night, Marge. Sorry to wake you."

Enid blew her nose and hid her valise back under the chair. She stripped off her clothes, dropping them not on her side of the cabin, but all over Margery's, then shimmied up to her bunk, wearing a slip and nothing else. She was snoring within minutes— proper snoring as well.

But Margery couldn't sleep. Clearly Enid Pretty was the last woman on the planet she should have hired as her assistant. And even though she hadn't actually been stealing from Margery, the thought was a seed of doubt cracking and sprouting in her mind. Stealing seemed exactly the kind of thing Enid *would* do, given half a chance. The ship was due to make its first port of call in a week: she would have to go. Margery would get another assistant.

The liner tilted. Her stomach went in one direction while the rest of her went the other. She glared at the washbasin, which seemed to be heading sideways, as did the mirror and also the lamp. Suddenly all she could think of was trifle.

She realized—too late—that she was about to be sick.

9

Stowaway

It was easy.

He had got on the train to Tilbury, same as her. He didn't see why she should think she could go to New Caledonia without him. Then he hung about on the quayside next to the RMS *Orion*, searching for the right kind of face. He noticed a steward helping a boy to catch a balloon. He waited until the steward was alone, and then he got talking with him and he said that his mother had always wanted to take a cruise. Could he have a look? The steward told him visiting was not possible, with all the passengers about to board. Mundic said yellow was his mum's favorite color. She'd had yellow flowers at her funeral. She'd loved yellow so much.

The steward said it would have to be quick.

He had shown Mundic the berths in first-class. There were proper beds and windows, and young men polishing the woodwork with little dusters on sticks, like that was all there was to do in life. Before they'd even got to the stairs, the steward said, "Well, sir, I'm afraid that's all we have time for. But you see what a fine vessel she is?" They were walking to the exit when Mundic elbowed a vase of flowers. It crashed to the floor, spilling water everywhere. The steward had to call for help, the dusting men dropped their sticks

and found mops instead, and Mundic slipped free. He waited in
the restroom until he heard the great noise of other passengers,
then came out to join the crowd that was surging through the ship,
like the sea itself, though he had to hold back when they came too
close.

It got on his nerves. All those people calling and laughing and
full of excitement, like the world was suddenly a good place. He
had to put his hands on his ears to stop the noise.

Mundic made his way to the bottom of the ship and found a
door that said NO ENTRY. That was where he went. Inside, it was all
engines, and smelled of oil. He crept under a tarp in a corner, and
he liked it because it was dark and hot. Then he saw a bit of rope,
and he started to shake and get the sweats, thinking it was snakes
but it wasn't: it was just rope. He threw up, and after that he felt a
bit better, and he told himself to sleep if he could. He told himself
the rope wasn't snakes, it was just rope. It was rope.

By the time he was freed from the POW camp, he hadn't known
himself. He'd got used to the other blokes with faces like skeletons
and their rib cages all bulging out, their skin scarred with the beat-
ings, but he hadn't believed he looked as bad. He was so ill, he
could barely remember the voyage home. There was supposed to
be a welcome party at Liverpool docks with the mayor and a brass
band, but the mayor didn't turn up. A few blokes said they would
change their names. Start a new life. Even immigrate to Australia.
They could do what the hell they liked. He wanted never to see
them again.

But he liked this. Being hidden down here, in the bowels of the
ship, under a filthy old tarp, where no one could find him. He had
his passport, so he was okay, and he had her map, with the cross
she'd made to mark the spot. He had his notebook and pencil, the
RMS *Orion* pamphlet, and the label from her tin of soup.

It looked like he was following her to New Caledonia.

10

So Much Vomit

"Help, Enid! I need the bucket again!"

Seventy-two hours at sea, and Margery had vomited her way through almost all of them. The red valise was forgotten, the missing passport was forgotten, and she still hadn't said anything about sacking Enid.

In all her years of teaching, Margery had never missed a day's work. Once, during the war, she'd been caught out by an air raid and found herself trapped overnight in a public shelter, the bombs so close it felt as if they were exploding inside her. It was too much. She'd begun to shake, and once she started, she couldn't stop. In the end, a woman opposite—Margery didn't even know her—had reached out and held her tight. In the coldest tone she could muster, Margery had asked her to kindly remove her hands. People had looked at the woman after that as if she were trouble; she didn't come back to the shelter. Later Margery had felt ashamed. She'd even wished she could have explained, though how she would have done that, she couldn't imagine. But the point was, she wasn't someone who gave in to weakness.

Now, trapped inside the tiny cabin, she could barely move her little finger. The ship rose. The ship fell. One minute she was flying up to the ceiling, the next she was crawling on the bottom of the sea. She had no idea how she would survive another four and a half weeks. Surely it would have been kinder to bash her on the head and leave her senseless. Meanwhile, cabin staff called by once a day, but flopped a mop and left in a hurry. It was Enid who fetched the bucket and emptied it. It was Enid who found remedies. She said she'd never seen so much vomit come out of one person. She actually sounded impressed. She set up card games, and when Margery refused to join in, she played Solitaire, though her relationship with the rules was loose to say the least and she thought nothing of cheating.

Enid was still anathema to Margery, like trying to read a map upside down. She rushed through life as if she were being chased. Even things whose whole point was slowness, like waking up, for instance, after a heavy night's sleep, she took at a lick. "Well, that was nice!" she'd say, leaping down from her bunk. "Rise and shine, Marge!" She joined every on-deck club available, including knitting for beginners, three-legged racing, and country dancing. She was constantly seeking her own reflection, even in the back of a spoon, and still she talked. On and on. Half the time Margery wasn't listening—she was just trying to keep the cabin in one place.

"Don't you love babies?" Enid might say. (Babies were her number one subject.)

And Margery would groan, "No. Not really, Enid, no."

"Don't you just want to hold them?"

"No. I can't say I do."

"Oh, Marge! You're so funny!"

It was hard enough, Margery thought, looking after herself. In the past, she'd even wondered why you'd want to bring a child into the world.

"Touch wood, I'll have lots of babies one day!"

That was another thing: Enid was spectacularly superstitious.

She said you should always try to do a good turn. It created a good feeling, and anyway you never knew when you might need help yourself. She was forever telling complicated stories about people in which lovely things happened that Margery was certain could not have happened. The widower they'd spoken to at dinner was a case in point.

"Guess what, Marge?"

"I haven't a clue, Enid."

He'd met a nice woman on the ship with a little boy. They were going to get married. Enid was so happy.

The only person she said almost nothing about was her husband. She called him Perce, but made no mention of where he'd gone or when he'd be back. Once she let slip she'd "got the shock of my life" because she'd seen a bald man who looked just like him, so Margery assumed he must be older than Enid was.

"I could have sworn he was following me," she said.

"Who was following you?"

"That feller. That feller with no hair."

"Why would a man with no hair be following you?"

Enid rummaged through her bag for a small bootee she was knitting: it seemed a colossal amount of wool for something so miniature.

"Did he say anything to you, Enid?"

"Why would he say anything to me, Marge?"

"About the beetle?"

"The beetle? Why would he ask about a beetle?"

They were going round in circles. There might have been an awkward pause, but Margery was stuck in a very small space with the world's most talkative woman: the chances of Enid falling silent were slimmer than bumping into an undiscovered gold insect. At that point, the liner jammed against something solid and Margery only just made it to the bucket. Enid didn't mention the man with no hair again. And the more she thought about it, the more certain Margery was that if a man was trailing Enid it was for the same reason every man trailed Enid, and that was for a better look.

They were well past the Bay of Biscay when another storm

struck. Margery was woken by the alarming sensation of everything Enid owned dropping on her, like coconuts. She hadn't
thought the sickness could get worse, but her body seemed not to
belong to her anymore. It just emitted without warning. Enid
washed Margery's nightdress, she broke into the laundry room to
get fresh sheets, she borrowed a bunch of flowers from first class,
but the stink of vomit had become part of the cabin. Not even
Enid's scent could kill it.

Portugal. Spain. The ship entered the Strait of Gibraltar and
docked for the night. Naples came next. Margery said nothing
about dismissing Enid. Instead, Enid took a boat ashore and
bought her first watermelon. The Strait of Messina, Stromboli, Na-
varino. At Port Said, they docked again. Still Margery said nothing.
Enid went ashore to try her hand at riding a camel and told Margery afterward how she'd been pointed at because of her yellow
hair. It took sixteen hours in convoy to cover only fifty miles down
the Suez Canal, but once they reached the Red Sea the weather
was glorious. Enid sunbathed every day and turned the color of a
toasted nut. The ship docked at Aden, where Enid bought a battery radio, though she came back appalled by all she'd seen: the
smells and poverty were even worse than they were at home.
They'd had to beat their way back to the ship through a sea of beg-
ging hands, she said.

But something else was upsetting her even more. Did Margery
know what had happened to the murderer Norman Skinner? Margery didn't. For the past few weeks, her world had been confined
to sweaty sheets and a bucket. She barely knew what had happened to herself; she certainly hadn't been following international
news. Well, Enid knew. She'd seen a British paper. Apparently, the
hangman had made a botch of his execution. Broke his neck but
failed to kill him. They had to get another rope and do it all over
again. "They wrote about it like it was a joke!" She dragged at the
contours of her face, looking desperate. And on the subject of terrible things she'd learned, here was another. They had the guillo-

tine in New Caledonia. They actually chopped off people's heads. "It's wrong!" She kept pacing the tiny cabin. "It's wrong!"

"Enid, just because they have the guillotine doesn't mean we can't go there. They have the electric chair in America. We have the noose. That doesn't stop people traveling."

It took another five days to get from Aden to Colombo. There were games to celebrate reaching the meridian and fancy dress; Enid made a tail to fit both her legs and then bounced along as a mermaid. Afterward she won her heat in the Miss Lovely Legs competition—presumably having removed her tail—for which she received a trophy decorated with the ship's logo. Meanwhile, Margery remained in the cabin, surviving on dried biscuits and water and trying to read her beetle books, though there were still things about Enid that didn't properly add up.

1. She kept making tiny woolen things that would fit a fairy. When Margery asked why she didn't do anything normal sized, Enid said she lacked the knitting skills.

2. For all her talk about finding the beetle, she didn't seem very interested in actually doing it. When Margery described the gold beetle, Enid yawned. "How hard can it be to spot a gold insect?" she said. Followed by "Would you say I'm getting fat?" And so far, she hadn't spoken a single word in French, beyond bon *shoor.*

3. There were two initials on the mystery valise, but they weren't Enid's: they were N.C. Margery noticed them once, though the next time she looked, they'd been hidden with a Band-Aid.

4. Enid didn't always come back to the cabin at night. She stayed up dancing. But there was a plus side: Margery was spared her snoring.

5. And this was more worrying: Enid had a thing about killing.

"So what's this for?" she said one day, reaching into Margery's Gladstone bag and pulling out the bottle of ethanol.

"It's highly poisonous. Please put it back."

But Enid didn't put it back. She studied the label in a myopic way. "What does this stuff do exactly?"

"It kills the beetle."

"Kills it?"

"You put the beetle in the killing jar with a few drops of ethanol." Margery felt tense suddenly. "Please be careful, Enid. It's all I have. And it's very powerful."

Enid put the bottle back into the bag as if it had changed shape in the short time they'd been talking. "I didn't know you had to *kill* the beetle."

"Of course you have to kill it. How else could we identify it?"

"You could keep it in a little matchbox."

"Enid, it would not survive in a little matchbox. And the whole point is that the specimen is dead. You can't identify it unless it's dead."

"Why not? A beetle is supposed to be alive. That's the whole point."

"But we don't know what they are until we identify them. And the differences are tiny. You need a microscope to see. It can come down to a few tiny hairs on a leg. Even the genitalia."

"You look at their *willies*? Do they even *have* them?"

"They do, actually. They're all different. And the males keep them inside their bodies."

"Well, good for them," said Enid. "All the more reason to let them live."

"Enid, think. If every animal in the Natural History Museum was alive, there'd be chaos. It would be like a zoo. They'd be running everywhere. And no one would know what anything was. So no one would know whether or not they'd lost it."

"Actually, I like the zoo. I took Perce once. We saw some chimps and they were having a tea party. Then the chimps got on the table and they threw the food all over the place. Perce laughed and laughed. Yes. That was a happy day." Personally, Margery couldn't think of anything worse, but Enid paused for a moment, staring into nothing as if she'd got stuck. Then she said, "So the beetle suffocates in the killing jar? Cos of the ethanol? Is that how it works? I mean, does it hurt?"

"What?"

"Does it pain the beetle? Does it feel like it's burning? Suffocating?"

"It's quick. It's the most humane way of killing."

"What? Quicker than hanging?" Enid gave a shiver she couldn't hide. "Well, I'm not doing it. If you ask me, it's wrong."

Already it was mid-November. They had been at sea for three weeks. With only two left to go, Margery woke one morning with the knowledge that something had changed. She felt thirsty, and not a polite kind of thirsty, but as parched as a hole in the desert. Enid was still flat out in her bunk after a late night, so Margery stuck her head beneath the tap and drank in guzzles. She didn't bother with a glass. Then: hunger. It hit like a freight train. She couldn't dress fast enough.

Hunger is the ultimate expression of hope, and Margery ate in the dining room that morning as if eating were her new job. Eggs, bacon, bread and butter, beans, pot after pot of tea, mopping her mouth with a napkin, only to stick her fork into another sausage. Seconds. Thirds. Sated at last, she staggered to the deck and collapsed into a chair where she sat, warmed by the sun, watching the sea. Never had she seen such blues that fanned out from the bow of the ship, each furrow divided from the next by a frill of white foam, slick and rutted and wreathing together. An entire school of silver fish leaped out of the waves as if it belonged to the sky. Back at home, people would be in coats, queuing for rations of tea and sugar. Margery dozed and came to with the feeling someone was watching, but when she looked, there was no one. Later she found Enid by the pool in her bikini, surrounded by new friends, so she went back to the dining room, where she wolfed lunch, shortly followed by full afternoon tea, then dinner.

She returned to the deck to watch the sun set until only a segment was left above the horizon, followed by the smallest clipping, and then, just as it disappeared altogether, the sky gave an explosion of green, like a blazing emerald. It came and went. If she hadn't seen it with her own eyes, she wouldn't have believed it.

"Oh!" she gasped.

"I know," agreed a woman in a hat. "Isn't life wonderful?"

Margery had survived a month with Enid Pretty. She had managed no more than a few pages in her journal and been sicker than she'd ever been in her life, but she was almost on the other side of the world, and that was more than anyone had said she could do. Already she had seen things she'd never heard of, let alone imagined. Things might work with her assistant after all.

But Enid had one more surprise up her sleeve.

11

Something Fishy

It was the blonde he didn't like. He didn't trust her.

It wasn't just because she'd got the job instead of him. It was something else: he knew a trickster when he saw one. He followed her on the ship, but she swung round sometimes, sharp, as if she knew he was on her trail. And she didn't drop clues, like Miss Benson did. He had a special page for her in his notebook and, so far, all it said was *Enid Pretty*. He wasn't even convinced that was her real name.

Mundic had managed to stay a few days in his hiding place on the RMS *Orion*. No food, but he was used to that—in Burma, he'd survived weeks on a bit of rice, and not white rice but yellow stuff that was crawling with weevils. On the *Orion*, if he'd needed water, he'd crept out from the tarp and taken it from a tap. But then a couple of boilermen found him, and he'd thought it was over.

"Hey! Hey!" He'd tried to run, but he hadn't a chance. He was still weak, even after five years of freedom. They'd come after him and pulled him back. "You could go to prison for this."

There was no point in fighting. He'd thrown a punch but it barely landed. He reckoned one of the chaps had been a POW. It was a thing that had happened since the war: you knew who'd been one, and who hadn't. And the chaps who hadn't got caught looked down on the ones who had, like they weren't real men. That was another thing that had happened since the war.

The two boilermen had walked away to talk it over. He'd heard them arguing about what to do. One said they'd have to turn him in. But the older chap said, "No. I'm not going to do that. Look at him. You've heard about the camps. Haven't you? You've heard how many of them died? It's a crime the way they've been left to fend for themselves." The one who wanted to turn him in had left, and the other had come over and said Mundic would be okay, no one would rat on him, but he'd need to keep his head down and stay out of trouble. And he held out his hands as he said it, like Mundic was a cornered dog.

After that, the boilerman left him bits of food, and when Mundic asked for soap and a razor, he fetched those as well so Mundic could shave his head. A clean shirt. Leftovers from the galley. Some nights they'd played cards. They didn't talk. Then the boilerman said he knew of an empty cabin, and why didn't Mundic sleep there? If he was careful, no one would know. So Mundic moved into the free cabin and it had a little bed and a desk, and he put his notebook and the map of New Caledonia on the desk. When the cleaners came, he said he was a private detective working under-cover, so he didn't want any trouble, and the man with the mop said, "Yes, sir," like he was important.

It was the first time he'd ever had a room of his own. As a kid he'd shared with his mother, just sleeping on the other side of the bed, though when he got too big, she'd moved to the chair. Some-times in the camp, he'd see a man huddled in a corner, not moving, and he'd say to himself the man wasn't dead, it was his mother, curled up in the chair, and it would be daytime soon, and she'd be passing him a lit cigarette, saying, "Wake up, sonny. It's another day." It got easier, if he cut off from things like that.

After a couple of weeks on the ship, Mundic felt stronger. He left the cabin when it was safe and stole a haversack, and another time he took a yellow towel, just as a souvenir, and a Panama hat and a pair of sunglasses, and he began to collect things to take with him to New Caledonia. He wrote about it in his notebook, and he listed what he ate, too, and when the ship stopped at Aden, he took a boat ashore to keep his eye on the blonde. She made her way straight to the Royal Hotel and rushed up the steps, as if she were a proper guest, and he watched her taking up a bundle of British newspapers and skimming through them, page by page, like she was hunting for something. After that, she sat for a while deep in thought until the headwaiter asked if she would care to come this way and escorted her off the premises. Then she made her way to a market and bought a cheap radio, and he thought, Something fishy's going on here, but he didn't know what, so he got out his notebook. But she must have given him the slip because he didn't know where he was: he was just in this alley all on his own, and hundreds of faces were staring out at him, and hands were poking through curtains, and he began to run but he couldn't get away, because all he could see in his mind were the faces of the men in the camp at Songkurai, and he couldn't tell anymore. He couldn't tell if he was still in the camp, or if he was free, until he took out his passport and looked and looked at it and said to himself he was a free man. He was free.

But today was a good day. He went on deck and he couldn't believe his luck because Miss Benson was asleep in a deck chair, and there wasn't a sign of the blonde. He watched from the shadows where she couldn't see him. It was like he was so empty there wasn't a thought or feeling inside him, and a strange peace came over him, and he wished he could have spent his whole life like that.

He stayed, for a long time, just watching.

12

The Truth About Enid Pretty

There was banging. Loud, frenzied banging in her head. Margery groaned and rolled over, trying to get back to sleep.

"Marge, help! Help!"

The banging was not in her head. It was coming from the door. She got up. She opened it. Enid stood on the other side, doubled over. Her face was like flint.

At the sight of her, Margery screamed.

"Ohnoohnoohno," wailed Enid, the words all stitched together. She pushed past Margery and staggered to the sink.

Perhaps it wasn't really as bad as it looked, but the mere sight of blood streaked down the lace skirt of Enid's frock made Margery's head swing. She felt incredibly light and incredibly heavy at the same time. She needed air. She needed it fast. She could kill a beetle and pin it, but when it came to blood, she was still unbelievably squeamish. At the sight of her first monthly, she'd screamed—she'd actually believed she was dying. It was Barbara who'd fetched a knitted rag, and told her what to do. So, instead of asking Enid if she was hurt, or even if she needed help, Margery grabbed her frock and put it on—inside out, as she later discovered—and threw herself from the cabin.

"Marge?" called Enid, but Margery couldn't stop. She lumbered down the corridor, practically trampling another passenger, until she reached the staircase. The steps were narrow and steep, with corrugated rubber treads, and she hauled her feet up them, one after another, telling herself not to think of Enid or her frock, or even what might have happened, but only nice things like blue sky and flowers, until at last the door to the deck loomed into focus. She reached for the handle and noticed her frock was the wrong way round and was so mortified she missed the door handle but still pulled, thereby successfully pitching herself back down the stairs, only this time without the benefit of being upright, and now she was falling, falling so hard, she couldn't remember which way was up and which was down, let alone inside out, but whatever it was, it seemed to be lasting forever. She hit her head on something sharp, and at that point things went a bit sideways.

"Are you all right?" someone asked, which she clearly wasn't—she was a large woman, lying at the bottom of the stairs—but people will ask these things. "I am fine," she said in her best BBC voice. And then she did the best thing possible in the situation. She passed out.

For a while, Margery had no idea who she was, or how she was, or why. She visited landscapes no one had ever seen before, and pinned hundreds of previously unidentified beetles. When she finally came round, she was in a freshly made bed in a room that was large and sunny and smelled not of vomit or Enid, but of lovely clean things, like disinfectant and menthol.

"You had a nasty fall," said a kind voice, while a nurse's hat loomed into focus, complete with a nurse beneath it. "Can you move?"

Briefly Margery thought she was a child again, back at the rectory, her mother in her bedroom, her father in his study, her brothers playing cricket on the lawn. "Where am I?"

"You are in the sick bay," said the kind nurse. "On the RMS *Orion.*" With a thud, Margery remembered: ship, Enid Pretty, villainous frock. She felt weak.

"How did I get here?"

"A passenger found you. Do you not remember?"

Now that the nurse said it, Margery did remember, but only faintly, as if the memory belonged to someone else. She remembered lying on the floor and wanting to stay there, with her eyes closed, until a man had helped her to her feet. She remembered the shame of being so helpless and how he had put out his arm to steady her, and how she had wanted nothing, except to remain asleep.

"You're lucky you're not on crutches," said the nurse. Clearly she was one of those Pollyannaish women who breaks one leg and is happy because the other is still functional. "Take it gently," she said, with a voice like ice cream. She was so lovely that Margery could barely resist the urge to ask if she fancied a one-off trip to New Caledonia. But she did: she did resist because she already had an assistant. It was just that she was covered with blood in their tiny shared accommodation somewhere in the bowels of the ship. Enid was less in the Pollyanna camp, more the Lady Macbeth one. Margery tried to move again and failed.

"No need to rush," said the nurse. "You're going to have a nasty bruise. And you'll be pretty sore, too. I'm going to give you iodine and some bandages. But when we get to Brisbane, you'll have to put your feet up. Have you got someone to look after you?"

Margery didn't even answer.

By the time she got back to the cabin, it was midday. Her assistant lay on the top bunk, wrapped in her prawn-pink dressing gown. As well as the iodine, Margery had a walking stick, which wasn't necessary but felt like having a backup leg. Miraculously her hip was in one piece, but her knees were badly grazed and it hurt to sit.

"Enid?"

Enid was asleep—or, at least, she was lying in a very still position with her eyes closed. Margery knew she was alive because she had an ashtray resting on her chest and it bobbed up and down, like a little boat, as she breathed. Her frock had been washed and was hung over the chair. She opened one eye. "What happened to you?"

"I fell."

"Oh," said Enid. Then she said, "In case you're interested, I think I must have lost my baby last night. So thanks for running away. Just what I needed."

Margery had the feeling of a lot of heavy objects falling on top of her all at once. It was everything she could do to stop herself passing out a second time. "Enid?" she said. "You were pregnant?"

Enid nodded, but not to Margery, only the ceiling.

"How far?"

"Does it matter?"

"I don't know, Enid. I don't know." Margery thought about Enid's miniature knitting and the way she'd touch her stomach sometimes, with a look of tentative awe. Then she tried to haul from her memory what she knew about Enid's husband, Perce, but all she found was that she seemed to know nothing.

"I wasn't sure," said Enid at last. "I wasn't showing or anything. I thought the baby might come about May."

"In *May*? Why didn't you tell me?"

"You wouldn't have given me the job."

"Of course I wouldn't have given you the job. This is a five-month expedition. We might not even have got home in time. And how could you possibly climb a mountain if you were pregnant?"

"Well, it's not a problem now, is it?" said Enid, with a snap in her voice.

"Did anyone know?"

"Beg pardon?"

"About the baby, Enid. Did anyone know?"

"No."

"Not your husband?"

Enid groaned, as if Margery was failing to spot something that was staring her in the face. But when she turned, her eyes spurted tears. "I lose them. I always lose them. Every time. Do you want to know how many I've lost? One, two, three . . ." Enid cradled each of her fingers, as if it were a tiny child. She counted until she got to ten, then stopped and just cried. "I want a baby. That's all I want. A baby. I thought this one would be different."

"Enid, I'm sorry. I'm sorry I didn't help. I'm frightened . . ." She couldn't even say the word at first. "I'm very frightened of blood."

Enid made a sarcastic noise, like an explosion in her mouth. "Well, that's great for a woman."

"I know."

"Still, Marge, you didn't even try to help. I know I'm your assistant, but I'm not your maid. In case you didn't notice, that went out with Queen Victoria. And you're no duchess, either. Your clothes are as shabby as mine."

Margery hung her head. She felt she had been called to give something of herself that was way beyond anything she had given to another person, but everything about her felt too big for the situation. Ideally, she would have liked to sit, only the frock had got to the chair first. Instead she dithered, waiting for Enid to get better all by herself. She asked if she might like a cup of tea.

Enid didn't hear. She spoke to the interesting patch of ceiling above her head. "I should have known I was going to lose my baby. I wasn't sick once. And that's a sign. It's a sign the baby's healthy if you're sick." She gave a laugh that had nothing to do with being happy. "Ha," she said. "Well, I suppose it's over for me. I'll never have a baby now."

At her mother's funeral, Margery had not cried. She was only seventeen. Her aunts had told her not to make a fool of herself in public, but she hadn't done it in private, either. She had watched the coffin being lowered into the ground and she had taken a clod of earth, just like her aunts, and thrown it down, but it had been like scattering mud into a hole. It had meant nothing. She had become aware of a strange snuffling, like a small animal being wrung at the neck, and, turning, had been astonished to find that the noise was coming from Barbara, who did not own a black veil like her aunts, but whose nose was red and whose features were mangled, as if her face had been shoved against a wall. Later, Margery had stared at her reflection in the mirror and screwed up her mouth like Barbara's and tried to cry, but nothing would come. She knew she missed her mother, and she knew she loved her, but missing her mother seemed to be in one place and Margery seemed to be in another, with nothing to join them up.

Enid was not like that. After her miscarriage, her crying was loud and messy. It wasn't just the pain, though sometimes she turned white with it and tensed her body like a fist. She said she couldn't believe her body was doing this. She couldn't believe it was taking away the one thing she wanted to keep. "It was a girl," she cried. "I know in my heart she was a girl."

Enid said she was afraid she was disappearing. When she was pregnant, she knew she was alive, and with every baby she lost, another part of her slipped free. Margery fetched treats to distract her, an egg sandwich, a bottle of nail color. It made no difference. Enid stayed on the top bunk, crying and beginning to smell, with her new battery radio pressed to her ear so that she could hear the General Overseas Service. A few people knocked on the door, but she wouldn't see them, not even Taylor. Margery had no idea you could be so slight and yet carry something so painful inside. And it wasn't as if what Enid wanted was glorious. She just wanted to be a mother, one of the most ordinary achievements in the world. When it had occurred to Margery in her late thirties that she would never have a child, she had not allowed herself to grieve. It had simply been another of those things that marked her apart.

And nursing. That didn't come at all naturally. Unlike Enid, who would happily have cared for every lonely or sick person who so much as coughed at her, Margery was uncomfortable with the role. No one in her life had ever asked for her help—in fact, they'd done the exact opposite: her aunts had endured illness as if it were vulgar to admit defeat—and Margery was afraid of getting it wrong. She suggested Enid might like a walk, but Enid said she couldn't bear to go where she'd see kids. She didn't want to be alone, either. So Margery hung up her frocks and put the lids on her jars, then sat on the yellow chair and talked about whatever she could think of, and since she ran out of things pretty quickly, she told Enid about the gold beetle, then showed her other specimens in her books.

"The gold beetle will be about the size of a ladybug but not as round. And it will have very long antennae, you see, because it is a pollinator. It lives on the white orchid. Now this one is a leaf weevil." She held up the book for Enid to see a picture. "It is bright green and covered with fine hairs. You see?" Or "This is a shiny rose chafer. It lives on rose petals." She went through page after page, showing her favorite beetles and describing them. "This is a rhinoceros beetle. Look, Enid. Look at its long horn. This is an African flower beetle. Do you see how green and red it is? Its big white spots? Or what about the devil's coachhorse? This has an orange head and large black mandibles." Enid would stare at every page and nod when she was done. She didn't exactly say she liked them, but at least she'd stopped howling.

"It's nice," she said once, in a small voice.

"What is?"

"This. You telling me about beetles. It's cozy."

So the last thing Margery expected was what Enid did next.

Three days from Brisbane, the party mood on the ship had changed. Many passengers were on ten-pound tickets to immigrate, and suddenly there was a lot of worried talk about the future. Rumors had begun to spread about migrant camps and the lack of work, how families were sharing Nissen huts. There was even a story about no lavatories in the whole of Australia.

Margery was reading when Enid crept down from her bunk. She had her slip on, nothing else. She looked shockingly pale.

She said, "I've changed my mind. I'm going to stay in Brisbane. As soon as I get a job, I'll send the money for my ticket. I'm going to try to have a baby in Australia."

All this Enid said clearly, hands behind her back and staring straight ahead, as if it were a bit of poetry she'd learned by heart.

Margery's mind went into overload, then jammed. She heard "Brisbane," "ticket," "baby," and the rest tipped over the edge. "But what about the expedition? What about your husband? And, in case you've forgotten, you don't even have a passport."

"I've thought it through. This is the best thing, Marge. You need to hire a new assistant."

And that—as far as Enid was concerned—was it. Margery waited, stunned, as Enid left the cabin to shower. She even wondered if she'd misunderstood. But when Enid returned, making a trail of wet footprints and with her hair turbaned in a towel, she began rummaging through her pots and bottles.

"I bet you'll be glad to see the back of me," she said, laughing.

"Is it because of the ethanol?"

"The what?"

"Is it because of killing the beetles? Because you wouldn't have to do that, Enid. I will do it. You don't even have to watch. I couldn't look the first time I did it." In fact, Margery had almost passed out. But she didn't say that.

"It's not because of the killing, Marge. I just changed my mind. Do you think you could pay me up front? I'm a bit strapped for cash."

After that Enid puffed up her hair and did her makeup, though after a month at sea her jars were practically empty and she had to whack them on her hand to get anything out of them. She wriggled into a frock, stuck her feet in her ridiculous little sandals, and off she went to find her friends. It was impossible to link the woman who had stayed in bed, grieving for her lost baby, with this whizzy updated version, who was going to start a happy new life in Brisbane.

Margery was beside herself. She actually felt that way, as if she was the anger and Margery was a stupid lump standing next to her. She tried staying in the cabin, but it was too small. She paced the deck—"Another lovely day!" called the happy woman in a hat—and Margery had to curb the urge to squash things. Enid had done only what Margery had been planning to do a few weeks previously—she had, in effect, dismissed herself—but Margery couldn't forgive the ease with which she had chosen to give up the expedition. Had she ever intended to go to New Caledonia? Or had she been using Margery from the start? And then to pretend she was doing her a favor by letting Margery down. That was the worst kind of cowardice. After all Margery had been through in her life, Enid's abandonment took on an intolerable weight, as if she was being injected with poison, limb by limb, and the life was being squeezed out of her. She felt stupid for trusting Enid. Stupid, too, for liking her. She paid her the cash she owed as wages, but she wanted never to see her again. She wanted the whole thing done.

So if Enid came into the cabin, Margery took her walking stick and left. The stick wasn't necessary anymore, but she felt an impulse to limp when she saw Enid, just to make a point. Meanwhile, Enid went to the beauty salon on board and had her hair dyed the color of a sherbet lemon. She spent more and more time with Taylor, who'd got fat and bought a cheap new suit. There was something absurd about the man, yet at the same time something else, a sort of arrogance that made Margery uneasy. She saw Enid chattering away with him on the other side of the deck, laughing at the dull things he said, clinging on to his arm as if she couldn't even walk a few steps anymore without his help, and it left Margery feeling dried up inside. Then the woman with the hat came over on the last day and said she'd heard about the awful way Enid had let her down.

"Between you and me, she's that kind of person," she said.

They approached Brisbane in a vicious southerly swell. Margery spent another night with the bucket—surprise, surprise, no sign of her assistant—and was just about to change the labels on her luggage when Enid waltzed in.

"Oh, hello!" she said. She seemed almost surprised to see Margery, as if they had bumped into each other at the bus stop.

She began shoving things into her suitcases, straddling them to fit the lids. The ship's funnel sounded for the last time, and she swung out her red valise—whatever she kept in there was very light. She said, "I know you're angry. I know you're upset. But I have to start again. I want a baby."

"Well, it seems to me you're going the right way about it. Though how you will settle in Australia without a passport, I can't think." Margery tried to get past, but Enid shoved her foot in the way.

"What would you give to find the beetle? Would you give everything you had? Cos that's how it is for me. I want a baby so much it hurts. I'm sorry I let you down, but you said it yourself. You said it the first time you saw me. I was never right for the job. Finding the beetle is your life's work and mine is having a baby. It's our vocation, Marge. If we don't do it, we'll die of sadness. Giving up isn't an option."

This was an exceptionally philosophical speech for Enid. Margery even wondered if she'd got it from a book, except she never read any. The word "vocation" stood out like fruit on a winter tree.

"Friends?" said Enid. "Let's part friends." She grabbed Margery's hand. And the way she held on, refusing to let go even though it hurt, fixing Margery with an expression that was both as frail as a bubble and stone hard, convinced Margery that Enid was right: it was the same for both of them. They would never be happy until Enid had a baby and Margery found the beetle. Despite their differences, they were the same. And it would take everything they had to get what they wanted.

It was too much, meeting herself in Enid like that. Margery made herself solid and pulled free. "Goodbye, Mrs. Pretty."

Enid staggered out with all her luggage. She didn't wave. Only as she closed the door, Margery caught her reply: "Well, fuck you, Margery Benson. Fuck you."

Margery picked up her insect net, her helmet, her suitcase and Gladstone bag. Suddenly the tiny cabin seemed to expand and swing around her head. She had not felt so alone since she lost her mother.

13

Father Spotting and
the Natural History Museum

It was strange. She'd never been much comfort to Margery, but her mother had been a solid presence in her life, like a piece of furniture that stands in the way of everything else. Whatever Margery did, her mother would be there, sitting in her chair at the window, the light shining through to her tender scalp, a cup of tea gone cold on the table. After her death, Margery had felt even more sheared off from the rest of the world. She'd also had another growth spurt. Her frocks hung inches above her ankles, and she was always cold. Sometimes her aunts stared up at her as if she were growing on purpose, just to be difficult.

By the time she was eighteen, her room was like the study of a mad biologist. Insect books everywhere, drawings pinned to the walls, her notes and journals, not to mention all the beetles living in her homemade insect houses and jars. She bought a sweep net for her birthday, and the moment she woke up, she went out. When she searched for beetles, she wasn't too big anymore or too strange. How tiny the world was when you were pressed up against it, how delicate and meshed and constantly changing. Crawling on hands and knees, eyes stitched to the ground, she thought of nothing except beetles. She disappeared, and so did people.

Then two things happened. She saw her father. And Barbara told her about the Natural History Museum.

Near to her aunts, there was a park with a lake and a bandstand, and in the summer there were often concerts. Margery was at the park one afternoon, on the trail of *Aromia moschata*, commonly known as the musk beetle, more than an inch long, rich green in color, thin as a stem, and with very long antennae. One of the few beetles to emit a nice smell. Also, frequently found on willow trees, of which there were many alongside the lake in front of the bandstand. She knelt and began to search. Time passed. A bird called. She looked up.

Her father was sitting on the other side of the lake. He was listening to the music with one leg stretched out. Until that day she'd forgotten one of his legs was stiffer than the other, and so he always sat that way. Everything in the park parted and disappeared and suddenly there was nothing except Margery by the lake and him by the bandstand. She felt incredibly warm, and happy, really happy. All she wanted was to watch, to be with him like this, both with him and not with him, until a little boy came into view, giving her father a ball, and then a woman, offering him a sandwich. Her father smiled kindly and took both.

It was as though a whip had been cracked somewhere deep inside her. Fury filled her mouth. A pain so bitter she could hardly breathe. How could he have walked through the French windows all those years ago and abandoned her? She was his daughter. Had she meant *nothing*? She stayed, nailed beneath the willow trees, her head dizzy, her mouth contorted, while the band played, and her father watched, and people came and went, and the woman fed him sandwiches, and the boy nestled up close and sometimes threw his ball then brought it back, until the concert seemed to be over because people were clapping and the woman packed up her picnic basket and the little boy put away his ball, and they helped her father to his feet, and left.

He wasn't her father. He was someone else's. A little boy's. But

it had upended her to see again what she'd thought she'd left behind.

She went back to the park every concert day. She knelt by the
lake; she waited. The man with the boy never returned. She wrote
to several hospitals, inquiring about her father, but there was no
record of him. She searched old newspapers at the library and
found nothing there, either. What she did find was a reference to
her brothers.

*Benson: Archibald, Hugh, Howard, Matthew. Killed 1914.
Mons. Unknown graves.*

It was like learning something in her heart that she had known
in her head all along. They were dead. Of course they were. Not
only that, so was her father. And not to have accepted something so
obvious felt like neglect of the worst kind. The chasm inside her
opened even further. She walked away from the library, where the
early-evening sun threw her thin shadow in front of her, and she
watched this strange elongated figure with the small faraway head
and was so overwhelmed with shock and grief, she had no idea who
it was. She didn't even know where she belonged. All she felt was
blankness. If she could, she would have walked and walked and
walked until at last she trod herself into the earth and disappeared.

"You should visit the Natural History Museum," said Barbara, a
few months later. "Go on. Stop mooching, and get out from under
my feet. Plenty of beetles there."

Margery did as Barbara told her. She was too scared not to. Barbara drew a map on the back of a Sylvan soap flakes box, and Margery held it out in front of her, like a prayer book or strange divining
rod, following it step by step while dressed in a frock that was now
a bit small and a peculiar hat. Arriving at the vast Gothic building
with its towering dark walls, its turrets and spires and hundreds of
windows, she almost turned away. It was too magnificent. Then a
crowd of schoolchildren swept past, and at the last minute she followed.

Inside she saw the skeleton of a blue whale. She saw polar bears behind glass. An aviary of colorful birds, suspended midair as if frozen in flight. The ostrich, the lion, camels, an elephant. Animals she'd read about but never dreamed of seeing. She climbed the vast stone steps and followed a long corridor where her feet echoed and, without even asking for help, she turned a corner and found herself in the Insect Gallery.

Was this how Howard Carter had felt when he opened the door on Tutankhamun's tomb? For a moment she had to shut her eyes. It was almost indecent, there was so much beauty. Beetles mounted in glass cases and displayed in drawers. Hundreds of thousands. Silver beetles, black beetles; red, yellow, metallic blue, and green beetles; mottled beetles, hairy beetles, stippled, spotted, striped, burnished; antennae like necklaces, mustaches, windshield wipers, clubs; antennae as slight as wispy curls, bobbled antennae; beaded, horned, spiked, and combed; thin bodies, fat ones, round as a bead, slim as a stem; long legs, short legs, hairy, branched, paddle-shaped or pincer.

Beetles that lived in the roots of trees, beetles that lived inside dung, beetles that fed on rose petals, beetles that fed on rotting flesh. Twice the size of her hand; no bigger than a comma. Why did people lift their eyes to the sky in search of the holy? True evidence of the divine was at their feet or—in this instance—pinned in glass cases and drawers, in the Insect Gallery of the Natural History Museum. She went from one to the next. Dizzy. Ecstatic. Overwhelmed. But nowhere did she find her father's golden beetle of New Caledonia.

The first time she looked up was when the bell rang for closing time. Watching her from the door was a short older man with one of those puffy faces that suggest there might be a handsome one hidden inside it.

"Do you like beetles?" he said.

14

No Place for a Lady Like You

The heat in Brisbane. It was like being sat on. Insects chittered like electricity.

Emerging at the top of the gangplank, Margery blinked. A sun such as she had not imagined pulsed down from the sky. Everywhere she looked people were meeting friends, shouting, waving, hurling suitcases, pointing which way to go. Gladstone bag in one hand, suitcase in the other, she was shoved along in a crowd of thousands toward the Health and Immigration Hall. Points of light shot from the water and burned her eyes. Her head hammered inside her helmet. A woman behind shouted down her ear that they'd be lucky to get out alive.

Margery was held for hours in a loud sea of boiling hot, smelly people—swatting flies and doing her best not to touch anyone—until finally a medical officer called her forward. "G'day!" he boomed. He examined her fingernails for the ridging that might be a side effect of TB. He asked her to roll up her sleeves, and inspected her arms, like meat on a stall, and before she could object, he shone a flashlight to her eye, his mouth so close they could have kissed. But when it came to her passport and tickets, the customs officer stared at the photograph, as if it were the world's most complicated puzzle.

Panic tightened her throat. She told him about the woman who had charged into the booth at the passport office in London when she was trying to have her photo taken. She explained that her tickets showed a berth for two people, but her assistant had already left. Her assistant had been an extremely unreliable person. A liar, you could say. She had been lying right from the start. So it didn't matter, she said. She was more than capable of managing by herself. She had done so all her life. When her aunts died, she'd inherited their flat, and also a maid, but then the maid had become ill so she wasn't really a maid. . . .

The words kept spewing out. Even to herself, Margery sounded ridiculous.

The passport official held up both hands, unable to take any more. "Whoa," he said. "Welcome to Australia, Miss Benson. I hope things get better for you, ma'am, I really do. It's a big country. You're bound to make a new friend." Then—before she could explain any more about her situation—he asked the next person to step forward.

The Marine Hotel was an ugly yellow establishment, close to the port. However, it took a long bus journey to get there and Margery couldn't open her window. Everything looked alien and too colorful—the trees were all wrong, and the flowers didn't make sense. Not even the sky seemed right. There didn't seem to be enough room in her head to accommodate so much that was different, and it hurt her eyes to keep looking. Worse, the bus was packed with happy people who insisted on cheering every time they passed a sign welcoming them to Queensland. At the hotel, a friendly young woman sang, "G'day, Margery!" as if she actually knew her, and offered to ring for the porter, but Margery—still smarting from Enid's rejection and determined to prove not only to herself but also to the southern hemisphere that she could manage without help of any kind—insisted on dragging her things to a room on the second floor. Sweat poured from every part of her. Her hip felt jackknifed. She could only hope that wherever Enid had ended up, it was not very nice.

There had been times at sea when Margery would have given anything to be in a silent room with proper windows and a bed, none of them shifting up and down. But now that she was in one, she could hardly bear to close the door. She told herself she didn't need Enid Pretty. "I don't need you," she said aloud, and since that didn't make her feel better, she said it more fiercely: "I can find another assistant." But the quiet seemed to spread into every corner of the room and swallowed it whole.

Margery unpacked her toothbrush and soap, and all she could think of were Enid's multiple pots and jars. For dinner she ate a steak the size of her head, and no one talked so long she felt an urge to snap things in half. The waitress asked if she was in Brisbane for a holiday and instead of being interrupted by Enid—who would have twittered away not just about the gold beetle, but the waitress's lovely hair, and then whether or not she had children, and did she have any photographs, and oh my goodness weren't they lovely—Margery said, "No," and the waitress took her empty plate and moved on. In bed, she opened her guide to New Caledonia and a scrap of paper floated free: *"GoOb luck, Marge! Finb the deetle!"* Outside, the trees gave a soft sound, like a whispered conversation that had nothing to do with her, while a thousand insects briefly switched to mute. It was like the silence before an air raid.

That night Margery dreamed she was carrying a red valise packed with her collecting equipment, but she couldn't manage to secure the lid, and bits of her equipment kept falling out and getting lost. In the end, all she'd had left was a useless pink hat. She turned over and went back to sleep and had the same dream yet again. At that point she gave up. She lay in the strange bed, in the strange room on the other side of the world, feeling so lost and unknown, she could barely move, while outside the insects buzzed, then paused, then buzzed again, as if following an invisible conductor. She couldn't stop thinking of the pink hat.

Enid was far from perfect. And yet it was suddenly clear to Margery, as clear as the light already sharpening at her window, that without Enid's help, she would never be able to find her father's beetle. And while Brisbane was big, it wasn't big enough to hide Enid Pretty: to do that would take a small continent. She had a whole day before the flying boat. Margery would find her.

"No," people said. "Sorry, ma'am. Never met that woman."

Margery described her, over and over. Yellow hair; strong to the point of physical violence; talks a mile to the minute. No one had seen her. The hotel porter asked if she had tried the motel. The motel receptionist sent her to a boardinghouse for women. As the temperature rose, Margery trudged from one street to the next. The sky burned down, glaring and white-hot in the streets, and her helmet was worse than an iron on top of her head. She tried cafés, milk bars, shops where women in afternoon frocks of blue and cerise bought whole joints of meat without whipping out a ration book. She had traveled through Suez, she had seen leaping fish and the green flash at dusk, she had heard about camels and watermelons and palm trees, and now here she was, alone on the other side of the world, looking for a woman with the yellowest hair—and she seemed to have vanished. Somehow, she had believed that her simple will to find Enid would be enough to invoke her spontaneous appearance. Then a man asked if she had tried the old American army camp out by Wacol that was now a holding place for migrants.

It was already midafternoon. Margery took a bus through dusty outer suburbs until the suburbs ran out, and all she could see was dust. By now she was a pool of sweat on her plastic seat; she was actually sliding up and down. She sat with her face toward the window. The great sweeps of space and the hard elemental colors almost blinded her. She still couldn't believe that trees were not the green things she knew at home, but these spindles with rags for leaves. Finally, the bus reached the gates of an army camp, surrounded with high coils of barbed-wire fencing and a hand-painted sign: WACOL EAST DEPENDANTS HOLDING CAMP FOR DISPLACED PERSONS.

The camp stretched for miles, a bleached town of Nissen huts with corrugated roofs, like great big tin cans sliced in half and set on their sides, the heat sizzling over them. She was stopped by a guard at the gate, wanting to see her paperwork, but when she asked after Enid Pretty, he consulted his record book and found no mention of her. It was only as a last resort that she tried Mr. and Mrs. Taylor, just arrived. He checked again. Yes, they were there. He pointed the way—keep on the main road until the fourth intersection. Take a left. Take a right.

Margery limped from one road to the next, from one pinch of shade to another. The air smelled of stew and reminded her of how hungry she was. She turned her eyes from peach and nectarine trees in pink bloom, and orange and lemon trees with proper fruit, to old petrol cans and broken bits of machinery and lines of washing that hung motionless in the heat. In one road, people were hosing their huts to cool them down. In another, they sat on front steps, fanning themselves and incapable of moving. She had no idea why she had come.

Then she saw a figure ahead of her. That figure was Enid.

Distance is an illusion. We stand apart so that we may know each other better: Margery had been away from Enid for a day and a half, and now she barely recognized her. If it weren't for the yellow hair and the clack of her pom-pom sandals, Margery would have marched straight past. Enid moved like an old woman. She was also being followed by several mangy dogs—another telltale sign—though she didn't seem to realize that. She seemed only half awake.

When Margery had imagined this moment, she hadn't banked on it hurting. She had assumed, too, that she would know what to do, but she didn't. She stopped, waiting for Enid to turn and make the discovery for herself, but Enid trudged on, slow as slow. Then she took a left—still followed by dogs—until she reached a hut and paused. She cast a frightened look over her shoulder, and slipped inside.

Margery waited. So did the dogs. They all waited. The sun got hotter. She sat a bit. Walked up and down a bit. Briefly a shadow moved on the opposite side of the road, then disappeared. Panting like heavy machinery, the dogs crawled off in search of shade. By now Margery felt parboiled. Stay there much longer, she would either pass out or spontaneously self-combust. She had no choice but to knock politely at the door of Enid's hut. The door turned out to be a canvas flap, her tap turned into a push, and without so much as a "Good afternoon," she crashed straight through.

If she had known it was a party, she would have brushed her hair. She would also have checked her boots.

"Christ, what's that terrible stink?" was all she got by way of greeting. A hundred lights seemed to shine on Margery. So there she was, standing in the middle of a Nissen hut that was lined with hardboard and hot as an oven, with a number of temporary beds inside it, while ten people gawped back at her. None of them were wearing pith helmets. None of them were dressed in purple frocks. And the terrible stink was Margery. A mix of her own sweat and the lump of dog business that she knew, without needing to lift her foot, was attached to the sole of her boot. Spotting her, Enid's jaw dropped.

"Marge?"

"Who's this, then?" said one of her new friends.

All Margery could see was Enid's face. Despite the makeup, it looked flat and empty. She said, "I need to speak to you in private, Enid."

Taylor pushed his way forward, and stood between them. "Whatever you need to say to her, you can say to me." He was sweating hard. It was even dripping from the end of his nose. He punched one hand over and over again into the cup of the other, his knuckles meeting his palm with a wet slap. It occurred to Margery that she didn't just dislike the man, she loathed him. Then a woman at the back laughed and asked if Margery had spotted any lions recently.

She said, "Beg pardon?" A stupid thing to say. She never usually said "Beg pardon?" but borrowing one of Enid's phrases was like holding on to a handrail.

"Marge, what are you doing here?" said Enid.

"Didn't you hear? She's looking for lions," piped up the unpleasant woman from the back.

Margery had no choice. She had to say her private word to the whole room. "Enid, I owe you an apology. I behaved badly. I let you down. But I'll never find the beetle if you don't come with me."

"Beetle?" laughed the unpleasant woman. "You lost your beetle now, lady?"

"That's right," said Taylor, laughing. "This crackpot thinks she's looking for a gold beetle."

Nothing she had suffered so far was as terrible to Margery as the laughter that met her now. She was one smelly, moist, furious lump of shame, and she had no one to blame but herself. Enid was the only one who didn't laugh. Her head hung low.

"You'd better leave, Miss Benson," said Taylor. "Walk her to the gate, Enid. And mind you come straight back."

Enid stepped forward and opened the canvas door. A slice of hot white light filled the room. "Come on, Marge. This is no place for a lady like you."

Outside, she picked up a shard of glass and scraped the dog mess from Margery's boot. Margery waited, balanced on one leg, helpless. Now that they were alone, she was sure Enid would say she had changed her mind, but she didn't, she just kept cleaning the boot and talking in a fast way about all the lovely people she'd met at the camp. It was late afternoon, and the sun still showed no interest in setting. There was one baby cloud in the sky that looked lost up there. Abandoned.

"Well, thank you for coming!" said Enid as they began to walk, sounding less like a woman in a migrant camp and more like a hostess at a cocktail party.

"Enid, I know I'm ridiculous. I do know that."

A huge bird flew past and settled in a spindly tree, bouncing up and down on the branches.

"I can't come with you to New Caledonia, Marge. I already told you that on the boat."

Now would have been the moment for Margery to open up, but there was no way of telling her story that would make it acceptable. Besides, she had been raised in a house of women whose skill at not saying a difficult thing verged on professional. The truth had become such an elusive entity, she could as easily talk about her feelings as ride a mule. So she said beetles had two pairs of wings. She knew it wasn't good but it was the best she could come up with.

"They have one set called elytra and they're like a shield on top of the second set. When the beetle needs to fly, the first pair splits and lifts, and then the second set—they're very thin, like film— unfolds. Nothing can fold as tightly as a beetle's wings."

"You're so clever, Marge."

"A beetle can't fly with one set of wings. It needs both. It needs the hard set to look after the complicated ones. Butterflies have it easy."

Enid gave a big sigh that didn't seem to produce any words. Then she said, "Look, I'm sorry. You have to get a new assistant."

"You've traveled to the other side of the world just to stop here?" Margery pointed at the Nissen huts and the baking hot road. Another dog limped past, covered with sores.

But Enid wouldn't listen. She had it all worked out. Taylor could put a roof over her head. He was just waiting for his paperwork. Then they'd leave the camp.

"So this is your life? It's like holing up with Bill Sikes."

"Who, Marge?"

"A man in a book, Enid. Not a very nice one."

They passed a group of women on chairs, with their frocks over their knees and their feet in a huge shared trough of water. The women were laughing about something, and when they saw Enid,

they waved and called, "What a scorcher, Enid!" and she waved
back. She said this was her friend Marge from the Natural History
Museum. The women called, "Hello, Marge from the Natural History Museum!" They trudged on.

"Enid," said Margery. "About that—"

But Enid interrupted. "You want to know how I got on the boat
at Tilbury? I stuffed some cash down my bra. That's how."

Despite the heat, Margery had to stop again. She didn't know
which was worse: that Enid had done such a thing, or that it was an
acceptable alternative to owning a British passport. "Why?" she
said. "Why?"

"Because I'm not the kind of woman you need. You'll only get in
more trouble if I come with you. Forget me, Marge. Start again."

They were almost at the gates. The high fencing was ahead. Ripping a page out of her notebook, Margery wrote the address of
the airport. "The flying boat leaves at eight tomorrow morning but
you have to get there early for the weigh-in. I think you'll be fine
with all your suitcases—you're small and the limit is two hundred
twenty-one pounds—though, to be honest, you could lose the fur
coat."

Enid took the piece of paper and stared, as if she was seriously
thinking about changing her mind. Then she said, "I should go
back. Taylor doesn't like it when I wander off."

"And what about your husband?"

This time, when Enid looked at Margery, her face was raked and
twisted. "It's too late, Marge. Anyway, Taylor has a gun. He's not
the kind of man you leave."

Here came that heavy feeling again, as if Margery were being
filled with sludge. They went the rest of the way without another
word. The gun had put their conversation into a whole new place.
Nothing she could think of was big enough to bring Enid back. At
the gates they shook hands, like polite strangers. Then Margery
opened her handbag and passed her a packet of traveler's checks.

"Here," she said. "Take this."

"You already paid me, Marge."

"Enid, please don't be a woman without your own means. Take the money."

Enid tried to object again, but Margery was already on her way to the gate. It was only once she was on the other side of the fence that she heard Enid shout her name.

"Marge! Thank you! I can't believe you came to look for me! No one else ever did that! Good luck! Find the beetle!"

Enid clung to the wire, continuing to laugh and blow kisses. Sick at heart, and far too hot, Margery trudged away and did not look back. She had come all this way to ask Enid to help her, when she should have been doing the opposite: she should have been rescuing Enid. Yes, she had given her cash. But she sensed that wasn't really the point; that, under the circumstances, much more was required. She remembered Enid on the morning of her miscarriage, how Margery had taken one look at her and run. She got the feeling she was always looking at life through a glass wall, but one that had bobbles in it and cracks, so that she could never fully see what was on the other side, and even when she did, it was too late. Then she thought of the group of women with their feet in the big trough and how easily they had sat together, as if they had no secrets. It occurred to Margery that something inside her was hurting, and the thing that was hurting was the knowledge that she would never be that kind of woman. She would always be on the outside.

The bus appeared, throwing up dust, and she clambered on. The driver wished her a happy day and Margery didn't thank him, she just paid for her ticket and found a seat. Enid had come into her life only to disturb it, and now that she had gone it felt not only smaller, and empty, but shabby, too. She pushed at the window but, again, couldn't open it, so she sat there, getting hot.

Her loneliness felt closer than her hands and feet.

15

Closer

He was so close he could touch her. He could reach out with his hand and go knock-knock-knock on top of her helmet.

When he was a kid, it was like he never understood the rules. Or, at least, not the ones the other kids knew. He'd push a boy in a fight, but he had to go a step further and kick him, then everyone would join in and pile into Mundic instead. Or he'd hear a joke and he'd go ha-ha-ha, finding it funny long after everyone else had stopped, so they'd poke fun at him and call him a retard. And it was like someone had struck a switch and there was this anger shooting up inside him and he had no idea how to turn it off.

His mother used to cry when she saw his bruises. It broke her heart. He was her special boy. Every time he got hurt, it hurt her, too, and he didn't want to hurt her. She said he had a flame inside him, but not everyone understood, so he must keep a lid on it like a good lad, or one day he'd get into serious trouble. But sometimes the flame was there before he saw it coming.

He had been okay until the ship docked in Brisbane. He'd had his little cabin on the RMS *Orion* and the bed. He'd found Miss Benson alone on the deck that time, and after that he had saved her life. He wrote all the facts in his Book of Miss Benson so he wouldn't get confused. Then he'd noticed the blonde with a new feller. He'd followed them and heard them talking about Brisbane. And he knew it was going to be okay now, because Miss Benson would need someone else to lead her expedition, and he was right there. He had the map and everything. He was ready. But then he'd lost her in the crowds at Immigration. The doctor took one look at him and moved him aside for questioning, and Mundic had to make up a whole story about how he'd been posted in France, and had never had a tropical disease. By the time he'd got out the only person he could spot was the blonde, so he took the bus with her, and it went all the way out to an immigration camp. But there was no sign of Miss Benson.

He'd got into trouble after that. It was seeing all those huts and the barbed wire. It took him right back. He found himself bang up against a bunch of guards. "What you doing, Pommie?" they asked. And instead of creeping off quietly, like his mother had said, he lashed out with his fist and felt the soft squash of a wet mouth, and he hit another right in the eye, until they grabbed hold of him and kicked and kicked, and he didn't do anything, just lay there till they'd had enough. There was blood in his mouth and on his hands, but he couldn't feel it. He had just stayed where he was and he was so hurt, it was like it was all peaceful and still inside him, so he could sleep.

Then today he had gone back to follow the blonde and he couldn't believe his luck because Miss Benson was there, and she was following the blonde, too. It was like they were all following one another.

It was really funny.

And he wanted to write that in his notebook but he couldn't because they were on the move and he didn't want to lose her again.

Then the blonde had gone into her hut and he'd watched as Miss Benson stood outside and she'd looked so big and hot, he'd

wanted to laugh again. He waited while she went inside the hut
and when they came out, he followed them again, and he saw Miss
Benson give the blonde money, then trudge away alone.

And now they were together on the bus. He was sitting right
behind and he was about to say, "Boo! It's me!" and go knock-knock
on her helmet, and then he remembered how punched-up he was
and he thought he'd better have a wash first. The bus stopped at
the Marine Hotel, and she got off and walked so slowly, it was like
she was made of lead.

Soon they'd be on their way. The blonde was gone. He was leading the expedition now.

16

London, November 1950

It was a neighbor called Mrs. Clark who went to the police. The house belonging to the couple on the opposite side of the road had gone quiet. The curtains had been closed for five weeks, there was a wad of post against the door, and so many milk bottles outside that the milkman had stopped coming. Mrs. Clark's husband, Mr. Clark, thought he might have seen the wife leave early one morning with suitcases, but his sight wasn't so good on account of being caught in a gas attack at Verdun, so he couldn't be sure. What was certain was that there had been no sign of life across the road for five weeks. Mrs. Clark had knocked a few times. She had checked round the back, though, to be honest, the wife had never been the kind of woman who paid too much attention to things like the garden—she wasn't even that bothered about scrubbing her front step. But a lovely young woman, Mrs. Clark said. Heart of gold. The husband was a bit . . . "You know," she said, wiggling her finger as if she were curling the air with a stick. "He has his bad days." It was the war. He was too old but he'd signed up anyway. Lost a leg during training. Didn't even make it overseas. Sometimes the wife put him in the garden along with the laundry, just to get a bit of sun on him.

"Lovely woman," she said again. "She works nights."

The police had barely broken down the door when the smell hit them. Not murderous, more like something rotting. This, it turned out, was exactly that. A vase of flowers in the kitchen that had turned nasty. There was no smell from the body because the house was so cold. At first, they thought he was asleep, but the inspector pulled back the blankets, and one of the younger officers threw up on the spot. It was a bloodbath. Mrs. Clark, who'd managed to follow them up the stairs, saw the sheets and screamed.

They calmed her down with smelling salts. "Just tell us her name," said the officer in charge. "You need to give us her name."

She took gulps of air as if it were medicine. One, two, three. "Nan," she said at last. "Lovely woman. Nancy Collett. Oh, God bless her. What has Nan done?"

Within two days, a notice appeared in *The Times*: "Wanted: Information relating to the whereabouts of Nancy Collett, last seen on 19 October, carrying a red valise."

17

Two Pairs of Wings

Almost dawn: Margery queued alone with her suitcase and Gladstone bag for the weigh-in at the port. Heart going thump, thump, thump.

Ahead, uniformed officials beckoned passengers to step, one by one, onto a giant weighing machine. The rule was the same for everyone. You mounted with everything you intended to take: the 221-pound allowance included both passenger and luggage. The longer she waited, the more anxious she got. Everyone suddenly looked small and neat, even the men, and none of them were carrying insect nets, let alone wearing pith helmets. And even though she'd lost weight during the first month on the ship, it had piled on afterward. If anything, she'd gained more.

For some reason, she couldn't stop thinking of Professor Smith, and she'd managed to not think of him for years, though the day she'd read his obituary in the paper, she'd sat in the staff room, unable to move, as if yet another part of her had been rubbed away. But maybe it was inevitable he should come into her mind now. It had been Professor Smith, after all, who had smiled at her in the Insect Gallery and then—over ten years—had taught her everything he knew. He had introduced her to the private archives he curated at the museum and even allowed her to help with his work. She had loved the display cases, as she pulled them out like drawers. She loved the orderliness of the lines, the tiny pins, the smell of preserving liquid, the minute white labels and the spidery writing with the Latin name of each specimen, along with the date and place it had been found.

Now, waiting for her turn to be weighed, she couldn't stop remembering the first time he'd shown her how to kill an insect. She had placed the square of lint on the bottom of the jar with a few drops of ethanol, just as he'd shown her, and then she had lifted the beetle with needle-eye tweezers, careful not to damage it in any way, and placed it inside the jar. She had screwed on the lid. But the beetle would not die quickly, as she'd expected: it flailed and sucked at the burning air, lifting its antennae, cramming its legs at the glass, calling her—or so she imagined—to stop, amazed and appalled at what she was doing after she had taken such care to lift it gently with her tweezers. In the end, she'd had to look away, until the beetle lay on its back, legs screwed up, wings tightly packed, as if it had never lived at all. She had gone so pale that Professor Smith had taken her to a tea shop, just to revive her.

"Miss! Miss!"

The man in front had already been weighed, and waved through the barrier. Now it was Margery's turn. The official signaled her forward as if she were a dangerous animal. "Miss! This way, please!"

She clambered up with all her luggage, only the step was higher than she'd thought and someone had to give her a shove from behind. The delicate needle on the scale moved more and more slowly—she seemed to be putting on weight, even as she stood there. Maybe it also weighed the heaviness in your heart.

Her total was recorded on a piece of pink paper by an official with shaving soap in his ear. He showed his notes to another man—this one wearing a toupee. He shook his head.

"No," said Toupee.

"No?" she repeated.

"You're too heavy. You can't get on the plane."

And that was it. She had suffered weeks of seasickness, lost her assistant, and just as New Caledonia was finally in her sights, she had met a dead end in the form of two bureaucrats with a bad wig and some shaving soap.

Then: "That bag is mine!" called a voice from the back of the crowd. "Let me through!"

Margery could have danced. Here came one pink travel suit, one perky hat, hair like a yellow lightbulb, three items of luggage, plus the red valise. In addition, a great big pair of sunglasses that seemed to prevent Enid from running in a straight line.

"Two pairs of wings!" she yelled.

No time to ask how she had got away, or what she had done about Taylor's gun, let alone the truth about her marriage and her husband at home. Enid leaped to the scales, tottering under the weight of not only her own luggage but also Margery's. Mr. Shaving Foam happily waved her through, without checking her weight or writing anything on his piece of pink paper, urging her to put down her heavy luggage because it was too much for such a lovely lady and would be loaded on to the plane separately. Before Margery could object, Enid had her gripped by the elbow, and was hurtling her toward Passport Control. There, she pulled out her purse and undid her top buttons, winking at the official, while saying to Margery, "I just need a quick moment with this feller," but Margery—who could not bear the thought of Enid exposing her underwear to any more officials—produced her passport and pointed at the photo, insisting Enid was the brown-haired woman in the background, while Enid put away her purse and fixed her top buttons, and now backed Margery up, or at least provided a smoke screen, with a complicated nineteen-words-to-the-dozen story about the wonders of hair dye, how nice the man was, how much she liked his lovely uniform, and how excited she was about her awfully big adventure with her friend.

The man hid his face. "Go! Go!" he cried, looking like a person who'd been kissed and told off at the same time.

They had done it. They were through.

• • •

A motor launch carried Margery and Enid to the flying boat. It was fully light, and the illuminated portholes reflected in the water like smashed jewels. As the driver cut the engine, the launch drifted beneath a high, broad wing. Inside, the fuselage was divided into cabins with comfortable seats and tables, and there was a heady smell of grease and paraffin. A nice stewardess showed them to their places and gave them a fully illustrated guide to air travel, while a steward offered barley sugar to stop their ears popping, though Enid—speeding now with excitement—swallowed hers without sucking and had to be whacked on the back to dislodge it.

"Let me get this straight," she said. "This thing lifts out of the sea and *flies*?"

One by one, the engines started. Slowly the plane began to move forward, twisting from left to right, stirring up a zigzag of foamy water, the port float rising a few inches as the wings tilted to starboard. Enid screamed and gripped Margery's hand so tightly that she lost all feeling from the elbow down. As waves buffeted the plane from both sides, it moved faster, water foaming at the portholes and filling the tiny interior with green light. Enid went from terrified to ecstatic in the space of a second. "Yes, yes, yes!" she shrieked. The nose began to lift, the sea level dropped down the windows, speckling it like pearls, and, with a scraping, boomy sound, the plane finally rose clear of the water and lumbered upward into the morning sky. Every muscle in Margery's body strained to keep the plane air-bound. Even the ones in her feet.

The plane climbed. Up. Up. Shuddering. Shaking. An improbable amount of noise. Margery's ears popped. The boomy sound seemed to have taken residence inside her chest. Do not look down, she told herself. Do not look down—

"Look down, Marge!" yelled Enid, also yanking her by the neck, so that Margery had no choice. She looked.

The plane's shadow traveled the ground below, like a black beetle. Already things were shockingly small. Houses had shrunk to the size of cotton reels. Roads were no wider than string, with dots for cars. Everything looked so fragile—she felt she could pick it up in her hands. And now here were clouds, little puffy things, while far down, the sea was a sheet of tin.

A tingle like an electric shock ran up from the soles of her feet. If the world was wonderful enough to contain jumping fish, and green sunsets, and these tufty clouds—even crazy, wild women with yellow hair—there must also be gold beetles . . . and then what else? How many other beautiful things were out there, waiting to be found? The stewards served lobster and champagne, followed by ice cream and coffee in little white cups, but she could barely tear her eyes from the window. Here was the endless expanse of the Pacific, cobalt blue, dotted with islets that floated like precious stones. Liners the size of the RMS *Orion* that were no bigger than ants. Then, at last, the archipelago of New Caledonia: emerald islands with pale coral frills as if a child had scribbled all round them with chalk, and—finally—one in the shape of a long rolling pin.

As the plane dropped, the emerald became a patchwork of dark trees with huge mushroom-shaped crowns. Pale scrubland, lagoons of clear water, a heart-shaped green swamp, pointing fingers of white sand and, running the length of it, a red mountain range like a bumpy spine.

The sight grabbed the breath from Margery's chest. For once, even Enid was stuck for words. Britain and rationing and rain seemed to belong to another planet.

"Enid, I have to tell you. I am not an explorer from the Natural History Museum. I taught domestic science for twenty years."

Enid barely shrugged. "That's okay. I can't speak French. I just know bon *shoor.*"

Suspended in the blue vault of the sky, and side by side with Enid, there was no other place that Margery wanted to be.

NOUVELLE CALÉDONIE,
LATE NOVEMBER 1950

SEARCH!

18

This Beautiful Isle

*A Short Introduction to the History of the Islands
by the Reverend Horace Blake*

Welcome to Paradise! New Caledonia, land of palm trees and coral reefs, home to the Kanak people, and where the kagu bird sings!

The first European to discover the island was Captain Cook in 1774. Since it reminded him of his homeland, Scotland, he called it New Caledonia. One hundred years later, Napoleon ordered the annexation of the islands as a penal colony. He renamed them Nouvelle Calédonie. This means New Caledonia, but in French. (See Chapter 5, "Useful French Phrases.")

The island's history is not a happy one. In the early part of the nineteenth century, the worst scum of the white race—whalers, sandalwood gatherers, blackbirders in search of slaves, and plain buccaneers—came to these beautiful, primitive islands, and left the white men's curses in the shape of vice, drunkenness, gunpowder, and disease. The indigenous Kanak people—handsome, hospitable, happy in Nature's abundant supply of all their needs!—were almost wiped out.

Today the islands—fertile and beautiful—abounding with forests and tumultuous waterfalls, are also inhabited by Europeans, mainly French, and South East Asians of Indonesian or

Vietnamese descent. The Kanak people live among tribes and have their own customs. They are a happy-go-lucky breed. It is quite all right to call a man "boy"! This is a widely used term. They will smile and wave in return.

Margery sat beneath a banana tree with the Reverend Horace Blake's illustrated pocket guidebook. It was as much use as a chocolate teapot.

Nouméa sprawled haphazardly: a golden-white beach on one side, palm trees with tops like feathery hats on the other. The mountain range stretched behind. It had rained in the night and drops hung in braids from leaves, while everything smelled of pine and frangipani. As the sun lifted, the sky flashed with bright colors that belonged to other things. Traffic-light green, birthday candle pink, egg yolk yellow, mailbox red. Briefly the mountains held those colors, too.

This mountain range . . . she'd never known anything like it. It seemed to go on and on forever, and light played across it, like emotion on a human face. At dawn, it was one pink mass, green by midday, with cloud shadows resting on it like mats, or even sliced off at the top by mist, blue at dusk, so black by night it seemed darker than the sky. She saw a peak with the shape of a triangle, another like a curate's hat, one like a sleeping elephant. But nowhere could she find any that resembled a blunt wisdom tooth.

Answered prayers can be frightening, suggesting—as they do—an obligation to act. Margery had her assistant again. She was finally in New Caledonia; they had been there almost a week, staying in a boardinghouse by the port. She had found a well-appointed bungalow in the far north of the island, called the Last Place, and paid six months' rental in advance. She had bought a new map and found a bus that made the journey twice a week. She'd seen French colonial buildings and narrow streets where houses were painted yellow and pink and blue; French cafés and bars, *boulangeries*, squares with palms and fountains. Fruits of every color. Fish of every size. Giant kauri trees. Palms with hairy trunks. Ferns with leaves as large as paddles. Flowers like lanterns. People dressed in all kinds of ways, some wearing light European clothes. Children bare naked. Men in skirts. Women with their breasts hanging out for everyone to see, others in missionary frocks that almost reached their feet. And insects, insects everywhere. Not just beetles, but flies, grasshoppers, moths . . . All this newness, this strangeness. This wonder. And yet now that Margery was ready to begin the expedition, she was completely stuck.

Problem one. Admin. She needed to get her permits stamped at the correct French government offices. She also needed an extension to her visa. Without the official permits, she would not be able to present the beetle to the Natural History Museum, and without the visa, she couldn't stay in New Caledonia for more than a month. But there were twenty-three offices to call on, and none of them seemed to share the same opening hours. *"The French Caledonian people,"* wrote the Reverend Horace Blake, *"are not like the British. They are very sociable. They enjoy fishing and cricket."* There was an illustration of a Kanak man holding a cricket bat, and another of a white man fishing, but nowhere did the Reverend Horace Blake mention that the French left their offices for weeks on end, and neither did he mention that they sometimes closed their offices and turned them into other things instead. L'Office Centrale de Permis, for example, was now a milkshake and hamburger restaurant. Margery had written twice to the British consul, asking for help, but received no reply. Every day she set out with Enid, following roads that turned into hot squares, then little alleyways and stone steps, where brightly colored washing was strung overhead like flags, and children carried baskets of chickens or pawpaw, and once a small pig. So far, they'd found only four of the twenty-three offices. Several, it turned out, had never been there to begin with, and others possibly didn't exist at all.

French. Another problem. Everywhere she went she heard words and sounds she didn't understand. Vowels that ran like small motors, tongues purring, explosive combinations of consonants.

She tried the everyday phrases in the guidebook, and no one had a clue what she was talking about. If anything, they looked concerned. She had no idea how to get it right.

Fortunately, Enid had a flair for communicating in a foreign language that took everyone by surprise, including speakers of foreign languages. She didn't give a damn about getting it right. She got the hang of basic words like *fromage* and *café au lait,* as well as *scarabée* for beetle, and the minute she got stuck, she mimed. "Bon *shoor*!" she would yell. "Have you seen *un* gold *scarabée*?" Or "Do you know *un* mountain *dans le* shape of *un* wisdom tooth?" She flapped her arms like wings; she pretended she had a great big beetle stomach; she even showed people her back molars.

Enid's inquiries could attract a small crowd, laughing joyfully and offering gifts she might like, such as fruit, or coconut milk, and once an old baseball cap. They also caught the attention of a smelly stray dog that was halfway in appearance between a white rabbit and a baby seal. Enid adored this dog and called it Mr. Rawlings. As far as Margery was concerned, it was the most useless dog she'd ever met, but it followed Enid like a shadow. She fed it scraps when she thought Margery wasn't looking and smuggled it inside the boardinghouse at night so that it could sleep on her bed.

Three. The very serious problem of Margery's luggage. Only her tea chest of food supplies and camping gear had arrived. All of Enid's luggage had been delivered, even the red valise—which she'd stuffed beneath the bed, quick as a shot—but there was no sign yet of Margery's suitcase, and no sign either of the Gladstone bag containing her precious collecting equipment. "But you did label it?" said Enid. Margery circumnavigated this question. She'd been on the point of labeling it as the RMS *Orion* docked at Brisbane, but then Enid had waltzed into the cabin. After that her mind had been on other things. Nevertheless, they went to the office of the airline every morning to inquire, and were told not to worry, the missing luggage would come that afternoon, straight after siesta, and every day it didn't.

(Siestas. Another mystery. Who knew that at midday an entire population could drop whatever they were doing, and pass out? Needless to say, Enid took to siestas like a duck to water.)

And there was one last thing, harder still to explain. Now that she was here, Margery felt overwhelmed. It wasn't simply the beauty of the island. The color. The smells and dazzling light. It wasn't even the paperwork and loss of her luggage. She didn't actually know what to do next. It went without saying that she was in New Caledonia to find a beetle, but it had been a lot easier to think about finding it when she was nowhere near it.

She couldn't admit that to Enid. She could barely admit it to herself. So she clung to her paperwork as if it were a lifeline. She needed to get the admin right. She needed it very much. Because as soon as she had the proper extension to her visa and twenty-three official stamps on her permits, everything else—including her suitcase and equipment, but, most of all, her faith in her own judgment—would turn up. She really believed that.

A pair of eyes blinked from the shadows. A green lizard emerged, the size of a dog. It lumbered toward her, and stopped to eat an ant. She couldn't believe how long it took. The little jaws, the flick-flick of the tongue, the great rippling pulse of muscle below the shoulder. Ant eaten, it turned and poked its tail at her and slunk away.

She went to wake Enid.

19

The Trouble Is That You Think
You Have Time

"I just don't understand why we're stuck in Nouméa," said Enid. "I thought you were worried someone else would find the beetle first."

"We are here because of our paperwork," said Margery. "And, anyway, I have no luggage."

"Why can't we go without that stuff?"

"Because I can't climb a mountain in my best frock, Enid. And I certainly can't do it without my equipment. You don't even have proper boots. Besides, we could get arrested without a visa. As soon as I have it all sorted out, we can go to the bungalow. The bus leaves every two days."

"The bus?" repeated Enid. "We came here on a flying boat, and now we're making the adventure of our lives *by bus*?"

"There's no other way to get there."

"Mules?"

"No, Enid. We absolutely will not go by mule. That will not be necessary."

They were taking *petit déjeuner* in one of the charming French cafés that lined the Baie des Citrons, but Enid had woken in a bad mood and was flipping through *The Times* without actually reading it. Not that there was any need. It was dated August 1950—everything it reported had happened when they were still at home. Apparently, British newspapers arrived in New Caledonia only spasmodically—it could be Christmas before anything new came. And even though Enid kept trying, she couldn't get a signal for her radio because of the mountain. Meanwhile, she would still say nothing about Taylor, or how she'd got past his gun, and if Margery asked about Perce, she simply shook her head. Out in the bay, white surf flicked a coral reef, and beyond that, the open sea was dark blue. Within the irregular arc of coral, the water was as still as a lake—blues of all shades, along with shadowy green and purple. Men were unloading fishing boats on the sand, and a woman was hunkered beside them, scooping out fish innards and slopping them into a bucket. Birds hopped round her.

"The kagu," said Margery, helping herself to another croissant.

"The what?" said Enid.

"That big white bird. With the spindly red legs. They're indigenous to New Caledonia. They can't fly."

"Oh," said Enid, remarkably unimpressed. "That's probably why they're indigenous to New Caledonia." She pushed away the newspaper and glanced left and right, as if checking for someone. "This is mad. We should leave. What difference does it make if you don't have your paperwork?"

"If you must know, I made a mistake once. I don't wish to make it again."

"What kind of mistake?"

Margery drew her mouth into a plum shape. "If you must know," she said again, because saying old things twice seemed safer than saying new ones once, "I stole my boots."

"You stole them? Where from?"

"From the school where I worked."

"You stole your boots from a *school*?"

"Yes, Enid. This is not a laughing matter. It is now in the hands of the British police."

But for Enid it was a laughing matter. She laughed a lot. "I can't believe you stole your boots. What came over you, Marge?"

"I don't know." It was a question she still asked herself but without ever coming up with an answer that she deep-down believed. "The point is, we can't just go. Besides, I'm waiting to hear from the British consul. I expect a reply any day."

"Why?"

"Because we're British. It's about connections, Enid. Who you know. The British consul will help us. He could sort out my visa."

Enid whipped a cigarette from her packet and lit it. A shot of smoke escaped from the side of her mouth as if she were on fire. She said, "Someone is still following me."

"No one is following you. Or, rather, everyone is following you, but you've only just begun to notice. Even mangy stray dogs follow you."

Enid ignored that. She just patted Mr. Rawlings and fed him half a croissant. She said, "He was on the ship. Remember? He followed me in Aden. And I'm sure he was there at the camp in Wacol."

"Who?"

"I don't know. I never really saw him. I think he had no hair."

"But why would he be following you?"

Enid shrugged. Or maybe she shivered. "The trouble is that you think we have time and we don't, Marge. We need to leave this place and start searching."

To Enid's relief, the lost luggage arrived at their boardinghouse that same afternoon. There was only one snag.

"It's not hers," said Enid. "And her Gladstone bag is missing."

The French delivery boy said (in French) that the luggage looked like Margery's. He was dressed in white with canvas shoes to match. Someone had sewn a brocade trim onto the shoulders of his shirt—presumably his mother, because he looked all of twelve. His skin was golden and fluffy, much like that of a peach.

"How could you possibly know what her luggage looks like?" said Enid. "You've never seen it." (This in English, but with a mime of a person looking for something and carrying a suitcase. The delivery boy was delighted. He sat down to watch.)

"Where is my equipment?" said Margery.

In answer, the delivery boy pointed again to the suitcase he had delivered. He could point as much as he liked; it still wasn't Margery's. For a start, it was brand-new. Enid said they should check the case anyway, but when she tried to open it, the lock wouldn't move. Margery was about to make an emergency phone call to the airline when Enid came up with a better idea. Enid's better idea was to pick the lock on the suitcase, open it, and see what was inside. It was inconceivable to her that they would return a suitcase that didn't belong to them without even taking a look.

Margery counted on the lock stumping Enid, but she might as well have laid bets against her running out of things to talk about. Enid examined the lock with one eye rammed against the shaft, fetched a bobby pin, and had the thing open in seconds. She pulled out sundry items: Bermuda shorts, short-sleeved shirts—some plain, some patterned with flowers—socks, garters, and a large jacket with pockets.

"Are you an idiot?" shouted Enid. "Of course this stuff isn't hers. Have you any idea who this woman is?"

The delivery boy shook his head, surprisingly upbeat for someone who had just brought a full set of male safari clothes to a hot lady and her volatile friend.

"She's a famous explorer," said Enid. "That's who. She's going to find a beetle and take it back to the Natural History Museum."

"But my equipment?" said Margery, again. The Gladstone bag contained everything she needed. She felt hollow. "Where is it?"

At this point Enid took over. Sensing disaster, she tipped the delivery boy and ushered him out of the room. She got Margery a chair and sat her down. "Marge, I need you to be calm. I need you to tell me exactly what you've lost."

"A killing jar, a pooter. Oh, no. I have no ethanol—"

"Marge, that's not being calm. That's flapping. Tell me what those things are for."

But Margery could barely think in a straight line. Without her collecting equipment, there was no way they could continue. "We might as well cut our losses and go home. I could try to get another teaching job." Her voice ran out even as she said it. She couldn't think of anything more desolate.

"No!" Enid practically shouted. She twisted her hands and paced up and down, followed at close quarters by Mr. Rawlings. "There has to be a way round this. Can we buy the stuff?"

"Where? And, anyway, I can't afford it."

"Okay, okay. What is a pooter?"

"What is a pooter?"

"Yes. Marge. What does it look like? Don't go blank on me. Think." Slowly, and with much faltering, Margery managed to explain that a pooter was a small suction collector with two rubber tubes going into it, one of which you placed over the beetle, the other you sucked.

Enid stopped her pacing and listened.

"How long are the tubes?"

"About eighteen inches."

"Like in a chemistry set?"

"I suppose like a chemistry set. Yes. I suppose."

"All right," said Enid. "What else?"

"Naphthalene."

"What is naphthalene?"

"It stops other insects from eating the specimens."

"Okay. Naphthalene. Got that. What else?"

"Pins. I need pins."

"Like ordinary pins? Dressmaking pins?"

"Yes, they would do. They must be very small."

"What else?"

Forceps. Tweezers. Pitfall traps. A sharp knife. A brush. Not to mention blotting paper, ink, pens. Her head began to spin. It was worse than being on the ship.

"I get the gist," said Enid. "There are a few inquiries I need to make, but I won't be long." Before Margery could ask anything else, she was out of the door.

Margery had no idea of whom Enid might possibly make inquiries in Nouméa. It was true she often wandered off and found something in the market: a bag of mangoes, a terrible painting of the Baby Jesus, a square of brightly colored fabric. And she always had a story of some poor, unhappy person she'd befriended on the way back. But she'd made no mention of meeting anyone normal, let alone a person who owned insect equipment.

She returned after ten minutes. She remained just as evasive after her inquiries as she had been before them.

"Well?" said Margery.

"All sorted out."

"What do you mean?"

"I mean, leave it with me." Enid changed into a pair of slacks and gloves and put on her baseball cap. Margery began to object that whoever she was going to meet, Margery should meet, too, but Enid cut her off. Margery had nothing to wear except a pile of clothing belonging to a big man they had never met. Either that, or her best frock. "And I'm sorry, Marge, but we need to sweet-talk this chap, not put him off." She kissed Mr. Rawlings and told Margery not to worry. When Margery tried to give her money, she said she still had her traveler's checks, so it would be fine.

Never had time passed so slowly. Enid was gone for the whole evening. The sun lowered and, in the distance, the mountains glowed like pink whales. Margery walked Mr. Rawlings beneath the palm trees, though he was so distraught he kept laying his head on his paws and letting out sighs that seemed to deflate him. He really was the most useless dog in the world. The last post was delivered—with one letter for Margery—but there was still no sign of Enid. By the time she turned up, it was dark. There was a full white moon, and low purple clouds lay over the horizon. She kicked the door open, bearing a box of supplies that was so big her torso was hidden. She was just two thin legs and a head with a baseball cap on top. Her face was popping with happiness.

Two bottles of ethanol, three of naphthalene, Kilner jars, Band-Aids and bandages, lengths of rubber tube, specimen jars, safety pins, a box of pins, a broom handle, scalpels and blades, scissors, tweezers, insulating tape, several small empty tins, as well as a pair of old soccer cleats—

"Enid? How did you get so much? Where's it all from?"

Enid mumbled something about a nice doctor who liked helping people. Then she threw herself onto the bed, like a child in snow. "You've got your equipment. I have a pair of boots. Now can we do this thing? Can we get out of here?"

Margery beamed triumphantly and stood taller in her girdle and stockings than she had ever stood before. "I, too, have news, Enid. My efforts have not been in vain. An invitation came in the evening post from the British consul. We are going to a garden party at six P.M. tomorrow."

20

Brisbane

He was stuck in Brisbane. She'd left the Marine Hotel and boarded a plane to New Caledonia without him. The first he'd heard about it was when he went to Reception, and said he was there to see Miss Benson about an expedition.

The receptionist had looked at him like he was dirt. "But don't you know she has already gone?" she'd said.

He had hit the desk so hard that the receptionist flew out of her chair, and the next thing he knew two big blokes in porters' hats were escorting him off the premises.

Mundic had hung round the harbor all week, but no one would let him board a tourist steamer without a ticket, and that would cost more money than a man could make in a month. He'd pulled off a cruise to the other side of the world, but when it came to a boat to a little island, he couldn't even get past the barrier.

At the jetty, a knocked-up old cargo ship had come in, heading for New Caledonia. The crew were loading crates before they let the steerage passengers on. He called up to the deck to ask how long it would take to get there. They said a month. He asked if he could take a look. They yelled at him to clear off.

He missed the RMS *Orion*. It was so crowded in Brisbane, with the blinding sea on one side, the cranes on the other, and all those people shouting and smelling of sweat. Then, mingled with all the noise and color, the heat and the haze, there were the faraway sounds, if you listened, of people eating and laughing. It got him confused. He couldn't remember sometimes where he was. He even thought he was in Burma. Besides, his feet were beginning to play up and he was afraid it was the beriberi coming back. It had started at the camp when they'd had nothing to eat but a cup of rice, and he'd got so weak and breathless he'd be throwing his guts up and it was like his legs were made of paper. There'd been times in Burma he'd had to tie a length of liana creeper from his big toe up around his knee, just to keep marching—he'd seen men fall over and die, right next to him, unable to take another step. Now all he wanted was to get to New Caledonia.

He'd slept on benches after he lost Miss Benson. Hung around the port. Tried to stay where no one could bother him. It was like he'd lost all direction. He kept his passport safe in his pocket, and he took it out and said to himself, "I am a free man," but he didn't write anything in his notebook. There was no point.

Ahead, the cargo ship was loaded up, and they were beginning to admit the first passengers. He scanned the crowd, looking for a weak link.

There was a delay leaving. A woman on the jetty began to kick up a fuss. She was shouting that her tickets had been stolen. Someone had taken her purse. The captain refused to let her board without them, and she said it wasn't her fault, one of her kids had been crying. She was getting hysterical. The captain made an announcement on the loudspeaker, asking if anyone had seen this woman's purse, and Mundic, who had got himself a seat right at the front of the boat, kept very still. He watched the shocked face of the man beside him, how his mouth dropped, so Mundic copied and made the exact same face, like he was shocked, too.

The ship pulled free of the jetty, and the woman with kids was left behind. But he had her purse now, so he could buy food.

Another month and he'd be in New Caledonia.

21

Time to Head North

The British consul had never heard of a golden beetle. And he thought Margery was joking when she asked for help with her visa. "I'm afraid that's not something I can do!" He laughed. "French bureaucracy!" Then he said, "It was smashing to meet you, Mary," and moved on.

His home was a large French villa on Mont Coffyn, overlooking the bay and Îlot Maître, a small rocky formation in the middle of the sea with the look of a hairy pimple. The consulate garden was beautifully kept, the grass as green as an English lawn, sloping down to a thicket of fig trees, bananas, and papery red hibiscus flowers, where someone had hung homemade Union Jack flags. It was a small party: men in tropical suits and old-school ties, dabbing their necks with handkerchiefs, as if they were covered in tiny cuts, and their wives in cocktail frocks that stuck out from the waist like lampshades. Dark-skinned staff moved between the guests, dressed as British waiters, with white gloves on their hands and hats attached to their thick hair.

"These people have *slaves,*" hissed Enid. Despite her reluctance to attend, she had sprayed her hair until it stood up by itself and put on a tight spotty outfit that left nothing to the imagination.

Meanwhile, Margery had washed her best frock. That was as much as you could say.

"They are not slaves, Enid. They are *staff*."

"I don't like this place, Marge. This is a very bad idea."

A waiter gave them drinks served in half coconut shells, with straws and foil umbrellas. Enid downed hers in one suck, and took another. "We don't belong here," she said again.

"Actually, we do. We are British."

"If this is being British, I'd rather be something else."

"Like what, for instance? What else could you possibly be?"

"Well, I don't know," said Enid. "But not this. I don't want this."

The consul's wife interrupted to introduce herself as Mrs. Pope. Mrs. Pope was one of those neat, thin women who made Margery feel the size of a tree. She tried to lessen herself by stooping. Now she resembled a hunchback. Meanwhile, Enid said she was off to check Mr. Rawlings, whom she'd left looking devastated at the gates. Secretly Margery was relieved. It would be easier to tell Mrs. Pope about the beetle and traveling north to Poum without Enid butting in to ask about babies. Besides, she hadn't said this outright, but when Mrs. Pope asked if she was from the Natural History Museum, Margery had nodded as if she might be.

Mrs. Pope laughed when Margery told her it was the dream of a lifetime to come to New Caledonia. "Oh, but it's such a hellish place," she said. "Absolutely nothing happens. And the north is even worse. You can go miles and not see a white face. Wouldn't you rather be anywhere else?" She introduced Margery to a group of women who were all variations on the theme of Mrs. Pope. Neat, immaculate, sweet smelling. And all blond—like Enid, but without the chemicals.

"Miss Benson is an insect collector," Mrs. Pope said.

"Gosh!" sang the women.

"She works for the Natural History Museum."

"Gosh!"

"She's going to find a gold beetle in the north. She is heading for Poum."

"Gosh!"

"I'm just waiting for my lost luggage and paperwork," said Margery. The women agreed that New Caledonia was an awful place. The heat and the insects, and it was so far from home—you could spend whole months without a scrap of news. Their husbands were there to manage the nickel mines. They couldn't wait to leave. Several wives had gone already. ("Emotional difficulties," said Mrs. Pope, tapping the side of her nose.)

"You should get in touch with my husband," said a woman with a little-girl voice. Her frock was covered with white frills. It was like talking to a wedding cake. "Peter manages a mine up north. Here is our address. He will be home for Christmas." She wrote her details on a piece of paper with their names—*Mr. and Mrs. Peter Wiggs*—at the top.

Margery had no intention of visiting them, but she put the note in her handbag out of politeness.

The women were desperate for the latest stories from home. ("The last British newspaper I saw was from summer," said Mrs. Pope.) Was it true things were as hard as they'd been during the war? There was still rationing? What did Margery know about the murderer Norman Skinner? Did the hangman really botch the execution, and have to hang him a second time? They reeled off great lists of things they missed. Queues, gray drizzle, properly stocked shops, Branston pickle, English fields. Or what about the Festival of Britain next May? Would Margery be back in time? Wasn't she *terribly* excited?

And Margery, who had never really enjoyed any of those things, even when she was bang in the middle of them, found herself saying, "Yes! Yes!" She couldn't wait, she said, for the Festival of Britain.

"You should join us for coffee," said Mrs. Pope. "We meet every Friday."

"Just the wives," said Mrs. Peter Wiggs. "We do craftwork. Don't we, Mrs. Pope? We make all sorts of things."

"We'll be hosting a Three Kings party on January the sixth to mark the end of the festive season. You must come."

"We all dress up as kings!" said Mrs. Peter Wiggs. "It's such fun!"

"How long are you here, Miss Benson?"

"Only three months."

"Oh, lucky you!" chorused the women. "Going home in February!" Then a waiter produced a tray of tiny sandwiches, and they held up their gloved hands. "No, boy! I couldn't! I couldn't!"

Margery wished she couldn't, either, but she was starving, and since the sandwiches were the size of postage stamps, she said yes, please, and took one.

Unfortunately, the sandwiches were not so tiny or stampish as they looked. As her mouth met one end, the entire filling spurted out of the other. She didn't even have a napkin. At the same moment, Mrs. Pope said, "I expect you've heard the shocking news, ladies?"

It must have been politeness, but Mrs. Pope chose to address her shocking question to Margery and consequently everyone was staring at her. She managed to say, "No," but with a mouthful of bread and a handful of egg filling, it was hard to express any further interest without also sharing the sandwich. She was mortified.

"There was a break-in at the Catholic school last night. Someone stole supplies from the chemistry department. As well as all sorts of equipment."

Briefly the world stopped and then started again at a different speed. There were scandalized gasps from the women.

"Have they caught anyone?" said Mrs. Peter Wiggs.

"Not yet, Dolly. But they will soon. It will be one of the natives. The GIs, Miss Benson, introduced the natives to all sorts of things. Life on the island isn't the same since the war."

"That's right," agreed the women.

"And it gets worse when you leave Nouméa. It's simply not safe up north."

"People have got lost," said Mrs. Peter Wiggs. "They go north and never come back. And aren't you worried about the cyclones? The whole island gets shut down."

"I assume you have a man with you?"

But Margery failed to reply. All she could see was her assistant, now on the other side of the lawn, surrounded by a group of husbands, like the brightly colored center of a pale wheel. She was telling them something hilarious. The British consul was laughing so much, he had his hand on her bottom.

Margery turned back to Mrs. Pope but too late. Everyone had followed the direction of her gaze, and they were all staring at Enid. Mrs. Pope's face was an aghast O. At this point, Enid gave a laugh that Margery wished she hadn't: exposing, as it did, even more of her already highly exposed cleavage. It was only a moment, but judgments are made in the blink of an eye, especially harsh ones, and Margery knew that Enid had been cast as an outsider, and trouble.

"Who *is* that person exactly?" said Mrs. Pope.

The women said they had no idea. Margery did her best to look like someone admiring the flowers.

"Weren't you speaking to her earlier, Miss Benson?"

"Oh!" she said casually, as if it were a small thing she'd just remembered. "Mrs. Pretty is helping me with my research."

"You mean you know her?"

"Only professionally. We are not friends or anything."

A waiter arrived with more sandwiches, but Margery was still trying to deal with the remains of the first. Besides, Enid had vanished from the garden.

Margery found her at the back of the house, smoking with the waiters and stuffing leftover snacks into her bag for Mr. Rawlings.

"Finished yet?" said Enid, barely able to hide a yawn.

"Let's go," said Margery. "Now."

The sun had begun to set. In the west, there were great masses of crushed-up rosy clouds, like another mountain range, and everything shone flamingo pink, even Mr. Rawlings and Enid's hair. They went along the Baie des Citrons where cafés and shops were closing for the night, and the streets were strung with red and green electric lights. Down on the beach, fishermen sat mending their nets. Water slapped gently against the hulls of the boats, and the waves were fluorescent curls. In the distance, lightning quivered in the sky. A storm was coming.

For a while they walked in silence. Or, rather, Margery marched, while Enid—even though she had hoisted her frock over her knees for ease of movement—mostly hopped. At every step, mosquitoes flew up, glistening like pink dust. Finally, it was too much. Margery said, "There was a break-in last night at the local school. But I imagine you know about that."

Enid said nothing.

"You think I'm an idiot? I have never been so ashamed."

"I was trying to help!" Enid swung round so fast Mr. Rawlings went crashing straight into her. "I was doing you a good turn! And how did you think I got all that stuff? Did you think I fucked a doctor?"

Margery bristled. She had never really heard a woman swear before. She still wasn't used to Enid's language. And the truth was, that was exactly what she'd thought, but she had been prepared to let it pass because at least she had her equipment.

"Anyway," said Enid, "you stole your boots."

For a moment, Margery felt kicked in the shin. She wobbled. But she rallied. "That is not the same. And at least I tried to give them back."

"So it's all right when you do it, but it isn't for me?"

"Tomorrow you will have to take everything back to the school. You will have to apologize and explain."

"And then what?"

Margery started to reply, but Enid cut her off. Why were they waiting to get her paperwork stamped? What were they even doing at the British consulate? Margery's return passage was booked for the middle of February. They had less than three months. "Three months!" she yelled. "That's all! And we've already wasted a whole week!" Margery wasn't going to find the beetle because she had an official stamp on twenty-three pieces of paper. She wasn't going to find it because she was hobnobbing with a load of expatriates. And she certainly wasn't going to find it because she was wearing the right frock. She was going to find the beetle because she was up a mountain, crawling on her hands and knees, lifting every stone, and praying for help. Enid's voice had risen an octave and turned thin and wiry. And she was so physical with it, putting her whole body into exaggerating each word. Even her hair looked cross.

And praying? Had she just said *praying*? Margery had not prayed since she was a child. Her aunts had done so much, she'd felt exempt. Besides, after realizing the truth about her father, she had given up on God. Or, rather, she had turned her back on Him. But this was not the time to contemplate whether she was an atheist or actually agnostic. Enid was still yelling.

"You know your problem, Marge?"

"No, but I have a feeling you are about to tell me."

"You're a snob. You're a complete snob. You're on a fool's errand, and you think you can do it by the book. Well, I don't give a toss about your paperwork. It's the first of December, and tomorrow I'm heading north."

"And how exactly will you do that? The bus doesn't leave for two days."

Enid didn't enlighten her. She stormed ahead, snapping off hibiscus flowers as she went, even tripping once because of her sandals, while Mr. Rawlings ran behind. At the boardinghouse, she tore off her clothes and got into bed. She didn't even bother with her mosquito net. She was asleep in seconds, and so was the dog.

Margery sat in her half of their room, feeling very hot and disliking Enid more intensely by the second. The lightning came more frequently now, but it still wouldn't rain. Worse, she seemed to be trapped with an insect that sounded like a flying motorbike. The air felt squeezed.

If it wasn't for Enid, she would still be at the cocktail party. And how dare Enid? How dare she call Margery a snob? The one with the problem was Enid. At least Margery didn't dress like a call girl.

At least Margery had been taught how to eat with her mouth closed, and use a knife and fork. That wasn't snobbish. That was just good manners. And what about Enid drinking tea with her little finger poked in the air, like a radar scanner? How snobbish was that? She could barely resist the temptation to wake Enid and point all this out. But she did, she did resist, because despite all her protestations, somewhere deep down it had begun to dawn on Margery that Enid might have a point. She herself had wanted to go to the British consul party's because she wanted the approval of the establishment, in the same way she wanted all her paperwork properly stamped. She wanted to get everything right. She wanted to please him. But the truth was that the British consul had barely noticed Margery. If anything, he'd treated her as a joke.

And a fool's errand? What was Enid doing here, if she really thought that?

Enid lay on her bed, flat out and snoring, her mouth wide open. Margery took up Enid's frock and put it on a hanger. It smelled of Enid—her incredibly thick, sweet smell—and there was a dot of pink powder on the collar that she rubbed off. It occurred to her that an item of clothing meant nothing until you knew the person who wore it, and then it became a thing by itself. And Enid's polka-dot frock struck her suddenly as one of the bravest things she had ever met. She straightened it on the hanger. Then she pulled the mosquito net over Enid, checking for gaps. She even patted Mr. Rawlings.

Afterward she got into bed but couldn't sleep. It wasn't the humidity that bothered her now, or the motorbike insect. It wasn't even the theft from the school. It was the way Mrs. Pope and her friends had stared at Enid, as if slicing her into parts, and the way Margery had said nothing. There she had been, sucking up to Mrs. Pope, when the one person who was true to her was Enid. Yet again, she experienced the dense feeling she had felt outside the camp at Wacol, as if she were always on the other side of a flawed glass wall and seeing the truth way after it was too late.

Margery had only five stamps on her paperwork. Her suitcase was still missing, and she had no extension for her visa. But Enid was right. It was time to stop doing things by the book, and head north. A peal of thunder banged overhead and here at last came the rain.

22

London, December 1950

It was only a week since the police appeal for help in *The Times*, but already there had been more than twenty reported sightings of Nancy Collett. The woman couldn't have been more helpful if she'd laid a trail.

The press conference was packed with reporters and police officers, amateurs and local rags, pushing to get a place on the balcony. The case had kicked off. Not just the murder itself, the victim being an old war hero who'd lost his leg, but because the killer was his wife. And then there was the fact that Nancy Collett was a person of dubious reputation, who wore revealing frocks and dyed her hair. Also, though this was not said in so many words, she was of the lower class. The words "cold, calculated, shrewd" were written on the blackboard at the front, as was "femme fatale."

"Before meeting the deceased," announced the superintendent, "Nancy Collett had a part-time job as a hostess at a local nightclub."

Much scribbling. This stuff was good.

"Her husband was ten years her senior, and before the war he worked as a solicitor. They were married for seven years. They had no children."

Only a few jotted down these details.

"It is now understood that Nancy Collett spent several days with the body of the deceased before she made her escape."

The superintendent said no more than that—he knew no more than that—but the pause he left was long enough for people to start filling it with ideas of their own. Pens went wild.

"She was seen by a neighbor leaving the house she shared with Percival Collett early on October the nineteenth. She was carrying three suitcases, and a red valise."

The officer in charge of the chalk now switched on the projector and showed a slide of a red valise, just in case no one was sure what that might look like.

It was the red valise that was of particular interest to the police, said the super. It was believed the red valise contained vital evidence from the scene of the crime.

Following this, another slide was shown: a plan of the interior of the house, with a cross to mark the spot—the bed—where the deceased had been discovered.

"There were signs of suffocation, as well as a prior vicious attack with a sharp implement, such as a scalpel or knife."

More intakes of breath. Fortunately, no slides.

"We believe Mrs. Collett made her way toward Fenchurch Street station, where she was seen waiting by a number of witnesses. At the station she asked for help from a porter but refused to let go of the red valise. It appears she then took a train to Tilbury to board a liner to Australia, but there were problems with her passport and she was delayed for questioning. We know she boarded the ship that same afternoon because she made lewd and inappropriate suggestions to several members of staff, while still holding the red valise."

With the news of her escape, there was a jeer from the upper balcony. Men felt they had been outwitted by this woman, and they didn't like it. But down at the front, some of the older hacks got ready to leave. "It's over," one said. "If she's already in Oz."

Then the superintendent said, "What we don't understand right now is the role of her female accomplice."

Those members of the press who had put away their notebooks took them out again.

Nancy Collett had been seen by witnesses at Fenchurch Street station greeting another woman. From the projector came a slide of a big lady without a head. So far, the superintendent explained, they were having difficulties finding any full images of this suspect. Her flat had been searched by the police and it appeared she was one step ahead. (No pun intended but, nevertheless, he got a laugh.) There was a flash of lights as press cameras went off everywhere.

"So what you're saying," piped up one of the older blokes, "is that you're looking for a femme fatale and a fat woman with no head."

Yes, said the super. That was about the sum of it.

"Bloody hell," said a chap in the front row. "This is hotter than the Norman Skinner case."

It was all over the morning papers.

23

You Have Very Good Legs

Enid had only gone to buy a watermelon for breakfast, but she came back driving an old U.S. Army jeep. Taking the corner at high speed, she appeared in a tide of red dust, accompanied by a loud screeching noise, and when she cut the engine and leaped out—the jeep appeared to have no roof—she was bright orange and so was the dog. It was even in his teeth and ears. A small crowd gathered to watch, including a woman with a pot on her head, and several toothless fishermen.

Margery could barely speak. "Enid? How did you get this?"

"I saw a sign. It was going cheap."

"I didn't know you could drive."

"Yeah, well, I drove an ambulance for a while."

"You did?"

"During the war. I used to be on the night shift. I took Pall Mall once at fifty miles an hour."

They packed the jeep until the rear end sagged. All the new collecting equipment, plus the tea chest of supplies and camping gear, and other miscellaneous items that Enid kept producing, like her Miss Lovely Legs trophy, the Baby Jesus painting, and her battery radio. She seemed to be in a hurry. She finished with the red valise, which she hid beneath a jack and a shovel, along with a couple of short planks for easing her way out of mudholes.

"Enid?" said Margery, as she loaded a last few things. "Have you noticed anything different? About me?"

She waited for Enid to finish ramming whatever she was ramming, and look. When Enid did, she shrugged, and went back to her ramming. "No."

"I am dressed in a man's clothes." Margery pointed at the Bermuda shorts and flowery shirt she was now wearing, along with her pith helmet and boots. The truth was that once she'd got over the shame of slotting one foot inside a trouser leg, and then the other, once she'd zipped up the fly and secured the button at the waist, and found it was not too loose but not too tight either, once she'd slipped her arms inside the lovely, colorful shirt and felt the generosity of the sleeve, she had given a large sigh, as if she'd just emerged from an underground hole and could finally breathe. She'd dug her hands into the pockets, and they weren't so small you could barely keep a thimble in them. They were proper places where you could store a compass, a ball of twine. Besides, it wasn't utterly strange to wear male clothes: it was just like being a girl again, in her brothers' hand-me-downs. She hadn't even put on stockings. "Would you say," she asked, beginning to color, "would you say I look odd?"

"No."

"Will people laugh?"

"Marge, you're looking for a gold beetle on the other side of the world. You think people haven't already laughed? Anyway, half the men in New Caledonia wear skirts. Now, are we going to stand here talking fashion, or can we leave?" She whistled for Mr. Rawlings, and scooped him into her arms.

Again, Margery balked. "The dog, Enid? The dog?"

"Of course. He'll sniff out danger."

Margery had never seen Mr. Rawlings sniff out so much as a ham baguette, but she let that pass. "You can't take a pet on an expedition. It's not fair."

Enid didn't bat an eyelid. She lowered the dog into the back seat and hopped in through the nonexistent roof. "It's me and Mr. Rawlings, or you go alone."

Enid went with terrifying speed for a woman who had once been an ambulance driver. Even if people had felt well when they got into her ambulance, they must have been very sick by the time they got out of it. And it was worse when she talked: she seemed to forget she was driving. Margery tried to object but got a mouthful of grit and dust. Meanwhile, Mr. Rawlings had scrambled from the back seat into her lap, still quite orange and nervous from the first trip, and now trembling uncontrollably.

"Enid," she managed to say. "Enid. This is too fast."

"You should close your eyes!" yelled Enid. "Get some rest!"

Margery could not have closed her eyes if she'd been drugged. Parts of the city whirled past at dizzying speed, like objects on a conveyor belt. La Place des Cocotiers—an elegant French square with fountains and flame trees—came and went with a flash of red. Palm trees were no more than a hairy blur. The jeep rattled past the market, kicking up more dust, and skidded over a curb, narrowly missing a street vendor with a selection of hens tied upside down by their legs to a pole. They reached the port, and careered toward the edge-of-town shanties, where banana trees leaned heavily over the road. After that it climbed upward, and there was nothing but forest. Pine and mangoes and huge banyans tangled with bougainvillea. Above them rose the teeth of the basalt cliffs, like black lace. According to the Reverend Horace Blake, they should take the coastal road that ran west of the island, snaking between ocean and mountains. *It will provide a delightful opportunity for the curious traveler to experience charming native villages, and colorful restaurants and bars.* There were illustrations of women in grass skirts cooking things on the fire, and several chieftains.

As far as Païta—about twenty miles—the road was in tolerably good condition. But there were no charming villages. No colorful restaurants. Certainly no women cooking things on the fire. And neither was there anywhere to refuel. From Païta to Boulouparis, another thirty miles, the road was broken and haphazard. Sometimes it was just a faint scar, or a spill of rocks indistinguishable from the rest of the mountain's rubble. At others it disappeared completely. On several occasions it gave up being a road and became a stream.

At Boulouparis, Enid spotted a makeshift store advertising food and fuel, and jerked to a halt. She leaped from the jeep and picked up Mr. Rawlings. Her hair stuck out in quills, and her mouth—when she opened it—seemed exceptionally pink against the rest of her.

"Coming?" she said.

Margery sat in shock. Even though the jeep was finally stationary, parts of her body still appeared to be on the move. She hauled herself out.

After the glare of the road, the store was very dark. Enid hunted for British newspapers but found none. In the end she bought a French fashion magazine.

"What kind of food do you sell?" she asked the owner, miming a very hungry person wolfing lunch. She paid for petrol and ordered an omelette and oysters from the menu.

They ate outside. Across the track there were a few mud huts, and some children came out to wave at Enid and point at her hair. Around them, trees were every color of green—from bright yellowish to one that was almost black, and the sky was hot blue. But there was still no sign of a mountain shaped like a blunt wisdom tooth.

"Enid," said Margery. "Is it necessary to travel so fast?"

"I'm just excited about getting there." Enid slurped an oyster out of its shell. She didn't even use a fork. "At least we should be safe now."

"Safe from what?"

Enid failed to answer. She took a mouthful of omelette.

"And you're sure?" Margery said. "About what I'm wearing? You don't think people are staring?"

"You're on the other side of the world. Who cares what people think? You can be what you want. Anyway, you look better in Bermuda shorts than you did in that frock. No offense, Marge—"

"None taken, Enid."

"—but you looked like a beached whale in that thing."

"I see. Well, thank you."

"I caught the way the women laughed at you at the British consul's party."

"They laughed? When did they laugh?"

"It made me sick. I had to walk away."

Margery paused a moment. All of a sudden, the awful picture that the schoolgirls had drawn turned up in her mind—the way things do sometimes, things that you're sure you've left in the past. She remembered hobbling like a hedgehog through corridors, unable to breathe. Then she looked at her arms, easy now inside a man's shirt. The memory of that day still hurt. And the idea of the British consulate women laughing—that hurt, too. But Enid was not laughing. She was tearing off chunks of bread and feeding Mr. Rawlings under the table. So the pain Margery felt was small, like a bruise that has turned yellow. It was bearable.

"And just so you know," said Enid, "you have very good legs. You ought to get them out more often. You're the one who should have got the trophy."

The road from Boulouparis worsened considerably. There was no change in the landscape: the mountains stretched to their right with the sea to their left, though between the road and the sea there was now an extremely vertiginous drop. The road kept climbing, twisty as a corkscrew, mist clinging to the lower slopes of the mountain, and suddenly they were looking down on thin spires of colonial pines, splashes of red poinciana, groves of coconut palms, the decorated roof of a thatched building, while the Pacific waited, blue as an iris flower, to their left.

They passed several large trucks—presumably there was a mine nearby: men hooted and waved at Enid to pull over—but then the land turned to a bald expanse of scrub where the forest had been cut down and burned to make way for plantations. It came as a shock, after so many trees, and the smell was awful. Enid glanced in her mirror. Her eyes grew wide.

"Is there a problem?"

"Not at all, Marge."

Not true. Margery checked over her shoulder. A police car had emerged behind them. The landscape was still very open and flat. But instead of slowing, like any normal driver, Enid stamped on the accelerator. Margery's heart dropped toward her bowels.

"Enid? That is a police car. We have to slow down."

Apparently not. Slowing down appeared to be the exact opposite of what Enid had in mind. Her face was set like a clamp. Her hair blew wild. The police car flashed its blue light. Enid went faster. The jeep rattled, bouncing over potholes. The police car followed, bouncing over potholes. Enid took a bend on three wheels. The police car sounded its siren and also took the bend. Enid zoomed faster. So did the police car. A tree appeared. More rocks. Several goats. Enid screeched the tires, only just missing obstacles as she flew past them.

"Enid! Enid!"

Margery couldn't take any more. Enid seemed to have lost her mind. Even though she had never driven a car in her life, Margery grabbed hold of the wheel and yanked it. They went swerving violently toward a precipice. The ocean flashed directly below, dotted with ships and fishing boats. Enid screamed and managed to swing the jeep back to the road just in time. It came to a skidding halt in another cloud of dust. "What the hell?" she shouted. "You almost killed us." There was no time to say anything else. The dust was clearing. The police car had drawn up. A policeman was getting out. Even the insects fell silent.

The policeman was as slow as a walking house. It took an age for him to reach the jeep. He knocked on Enid's window. An unnecessary preliminary since, of course, the jeep had no roof. She wound it down a few inches. Also, unnecessary. Politely he leaned over the window.

"Bon *shoor!*" said Enid. She gave a huge smile and revealed a pair of dimples Margery had honestly never seen before.

The policeman replied in French.

"What did he just say?" said Margery.

"I have no idea. Keep smiling."

Momentarily the policeman wiggled his finger in his ear and then examined whatever he had found there. At least he seemed distracted.

But Margery was not distracted. She felt made of wire. She whispered, "Paperwork."

"What about it?"

"Enid. We don't have any."

"Marge, could you possibly look less terrified, and just smile?"

The policeman had now finished his ear inspection and was ready to give Enid his full attention. "Bon *shoor,*" she repeated, incredibly sweet.

He said something French again.

Margery fumbled through her handbag. She pulled out her guidebook and flipped to the Reverend Horace Blake's Useful Phrases. They included *"Can you direct me, boy, to the nearest lighthouse?"* Also, *"Help, help, I am drowning!"* and *"I am going to the next village to sell my grandmother's hens!"* She abandoned the Reverend Horace Blake and produced her passport. She began to explain in very clear English that Enid was the brown-haired woman in the photograph, but the policeman was not remotely interested. He patted the hood of the jeep as if it were an extension of Enid. He said, *"Voiture?"*

Margery slunk down in her seat. "It's because of my clothes," she said hopelessly. "He has stopped us because I am dressed like a man."

"Marge, this has nothing to do with the way you look. It's because we have no license plate."

"Why do we have no license plate?"

"Because I took it off. When I stole the jeep."

"You stole the jeep?"

"Marge, please stop shrieking. Yes, the jeep is stolen. You think I'd pay for this?"

Margery's heart had lifted from her bowels and was now banging wildly in her throat. Quite a lot appeared to be going on. Not only had she been stopped by the police—when she had no paperwork, no extension to her visa, and was dressed like a man—but she had also just discovered she was traveling in a stolen vehicle. "Cash," hissed Enid, still smiling sweetly. "Try giving him cash."

"Are you suggesting I bribe a member of the French police force?"

"Yes, Marge. That's exactly what I'm suggesting. You were the one who caused the jeep to stop. I could have shaken him off if it hadn't been for you." She went back to smiling at the policeman. She adjusted her top as a form of distraction. It worked. His eyes rooted in her cleavage and flowered there.

Margery pulled out her purse and found loose change. Her hands were shaking. She held out the coins, in the midpoint between Enid's bust and the policeman. It felt like offering cake to a vulture.

"Are you serious?" said Enid. "We are *bribing* him, not giving him his bus fare home." She grabbed the purse.

It took ten notes. He counted each one solemnly and, for some reason, also licked it. Satisfied at last, he beckoned them out while Enid reversed, the way men do sometimes, as if a woman cannot successfully maneuver a vehicle unless someone gesticulates wildly, while at the same time standing in the exact space she needs to get into. But he could gesticulate as much as he liked. They were free.

"Well, that went smoothly," said Enid. "Next stop, Poum."

She was right, of course. They were safe. But it took several minutes for Margery to regain the power of speech, and even then, her words came in a rush and in the wrong order. She told Enid this

was too much: there must be no more stealing, and no more brib-
ery. "I am an amateur beetle collector, Enid. I am out of my depth."
In turn, Enid said she was awfully sorry, she wouldn't do it again,
but at least they would soon be free to start looking for the gold
beetle. She gripped the wheel tightly as they took another bend.
"You said you'd do anything, remember? You told me you'd risk
everything to find what you want."

This was true, though it was beginning to occur to Margery that
her notion of everything was not Enid's. When she'd decided to
stop playing by the book, she hadn't meant to lead the life of a
criminal.

"Anyway," continued Enid, "we can hide the jeep. Once we get
north, there will be no need for it. Now, why don't you start looking
for your mountain?"

Margery kept her eyes fixed on the horizon—the mountains
rose like waves as far as she could see, many bladed, but there was
still no sign of one shaped as a wisdom tooth, blunt or sharp or
otherwise. As the sun sank, the entire range gave one last bright
flare of gold and then the sky went the color of a blackberry and
night happened so fast it was like someone had switched off the
light. The jeep's headlamps poked through the dark. Above, the
dome of the sky was crowded with stars, occasionally fractured
with faraway splinters of lightning. Enid slowed. Even in the dark,
Margery could sense her excitement, and though she could not see
the mountains, she felt their presence all around, sloping and peak-
ing and falling, more ancient than life itself.

"Look at that. Just look, Marge. Did you ever see anywhere so
beautiful?"

It was nine before they reached Poum. *"Delightful Poum,"* wrote
the Reverend Horace Blake, *"where the native huts stand on stilts
and the Kanak people spear tropical fish and dance merrily by the
fire."*

Margery was beginning to wonder if he had actually been to
New Caledonia. Poum wasn't even a town, it was so small. It was

just a few ramshackle sheds, some old men, and a lot of goats. Since the café where they were to collect the key for the bungalow was closed, they had to sleep in the jeep, covered with a net and interrupted only by mosquitoes, the sound of the ocean, and the odd murmur of drunken laughter.

At dawn, they washed in rust-colored water from a tap in the square while a silent group of old men—both Kanak and lonely Europeans—gathered round to watch. Afterward Enid led the way to the only shop, which had a total of two shelves, selling eggs, corn and guavas, yams, coconuts, small sweet pineapples, and green bananas, alongside bags of salt, hardware, batteries, and some old tins with a picture of a fish on them. Margery bought fruit.

Since the café was still closed, they walked to the water's edge where the Pacific met the Coral Sea, and the waves were the biggest they'd seen yet, hitting rocks and sending up towers of spume. Ahead, islands of diminishing size poked out of the ocean, like broken-off fragments floating toward the horizon. It really was the end of the world.

Enid climbed onto a wooden jetty, hopping between the missing slats while the breeze tossed her hair. Britain seemed another life. And it wasn't just home that was as far away as it could be. Neither of us, Margery thought, is the woman we were when we met.

Enid must have been thinking something similar because, as she jumped down from the jetty, she laughed.

Then they turned their backs on the ocean and faced the mountain. It looked so close suddenly, rising to the highest point where nothing grew—there was just red stone—and topped—exactly as the missionary had described it—like a blunt wisdom tooth. Enid reached out as if she could touch it.

"You're going to find the beetle," she said. "And I'm going to have a baby. I know it in my heart."

They set off to collect the key for the bungalow.

24

Back on Track

Every day, he was closer to New Caledonia. And this time he didn't hide. He sat at the front of the cargo ship where he could see the horizon, his big hands overlapping his knees. He hardened himself so that each muscle in his body was rigid and strained. He spoke to no one. He sat in silence, waiting.

Mundic had his Panama hat and sunglasses and wrote in his notebook about the weather, what he ate, and the things he saw, like the fish. Sometimes he watched other people, just so he could collect their names and put them in his Book of Miss Benson. He heard their voices and the splintering of the waves against the ship's sides, and sometimes he got the oily whiff from the engine room or a rancid smell of half-dry coconuts, but he let it wash over him as if it was all part of the same thing. There was a berth below but the men were Dutch, in the sandalwood trade, so Mundic stayed on deck, and at night he coiled himself under a bench and slept there.

One of the crew came out every morning to read a letter. He would take it out of his pocket, read it, and wipe his eyes. Then he would fold it carefully and put it back in his jacket.

Watching him, Mundic remembered the faces of the lads in the camp when a Red Cross parcel got through and they read their letters from home. They'd talk about a sweetheart, or a wife, or their kiddies. Mundic had been glad he had no letters. Everything about Britain had seemed off the point when you spent your nights in a hut, not even with a proper roof on it, rats running over your head and men crowded all round you, like cattle, and dying.

And sometimes one of the deckhands would sit and play his harmonica and that would get Mundic remembering the camps, too. In his mind, he'd see the blokes who had tried to keep themselves educated. Playing music and reading books, like they were clever. But it didn't matter how clever you were if a Jap was beating you with a stick.

And then Mundic would get so lost in remembering, the old thing would happen again, and he couldn't tell. He couldn't tell if he was on a boat or if he was back at the camp and dreaming about a boat. He couldn't tell if the men laughing were Japs or the Dutchmen in the sandalwood trade. And he'd have to knock his head and take out his passport and say to himself, "I am a free man. I am a free man," before the flame blew up inside him and he lashed out.

Now he sat very still on the boat, waiting for the memories to pass. He didn't write them down. He wrote only the facts. He put that the sea was blue and he could see a white bird. He would be okay, so long as he stayed in the present.

25

The Last Place

In order to find a new beetle, Professor Smith had told her once, you needed three things. The first was knowledge. You needed all the knowledge you could get your hands on. Second, you needed to be where you thought the beetle was. Last, you needed courage.

Staring at the bungalow, Margery felt every drop of it evaporate.

"Oh, Enid," she said.

"Fuckadoodledoo," said Enid.

The clue was in the name: the Last Place wasn't just the last bungalow on the track. It was the last place in the world anyone would want to live. They had collected the key from the café in Poum—the owner was possibly the biggest man Margery had ever met, and also the hairiest. He had clasped Enid and Margery in his arms as if they were long-lost daughters and roared something in pidgin French that had made no sense to either of them but turned out to be an insistence that they must eat. He'd brought them a giant plate of cooked prawns and lobster, then pointed the way. After that they had followed a dirt track past a shantytown where a gang of small boys raced alongside the jeep, dressed in scraps, waving madly, shouting madly, and holding up a selection of domestic animals—mainly flapping ones—that they appeared to want to sell. After another few miles, the track had petered out completely, and there was nothing but the bungalow. It was surrounded by thick, high elephant grass and kauri trees as tall as towers. The two-pronged mountain loomed just behind.

Enid cut the engine. No sound other than a million trillion insects.

This was no bungalow, or at least not the lovely British kind. It was a wooden hut standing on stilts six feet off the ground, with broken steps that led to a broken wraparound veranda. The roof was a mishmash of tiles, tarp, and banana leaves, while the door was held in place with a broken padlock; the key in Margery's handbag was a red herring.

Enid leaped out of the jeep and went ahead, clinging to the rail with one hand and holding Mr. Rawlings with the other. Margery trudged behind.

Inside, the bungalow was in better structural condition, though it was piled with rubbish and the smell was foul. From the veranda, they entered a long room with a cupboard-sized room next to it, and behind that they found three smaller rooms that opened off a narrow passage, each with a moldy bed and a window. The running water was mainly what it said: gaps in the roof that let in rain, and some wonky pipes; the bathroom facilities were a lavatory attached to another pipe that went straight to a hole in the garden.

"I've seen worse," said Enid. "Yes. I've seen worse."

"When, Enid? When have you seen worse?"

"During the war, Marge. I saw a lot worse. At least it's nice and private. At least it's out of the way."

"Out of the way? Even hermits would avoid this. Nothing's lived here for years."

Untrue. Clearly a lot of things had lived there. It was just that none of them were human. Margery tripped over a tin can, and a flood of cockroaches came out. Dead insects were collected everywhere in powdery piles, and paper curled off the walls, half chewed. A thick web filled an entire corner, loaded with flies, like a serial-killer spider's pantry. There was even the bottom half of a bird.

"It doesn't matter, Marge. We're not living here. We'll be up the mountain in our tent."

"But this is our base camp. It's where we store our collection. It's where we come every week to clean up and refresh supplies."

In time, Margery would love this place, just as she would love the view as she sat on the veranda with Enid after another week of hard toil. Sunsets like a sky of geraniums. A mosaic of light and shadow on the trees. The sky snowing butterflies. She'd make Enid some eggs and fetch a bucket of water for Enid's feet, and they'd sit together watching the sky turn purple. Later, as threads of cloud laced the moon, Enid would shout, "Look, Marge! That's a beetle-shaped one! Make a wish!"

But right now Margery hated it. She was furious with herself for getting it wrong, furious with this filthy hovel for not being a well-appointed bungalow. She even kicked it, which was silly, really, because her foot went through the floor, causing a hole with a six-foot drop beneath it, and that was just another thing to deal with.

Outside, a bird gave a squawk, like a person being slowly strangled.

Enid became a different woman. Literally. She pulled off her frock and, in no time, was in a leopard-print bikini with an apron round her middle, running backward and forward. She was like Miss Lovely Legs on turbocharge. ("Don't you think you should put some clothes on?" said Margery. "Marge," said Enid. "Relax. No one's looking.") Followed by Mr. Rawlings, she lugged water in pots from a freshwater creek beyond the bungalow. She pulled from the jeep anything that vaguely resembled a cleaning object, and by the afternoon she had scrubbed every inch of the bungalow with water and pink soap, not stopping once to lie down, or even say very much. She hauled out the pieces of scrap iron and pushed an old mangle over the veranda. She collected a load of cigar butts and porn magazines, and made a fire of them in the garden, then scrubbed the bungalow a second time until it smelled almost entirely of pink soap. She caught an assortment of lizards in a net and took them to the other side of the track, where she set them free, convinced that lizards were either too obedient or frightened to cross roads. (They followed her straight back.)

In the garden, she found two old cane chairs that she hoicked up to the veranda. There, she said, it would be possible to rock gently and admire the view, not because they were rocking chairs but because they had dodgy legs. She dragged two mattresses out to the balcony and whacked them free of dust and mildew, then made up the beds with sheets from the jeep and mosquito nets. Now that it was semi-clean, the bungalow seemed much less frightening. She said a table could go here, the hurricane lamp there, perhaps some shelves. It was as if Enid, with all her bashing and scrubbing, had jolted it back to life. And Margery, who had for most of the day followed Enid in a completely useless way with a broom, and attempted to make something edible out of yams—which was so awful that even insects steered clear of it—now carried heavy items up from the jeep. Somehow in all of this she had become Enid's assistant. She had become her assistant's assistant.

Enid drove to Poum for nails and matches, and returned with a selection of boys from the shantytown—"They wanted a ride"—as well as an old rug. The boys came into the bungalow and made a thorough inspection of all their camping gear. They touched the tent, the hammocks, the Primus stove, the pots and pans. Enid handed out chewing gum and sent the boys packing, though they came back later, trying to sell her a goat. Enid said no to the goat, but did her expert mime of the gold beetle, which the boys enjoyed so much they returned yet again with lots of friends and a selection of clown beetles, as well as a giant coconut grasshopper that was the size of her hand. It took more chewing gum to get rid of them. She put her Miss Lovely Legs trophy on display, and nailed up her picture of the Baby Jesus, with his fat legs and fat feet, a look of sweet pleasure on His face, as if He was full of milk.

So it was that Enid, who had been wildly sloppy on the RMS *Orion,* became passionate about this hovel she now shared with Margery. By the end of the day, there were two semi-habitable bedrooms at the back, a makeshift kitchen, and a washing line in the garden. She even found a sheet of old hardboard under the bungalow and repaired the damage Margery had done to the floor, though it would always be a weak spot. To avoid a fatal accident she put the rug over it as a reminder.

"Look!" she said. She was covered with insect bites, like spots, all over her back. "Look, what I made you! A study!" She bounced to the little room at the front, swatting things as she went.

For the first time in her life, Margery stood in her own study. Through the window, ferns the size of trees bowed as if welcoming her, and the air was laced with pine. Enid had already unpacked the naphthalene and the wooden trays for storing specimens, as well as Margery's books. She'd even donated some of her empty bottles and jars.

"Do you love it?" she said.

Margery was overcome. It was possibly the kindest thing anyone had ever done for her. She had no idea how she deserved it. And she didn't know if it was because she was dressed in shorts, like a man, but Margery took in that view and got the strangest sense that everything she wanted was ahead and available, so long as she was brave enough to claim it. Then she thought, No. It's not because I am dressed as a man. It's because I am a woman who is ready for adventure. I'm not here because I am someone's wife or sister. I am here because this is what I want, and now I have a place for my work.

She said, "I love it. Thank you, Enid. I love it."

It took ages to get to sleep. She was nervous about the next day and in the dark the room felt even more alien, and then she had to move the mattress because something was chewing the roof directly above her head. Clearly it wasn't enough to worry: she also had to lie awake worrying because she was worrying. But she must have drifted off in the end because she was woken by Enid asking if she was asleep.

"I had a nightmare, Marge."

Margery struggled to switch on her flashlight. Moths with wings like paisley shawls flapped out of nowhere and banged uselessly against the walls. Blue moonlight poured through the window and lit Enid as if she were a ghost. The night was quiet.

"What was your nightmare, Enid?"

"I dreamed I only had a year left to live. It was terrifying."

"But that was a dream. It wasn't real."

"Supposing it wasn't? Supposing it was one of them things?"

"A premonition?"

"Yeah. Suppose my head knows something, and I don't." Enid plumped herself on the end of the mattress and drew her knees up to her chin, but her foot kept jigging. Even in stillness she was full of movement.

"I don't see how a dream could be a premonition, Enid. I don't see how your head would know a thing like that."

"Well, it put the wind up me, Marge. How could I have a baby if I only have a year left to live?"

"But you don't have a year left, Enid. You're young." Enid was the most alive thing Margery had ever met. Like grabbing hold of an electric current.

"I'm twenty-six, Marge."

"Exactly, Enid."

"My time's running out. What were you doing when you were twenty-six?"

"Nothing, really. Research."

"Exactly. You were fulfilling your vocation."

"Your dream wasn't a premonition, Enid. You're just nervous because we're going to start searching tomorrow. I'm nervous, too. It's natural."

"What would you do, if you only had a year left? Would you keep looking for the beetle?"

"Of course. Wouldn't you want to be a mother?"

"But how could I look after her if I only had a year left? Who would love her when I was gone?" Enid flexed her toes. She stared as if she hadn't seen them before. "What about if you had a month? You'd still look?"

"Yes."

"One day?"

"What about it?"

"If you only had one day, wouldn't you want to give up?"

Margery shook her head. She didn't even think. But Enid sighed. "If I had one day left, I'd give up on my dreams. I'd just want to hold another human hand."

Margery stared. Enid was telling the complete truth. She remained lit by the moon, jigging her toes, her hair almost white, her arms slick with sweat. Faraway thunder rumbled; a flash of lightning struck the room. And despite the closeness of the air, sharp pimples stood out over Margery's skin because she saw that Enid knew herself far better than Margery did. The fact was that she had no idea what she'd do if this was her last day on earth. Probably dig a hole and wait for the end, hoping it wouldn't hurt too much. And it hadn't really been true to say she was fulfilling her vocation when she was twenty-six.

She said, "We should sleep. It's a big day tomorrow."

"Can I stay with you? I hate being alone."

"If you like."

"Will you tell me about them beetles? Like you did on the ship?" So Margery told her about the African Goliath beetle, as big as a hand. The flightless bess beetle; the blue *Lepicerus inaequalis,* so tiny it could pass through the eye of a needle. Enid was snoring in minutes.

But Margery couldn't sleep now. She sat, head bowed. All she could think of was Professor Smith.

26

Killing the Thing You Love

He had taught her all she knew, this man who was old enough to be her father. They talked beetles, beetles, beetles. It started with him smiling at her across the Insect Gallery, and after that he invited her for tea. No man had ever bought her tea and cake, and no man had ever asked so many questions. Where did she live? Were her parents alive? When had she first become interested in entomology? She kept gulping and flapping her hands, unsure how to keep her mouth closed to eat her cake, while also opening it to reply. They met the following week, the week after that, and it became their routine. When she was with him, life seemed to move at thirty miles an hour, shimmering with so much color she felt breathless. Everything was beautiful, even the hook where he hung his coat. He was maybe in his late forties, but she couldn't be sure. He lived for his work, and the thought of his loneliness made her heart contract, as though squeezed by an invisible hand.

He explained that the discovery of new species was increasing at a fast rate, but so was the disappearance of known and unknown ones. Species were vanishing without ever having been found. In order for scientists to understand what they were losing, and why, they needed to discover first what they'd got. It was a race against time. He showed her beetles that before now she'd only read about; he taught her the hundreds of thousands of tiny differences that marked them apart. And when she dared at last to mention the undiscovered golden beetle of New Caledonia, he didn't laugh at her or say no. He promised to make inquiries. In that moment her life seemed to balloon outward because it was possible: the glory she had imagined the first time her father had shown her his book of incredible creatures was not a fantasy or a pipe dream; it was within her reach. It was everything she could do not to hug him.

Professor Smith wrote to a colleague in Belize. His colleague in Belize wrote back. The next time they met, he was so excited he forgot to take off his hat. "We know there are golden scarabs. We know there are golden carabids. Golden weevils. There's also the golden tortoise beetle, of course. But as far as we know, no one has ever found a golden soft-wing flower beetle. To find it would be something special. And important, too. It would be very important for the museum."

She laughed, he laughed. And it was so tremendous to see him happy, and know that it was at least a little bit because of her, that she could feel herself blooming inside, like a new flower.

"Now find your evidence."

So she did. She found it. Suddenly her life had purpose. He sorted out a pass for her, and she was in the British Library every day. She discovered Darwin's private letter to Wallace, the missionary's journal, and the account by the rare orchid collector. She learned about other entomologists who'd collected in New Caledonia—a French priest, Xavier Montrouzier, who had lived on the island from 1853 until his death in 1897; Émile Deplanche, who had made two trips between 1858 and 1860, along with the ship's pharmacist, Monsieur Bavay. There had also been Alexis Saves, and Monsieur Godard and a Mr. Atkinson, as well as, more recently, several GIs who'd got interested in beetles while they were posted there. She scoured their notebooks, their journals, their letters. Several had heard of the gold beetle, but none had made the link with the white orchid.

"Now work out why the beetle will be there," he said. "And no-where else."

She did that, too. It was like piecing together a mystery. She fol-lowed every clue, and when she met a dead end, she didn't give up; she retraced her steps and started again. If the orchid collector was right, the male probably fed on the nectar of the rare white orchid. The female might bury her eggs in the damp leaves surrounding it. And so the larvae probably fed on the invertebrates that would otherwise eat the seeds of the white orchid.

At last, she presented him with a set of notebooks. "It's amazing. The white orchid needs the gold beetle as much as the gold beetle needs the white orchid." She could barely breathe.

"Good work. Very good." He brushed her arm by mistake—she blushed. "Now find out more about the orchid."

She spent months researching orchids of the world. There was one, a small white orchid, that had only ever been seen growing at high altitude on a mountain in New Caledonia. "Very good. So where is the mountain?"

She discovered an unnamed peak in the most remote and north-ern part of the island. It looked like a blunt wisdom tooth. No Eu-ropean collectors had gone that far. Or they'd tried and been eaten.

"Fortunately, cannibals aren't a problem now," said Professor Smith. He was being humorous. She laughed way too much. Hic-cups followed. He offered her his handkerchief. It smelled of him. A surprisingly feminine smell. She kept the handkerchief.

"You must go to New Caledonia. You must find this beetle."

"With you?" she wanted to say, but she didn't. In her mind she already pictured him leading the way on a mule, her following, not on a mule but very happily on foot, bearing cooking pots and equip-ment and whatever else he might need.

"And, of course, you will have to kill it. I know you won't want to. But you will have to do that, Margery."

She didn't need to hear the argument, but he gave it anyway. If the golden beetle of New Caledonia was real, it was her job to know as much about it as she could. And you couldn't find out everything you needed to know by simply watching it chew a leaf. You needed to study it under a microscope. You might need to discover what was inside. She would have to bring home three pairs. That was all. Besides, beetles multiplied rapidly. Three pairs were nothing.

She nodded: he'd said it so many times that she knew the argument word for word. But she let him talk. Even if he talked, and she didn't, it still counted as a conversation.

"The entomologist is not a beetle murderer. It is a case of killing what you love in order to preserve the whole species."

Love. The word turned her pink. Her visits weren't once a week anymore. She went to the museum at least two or three times. The aunts remarked occasionally that she was late for dinner or running too fast up the stairs, but they never inquired what she had been doing all day. They probably didn't want to know. She accompanied Professor Smith to the private archives of the Entomology Department, where she took notes for him. She pinned new specimens. She described them exactly as he'd taught her. And even though this wasn't an official job, she knew she was lucky. Most women behind the scenes at the museum were either pot washers or cleaners.

She was in love with a middle-aged man who was devoted to his work, and no one knew anything about it. Not her aunts; certainly not him. If Barbara knew, she referred to it obliquely. A paperback manual once appeared on Margery's bed, *Mainly for Wives,* with chapters on how to cook a proper meal for your husband, and how to look attractive when he came home from the office. Margery read it from cover to cover and discovered she needed to be more interesting and also wear rouge. But really there was no hope of being his wife: he was much too clever for marrying. She resolved on secrecy—whatever happened, he must never know her true feelings, must never realize how daft she was. In silence and with every part of her, she loved the mumbliness of his voice, the brilliance of his mind, the way he combed his hair to hide the bit of his head where there wasn't so much. And when his hand reached for her leg one day beneath the tea table, she sat very still, certain it must be a mistake and too polite to point it out. If she could have cut off her leg to spare him embarrassment, she would.

But it seemed to be a mistake his hand kept making. After that first time, it was always reaching for her leg beneath the table. Sometimes it even stroked and squeezed.

Margery said nothing. She would happily have spent the rest of her life with his hand on her knee, if she could remain at his side, helping with his work.

27

Mist, No Mist

She was woken by a block of white at the window. No trees, no sky. There wasn't even a mountain. The world had apparently vanished in the night. She rushed to the door.

Pressed against the bungalow on all sides was a thick felty whiteness that sucked the sound out of everything. She couldn't even hear insects. The air smelled oozy, and was very cold, while the ladder from the veranda seemed to disappear after two steps. For a terrible moment she thought the bungalow had cut loose and drifted into cloud. They'd crossed the world to find a beetle and suddenly they'd be hard put to spot their own feet.

The world stayed white and not-there for three days. There was no way they could start the expedition. Enid tried to drive the jeep to Poum but bumped into a tree, and decided to walk. Margery sat in her study under a blanket and wrote notes in her journal, but there wasn't anything to report beyond that they were stuck. Even her watch had stopped working. Enid came back from Poum with a new battery for her radio, followed by yet more boys from the shantytown, who took advantage of the mist to climb up the bungalow and peer in at the windows: Margery found six pairs of eyes watching her and shrieked. Enid tried to get a radio signal but failed. In her boredom, she arranged the tinned food into towers; five in all. They went over how to identify the orchid and the beetle—Margery drew Enid an oval-shaped specimen with long antennae. Enid even had a practice at sucking things up with the pooter. But it was the worst kind of waiting. They were lost and they hadn't gone anywhere.

Then, as suddenly as it had come, the mist went. The mountain came back, the trees, the boundless blue sky. Margery saw things she hadn't even spotted before. A red flower shaped like two hands in prayer. A cactus as tall as a person. But it was a lesson: a lesson that the weather was bigger than her and must be treated with caution. Unlike Margery, it could change in a moment. They packed their haversacks and took an early night.

Dawn, the next morning. A completely different world: the mountain was ambered in a deep, shifting light. Everywhere there was a smell of ripeness and the booming and sawing of insects.

Enid paced the veranda in a pair of orange shorts and a bright pink top, her baseball cap on her head, her boots on her feet, and a bush knife in her belt. You could spot her a mile off. But it was the dog that was the worry. They hadn't even left, and its tongue was hanging out. Before Margery could say anything, Enid scooped him up. "He's coming with us," she said. "He's lucky."

"That dog cannot be lucky, Enid. I would lay bets on it."

Ignoring Margery, Enid reached for her haversack and hauled it on to her back. Margery checked one more time. Two hammocks and the tent, hurricane lamps and spare paraffin, towels, mosquito nets, enough tinned food and oatmeal to last a week, as well as jerricans of water, first aid kit, cooking pot, plates, journals, pencils, specimen vials, and the killing jar. Slowly, they climbed down the steps of the bungalow.

The boys from the shantytown were already waiting. They were even up in the trees. But for once they weren't waving or performing backflips or even trying to flog half-dead animals. They were wide-eyed and tense, staring at Margery and Enid as if they were prisoners being led to execution.

"Do we lock up?" said Margery. In the silence, her voice came out unnaturally loud. Like addressing Enid through a megaphone.

"Lock up? What for?"

"Because almost everything we own is inside the bungalow."

"If those kids want to break in, they can stick a foot through the wall."

"What if they follow us?"

"They won't. They think the mountain's haunted. They won't go near it."

They pushed through the elephant grass and ferns at the back of the bungalow, tunneling between the stems and rough fronds that grew above their heads. Even that took ages. Enid was right about the boys from the shantytown: they didn't follow them beyond the bungalow. Ahead, the forest was as thick as a wall and making strange sounds of its own. There was not the faintest hint of a path. The air was dark.

"Good luck, Marge."

"Thank you, Enid."

"We might find it today."

"We won't."

"We might, though. If we think positive thoughts. It's exciting. Don't you think? I'm excited."

"Enid, we won't find it because we are thinking positive thoughts. We'll find it because we've got to the top."

"You know your problem?"

"No, Enid."

"You're too down in the dumps. You think the glass is half empty when it is really three-quarters full."

"Half full."

"Beg pardon?"

"The phrase is 'half full.' And, anyway, science has nothing to do with positive thoughts. It is to do with hard evidence. Now, shall we start?"

"Yes, Marge."

"From now on, I need you to be quiet."

"Right, Marge."

"I need to focus on the climb. I need you to stop talking. Is that a possibility?"

"I can try."

Margery reminded her that the plan was to forge a path upward until the trees began to clear and they could start looking for the white orchid. They would stop to collect other specimens along the way. They would set traps. Search dead wood. But if Enid caught sight of a gold beetle, or even something remotely similar, she must stay absolutely still. She must raise her hand. She must not shout, or flap her arms, or in fact do anything that she would normally do: she must simply wait for Margery to bring the sweep net and killing jar. Above all, she must not rush ahead.

Enid nodded. "And we go back to the bungalow after a week?"

"Yes. With any luck, we'll have found a few beetles. We might even reach the top by Christmas."

At the mention of the word "luck," Enid's hand shot to her collar. It was another superstitious thing. She would have to keep hold of it until Margery said Enid's special code.

"White elephant, white elephant, white elephant."

"Thank you, Marge."

They began, Margery first, Enid—plus dog—at the rear. They set down their haversacks and took out their bush knives. They would hack a bit, then go back for their equipment, then hack more. Trees surged closer on all sides, losing themselves in the distance in a swampy green dusk. Creepers dropped in thick, matted curtains; climbers flaunted huge red blooms. Roots ran everywhere like tangled cables beneath their feet, while trunks as tall as poles bore pale flowers all the way up to the canopy above.

It was awful. Infinitely worse than Margery had thought possible. After ten minutes, she was panting for breath and drenched in sweat, and her fingers were fat with heat. Even the leather of her belt swelled, and in spite of a neckerchief, ants slithered down her collar and got inside her shirt. She pushed aside a creeper; it swung straight back and almost knocked her out. Pausing to check that none of the shantytown boys were following, Margery found herself rolling backward.

Their knives were blunt in no time. They might as well have brought wooden spoons. Monstrous tree trunks, circled with tendrils and coils. Bromeliads the size of pots. The hanging roots of the great banyan trees, jutting out elbows and knees from plaited windings of stems that were so intricately knotted it made her eyes blind to try to follow them. Lianas of all thickness, from several feet to those of the finest hair's breadth. Sometimes the only way to continue was by untying each one.

Clouds of insects trailed them in the hot air. A branch blinked a blue eye, and turned out to be a gecko. If a breeze came, they stopped with their arms wide, their mouths open, and took it in, like water.

For a while, Enid managed to say nothing, though she more than made up for it in sighs. Maybe it was nerves. After keeping silent in a loud way for another half hour, she interrupted to ask if Margery had ever had a pet.

"A pet?" Margery smeared the sweat from her neck. Her shirt was glued to her back.

"Sorry. I was just thinking. I must have talked by mistake. Have you, though?"

"Have I what?"

"Ever had a pet? You could just answer yes or no. Then I wouldn't have to think about it anymore."

"Enid, I have never had a pet. I wasn't allowed a pet."

"You weren't allowed a pet?"

"My aunts were very strict."

"That's so sad, Marge."

"Yes, well, I got over it. Can we go on?"

"Beetles?"

"What about them?"

"You kept beetles. Weren't they pets?"

"They were specimens."

"You mean you killed them?"

"No. They died. They don't live long."

"So what about the gold beetle? Will you kill that?"

"Enid, I will have to, in order to take it home and present it to the museum. We've been through this. But you don't have to look. I will do it."

Enid gulped. She nodded. "I'm emptying my mind."

"I see."

"Otherwise my thoughts get in my way."

"And is your mind fully empty now?"

"Not quite. I had two mice. The wife died and the man was so sad. It broke my heart. Animals aren't supposed to be alone. And then I had a cat once—"

"Enid, this is a full-blown conversation."

"All right, Marge. I've finished."

They forged on. The forest closed over their heads and was as pathless as water. And being silent next to Enid was worse than waiting for a dormant volcano. She began to hum. Just quietly under her breath, like a reminder she was alive. The cruelest thing you could do to Enid was not notice her.

Two hours more. It got worse and worse. Hacking, clearing, climbing. Another step. Another step. Why had she left it so late in life to do the thing she'd always wanted? Everything that could bite flew straight past Enid and went for Margery. Even little insects that looked too small to leave their mothers, let alone paralyze a human arm. She crouched to pee and couldn't do it fast enough, desperate to cover her rear end. Doing the other business was even worse: a wild pig appeared, and no small pig, either, but a great big hairy one, built like a tank, and stood waiting for what she was straining to produce, even though she shouted and threw stones. Meanwhile, the forest was so dense there was barely light— Enid was dull green and so was her dog. When a parrot shot out of the undergrowth, screeching and flapping, its cries echoed through the entire forest.

Midday, they stopped to eat. She cracked open a tin each of Spam, which Enid mixed with curry powder to put off the flies. It was possibly the worst thing Margery had ever eaten, and they had barely covered half a mile.

Enid asked if it was okay to pick up on their conversation, now that they were resting. She said she'd been thinking all morning of the babies she'd lost. She'd been thinking, too, of her twin sister, the one who'd been born dead. Her voice went up and down, like a song.

"Every time I see a butterfly, I say to myself, 'That's her.' I know my sister's here. And my babies, too. They're all with me."

Enid pointed at a blue butterfly, fanning its wings on a leaf. If Margery had seen one that morning, she had seen hundreds. She tried to imagine her brothers as butterflies. It was as absurd as saying they were still alive. If she thought of them too long, or tried too hard, she could barely see their faces. But it was too hot to think. It was too hot to listen. And she didn't like to break it to Enid, but most butterflies died after a couple of weeks, even great big blue ones.

They spent the rest of the afternoon hacking their way up a steep ridge that turned out to be a tiny plateau. By now, her haversack was so heavy she felt as if she were carrying a dead person on her back, and her clothes were so thick with sweat and dust they hurt. She said nothing to Enid—who had overtaken her and was now forging ahead, yelling every time she spotted an insect—but her hip was beginning to seize up. Mr. Rawlings looked back at her as she lagged further and further behind. Worse, they had finished the water, and it was all she could think about. Her throat felt sliced. Her mouth was filled with thick white paste. Then, briefly, the trees cleared and the mountain peak rose straight ahead, two-pronged, like a blunt wisdom tooth.

It was just as high as it had been that morning. If anything, it seemed to have grown. At this rate, it would be February before they even got to the top, let alone began to search for the gold beetle.

Enid cocked her head. "Water!" she yelled, and with that she went thrashing and cutting through the undergrowth so fast Margery could barely thrash and cut fast enough to keep up.

But she was right. Margery heard water before she saw it. A sizzling, like oil in a frying pan. In her joy, Enid pulled Margery up a boulder; her hip practically split in half. But down below lay a clearing of light: a place where the trees parted and sunshine fell onto a pool of water so deep and blue she could see the bottom; water making a crisscross of paths down a sheer rock face and sending up a mist of spray that held the colors of the rainbow. Carefully they picked their way down, though Enid got fed up with being careful and slid the last part on her rear end. They scrambled to the water's edge and were soon kneeling in the sunlight and making cups of their hands. It tasted of stone. It was possibly the coldest thing Margery had ever drunk. Then Enid pulled off her clothes and hat, and, before Margery could object, was tearing bare-naked into the shallows, shrieking and laughing, "Yahoo!" as if she'd just leaped out of a wild Western. Her skin was white where her clothes had been, her breasts full and blue-veined, a swatch of dark between her legs. By the look of things, she'd actually put on weight.

"Yahoo! It's beautiful! Come on, Marge! Come in!"

Margery had never swum in her life. She hadn't even paddled. "No, Enid."

"Come on, Marge!" Enid smacked the water with her fists and shouted to make echoes. "Yahoo! I'm alive!" Then she plunged underwater, and her hair moved like a sea anemone.

Mr. Rawlings looked up at Margery. She looked down at him. He closed his mouth and stopped panting, as if he expected her to say something.

"After you," she said.

He continued to stare at her. He clearly had no intention of getting wet, and neither did she. But he was a dog, a useless one, and she was a human being. In order to prove herself the superior species, she took off her boots and shorts, though she drew the line at removing her top—or, indeed, her underwear. The water was ice cold. It was like being bitten. It even seemed to snap at her bones. But she held on to a root until it broke in her hands and she lost her footing and suddenly the water was not up to her knees, it was up to her chest, then her chin, it was in her mouth, ice-cold water, and her head was going under. She threw out her arms. She struck furiously. She began, if not to swim, then at least to stop drowning. Once she choked and went under again but kept going. She reached the other side where she could touch the bottom, but she did not get out, she stayed, staring up at the thundering cascade of water and dark green pine clumps and, above them, the sky as blue as a piece of glass.

And just for a moment she could have sworn she heard something inside her, groaning with pleasure and whispering, "Oh, Margery Benson, what was this beautiful crazy thing that you just did?"

28

A Gun Is Not an Option

Dusk came fast. Or, rather, day went. One minute there had been occasional pins of light between trees; the next darkness was flooding in. Enid rushed to find the hurricane lamp. Once lit, it shone like a small moon.

"What I don't understand," she was saying, "is why you never tried putting up this tent before?"

"Because," Margery was saying, "I didn't need to. I live in a flat."

"You taught domestic science for twenty years."

"That doesn't mean I put up tents. I taught girls how to iron men's shirts, and boil vegetables."

"That's all?" said Enid. "That's all you taught them?"

They had filled the jerricans and moved on from the bathing pool. The forest was thick again; so was the insect life. And even though Margery had brought towels, the humidity had got into them and they were soaked. The euphoria she had experienced in the bathing pool was gone. Now all she felt was very wet. Meanwhile, the separate pieces of the A-frame tent were spread at her feet. The truth was that she hadn't dealt with the tent before now because she'd had no idea what to do with it, and so—in her mind, at least—this was a task she had allocated to her assistant. But her assistant was currently busy unrolling the hammocks and studying the ropes and hooks.

"I would just have expected," continued Enid, "that you might at least have tried the tent before now."

"You may not be aware of this, Enid, but I had a flat filled with tinned supplies and equipment. I could barely move."

Margery fitted the poles together and threaded them through the tent's roof. Now what she had was a piece of canvas on a stick, more like an enormous flag than accommodation. Margery took it apart, tried again. She rammed the poles through the sides. She tried to pin the ropes into the ground to keep it upright. Mr. Rawlings brushed past. The tent keeled over.

"You have done this before?" said Enid. "You have put up a tent before?"

"No."

"You haven't?" Enid paused. "But you've led an expedition?"

"I haven't."

"But you've been on one?"

"Not exactly."

"You've never been on an expedition?" repeated Enid, spelling this out with such force she might as well have hit Margery over the head while she was at it.

"What? Never?"

"No, Enid, I have never been on an expedition. I told you. I was a teacher."

"Bugger," she said, followed by a slower "Okaay." She sucked the end of one of her plaits. "So maybe we should cut our losses and go to the bungalow tonight."

The idea of dragging her body one more step appalled Margery. Besides, she wasn't entirely sure that if she went down the mountain she'd ever come back up it. "No," she roared. "We can't go to the bungalow. The whole point is that we keep moving forward."

Enid held up both hands as if stopping traffic. "Suits me. I'll sit and watch you put up the tent. It's very entertaining."

"Enid, you could at least do something useful. You could put up the hammocks."

"Marge, I don't want to upset you again. But aren't the hammocks supposed to go *inside* the tent?"

"Enid. Why don't you just work out how to put them up?"

And she did. She had them hanging securely in minutes, just like that, two perfect hammocks, strung low between trees, as if Enid had camped in tropical rainforests all her life. She even draped them with mosquito nets. Afterward she took Mr. Rawlings to fill the jerricans with more water from the bathing pool, and then she gathered stones the size of Ping-Pong balls, which she arranged into a fire pit, laying it with fronds of dried palm, though the flames wouldn't take and she wasted one match after another. Since they had no heat, they had to mix the dried oats with cold water, which just floated like bits of sawdust in a bowl. After that they had more Spam, spiced up with more curry powder. Occasionally one of Enid's matches took light and a leaf burst into flame, while above glowed the enormous pines and giant ferns, freckled with quick shadows, but never long enough to last.

Margery was too exhausted to write anything in her journal apart from a brief description of the terrain. Bolts of pain seemed screwed in the space between her eyebrows. Besides, the pages of her book were sopping wet, and the pen just made holes. Meanwhile, the tent—despite her best efforts—resembled a coffin. They could either sleep in the open on Enid's perfectly assembled hammocks, or lie squashed beneath a bit of canvas. It was already crawling with red ants.

Margery took off her boots. Her bare feet were mushy and hot and the smell was rancid, like something that had been kept in a dark place for too long. She smothered them in talc.

"You need to do this," she said, passing the tub to Enid. "You don't want to get foot rot."

Enid's feet were red, a few blisters forming on the heels. She sprinkled them with so much powder they looked like socks.

"Do you want to know," she said slowly, "how I got away from Taylor?" She lit another match. "I left while he was asleep."

Margery nodded. It stood to reason that you wouldn't leave a man like Taylor while he was awake.

"You were right, Marge. He was not a nice man. It's a habit I have."

"What is?"

"Falling for men who aren't nice. I do it every time. It's like I can't help myself."

"Is your husband like that?"

"No." Enid balled her hands so hard the knuckles went white. It was like looking straight at the bone. Then she said, "I don't know what I'd have done if you hadn't come to find me. I'd have got myself in all sorts of mess. No, Taylor was not a nice man. He tried to lock me in after you left the camp. And he took all the money I had. But at least I got his gun."

For a moment, the entire forest seemed to fall over. Margery was aware she needed to sit, then realized she was already doing that, so probably what she needed was to lie down. "Enid? You stole his gun?"

"It's in my haversack."

"You mean you have it with you?"

"I thought we might need it."

"No, Enid. We do not need a gun. We will never need a gun. A stolen jeep I can manage, but a gun is not even an option."

The words came from Margery with a force that shocked her. And—as if that wasn't enough—here were . . . not tears as such but noises like gulps, as if she were drowning. All she could see were the open French windows of her father's study.

Enid threw out her arms and grabbed hold of her. She held Margery's head clamped against her chest. It was both painful and strangely reassuring, like being a football. She could even hear the wild thump of Enid's heart.

"I'm sorry. I'm sorry. I never meant to upset you. Here." Enid

passed something improbable that turned out to be a handkerchief. It would barely cover a nostril. "Blow."

Margery did. She blew as small as she could, though technically
there was nothing to blow out, she was just overcome.

"Better now, Marge?"

"Yes."

"We'll get rid of the gun."

"Thank you, Enid."

"We'll bury it in the morning."

"Thank you."

"There's one more thing I need to say."

"Is it as bad as the gun?"

"Marge, it's my husband—"

But Margery interrupted. For a terrible moment she'd been
convinced Enid was about to confess to further weaponry. "Oh,
Enid, I've worked that out."

"You have?"

"I worked it out ages ago."

"You did?"

"Well, of course you're divorced. You don't even wear a ring. I
don't know why you tried to cover it up."

In reply, Enid said nothing. Lit by another match, she looked
only half familiar. Her eyes blazed, like chipped glass.

"Enid? Whatever happens, we won't need a gun."

"You really think that?"

"I do."

"Hm," said Enid. Just a noise.

"Come on. We should sleep."

How does a woman get into a hammock, when she has not got into
a hammock before? Enid asked if she needed help, but Margery—
still piqued after the business with the tent and also her confession
that she had never been on an expedition before—insisted she
could manage. Enid seemed to mount her hammock with no difficulty whatsoever. One moment she was on the ground. The next

she was in a hammock. She even had Mr. Rawlings with her, his ears glowing in the dark.

"Sleep well, Marge!"

Margery's hammock was less amenable. She tried one leg first. It went swinging off with her a little bit on it, but mostly not. She tried taking it by surprise, mounting suddenly. The hammock accepted her weight, then performed a full cartwheel and tossed her out the other side, dumping her in a load of spikes. In the end, she gave a leap and pitched herself. She landed on her front, her mouth mashed against the canvas, rocking violently, but still, she had done it. Technically she was in a hammock, no one could argue with that, though she could barely move without the risk of depositing herself back on the ground. It took a lot of effort to roll herself the right way up. She pulled the mosquito net round her.

But sleep? How could she possibly do that? Who in their right mind would even close their eyes? The bungalow was one thing, but at least there had been the pretense of a roof and some walls. This was terrifying. Her senses felt sharpened like pencils—her flashlight was about as much use as a paddleboat in the ocean. She heard whistles and screams from creatures she'd never even had nightmares about, let alone seen. Rough cawing, lunatic whooping, once a clang. When a pale shadow took shape, she lay taut as a trap, her eyes so wide they could have popped, until it gave a snort and became a pig. More whistling. More twitching. Another animal that screamed as if it was being eaten alive. She thought of Enid, the gun. Then something landed on her face.

Possibly it meant no harm. Possibly it mistook her for something friendly, or at least inanimate. But Margery did not feel friendly, and neither did she feel inanimate. Her first instinct was to bat it. Unwise. It got meshed in her net. Flapping and squeaking. A bat. She had batted a bat. And now Margery was panicking and the bat was panicking and there was something in her mouth, but it was not a bat, it was her net, and even though the bat had flown free, she was swinging wildly—up, down! Up, down!—like an awful ride at the fair, while a hundred mosquitoes zoomed in to bite her.

The dawn chorus came miles before dawn. It was actually the middle of the night. Nevertheless, every bird in New Caledonia woke early and decided to sing about it. Then the cicadas joined in, less a chirruping than heavy marching. Gradually, silver light seeped into the dark, and shapes came to life. A banana tree. A rock. The birds went back to sleep. The cicadas settled down. She told herself that if anything was going to eat her, it would surely have started by now, and dared to close her eyes. She managed thirty minutes. Then she woke again. Rain was falling all over her.

It had been the most awful night of her life. The gap between making a plan and actually doing it was unbridgeable: nothing Professor Smith had taught her had prepared her for this. Nothing she'd read had prepared her, either. She was covered in insect bites—they had even got inside her ears. She was soaking wet, possibly rotting, and she felt wrung out from lack of sleep. Worse, her body had seized up. The only way to get out of the hammock would be by extending herself in segments, like a foot rule. She had no idea how she would walk another step. Already she knew she was in something she was not made for.

She thought of the British wives at the consulate party listing everything they missed from home: Branston pickle, gray drizzle, perfect English grass. They were right. Faced with the rainforest, she felt desolate. Back at home she had a flat with a bed in it, clean sheets, and a nice bedside lamp. She missed streetlights, windows, curtains, roads with proper names. Rationing was better than this. And even though her aunts had taught her it was wrong to cry— even though she hadn't done so at her mother's funeral—a million tiny dots seemed to prickle her nose, culminating in a salty rush as tears filled her eyes. She hadn't a clue why she was lying in a hammock on the other side of the world, already half crippled, looking for a beetle that had never been found—she could die out here, under these alien stars, and no one would know. She thought of her father, her mother, her brothers. She thought of the professor, Barbara, and her aunts. And the more she thought about the people she'd lost, the more she wanted them back. Her crying wasn't about missing home anymore. It wasn't about Branston pickle, or green grass, and roads with proper names. It was something else. It had been with her ever since her father had walked out of his French windows and left her behind. You might travel to the other side of the world, but in the end it made no difference: whatever devastating unhappiness was inside you would come, too.

Margery lay in her horrible hammock and sobbed.

29

Cutting Paper Shapes and Stars

In Nouméa, the British wives had gathered at Mrs. Pope's for Friday craftwork before the day got too hot. The meetings gave them something to look forward to, especially in the cyclone season, when the weather could turn without warning and, before they knew it, thoughts of Christmas at home could balloon into despair. It was no wonder some of the wives had already been sent away.

Weekly coffee allowed them to show off a new frock, exchange a recipe, and share an activity, though the knitted space rockets for the local orphanage, their last project, had turned out looking like woolly condoms, and the women had been a laughingstock. Even the Australians had laughed; Mrs. Pope still hadn't got over it. Her husband had suggested she might invite other wives—New Zealanders and Dutch. After all, they spoke English—but Mrs. Pope said no. Speaking English was not the same as being British. Besides, they themselves were a small number, and when you were in a minority, you had to stick together.

Since it was nearly Christmas, they were cutting out paper chains to decorate the British consulate for Mrs. Pope's Three Kings party. They talked about their fancy-dress outfits—Mrs. Pope would be wearing gold this year—and the news from home,

though the latest papers still only went as far as October, so strictly
news wasn't new, it was just more of what they'd already heard.
Rationing. The Festival of Britain. The Norman Skinner trial.
Then they returned to things more local. Apparently, there'd been
a development on the theft from the Catholic school. The French
police had a new lead.

"No!" gasped the women.

"Yes!" said Mrs. Pope. She cut out a paper star. She knew how to
milk a moment.

"Do tell us!" chorused the women.

Mrs. Pope put down her scissors and leaned forward. She said in
a low voice, "Maurice says they think the suspect is British."

"British?" Absolutely no one could believe it. They had to say it
again. *"British?"*

"I can't believe they think a British person did it," said Mrs.
Peter Wiggs. "I thought it was one of the natives."

"It appears not," said Mrs. Pope. "Of course, it's frightfully embarrassing."

The women agreed the whole situation was both frightful and
embarrassing, almost as if the entire British community had been
accused of theft.

"What will the French police do? Will they interview us?"

Mrs. Peter Wiggs, also known as Dolly, was Mrs. Pope's right-
hand woman. She was a sweet person, but her intelligence she
saved for special occasions.

"No, Dolly. They won't interview us. Not unless we are behaving
suspiciously, which we are not, because we are British citizens and
we didn't commit the crime. But I hear they are looking at the paperwork of all new arrivals."

"It seems an awful lot of trouble," said Dolly. "Just for a theft."

"It's the principle, Dolly. Besides, the French have always had it
in for us." She put some glue and sparkles on her paper star. "If you
ask me, they never got over Waterloo."

"What about those two nice women? From the Natural History
Museum?"

"What about them, Dolly?"

"I hope they're not suspects. They seemed so nice."

"Nice?" repeated Mrs. Pope. "Did you not see the assistant? She was practically a call girl."

"I liked her hair," said Dolly.

The housemaid arrived with a plate of mince pies, but Mrs. Pope waved them away. The pastry was soggy and the woman had misunderstood and put stewed goat inside them instead of paw-paw.

She said, "Those two women won't last up north. They'll be back before Christmas. Mark my words." And then she said, as if the two thoughts had suddenly become connected, "I fully intend to find out who broke into the Catholic school."

Across the table crawled a strange insect with a long proboscis and feelers on both sides. It was dragging another insect with it. Mrs. Pope watched a moment, the way it carried the other, testing the way, like the blind. She lifted an old newspaper and flattened it.

30

Every Day We Keep Climbing

"Morning, Marge! Rise and shine!"

There was only one thing worse than being stuck in the rainforest on the other side of the world, and that was being stuck in it with Enid Pretty. Enid had just enjoyed the best night's sleep of her entire life. She loved sleeping outside—she hadn't even noticed the rain. Now that it had stopped, the forest was rayed with light. Soft mist hung in threads between trees. Raindrops hung everywhere like silver fish.

"Do you need help getting out of your hammock, Marge?"

"No, thank you. I'm fine."

"Only you look a bit stuck."

"I am admiring the tropical scenery, Enid."

"Have you been crying?" Enid was now peering over the edge of Margery's hammock. She was holding her well-slept dog, and her hair stood out in a halo.

"Of course not."

"I think I might go for a lovely morning swim to freshen up. Do you want anything?"

"Like what exactly? A bowl of cornflakes?"

Enid laughed and laughed. Her dog wagged its tail. "See you soon, Marge."

As soon as Enid was safely out of the way, Margery took her life into her hands and deposited herself out of her hammock. The only way was to swing! swing! swing! then toss. She landed in a heap that hurt, and crawled to her feet. She had been right about her hip: it would have been easier to saw off her leg than walk on it. And after all her crying, her eyes felt like red stones. She fetched a clean wet shirt out of her haversack. She took a button and lined it up with a buttonhole. She zipped up her shorts. She tucked in the shirt. She shook her socks to lose the ants. She knocked the insects out of her boots, and slotted her feet inside them. She tried to focus on these very small things while knowing that within her there was a colossal thing, and the colossal thing was telling her, "This is useless. There is no way, Margery Benson, in which you can keep going."

Enid returned from her swim with a bundle of green bananas, and then had more luck with the fire and managed to heat enough water to brew a pot of coffee that was so strong Margery might as well have eaten the powder. Apparently something with teeth had made holes in everything inside the tent that wasn't a tin, so all they had left on the menu was Spam. Enid mashed it with the bananas. It was even worse at breakfast than it had been for lunch and tea. Margery's stomach went into spasm.

"I never realized before how versatile Spam is," said Enid, happily digging into it with her spoon. "I think I could eat Spam for the rest of my life and not get tired of it. But there's one more problem. It's our supplies of lavatory paper."

Margery's heart dropped. Or maybe it was her stomach. Hard to tell. Since drinking Enid's coffee, her insides had begun to swap places. "What about our supplies of lavatory paper?"

"They've been eaten as well. Covered in holes. We'll have to use leaves."

"Leaves?"

Unperturbed, Enid fixed her hair and makeup with the aid of her compact mirror. Meanwhile, she broke into a nonstop monologue about a man she'd seen once at the circus who could ride a pony while carrying an umbrella and a lion cub. It had absolutely nothing to do with anything. It probably wasn't even true. "What happened to your face? It's swollen up, like a punching bag. Looks like you've been bitten all over."

"I have been bitten all over."

"Hm," said Enid, again. "At least it's a nice day. At least we're safe." She looked up at the basketwork of trees and lianas above their heads. An enormous leaf slowly fell, like a pterosaur pierced with an arrow.

"Safe? How can you possibly call this safe?"

There was no time to wait for the answer. Margery's sudden need for the privy was monumental. She felt ready to explode. No choice but to run for the undergrowth.

By the time she came back, she had lost substantial amounts of herself. Worse, she smelled like a goat. Enid had already packed the hammocks and the tent and what she could retrieve of their supplies. She stared at Margery, up and down, in the way that car mechanics look over old bangers before consigning them to the junk heap. "You okay, Marge?"

"Yes, thank you."

"You seem to have a bad limp."

"No. I am fine."

"You know, we don't have to bury Taylor's gun. Maybe you'd feel safer if I kept it."

It was too much. The last straw. Margery had thought the hammock was the last straw, and the bat, followed by the night itself, and the crying, then possibly the Spam, as well as the diarrhea, but they had not been the *last* straws, they had simply been a succession of penultimate ones. It felt as if the air was thickening to the point at which she could no longer breathe. Her voice came out in a wobble. "Enid. I do not want a gun anywhere near me. A gun is a terrible thing. I don't want to think about the gun. I don't want to see the gun. Do you not understand? I do not want a gun in my life."

Enid straightened. She stared at Margery as if she was seeing beyond the insect bites and her skin, as if she was seeing right through Margery and into her heart. She said slowly. "You lost someone, Marge. You lost someone because of a gun. That's why you can't stand the sight of blood."

"Can we please drop this? Can we please not have this conversation? Can we please just keep searching?"

Enid nodded. She chucked the dregs of her coffee onto the ground. She said quietly, "Sure, Marge. I understand. I'll bury the gun."

And she did. She took it and buried it straightaway. When she came back, her hands were empty.

"No more gun," she said. "All right, Marge?"

They kept going. Margery plastered her bites with witch hazel. She rubbed her legs so hard they seemed to produce their own electricity. She put on her helmet. Off they went. Day number two.

"Maybe we'll find it today!" sang Enid.

Hour after hour. More cutting, more climbing. Dripping with sweat, as if Margery was permanently in a shower. Her hip seeming to scream. One of her boots chafing badly. Her head too heavy, her head too hot. Her stomach in knots, her rear end like a tap. Hands blistered. Hands cut. Trees as far as she could see, with roots like huge webbed feet, and branches thick with liana creepers. The heat was a pall.

Meanwhile, Enid did not get bitten. Enid did not get stung. Enid didn't even sweat that much. She was having the time of her life. She forged ahead in her baseball cap with the dog—sometimes no more than a happy fluorescent streak in the canopy of green—clambering over rocks, up and down gullies, splashing through water. "This way, Marge!" or "Quick! Quick, Marge! Over here!"

She was a woman possessed. She spotted gold beetles that turned out to be no more than a play of light. And if she wasn't spotting nonexistent beetles or saying hello to butterflies, she was leaping streams and swinging on lianas and knocking the top off a coconut to drink the milk. Margery crawled further and further behind, lifting every stone, peering under every leaf. With each step, she knew pain. But she focused on one after the other, just as she had focused on one button after another on her shirt, and by looking only at the small things that were straight ahead, she kept going.

It was Enid's idea that they should set up their hammocks before it began to get dark. She managed another fire, and the flames took. She found a flat piece of rock where Margery could write her journal. She even blew on the pages to dry them, though with the humidity they felt Bible thin. She insisted on giving Margery a leg up into her hammock. She even arranged the net. And then, as if that weren't enough, she talked on and on and on about anything that came into her head, until Margery couldn't bear any more and passed out.

She slept. She slept the entire night. Rats might have run over her. Bats might have landed on her. Mosquitoes might have taken enough blood to fill a tankard. She had no idea. In the morning, Enid found another place to swim, then came back and made black coffee so strong it could have brought a dead horse back to life, and the only reference she made to the gun was oblique.

"I understand you have secrets in your life, Marge. That's okay. We all have secrets. But I don't think you should stop looking for the beetle. You would never forgive yourself if you gave up on your vocation."

They went on. Day after day. Caked in red dust and sweat. Permanently wet. Bitten all over. Stung all over. Followed by pigs. Followed by lizards. Followed by rats. Stomach cramps, foot rot, diarrhea. When it rained, it fell in bucket loads. When the mist came, they couldn't move. Enid said that in order to find the beetle, they should think like a beetle. Margery said that in order to find the beetle they should keep their eyes peeled and not talk so much.

But there were moments of joy. Even at its worst, life will offer such moments. After day four, they slept all night in a clearing and afterward managed to boil a pan of water, and drank hot coffee, talking softly, in the first glow of light.

"What is your favorite nail color, Marge?"

"I don't wear nail color, Enid."

"But if you did, what would it be?"

"I don't know. It's not something I think about."

"Red?"

"No."

"You're right. Red wouldn't suit you. You're more a pink kind of person."

"Pink? I don't think so."

"I don't mean blancmange pink. I mean that kind of pink." She pointed at the sunrise. It was the color of Enid's travel suit.

"Okay, Enid. Yes. I think I would like that pink."

"You see? I told you you'd like nail color. Just because you've never done something doesn't mean you can't start. We'll get that pink for you one day."

There was the moment hundreds and thousands of blue birds exploded out of the trees, weaving through the air, like a piece of silk, and the two women watched and watched. Afterward Margery found a blue feather she gave to Enid, and Enid tucked it into her pocket and said, "Oh, Marge. Is that really for me? That's the luckiest feather in the world. I'll keep it my whole life."

And there was the night they lay side by side in their hammocks and watched a comet speed past, eating its way through the constellations, and Enid said, "That's a sign, Marge. It's a sign we're going to find the beetle."

At the end of the week they returned to the bungalow, empty-handed, desperate for salt. It had taken all Margery's courage to keep going. But however much she hated it, she had not given up:

she had continued to limp after Enid and the dog, and while it had rarely been what she would call pleasurable, she realized she had a supply of endurance she wouldn't otherwise have known about. As expected, the boys from the shantytown had broken into the bungalow while they were away: nothing was taken, but it had all been slightly rearranged, and in a few instances, it had even been tidied. Margery checked the box where she kept her passport and money: everything was safe. The women washed their clothes. Restocked supplies. Margery slept for fifteen hours. Enid drove to Poum and came back with salt, eggs, yams, watermelon, and French pastries. They ate so much they fell asleep in the sun on the veranda.

Then: "Ready, Marge?"

"Yes, Enid."

"Got your helmet? Got your net?"

"Yes, Enid."

Another week on the mountain.

This time they turned more serious. They didn't just hack a path. They laid insect traps. They examined dead leaves, fallen branches, rotten logs, pig droppings. Margery showed Enid how to use the pooter, though in her enthusiasm Enid kept swallowing insects and had to stick her fingers down her throat to get them back. They cordoned off areas, searched on hands and knees. They whacked branches and caught what fell out in a tarp. When it was dark, they held up the hurricane lamp, and as insects buzzed and flapped toward its light, they caught them, too. They now had ten species of clown beetle and an extremely rare *Rhantus alutaceus*, the size of a black bean with pale reddish marking. Margery dispatched them, while Enid closed her eyes and hummed. By the time they returned to the bungalow at the end of the second week, the boys had broken in again but taken nothing except more chewing gum. Margery soaked her specimens, ready for pinning. She made drawings and took notes. Enid washed and dried the nets, and drove to Poum to restock supplies. They went back up the mountain.

Dawn until dusk with nothing, surviving on a Spam and coffee diet that they supplemented with as much coconut and fresh fruit

as they could carry, and edible green leaves: Enid was forever trying them and found one in particular that she insisted had a taste
of honey. They also found a rare clown beetle and two specimens
of *Uloma isoceroides*, like shiny brown nuts. They identified three
types of pink orchid.

Time changed shape, inelegantly and without Margery's permis-
sion. Days passed and sometimes they felt like weeks and sometimes hours. When had she gone into the bathing pool? Was it last
week? Or the one before? Her watch hadn't worked since they
arrived at the bungalow. Nothing seemed present anymore, except
the place where she found herself—and she knew, as she moved
away, that that, too, would quickly become unreal. The only con-
stants were Enid and the search for the beetle.

Enid led the way, scrambling ahead with the insect net. Her dog
kept at her heels, looking neither left nor right. Meanwhile, Margery's feet were rotting. Her skin was so burnt it was coming off in
flakes; she was using Pond's Cold Cream just to stick it back together. The damage to her notebooks was even more serious. The
covers were soggy, and the pages were approaching a state of such
pulpiness she had to peel them apart. But then again, she could
barely hold a pen. And the heat, the rain, the bites. The one thing
there hadn't been was a cyclone. Grimly she kept going.

Enid talked about the future when Margery would have a job at
the Natural History Museum and be a famous beetle collector. Another time, she said, "Marge? Do you really think you'll want to kill
the gold beetle? I know it's important. I just don't see how you'll
bring yourself to do it."

But by the end of the third week they had five specimens of rare
weevil to add to their collection, plus two leaping beetles Margery
had never seen before, and a number of tortoise beetles. This time
the boys hadn't broken into the bungalow but they were all waiting
outside in a surprisingly neat line, and wanted to sell Margery a
basket of live freshwater eels. She said *non* to the eels. The boys
decided to leave them as a gift instead. Enid carried the eels to the
freshwater creek but they kept coming back—it was the light of

the hurricane lamp that drew them, and it was always worse after rain. They would even come up the water pipes and then get stranded in the bungalow: in the end, Enid had to set up a bucket in the front room in which to save them.

Enid washed their clothes, did her best to dry out the hammocks, restocked supplies, and repacked. Margery pinned specimens, made drawings, took notes. They slogged back up the mountain.

At night the shadows were so black, it was as though pieces had gone missing from the world. Early morning: mists blocked out the trees. By day, light sliced the undergrowth, like a trip wire. Enid began boiling the leaves she picked to make healthy soup.

"Marge?" she said in her hammock once. "I slept with other men. Not my husband. Perce liked the lads. If you know what I mean. We both did. We both liked the lads. You see? Sometimes we even got jealous."

It was everything Margery could do not to fall out of her hammock, but she didn't: she lay very still. She took in what Enid had told her.

Another time Enid said quietly, again in the dark, "Men weren't always nice to me. You know? When I was a kid? They weren't always kind."

Margery felt the old heaviness again. The war was over and yet there seemed to be no end to the suffering that had to be endured—and not even in full view: behind doors, where no one could see. Yet in the morning, Enid sprang out of her hammock and did her makeup, same as always, with her compact mirror resting on a tree trunk, and brewed her incredibly strong coffee. It occurred to Margery that this was how it was, that there was always darkness, and in this darkness was unspeakable suffering, and yet there were also the daily things—there was even the search for a gold beetle—and while they could not cancel the appalling horror, they were as real.

Margery said none of that to Enid. What Enid had told her was like something she'd slipped into Margery's pocket. She got the feeling Enid did not want to say any more on the subject. Instead Margery asked for a second cup of coffee and complimented her on her skills as an insect collector. ("Do you really mean that?" said Enid, her mouth wriggling with pride even though she was doing her best to appear modest.) But it was by continuing to focus on small rewards that Margery got through the next few days. A comb of sunlight cutting between trees. Another bathing pool. The time her foot slipped, and she didn't fall.

Two days before Christmas, Enid scrambled ahead to the summit. Trees cleared. The ground was soft and red and bare, apart from the odd cactus. The twin peaks rose like two bright orange chimneys. Margery crawled to Enid's side. No sound but the wind.

"We did it!" Enid yelled. "We did it, Marge! Yahoo!" She tossed her cap into the air.

She was right. It had not taken until February, as Margery had once feared: they had cut a winding path right from the bungalow to the very top. For days and days they had been struggling uphill looking into the slope, until the view that had only been behind them had expanded to encompass them on every side. From up here, they could see everything—the whole world seemed to lie at their feet, more colossal and remote than she had even imagined. The endless canopy of trees. The flashes of red poinciana. The tiny rooftops of Poum. Soft trails of mist. The mountain range poking up for miles and miles, as far as she could see and beyond, disappearing into the blue horizon like an infinitely bumpy spine. The ocean as bright as liquid turquoise. The pale fringe that would be coral. The many islands. Faraway, a cargo ship coming in to dock.

But nowhere was there any sign of a white orchid or the golden beetle of New Caledonia.

31

Terrible Business

Nearly four weeks at sea, and finally he could see the island. From a distance, it had shone pink and gold, but now that he was close, it was just black rock and scrubland, here and there a white beach, a fringe of palm trees, a hut. It wouldn't surprise him if the whole thing vanished, and nothing met his gaze but the loneliness of the Pacific.

A crowd thronged the wharf at Nouméa as the cargo ship drew alongside. Everywhere there was too much noise, too much color, too much smell. Mundic cowered with his haversack, trying to keep it all away. The stink of salt and fish and sweat, the sun burning riotously bright, the ocean behind him and the mountains ahead.

He thought he would find Miss Benson on the quay. He really believed she would be sitting there under an umbrella, waiting. He walked up and down and he looked in all the little French bars and a milkshake shop but there was no sign of her. He couldn't make sense of it. And suddenly it was like the day he got home from the war and found out his mum had died, but no one had written to tell him, or the times the guards had made them stand in the full blare of the sun just because someone had stolen a bit of food. And he didn't know how to keep on his feet. He didn't know where to put the things he felt inside.

He got drunk and he saw a chap laughing at him, and he felt the flame. The next thing he knew he was being dragged off the bloke by the police.

They took his passport and put him into a cell. There was a pail in the corner full of someone else's piss, and the walls were crawling with cockroaches. "My passport!" he yelled. "Give me back my passport!" But it wasn't like the POW camp. There were no sticks. No clubs. In the morning the guards gave him coffee and pastries. Even a clean bucket. He shouted because he had the runs, and another time he thought there were snakes, but they let him keep his notebook. And when his pencil broke, they gave him a ballpoint pen.

He couldn't think of anything except Miss Benson, making her way north on her own. It made him mad. He didn't even know the name of the town where she was going. All he had to guide him was the stupid cross on her map. He shoved his fist into the wall and it sprang out like a ball. "I am a free man! I am a free man!" he shouted. "Give me back my passport!"

The next day the guards fetched him out of his cell and took him to an interview room. A man in a linen suit was sitting there, pale as a goose and mopping his face. Mundic said, "You can ask as many questions as you like. I still don't know what the hell you're talking about."

And the fat guy said, "I am the British consul and I will thank you not to swear at me, Mr. Mundic."

Apparently there had been a break-in at a local school almost a month ago. "Naphthalene was taken and also chemistry equipment. The next day, a jeep was stolen. You are, I am afraid, the leading suspect."

Mundic laughed. "Me? I've only just got here."

The British consul said it was no laughing matter. "A British traveler's check was found close to the school. The police believe it is a clue. And there aren't a lot of British out here. It's a very embarrassing business."

"Well, it wasn't me, sir. I've come on a job."

"Really? What kind of job?" The British consul stared so long and hard that Mundic squirmed in his chair. "Where exactly were you posted?"

"The Far East."

"I thought as much. Terrible business."

"Yes, sir."

"You were lucky. At least you're alive."

"Yes, sir." After that, Mundic couldn't even look the British consul in the eye. He just squeezed the hand that he'd punched into the wall, until the pain was shooting all over his arm, but it still didn't hurt. It was like the pain was there and it wasn't.

"You're right, of course. I don't see how they can keep you here if you weren't even on the island a month ago. I have your passport. Where are you staying?"

"I'm heading north. Do you know the name of the town up there?" But the British consul wasn't listening anymore. He had opened Mundic's passport and was staring at the page. "But you have no visa. You can't stay in New Caledonia without a visa. I don't know how the police failed to notice. Well, let me see if I can pull a few strings. It's the least I can do, though everything closes, of course, because of the season."

"What season?"

The British consul laughed. "Good heavens, man. It's Christmas. Have you forgotten? Report back to the British consulate in a week."

"Can't I travel without a visa?"

"Unfortunately not. They're very strict here about things like that." The British consul was already hauling himself to his feet. And he still had Mundic's passport. Without it, he felt cut loose. He didn't know how he would survive without his passport.

"What am I supposed to do now?"

"Enjoy the lovely weather. Any problems, here is my home address. But you need to control your temper, Mr. Mundic. I hear you shout a lot. There is no need for that kind of behavior now."

"No, sir."

"Good man."

They shook hands and the British consul passed him twenty francs, just to cover his needs. Then he departed in a hurry, leaving the door to the interview room wide open. So much light that everything seemed either black or dizzying white—Mundic had to back away. He was free to go, just as he'd been a free man in Songkurai when the Allies came. Back then he had stood in a crowd of prisoners, watching the guards who'd made their lives hell being marched away, and an Aussie next to him had laughed. "They're for it now," he'd said.

But war was not over just because someone signed a truce. It was inside him. And when a thing like war was inside you, it never left.

Mundic found a barber to shave his head. After that he felt clean again, and ready to eat. On the jetty, men were unloading a batch of newspapers from a new boat. They called out, "Breeteesh newspapers! Breeteesh newspapers fresh from Great Breetain! *Vous voulez?*"

Mundic walked past. He didn't give a damn about the news from home. The last thing he needed was another story about some POW who'd hanged himself. He just wanted to get his passport back, and find Miss Benson.

32

London, December 1950

Ever since it broke, the British newspapers had been full of the Nancy Collett story. People couldn't get enough.

Repeatedly she was described as shrewd, cold, and calculating. There was an old photograph of her in the *Sunday Mail*, sitting with her husband, surrounded by chimpanzees at a tea party. She didn't look shrewd or cold or calculating. She was wearing a spotted head scarf. She and her husband were eating ice cream, and they were laughing.

Another photograph had taken up the front pages of the *Daily Mirror*, the *Yorkshire Evening Post*, and the *Sunday Dispatch* of Nancy Collett before she dyed her hair. Almost unrecognizable. A plain young woman, wearing a hat with some plastic cherries on it. If anything, the hat was the bit you noticed.

A third: her wedding day, featured in *The Times*, the *Daily Sketch*, the *Manchester Evening News*. Her face was hidden by a bunch of flowers, but her husband (Percival Collett, forty-two, deceased) was wearing a suit. She had her arm through his. She looked very young. Full-faced. She was standing on tiptoe.

Nevertheless, Nancy Collett was repeatedly described as a sexual predator. At least thirty gentlemen had come forward, confessing to knowing her in intimate ways. Later, the same photograph had been splashed all over the daily and Sunday papers, showing her posed on a settee. She was dressed in a frilly blouse, suspenders, stockings and high heels, no skirt. She was leaning her head on her hand—that was certainly provocative—but her neck looked taut, and her smile was stiff, as if she would rather she still had her skirt on.

The crime was talked about, over and over. Frustrated by her husband's war injuries, Nancy Collett had taken many partners for her pleasure. (MY CLOSE SHAVE WITH A KILLER ran one of the headlines.) Then, on the night in question, Nancy Collett—who was drunk in some versions of the story, but stone cold sober in others—had gone upstairs with a sharp knife and attacked him repeatedly while he was asleep. She had killed him because she could, and then sat gloating over the dead body before she made her escape in broad daylight.

Nancy Collett represented passion unleashed. She had spurned the restraints of civilized society and given in to animal instinct. The British public was appalled by what she'd done, and also fascinated. They bought every edition of the papers they could lay their hands on. They even went to gawp at her house. A neighbor stood outside all day retelling the story of how she'd come across the dead body. She was flogging bits of wallpaper from the scene of the crime.

WHERE IS NANCY COLLETT?

THIS WOMAN MUST HANG.

BRITAIN'S MOST WANTED CRIMINAL.

The truth was that even though she'd been spotted on the RMS *Orion* in mid-October, there was no record of Nancy Collett on the passenger list, and no record of her arriving in Brisbane. She had disappeared. Possibly under another name. No one had a clue.

Which was why the British papers had begun concentrating on her accomplice, the Woman With No Head. Very little was known about her, either. She lived alone. She'd been employed for twenty years as a teacher of domestic science. According to police records, she was some sort of petty thief. SPINSTER TEACHER IN DARK LOVE TRIANGLE! In the absence of a photograph, the cartoonists had a field day.

Nancy Collett was the big story of 1950, even bigger than the Norman Skinner case. It got so big she was mentioned on the wireless just after the king's Christmas broadcast. "Scotland Yard are continuing their search for the murderer Nancy Collett and her mysterious accomplice."

33

Merry Christmas, Margery Benson

Enid was ashen. "How long does it take," she said, "for British newspapers to get as far as New Caledonia?"

They were in the bungalow. She was holding her battery radio—she'd got a signal at last. She was also wearing a homemade paper crown.

"I don't know, Enid. A few months?"

Christmas. A day off. They'd exchanged presents—Enid gave Margery a pink cloth for a neckerchief. Margery gave her a pineapple. They ate yams and eggs and sweet bananas; not a tin of Spam in sight. Afterward Margery had pinned the new specimens they'd found that week; the boys from the shantytown crowded round to watch. The rest of the day she'd spent with her feet in a bucket of water and a compress on her hip. Her legs didn't feel like legs anymore. She hadn't said anything to Enid, but the pain in her hip was gigantic. Also, the skin on her lower legs had turned purple and swollen—she was worried the insect bites were infected.

Anyway, she must have dozed. She was aware that Enid had said something about trying to tune in to the General Overseas Service on her radio—she wanted to catch the king's Christmas broadcast. Then something else had happened. One minute, Enid was saying,

"I've got it! I've got a signal!" The next moment she yelped, as if her radio had just bitten her.

She sat now in silence, with it buried in her lap. She said again, "Do you think the British newspapers will be here soon?"

"Is something wrong, Enid?"

"No, Marge."

"Is there bad news from home?"

Enid swallowed. She shook her head. She didn't look remotely convincing.

"Not another war, Enid?"

Margery had lived through two, and peace seemed fragile. There'd been talk about Korea before they left. Not to mention Russia.

"No, Marge. Everything's fine. There's no war back home."

Enid went outside to smoke, but when she came back, she still looked ill. "Even if the British papers are in Nouméa, I suppose it'll be ages before they get all the way up here."

"Enid, I have never seen a British newspaper in Poum. The only things you can buy in Poum are yams and eggs and tins with a picture of a fish on them. And they look pre-war. I wouldn't eat them if I was desperate."

It was a joke, but Enid didn't laugh. She pulled her hand through her hair and found her paper crown. She took it off as if it was silly and bunched it up.

"Enid? Why are you worried about British newspapers?"

"I'm not. I just don't want to have to read them. I don't want to know about home."

That made no sense when she was always trying to get a radio signal, but she was twitchy and Margery didn't want to make it worse. She said, "Would you like some ice cream? We could drive to Poum?"

"Actually, Marge, I think we should stop using the jeep for a few days. I think we should lie low."

Another thing that made no sense. Enid loved driving the jeep. Besides, the idea of her lying low was ludicrous. But she was pac-

ing the room, and it was hard to keep up. After that she put away
her radio and fetched a beetle book. She picked up Mr. Rawlings,
sat at Margery's feet, and asked her to talk about beetles. They
were what really mattered. A little while later she said quietly,
more to herself than to Margery, "We'll be fine so long as we stay
north."

Enid didn't listen to her radio again. She gave it to the boys from
the shantytown. She didn't need it anymore, she said.

Ten days later they were back up the mountain, following their
path to the peak. The air was as thick and fat as a pig. Even flies
looked stuck—Margery had to tie a scarf round her mouth to stop
accidentally swallowing them. After Christmas, the weather had
changed: silent tongues of lightning in the distance, constant rum-
blings of thunder. There'd been sunsets, too, with new colors: bil-
liard table green, egg powder yellow, tomato soup red. For a few
days there had been constant insect activity, and they had caught
six new specimens of hister beetle. But suddenly there was this
awful stillness, as if the forest knew something Margery didn't. It
seemed to be holding its breath. She couldn't even hear water.

And it wasn't just the weather that was strange. Enid had
changed, too. Ever since she'd got that signal on her radio, she was
a different person. She wasn't scrambling over rocks anymore. She
wasn't happily leaping streams. It could take her a few goes just to
get into her hammock. At night she kept calling to Margery to
make sure she was still close. Other times she opened her mouth
to speak, then sighed. And this was Enid, who could once make an
entire monologue out of a shopping list. She'd started going so
slowly that Margery, despite her hip and infected bites, was in danger of overtaking her.

Enid threw off her haversack and lay flat on her back. She stayed
with her arms and legs spread out, like a star, as she stared up at the
sky. Mr. Rawlings settled next to her. He stretched on his back with
all four paws tucked up, exposing the full pink barrel of his belly.

Clearly neither of them planned to move in a hurry. Margery lowered herself with great difficulty. Now that she was down, she wasn't entirely sure how she would get up, but that was minor so she let it pass. She eased off her boots and powdered her feet. All around her, ants were flooding into holes in the ground. Their nests were like piles of coffee grains. Something was definitely happening.

"You've guessed, haven't you?"

"Guessed what, Enid?"

"My news."

"What news?"

"Oh, God," said Enid. She sighed multiple times.

"Are you okay?"

"I'm still pregnant."

Margery had to cover her mouth, as if a part of her was about to fall out. Had Enid just said she was pregnant?

"Yes," said Enid, implying she'd become a mind reader as well. "I'm having a baby."

Margery felt as if she were drowning. As if looking down had now become looking up. She had no idea what was going on. She knew Enid prayed sometimes and was very superstitious. She knew she was resourceful. But not even Enid could get pregnant all by herself and at the top of a mountain. Besides, she had spent the best part of a month scarpering up and down rocks and gullies. If either of them had been acting like a pregnant woman, it was Margery.

She took her hand from her mouth, but it was still wide open. Barbara would have said something about catching flies. And suddenly, thinking of Barbara, she really missed her consistency. Unlike Enid, Barbara was incapable of surprise—even if she'd had something nice to say, she still managed it without smiling. Barbara had been the last of the household to go. She had suffered cataracts, then near-blindness, and had stayed with Margery to the bitter end, though every time she picked up a kitchen utensil Margery had had to make a dash to rescue her. She'd died penniless and without anything to call her own except a pair of new shoes, both of which she had left to Margery.

Fortunately, Enid didn't notice Margery's distraction. She was busy talking. She was staring at the greener-than-green trees, and saying she knew this was difficult to understand. She knew it was a shock. To be honest, she was shocked, too. She'd genuinely feared she'd lost the baby on the RMS *Orion,* but after Christmas she had begun to realize she might have been wrong. She hadn't dared to say anything until she was sure, she didn't want to tempt Fate— saying the word, she crossed both fingers and held them up—but now she was certain. She'd felt the baby moving. It was moving all the time. It was a miracle, she kept saying. This baby was a miracle. She'd been afraid on Christmas Day that everything was over for her, and now suddenly there was this. Her baby was still alive. Enid had been given a second chance. Finally, she paused. "Marge? What are you doing?"

Words had disappeared. Margery felt an overwhelming need to straighten her socks. She pulled them over her knees, and adjusted the garters. She just had to get her socks straight. The line of the wool wasn't right. It was all she could think about.

"Did you hear what I said? This is my second chance."

"So you didn't have a miscarriage on the boat?"

"No. I got it wrong."

An ant stung Margery's thigh. She picked it up and looked at it very closely. "I see."

"What's up, Marge?"

"Nothing's up, Enid."

"You're not pleased."

"I am."

"I thought you'd be happy for me."

"I am."

"We'll be okay. We can still find the beetle."

Again, the world seemed to tip upside down. "Still find it? Are you mad? We're at the top of a mountain. You can't be pregnant up here." Enid sat. She stuck her hands on her hips. She looked like a jug, with her wide-open mouth as the spout. And somehow—was this even possible?—her belly was popping over the rim of her shorts. As if it had been in hiding until she had broken the news and was now freely bulging all over the place.

"So what are you saying? Are you saying we should stop?"

"You can't look for a beetle when you're pregnant. When exactly will the baby be born?"

"I don't know."

"You don't know?"

"I'm a bit hazy with my dates."

"On the ship you said May."

"Well, it's May, then. May."

"You don't sound sure."

"I am sure."

"And we're not leaving until February."

"So? That gives us ages."

"Don't be ridiculous, Enid. You can't be pregnant up a mountain. Suppose you fell?"

"Suppose I fell? What about you? Your legs don't even work. Do you think I don't notice you every day? Crawling behind? You're the one who should be in a hospital."

They were shouting. They were up a mountain, on a small tropical island, on the other side of the world, et cetera et cetera, having a full-blown argument. Minutes previously, she'd been sitting side by side with Enid, possibly incapable of getting up again, but happy, now that she thought about it—or at least at peace—and suddenly she was yelling at Enid and Enid was yelling back at her. She didn't need a mirror to know she was red in the face.

"Enid. You've done some mad things. You broke into a school. You stole the car. Bribed a policeman. You even buried a gun. But this is insane. We have to go."

"Go where exactly, Marge?"

"Home, Enid. Home. The expedition is over. It is a mad idea. It always was. The orchid is not here. The beetle is not here. I don't even have a visa anymore. We have to go."

There. She had said it. She had said it at last. They should stop. The beetle meant everything to her and they had tried, they had really tried, to find it—she had endured things she'd never even imagined—but now they should give up. They should not go on. And it was not because of Margery that they should stop. It was because Enid was pregnant, and it was no longer safe. To her astonishment, it didn't even hurt to say it. If anything, it came as a relief. In her mind at least, Margery was already packing her things.

But this was Enid she was talking to. Wild and unpredictable and completely illogical Enid. She scrambled to her feet so fast, her top popped open. She looked feral, possibly dangerous. Her hand flew out to Margery's shoulder, yanking her back, and squeezing way too hard to be friendly. Her eyes flashed.

"Margery Benson, where is the woman who stole a pair of boots? Who organized an expedition to the other side of the world? Who put on a man's shorts? This is your vocation same as mine is having a baby. You think you can just walk away? What happened to your *gumption*?"

Clearly these were not actual questions, they were rhetorical: even though Margery tried to answer, Enid barged on.

"Marge, this baby will not happen unless we find the beetle. I know it in my bones. I've lost ten babies. I did everything you're supposed to do—I put my feet up, didn't lift anything too heavy— but I still lost them. And I was certain on the boat I'd lost this one, too. But I was wrong. She held on. We have climbed up and down a mountain every day, Marge, and this child has held on. She wants to live. She wants it, Marge. So cut the crap about giving up. You brought us here. Now get on with it. Find the beetle." In her fury Enid practically flung Margery aside. Then she stooped to pick up the dog. She patted him, like a soft toy. She even rubbed his ears.

Margery held her fists tight and looked up at a diamond spot of sunlight. She counted in her mind the time they had left. One, two, three, four . . . seven weeks. Seven weeks until the middle of February. It was nothing. The chances of finding the beetle were so small they were practically nonexistent. She thought of all the extra things she would have to do now that Enid was pregnant. Carry both haversacks. Put up the hammocks at night. Not to mention taking the lead. She was not up to it. She knew she couldn't do what Enid had done. She held her fists so tight they felt ready to crack.

"Enid," she said. "I'm sorry. I can't—"

But Enid interrupted: "What's that noise?"

A sudden coldness swept through the forest and seemed to reach into the heart of her. The air smelled damp and acrid. In a flash it dawned on Margery that the thing that had been wrong was the silence. The lack of insects. Now the air was full of movement, and every tree was roaring, like the *whaps* of a helicopter's propeller, a million swishings. The sky turned solid. Black. Enid couldn't have been expected to know, but Margery should: a storm was on its way. They should have got off the mountain ages ago.

As if on cue, Enid's hair flew out. She clutched her belly. She shrieked. "Shit, Marge! What can we do?"

34

January 6, the Three Kings Party

It was the worst in years. Everything the cyclone could destroy, it did. Within hours, there was flooding all over the island. Rumors of landslides. Trees came down. Rivers burst their banks, a nickel mine collapsed, and the two major coastal roads from south to north were closed. Houses in Nouméa went without electricity, while whole shantytowns were flattened. The ocean was vast, breakers crashing all the way up the beach, ruining shops and restaurants. The British consul sent out a reminder not to drink water unless it was boiled, with an offer of free blankets and food.

Despite the heavy wind and rain that were still raging outside, Mrs. Pope's Three Kings party went ahead. Her paper chains remained intact, as did her nativity scene and Christmas tree. She told Mrs. Peter Wiggs, also known as Dolly, that she was expecting at least fifty.

In the end it was over two hundred. The consulate villa was packed. Maurice must have invited every waif and stray he'd ever met. Mrs. Pope had a little quartet playing Christmas carols in the hall and wore her gold king costume, but she ran out of mince pies after half an hour. Worse, barely anyone had bothered to dress up. All people wanted to talk about was the cyclone. Either that or the big story that had just reached New Caledonia about the call girl Nancy Collett and the Woman With No Head. ("Though technically she *must* have a head," said Mrs. Pope to Dolly. "It's ridiculous that the newspapers have given her a name like that."

"It's because she's a woman," said Dolly: "If she was a man, they wouldn't make a joke of her.")

The British consul introduced his wife to the POW who'd arrived recently. It was a trick he often pulled: Maurice would drag her over to meet some social misfit, then disappear. This man had been hassling them for days, ever since Maurice rescued him from the French police. He just kept showing up at the front door, asking if his passport was ready. Maurice had given him a change of clothing. Some extra currency to tide him over. But he kept waiting outside. Mrs. Pope had even spotted him asleep at the end of the garden.

He proudly showed her his passport. He turned to the page with his new visa stamp. He said he'd only just got it.

"And you're hoping to travel north now?" she said, to make conversation. There was something not right about him. His hair was shaved too short and he had a habit of speaking over her shoulder. He was also sweating hard and as thin as a rake. Obviously, one had to be kind to the man because he'd been a POW and everything, but she couldn't help wishing he was a bit more civilized. "I think you'll be lucky after the cyclone. There are only two roads that go all the way to the north and they are both closed, Mr. Mundic."

He mumbled something she couldn't catch. She thought it might be about a person he was looking for. A British woman.

She said merrily, "Well, we have quite a few of those here!"

But he didn't laugh. He said something about a beetle.

"Oh, do you mean the two women who went north?" she asked. "But they left over a month ago."

"Two?" He knocked his head, as if he had something inside it that shouldn't be there. "Two of them?"

"Yes. They came for cocktails."

"Two?"

"That's right."

"No. You're wrong. Miss Benson's traveling alone."

"No. She has her assistant, Mrs. Pretty. Do you know her, Mr. Mundic?" She asked this question only because he had begun to do something very odd. He was rubbing his fingers, twisting the joints, and clicking them. She'd never seen such vast hands. Then he did something even more strange. His eyes filled with tears. "Why?" he said. "Why? Why would she say that? I'm leading this expedition. I saved her life."

Mrs. Pope glanced over her shoulder for her husband, but he was deep in conversation with some young woman she'd never seen before. She said vaguely, "Miss Benson never mentioned that."

"She didn't?"

He pulled an old notebook out of his pocket. It was a tatty thing, and the pages were crammed with writing. Not just sideways, but even up and down. He wiped his eyes with his sleeve, then flicked through, trying to find a fresh page. "Where were they going?"

"Poum," she said, to rhyme with "room."

"How do you spell that?" He shoved his notebook against the wall. In the end she had to give him the word letter by letter; he couldn't get it right. He kept crossing it out and trying again.

She said, "I do hope they survived the storm. We warned them not to go. Maurice didn't mention you were from the Natural History Museum."

He ignored her. He just kept trying to spell Poum. Such a small word, yet he couldn't get the letters in the right order.

"They were held up here for a whole week. There was a problem with her luggage. It got lost. Do you know if she found it?"

Now he turned. He cocked his head. "Not her collecting equipment?" he said. And to her confusion he actually laughed, his thin face raked open, as if he knew something she didn't, which was not a situation Mrs. Pope liked. On the whole, it was the other way round. She changed the subject.

"Will you be here for Valentine's Day, Mr. Mundic? We'll be

having another special party at the British consulate. Lots of paper hearts. Terribly jolly."

Even as she said it, she regretted it. She had no idea whom she could pair the man up with. And she liked to do a little matchmaking on Valentine's Day. She had once dressed up as Cupid, wings and all.

Fortunately, Mr. Mundic said he wouldn't be free. He was heading north. "Poum," he said. And again he stared at the word he'd written in his notebook. "Is it a big town?"

This time it was Mrs. Pope's turn to laugh. It was the idea of Poum being a town. She hadn't heard anything so funny in ages. She couldn't stop. "A town? It's no more than a few huts. You'll find your colleagues in no time."

But Mr. Mundic wasn't laughing anymore. He stared at her, stone cold, as if she had insulted him, then elbowed his way out of the room, and left.

Later Mrs. Pope called a private meeting of the British wives in the kitchen. The staff were washing up, but she kept her voice low so they wouldn't understand.

"Something is going on," she said. "Those two women in the north are up to something."

"Do you mean espionage?" cried Dolly, who read too many thrillers.

"I don't know, but whatever they're doing, I don't think it's about beetles. There's something suspicious about the man who's joining them."

But here she was interrupted. One of the servants was wailing about the carving knife. It had gone, she said. It had gone from the drawer. Someone had walked out of the British consulate with the British consulate's carving knife.

35

We Will Die Here!

They were lucky to be alive. They made their way down the mountain slowly, stunned, exhausted, gripping each other tightly, too shocked to feel hungry. Their clothes hung wet and shriveled to their bodies, and their boots creaked. All around there was nothing but felled trees and uprooted trunks and moving channels of water. The bungalow—if they ever got to it—would have been flattened and carried away.

"Are you all right, Enid?"

"Yes, Marge."

"That's it, Enid. Another step. It's nearly over."

They had been caught up the mountain in the storm for forty-eight hours. Forty-eight hours of gale-force winds and rain. *"In the case of a cyclone,"* wrote the Reverend Horace Blake, *"be sure to secure all doors and windows. It is advisable to sit under a table or mattress for the duration of the storm. Unplug all electrical appliances. Do not on any account go outside."*

It was everything they could do to stay upright. Margery had found a deep crevice between two boulders, and there they had wedged themselves, clinging to one another, the dog, and as much of their kit as they could grab. They had lost one net. Several traps. A bottle of ethanol. Even Enid's baseball cap. The noise had been a roar. Margery had never heard anything like it. Wind had come in slashes—pointless wearing her helmet: it was worse than repeatedly knocking herself on the head. The tallest pines bent at an angle, and bananas shot through the air, along with coconuts, leaves, branches, a flock of birds. Splinterings, crashings, hissing, sucking, cracks as loud as gunfire. Now and again came the faraway roar of breakers against the reef. Incessant lightning—flashes of violet, yellow, silvery-white that briefly lit some new part of the forest and then snapped it away. The storm was so intense it was hard to see how it could ever stop. Their hair flew wild.

"We will die!" Enid had shrieked. "We will die!"

In her terror, something happened to Margery that had never happened before. As everything imaginable whipped through the air, too fast for her to see, she began to talk. And not even about anything meaningful. She said to herself, "Margery Benson, you are now a talking machine and you will not give up." While Enid cowered and sobbed and screamed that it was over, Margery voiced whatever came into her head. She named an animal for every letter of the alphabet. She did the same with countries of the world, market towns, and capital cities. So long as she talked, she kept her terror at bay.

"Marge?" Enid shrieked. "What does it matter? What do I care if you can think of an animal that begins with X? Shut up. We are going to die!"

But Margery did not shut up. She kept talking. Stuck up a mountain in a cyclone, Margery felt she and Enid were like kites flying in opposite directions while held by the same hand. But it was vital that she did this. It was vital that she kept her terror at bay, and looked after Enid, who was not only pregnant but also convinced this was her last day on earth. So Margery leaped from one subject to the next, while Enid continued to scream that it was over. And the more Margery talked, the more she voiced every word in her head, the more certain she felt that she was alive, she was not going to die, and she would not let Enid die, either. All she had to do was keep talking.

Boys' names. Girls' names. Dates of famous battles. The wives of Henry the Eighth. Every British king and queen since Alfred the Great. Lists of saints. Lists of poets. Lists of ingredients for wartime recipes. Lists of anything she could think of.

Night fell, the wind howled; Margery kept talking. So cold now she was shaking from head to foot, Enid cried, "We're going to freeze to death!" But Margery would not give in to the cold in her toes, the cold in her ears, the cold that was so cold it began to feel like heat and made her want to sleep. She held Enid hard and bullied her to keep awake by listing months of the year, then spelling them backwards until it occurred to her to list entire families and subfamilies of beetle species, including all their Latin names. She had thought she was at the end of her tether, had believed she wanted to give up, but faced with the very realistic possibility of death on a mountain, and with Enid's terror at losing another baby, she had realized she was not fragile and neither did she want to die. She wanted to live. She wanted Enid and her baby to live. She wanted that so much. All she had to do was keep talking.

As the wind screamed to new heights, the palest light showed in the sky and began to brighten, very slowly. She could not tell exactly how long it took to get light enough to see, but it was a long, long time.

Then the rain came, and it was like no rain she had ever felt, not even in New Caledonia. It fell from the sky in rods. It coursed down the trunks of trees, it tipped from leaves, it hurtled down as far as she could see, drowning the forest, crushing and mashing it, until the roar filled her head. It bounded from the summit in foamy red brooks, exploding before her eyes. Now trees were not flying past, and neither were boulders: they were swimming, tossed and bullied and half submerged by the water. Nothing seemed rooted or solid anymore. "We will drown!" Enid cried. She cried again when she dirtied herself. "We will get hit by rocks! We will get hit by trees!" Enid clutched her belly as if the storm might take that, too. And throughout all this Margery continued to talk.

Did Enid know how many different types of beetle antennae Margery could name? "No!" Enid yelled. "I don't!" Never mind: Margery would take Enid through every single one of them. And she did. Short. Stubby. Resembling a toothbrush. Resembling a feather . . . Another hour was gone.

Did Enid understand the complicated mating patterns of the stag beetle? Did she understand the differences between a weevil and a carabid? "Of course I don't, Marge!" Excellent. Sit tight, Enid. We'll run through those as well.

Then the mountain gave a monumental crack and the earth swayed and a whole side seemed to break off and slide past, like a table upended. Tree trunks, broken-off branches, boulders, a boiling avalanche of water and leaves and stone. Margery clung to Enid, and Enid clung to her dog. They cowered in their hiding place while the ground shook and roared as if the entire earth was being washed away, while Enid sobbed and sobbed, and Margery continued to talk about the anatomy of a beetle. Never in her life had she been so grateful there were so many species. If necessary, she had enough source material to go on for weeks.

Toward the end of the second day, the wind dropped and the rain paused. The return of calm felt like a question in the air, waiting. Margery dared to crawl out to check the path but had barely gone a few yards before the wind took up again. It was even worse than before. Too late it occurred to her that this was the eye of the storm, the dangerous moment of hiatus before things got even worse. The wind snatched the hurricane lamp out of her hands and smashed it on the ground, where it went crashing and shattering as if it were at least twenty times its size. She lifted a foot to get back to Enid, and was hurled to the ground. Crawling on hands and knees, she was assaulted by branches and leaves and stones. She even accidentally punched herself. "We will die!" roared Enid, for the twenty-three hundredth time. "We will die and no one can help us!"

Another night on the mountain. Another night of talking. Then at last the wind lowered, light came, the cloud drifted away, rain fell more softly. Margery pulled herself out of the crevice, then helped Enid.

Now they made their way down, moving as if tied together by a rope. Enid was weak. Margery's voice was hoarse. Somehow the killing jar was still safe in her haversack and so were her helmet and the insect net. The dog was also safe. But they had lost nearly everything else. The path was filled with rubble and stones and fallen trees. Giant boulders the size of furniture blocked the way. Stones rattled beneath their feet like china, and in other places rivulets came up to their knees. Steam rose from every part of the earth. The air was filled with whistles and birdsong. Margery took both haversacks. She helped Enid over one fallen tree after the next; they waded through water, while Enid held her tummy with one hand and Margery with the other.

"Enid? Is the baby all right? Can you feel it moving? One more step, Enid. You're doing so well. Keep going. One more step. That's it. And another. Keep going, Enid. Look. The wind has almost gone. We did it. We're safe. Are you all right, Enid?"

"I'm okay. The baby is, too. But could you please stop talking, Marge? I can't *think*."

A bird of prey circled overhead, wondering if they were dead enough to eat.

A miracle. The bungalow was in one piece. It was still standing. In fact, it looked the same—if not slightly better. A few palm leaves were missing, but they could be fixed. There were no broken steps because the steps had already been broken; the same with the wraparound veranda. The tarp on the roof had not flown off but slightly flattened itself. The door seemed to be hanging at less of an angle. The bungalow, it occurred to Margery, had been through so many cyclones, it couldn't get any worse. It was, in effect, cyclone proof. And seeing it again, she felt a whoosh of love. It struck her as the best bungalow in the entire world.

"Home!" yelled Enid. "Marge! We did it! We're home! We did it!" But she couldn't make the steps. Margery practically had to lift her to the top. Afterward she had to go back and fetch the dog.

Enid wasn't just weak, she was jumpy, too. When Margery opened the door and a quantity of wildlife spilled out, including an eel, she shrieked. Then she blinked, bewildered, at the threshold, surveying the mess. The floor was a lake of water and strewn with branches, papers, tins of Spam, and the floating remains of all the specimens they'd risked so much to find. The Baby Jesus painting had fallen from the wall. Some of Margery's display cases and jars had been blown from the study, and many were smashed. Her books were soaked.

"It's not so bad," Margery said slowly. "It's not so bad, Enid."

"Isn't it?"

"Not at all. I've seen worse."

She led the way. The most important thing was that she did not despair: Enid was watching her like a hawk. Her boots swished through the water and cracked on broken glass. But the roof had kept hold at the back of the bungalow. The bedrooms had not been flooded. The mosquito nets were intact. It would not take too long to set things straight. "Yes, Enid. It's all right."

"We did it! We did it, Marge!" whispered Enid, who had switched to happy again but only on a faint setting. She clung to Margery's arm.

In her bedroom, Margery helped Enid remove her boots. She peeled off her shorts and top. Briefly Enid ducked to check her red valise was safe beneath the bed, then allowed Margery to help her into a slip. It was the first time Margery had seen Enid naked since the day she'd swum in the bathing pool, and her body was dark and thin and muscled, except for the very pale torso, which looked like a vest. Her breasts were fat and blue-veined, her belly already swelling. Suddenly she seemed too small for it. Despite herself, Margery laughed. Maybe it was just relief. The relief of being safe. Enid gazed down at her belly and stroked it as if she was proud of it, and laughed, too. Then Margery rigged a canopy above the bed with a tarp and sticks so that Enid would stay dry if it rained again. She pulled the insect net all round her.

"Marge, we did it!" whispered Enid, in weepy wonderment. "There's nothing that can stop you and me finding the beetle now." She dropped off instantly, one hand cupping her belly.

Enid slept on and off for the rest of the day. She got up to eat, and drink a gallon of water, then picked up her dog and went back to bed. She said she just needed to rest. After that she'd be ready to keep searching.

In her absence, Margery became a swarm of activity. She actually made herself dizzy. She swept away the broken glass, mopped the water, banged in hardboard at the broken windows, and another nail to rehang Enid's precious Baby Jesus painting. She made new towers of what was left of the tinned food and threw away the packets of oats that were inedible. Outside she collected armfuls of sweet bananas to feed to Enid; she fixed the leaves back on the roof and secured them with rope; she fetched more water from the freshwater creek, which had swollen considerably with the rain. She scrubbed their clothes to get the red and sweat out of them— though their original colors had mostly gone now. She patched the worst of the holes, and used Enid's knitting needles to pierce their boots so that when they got caught in rain in the future, the water could run through. She made something with yams and eggs that smelled so good Enid got up and ate it without talking. She hung out everything to dry.

As darkness poured in, she lit the only remaining hurricane lamp, and focused on her beetle collection. She found the specimens she could salvage. She wrapped them carefully, ready for transporting home. She retrieved what she could of her books and paperwork, and nailed loose pages to the walls to dry them. She sat up into the early hours of the morning, rewriting her notes. Outside, the sky was a huge glass ball, very dark, with sprinkles of stars. There was the murmur of insects and, far away, the ocean, and everywhere the scent of the very sweet flowers that seemed to be opening in the dark like candles, and pine.

Enid had been right. They could have died up the mountain. But they hadn't. They had not been killed by floodwater or falling rocks or bouncing coconuts. They had survived. Margery had failed Enid on the ship, she had failed her at Wacol, she had failed her repeatedly on the mountain—it was shameful how much she'd failed—but now she was going to take charge. Wherever life had seemed to be going before, it was going to get there differently, with Margery at the helm.

It was as if forty-eight hours of nonstop talking had unlocked something new, and she felt not only big on the outside but big inside, too. So even though she had begun to fear she was wrong about the beetle—that it might not be in New Caledonia, or if it had been there once, it wasn't anymore—she was going to get back on that mountain and keep searching. Who cared about a visa? This was her second chance.

Something about the words "second chance" pulled her up short. They seemed familiar. She had to stop and think hard. Then she remembered. When Enid had confessed she was still pregnant, just before the cyclone, she said she'd been afraid on Christmas Day that everything was over—and then she'd realized that the baby was her second chance. But there was something strange about that. Why would Enid have thought everything was over? She'd done nothing on Christmas Day except make paper hats and fiddle with the radio, trying to find a signal. Margery wished she could ask Enid exactly what she'd meant.

But even if Enid was awake and they were sitting on the veranda, Margery realized she wouldn't ask. The differences between them—all those things she'd once found so infuriating—she now accepted. Being Enid's friend meant there were always going to be surprises. Her red valise. That was another one. As she'd watched Enid doing her best to wriggle beneath the bed to check on it, she'd wanted to laugh and say, "Enid, what on earth do you keep in that thing?" But respect for Enid had stopped her. However close they were, it didn't entitle her to Enid's memories, and neither did it allow her to be part of Enid's life before they'd met. Being a friend meant accepting those unknowable things. It meant saying, "Look! Look how big my leg is! And look how small yours is! Look how marvelously different we are, you and I, and yet here we are, together in this strange world!" It was by placing herself side by side with Enid that Margery had finally begun to see the true outline of herself. And she knew it now: Enid was her friend.

She took a pencil and paper and counted how many tins they had left. Enough for a month. No more. That would get them as far as early February. She fetched her purse and counted the money. If they were careful, she could afford the fuel back to Nouméa, with a little extra to spare. Their clothes and boots were in a bad way, and one of the hammocks would last barely another week. But it was her legs that were the real problem. She fetched the magnifying glass and a knife.

Margery unrolled her socks and took off the bandages. The skin was red-hot and swollen where the bites were infected. She took a pen and drew a ring around each one. Ten in all. Then she placed the tip of the knife over the first, and looked away as she sliced the blade into her skin, as if it were a peach, trying to lance the pus. Pain showered right through her. It was like nothing else—though, conversely, she completely forgot the agony in her hip. Afterward she washed the wound and applied iodine. She wrapped it in lint and a clean bandage, but it went on stinging like mad. Attracted by the blood, a cloud of mosquitoes billowed up.

Only five weeks ago, she'd spent her first night in a hammock and felt desperate to stop. Now her assistant was pregnant, and Margery's legs were a write-off. Most of her equipment was gone, and they were down to the last of the tins. But she was hanging on by her fingernails to find ways to keep going.

She took the knife, wiped it, and braced herself to lance another bite.

36

Easy

He had the carving knife, the Panama hat, and the yellow towel from the RMS *Orion,* as well as his notebook, the map, and his passport with the new visa stamp. He crouched low, where he could keep the bungalow in view.

It had been easy getting north: the British consul's wife had been wrong. And she'd had no right to laugh. He had left their villa with the things he wanted—the knife, the British consul's wallet, and a bottle of red wine—and hitched a lift with two Dutchmen heading north for the mines. He showed them the word "POUM" in his notebook, and then the cross on his map, and they said they could take him halfway, if he sat in the back with their kit. They tried the west coast road but it was closed because of the cyclone, so they crossed the island to the east coast road instead. They asked if Mundic was there for work, but he'd had enough of talking, so he pretended he was asleep. After a few hours, they dropped him off and said something he didn't understand about a river. But it didn't matter because he had taken one of the men's binoculars from his kit bag, as well as a spare battery. He didn't want the battery, but he took it anyway.

After the lift with the Dutch, he had walked until he came to a

little town with some shacks and a café. He ordered a plate of fried
fish and wrote it down in his notebook so he wouldn't forget, and
he wrote about the two Dutchmen, and then he showed the man
at the bar the word "POUM" but the man said, *"Non,"* like it was
closed. Then he took hold of Mundic's notebook and drew a picture of a river. He pointed up, like the river was in the ceiling.
Then Mundic got it. He understood. It was like the men in the
camps when they had code words so that the Japs wouldn't understand when they were planning an escape, and he realized the fellow was telling him that the river was not in the ceiling, it was
north. The river was in the north. The guy said, *"Non,"* again. And
Mundic began to understand that the river was blocking the east
coast road because of the cyclone and there was no way he could
get past.

So he drew a picture of a boat, and the man rubbed the tips of
his fingers, like he wanted cash.

But the cash wasn't a problem because he still had the woman's
purse from the cargo ship—he didn't even have to bother with the
British consul's wallet.

The next thing he knew he was getting into a little fishing boat
with an old chap in a hat and he was saying, "Poum," and pointing
at the word in his notebook, and the man was laughing and saying,
"Poum wee wee Poum." And it made no sense but Mundic pulled
out the bottle of red wine from the British consulate, and the sky
was so starry it was like it was filled with holes, and he drank the
red wine, and he watched as the stars split up and down, and the
oars of the little fishing boat pulled through the water, and even
though it was choppy because of the wind, a great happiness surged
through him. He had been a free man for five years, but this was
the first time he truly felt it.

And now here he was. In Poum. The boat had docked by a broken jetty and he walked until he found some old men and some
goats, and he had drawn a picture in his notebook of two women,
and a big bloke in an old café had pointed the way down a dirt

track. So he had walked another few miles, and there were banana trees and red parrots and ferns that were as big as towers and cacti the size of people, and far away he could hear the ocean. He went past a shantytown, and when the boys ran out to shout, "Hello, Monsieur!" he yelled at them to clear off, like the men in the cargo ship in Brisbane had shouted at him. He had walked through the red dust until the track came to a stop and all he could see were the trees and all he could hear were the insects—and there it was, this horrible little bungalow. He thought it was all a mistake.

Then there was Miss Benson. She was ahead of him on the veranda. And she was dressed like a man, and helping the blonde, and at first he wanted to wave and say, "Hello! I made it! I'm here now to lead the expedition!" But he didn't because he saw that Miss Benson was helping the blonde, like she was very sick, and he drew back, slashing his way through ferns and elephant grass with the knife, to a place where he could hide and find out what was what.

He stayed a long time, and he felt strangely powerful, watching the bungalow when they didn't know, writing facts about them in his notebook. Later he went to Poum, found himself a room, and slept, then remembered to buy fresh fruit because of the beriberi. The next day he came back, and knelt in his hiding place and took notes. Sometimes the blonde appeared with a mangy dog, but she looked dead on her feet, and she held on to her belly, and he saw now what the problem was. She was up the duff. She was a lousy assistant.

And he thought of the men at Songkurai and the march to the railway lines and how, when someone fell at your side, you couldn't stop. You couldn't even look. You had to go on without them. He thought of laying the tracks and how, with every piece he'd carried, another man seemed to collapse. He thought of the rock they'd hacked through every day, and the river water at their feet, and the jungle that was so dense he'd thought he'd never see his way out. He thought of the dead lying on rice sacks and the stench of broken bodies. And the thoughts came so fast he had to sit very still with his arms round him and say, "You are a free man, you are a free man. It's okay, son, eat your fruit."

Three days of watching Miss Benson. He wrote his observations in his notebook, like what time she got up and what time she picked bananas and what time she put out the lamp at night. And it was all right when he fixed on those things. He was back in the present.

Now he lifted his binoculars for a better look. He could see her burnt arms as she leaned on the broken railing of the veranda. The splits in her boots. He could see the bandages up her legs, and the way she had to hold her hip so she could walk. He guessed she hadn't found the beetle.

It was different now that he knew she'd stolen her equipment. The rules had changed again, just like they'd changed when he'd saved her life on the ship. There was this new secret feeling between them. He lay back and closed his eyes, and he could hear the insects, he could feel the heat, and it seemed he sank down into a place that was warm and red and full of comfort.

He just had to work out how to lose the blonde.

37

A Change of Plan

They drove to Poum to celebrate being alive. That was Margery's idea. She went with her hair dyed: that was Enid's. Margery did not want new hair, she liked her hair the way it was, but Enid had flown into a rage when she said no—she absolutely refused to go to Poum unless Margery changed her hair—so Margery had caved in. She caved in mainly because they needed to eat something that wasn't Spam or bananas. Enid had one last bottle of bleach left, and the transformation of Margery's hair took thirty minutes. She'd had no idea you could do so much damage to a human head in so little time. Her hair was bright yellow. Her eyebrows, by contrast, seemed dark in an evil way. She looked like a child killer. Enid, however, was oblivious to that. She was delighted.

"No one will recognize you," she said.

Yet another Enidism that made no sense. Even if no one had noticed Margery before, they couldn't fail to spot her now. But it was not the time to cross Enid. It had been nearly a week since the cyclone, and she could pass from happy to preoccupied to fierce in the space of a jiffy. Also, she tried to hide it but she was unsteady on her feet. It wasn't just her belly that had swollen, but her neck and wrists and ankles. She carried herself like a pot of water that she didn't want to spill. It could take ages for her to get down the steps of the bungalow, and her pockets were weighed down with shiny stones and feathers for good luck. She refused to see a doctor, even though Margery said they had enough money to drive back to Nouméa.

"There's nothing wrong with me," she would say. "I'm pregnant. It's not an illness." In an ideal world, she'd have spent all day on the veranda, talking babies and knitting tiny clothes.

Whenever Margery suggested getting back to the expedition, Enid agreed, then came up with a good reason as to why they shouldn't: either the mist, or Margery's limp, or just a feeling she had that this was not the right time. But ever since the cyclone, the weather had been beautiful. The sky was a clear blue, like the inside of a shiny bowl, sunlight fanning between the trees, and the air was as clean as a knife. Margery often stood gazing at the mountain, the two prongs at the top that she knew now resembled a pair of chimneys. She watched the clouds pass overhead, their shadows crossing the land beneath, or the early-morning sun—a slice of gold rising above the horizon, taking shape and spilling light like treacle. Despite the constant pain in her calves and hip, she was impatient to get back.

Enid borrowed Margery's best frock to go to Poum because everything she had was too tight. Her hair wasn't so yellow anymore—it was laced with black—but she'd overdone it with the makeup. She didn't look evil, as Margery did: more like a woman who'd been at the same party for three weeks. Now she hauled herself into the jeep. Maybe it was the purple frock but she seemed massive. She'd put on her pom-pom sandals as well. They seemed tiny.

"Are you sure you're fit to drive, Enid?"

"I'm not an invalid, Marge."

She asked Margery to look after her handbag and yanked the jeep into first gear. Then she drove at an incrementally slow pace down the track, traveling all the way to the left side to avoid the smallest holes on the right. They weren't so much driving as treading water. It would have been quicker to hitch a lift with a tortoise. Even trees had more movement.

Margery had barely seen the boys from the shantytown since the cyclone. They had visited the bungalow a few times, once trying to sell her eggs—she'd bought them to feed Enid—and then trying to sell her Enid's old battery radio. She didn't want the radio so she gave them chewing gum and sent them packing. Now, when they appeared, shouting, "Hi-ya! Hi-ya!" they didn't even need to trot to keep up with the jeep, though, out of politeness, they went backward just to give Enid a fair chance of getting ahead. Meanwhile she clung to the steering wheel and sat with her seat jammed forward, peering at the dirt track as if it were the middle of the night.

"You think I'm a bad driver."

"I have never said that."

"You think I'm not safe."

"Enid, we couldn't possibly hit anything, even if it lay down on the track and waved a flag."

Enid stamped on the brakes. The shantytown boys crashed into one another, like dominoes. "That's exactly what I mean. You're criticizing me." She began to cry.

"I think you're the best driver in the world."

"You do?"

"Yes. But I think you need to eat something. You look starved. Also, there's something I need to speak to you about."

"Are you saying I can't be a mother?"

"No, Enid. You'll be a wonderful mother."

"Do you think my baby's all right?"

"Of course your baby's all right."

"I love you, Marge."

"Thank you, Enid."

"I never had a friend like you."

"Thank you."

"You saved my life. You saved my baby's life. You never forget a thing like that."

"Enid, I just did my best. Can we drive to Poum now? It would be nice to get there before dark."

Enid smiled like an angel, put the car into first gear, and on they went.

The shantytown was still strewn with palm leaves and debris, and its inhabitants were busy fixing their roofs and walls. It struck Margery how little she'd understood when they first arrived. The mud huts and sheds looked as they did because they had withstood cyclones. Poum was the same. Buildings were covered with tarps and ropes, like wrapped gifts. It was not a scattering of ramshackle sheds. It was a small town that knew how to survive. They went to the café, where the owner greeted them joyfully as if they had just returned from war, and ordered a feast: a plate of fried oysters, boiled mud crab with fire-red claws, bright yellow lemon chicken with yams, and a salad of choko and sliced pawpaw.

Margery wanted to take Enid to lunch because she had news to break to her, and she felt safer doing it in a public place. She'd been dreading saying it, but it could no longer be avoided. She'd been thinking carefully about the expedition and, from now on, Enid would have to stay behind at the bungalow. It was far too dangerous for her up the mountain. There might easily be another cyclone, and if Enid fell she could lose the baby. Clearly Enid was in conflict: she needed to find the beetle because—having lost so many pregnancies—she was trying to make this one different. But she was ignoring her physical condition. So Margery would take the decision out of her hands. She was going to dose herself up with aspirin for the pain and do the rest of the expedition on her own. She would return every few days with new specimens; Enid would rest. She'd be safe and she'd have her dog for company. No harm could come to her. Then in February they would go back to Nouméa—possibly not in the stolen jeep—and she would make one last attempt to complete her unfinished paperwork before they began the journey home.

However, when Margery had carefully planned this conversation, she hadn't carefully planned it with Enid on the receiving end. It was so much easier to have difficult conversations with Enid when she wasn't there. Now that they were sitting at the table,

Margery couldn't get a word in edgewise. Enid talked nonstop. A crowd of old men gathered, setting up chairs just to watch. For every mouthful of food, she said about fifty words. Margery found herself taking deep breaths on Enid's behalf.

"Marge, I never had someone like you. I never even had my own family. I wish I'd known my mother." Gulp. "I think a mother would have told me what to do. She would have loved me. That's what mothers do." Slurp. "I was just passed around other families. But the men always got ideas. You know what I'm saying?" Swallow. "And the women didn't believe me. They treated me like I was trouble and got rid of me." Slurp. Enid cracked open a crab claw, scattered more salt on her fried oysters, and crammed them into her mouth, one after another. "Perce was the only person who was kind. We had such fun. I know he liked the lads an' that, but it wasn't about sex for us. We were pals. He said being a mother was my vocation. I wish you could have met him. Don't you want your chicken?"

"No, Enid. You have it."

Enid took Margery's plate and tucked in to a drumstick, then went on to the subject of the beetle. She couldn't stop saying what a great team they were. She couldn't wait to get back on the mountain. She knew this time they would find it. She had her free hand on her belly, and she patted it like a kitten on her lap. Even in the time they'd been eating, she seemed to have got more pregnant. Then she said, "What was the thing you wanted to speak to me about?"

Margery reached for her glass. There was nothing in it, but she drank it anyway.

Enid started talking again. "No one else would've stuck by me. But you're my friend, Marge. The thing about friends is that they don't give up on one another. We're a team. We're stronger together than we are on our own. We are going to find the beetle, and then I will have my baby."

The inside of Margery's head bent, like a spoon. She thought she had learned things since meeting Enid, but once again she had that feeling of being in something that was too big. "Enid, the beetle has nothing to do with your baby. Don't you see?"

Enid reached for Margery's hand. Her grip was a vise. She might be an expectant mother, but she could still really hurt a person. "I *know* it is. My baby won't be safe until we find the beetle." Even when she let go, her hand still seemed to be round Margery's. "We have to find it, Marge. We still have time."

There was nothing Margery could say. In the absence of anything holy, and probably also in the absence of much that was kind, Enid had built her entire world around superstition. It would be as hard to knock it down as flatten a cathedral.

Enid finished the chicken and soaked up the sauce with an entire basket of bread. Then she laughed as if she'd just thought of something funny. "When you said we should come to Poum, I thought you were going to tell me you wanted to do the rest of the expedition on your own. I know I've been holding you up these last few days. I know I've been difficult. And up and down, too. I know I've been up and down. The truth is, that cyclone put the wind up me, Marge. But I'm ready. Now that we've had this lovely feast, I'm ready again. I'm sorry I doubted you. It's because I've had too many bad people in my life. But you're different. You and Perce. You're the only good things. We came out here together, Marge, and we're going to finish this together, too." At this point, Enid pulled out her handkerchief and burst into tears.

Margery couldn't take any more. She trudged inside to pay the café owner. Seeing her, he did a double take, as if something terrible had landed on her head and he didn't like to alarm her. In all the tension, she had forgotten about her hair. Her eye drifted to the window and found Enid, caught in a bright slant of sunlight as if she were lit up on a stage. Enid had picked up a newspaper and was leafing through it in a hurry. She read with a strange, terrified look on her face, holding it at arm's length like something she could not bear to look at too closely.

But the café owner was still talking in French to Margery. He seemed to be asking her a question. He kept doing a mime of someone searching for something. Then his hands shaped the silhouette of a very thin person, and he did another gesture, pointing at his own thick hair and then shaking his head, as if he was trying to say he had lost it. Or maybe he was referring to hair dye again. She had no idea. Besides, she was trying to work out what was going on with Enid. She had two people who made no sense, one inside the café and the other out.

By the time Margery made it back to their table, the newspaper was gone. Enid scrambled to her feet, closing her handbag.

"Did you find a British newspaper, Enid?"

"No." She didn't even flinch. Instead she made a salute. "Enid Pretty reporting for duty!"

Mr. Rawlings turned and began to bark at nothing. This should not have been odd: he was a dog after all. But Margery had never seen him do anything in his life that was even vaguely doglike, except trot after Enid with his tongue hanging out. Enid picked him up and covered him with kisses. "What's all that fuss?" She laughed. "What's all that fuss, you silly dog?"

Margery watched Enid, dressed in the purple frock that was so big on her it trailed the ground, and her tiny sandals. Behind: the ramshackle sheds and buildings, the old men, the tall pines, the odd goat. The sky was a pure spangled blue, with the outline of the peak firm against it. It was one of those moments when you see a person you know as if you've never seen them before. Maybe it was just the way she was caught in the sunlight or the brilliance of the sky. Whatever it was, the sight of Enid gathered up Margery's breath and hit her like a graze or a rip in the air. Once again, she had changed. Enid was not the woman who had leaped off the jetty on that first morning in Poum. She had entrusted Margery with her life. She had followed her to the other side of the world, then up and down a mountain. And seeing her now, in the terrible old frock, Margery felt a rush of tenderness. So even though she knew in her heart it was the maddest thing she had done yet, she gave in. Of course, she would take Enid with her.

Mountain: here we come.

38

Shoes with a Buckle

In one week alone, they found more than a hundred specimens. They were like a machine. A beetle barely had to move its antennae, and zip: Enid was sucking it up with the pooter. She wasn't even swallowing them. Margery dispatched them in the killing jar; afterward Enid wrapped them carefully. If Margery needed something, she didn't have to ask: Enid passed it. They had been together so long their differences seemed to dissolve. And while they couldn't share their past lives, they existed inside each other's thoughts and work.

When the dust blew, they closed their eyes to slits. If the path was steep, they took it, arm in arm, like a crab. In the places the cyclone had destroyed it, Margery started again, hauling back the rocks, slicing through undergrowth, untying the toughest scrolls of creepers, while Enid put her feet up. Neither of them was in a position to make rapid progress, and Margery knew that if they did, they might miss what they were looking for. They tossed a coin every night as to who should get the good hammock, though she often cheated so it would be Enid—her belly had grown yet again. She found it hard to sleep at night, and she was always peeing. Margery donated most of her supplies of Spam, and stuck to coffee and bananas. It might have been seen as a sacrifice but, in fairness, she would happily never set eyes on another tin of Spam in her life.

Their boots were worn to the point at which they could see the shape of their feet inside them; for some reason Enid began to talk about shoes. They were in the middle of a rainforest, soaked with sweat, on hands and knees, their clothes not even patterned anymore, but so filled with dust they were just red, and suddenly Enid said, "Marge?"

"Yes, Enid?"

"When you're a famous beetle collector at the Natural History Museum, what shoes will you wear?"

"Boots?"

"I don't think you should wear boots at the museum. I think you should wear a small heel. The good thing about a heel is you can hear yourself walk. I never like people with quiet shoes. It doesn't feel honest."

"But could I pull off a heel? You think that?"

"Definitely, Marge. You have the legs."

"Maybe you're right. Maybe I should try. What about you? When you're a mother?"

"Well, it's important I have comfortable shoes. But I don't see why they can't be a nice color. Or have a gold buckle or something."

Then, back to collecting beetles.

Besides insects, Enid found other things she claimed were lucky and would help her keep her baby. A heart-shaped stone. A gold feather. She made little bargains with the world that she repeated to herself as she went. She'd say, "If a bird flies overhead in the next minute, I will keep my baby. If a spider lands in my dish, I will keep my baby. If I touch that tree three times, I will keep my baby." She was constantly greeting butterflies and asking them to bless her child and look after her. Meanwhile, Margery kept pouring iodine onto her legs and binding them. The pain had reached a level where it didn't seem painful anymore, and at least the infected areas weren't getting worse.

She would always be a big woman. She would never be light on her feet, and even in her dreams she wasn't jumping over gullies and streams. But she felt she'd found her rhythm at last. Margery loved the vastness of the forest. The aristocracy of the trees seemed to link with something inside her, and she had the strangest sense that, even though she was on the other side of the world, she was in a place she'd known all her life. The more time she spent in the forest, the higher they traveled, the smaller she felt, overwhelmed but also liberated by how much space was around her, as though the trees went on forever. She loved Enid's ridiculously strong coffee—especially the first cup of the day. She loved lying in her hammock at night, side by side with Enid and the dog, listening to the rustling of palm leaves and the pines high above and beyond them the fretwork of stars—sometimes she woke just to watch and listen and know they were there. Her favorite time was still that brief stretch before full daylight when silver filtered into the sky, light blossomed where the stars had been, the air was sweet and fresh, and everything came back to life. It seemed full of such hope.

Sometimes she paused, thinking a wild pig was close, or a giant lizard, or maybe even one of the boys from the shantytown, but seeing nothing, she pressed on. Sometimes Mr. Rawlings turned and barked and wouldn't stop until Enid picked him up. It left Margery disquieted, with a pricking sensation she couldn't quite identify. She watched Enid, trying to read her face for the same uncertainty, but Enid's head was bowed, her hand was on her belly, and she was telling herself little things as she lifted herself over one rock after another, doing her best to keep up. Clearly her attention was in another place. Often she was so lost in thought, she didn't even notice the flies in her hair—it was Margery who flicked them off. They pressed on, and then Margery would become so swallowed up by the search, she'd forget the unsettled feeling.

At the end of the week, they began following the familiar path back to the bungalow. The haversacks were empty of food, but stuffed with specimens; Margery was even carrying them in her pockets. She helped Enid over the larger stones and held back the ropes of liana so that she could pass. They were almost there when Mr. Rawlings scampered ahead, barking.

"Quick!" said Enid. "Catch him!"

Margery struck forward, thrashing through the undergrowth. She ducked beneath creepers, brushed past ferns, followed at a distance by Enid. When she finally caught up, she saw he'd found the bathing pool where they'd swum on that first day. It lay below, as blue as a peacock, reflecting the half-forgotten sky, with the waterfall knifing down a wall of rock and sending out spray. Enid hauled herself to Margery's side. She didn't have to say anything. She just looked.

"You want to swim, don't you, Enid?"

They clambered over some rocks and made their way toward the pool, carefully sliding down on their backsides. The trees were silver and green, leaves sprouting out in giant fans. Mr. Rawlings stayed at the top.

Enid threw off her clothes. She didn't even think about it. Her body was soft and pulpy, the skin streaked with silver threads. Her stomach swelled out from the rest of her, her belly button sticking out, like a doorknob.

Margery removed her shorts and her top. She folded them carefully. And even though Enid was wearing nothing, Margery had the strange feeling that keeping on her bra and knickers made her the naked one. She stepped out of the knickers. She unhooked her bra. Her bosoms fell heavily, and she felt the warmth of the air. But it was a good feeling. She liked it. While Enid admired her belly, Margery quickly untied the bandages from her legs. Then they held hands and waded into the pool, their full-fleshed bodies in the sunlight, and lowered themselves into the ice-cold water and sang out, "Yahoo! Oh, Jesus!" then lay in the water and disappeared and came up, the wet shining on their skin, their hair. Margery pushed off and swung her arms and swam a few strokes, though she kept one foot close to the stones on the bottom, so maybe it wasn't quite swimming, but whatever it was, she felt heavy and clumsy but also graceful and free, as if the water was holding her. It even seemed to freeze the bites on her legs and lance the pain. Then Enid lay on her back and began a stroke that made her look like a delicate bird with a large boiled egg on top of her, and her hair frilled out around her. Margery lay on her back, too, and tickled the water with her hands, just like Enid. She stretched out with her eyes open to the blue sky above. There they floated.

"Do you mind?"

"What, Enid?"

"That I have my baby and you don't have your beetle yet? I know what it meant to you. Of all people, I know that."

Margery wiped her face. Tears pricked her eyes, and she didn't want Enid to see. "No, Enid. I have a good collection. Even if I don't have the gold beetle, it's still a very big collection. And it's worth a lot of money. Any entomologist would be proud."

"Is that right, Marge? It's worth money?"

"If we sold it privately, we could make a few hundred pounds."

"But we won't."

"No, Enid."

"We're gonna take it to the Natural History Museum."

"We are."

"We can wear our nice shoes."

Margery didn't know why she was so moved, other than that she was on the other side of the world and this was a place so beautiful it almost hurt to think about it. She was lucky, she was so lucky, yet Enid knew her well enough to understand that a part of her still longed to find her father's beetle. And then there was the fact that Enid was going to have a baby when they got home, and there would be a day when they went to the Natural History Museum, both wearing new shoes. Somehow it was all too big to take in, and maybe that was why the tears had come. She couldn't honestly see how life could be more perfect.

Enid was still floating with her hand on her belly. She was singing. Then she said, "Did you really never want kids, Marge?"

"No, Enid."

"Were you a good teacher?"

"I was terrible."

"Your cooking is very bad."

"I know."

"But you were in love? With the professor? He broke your heart?"

"There were complications."

"Complications? What does that mean?"

"I don't know. Some people are born to be left."

"Oh, sod that," said Enid. "That's an awful thing to say. It's like saying it's a woman's duty to suffer."

And, actually, Margery could see that, even though this was indeed the belief on which she'd been taught by her aunts to build most of her adult life, Enid might be right: there might be a weakness somewhere in the foundations, a flaw. But she wasn't able to think of that yet. "Well, it doesn't matter. It happened years ago."

Enid fanned the water toward Margery, like a gift. Margery took it. Then Enid went quiet but not in a normal way, more as if she had a hundred things to say and hadn't a clue where to start. "Have you ever—"

"What?"

"Have you ever done anything terrible? Have you ever been in a real mess?"

"I was in a mess after the professor. I gave up on everything. Why? What about you?"

"Me? I've been in loads of trouble." Enid laughed. Then the laugh stopped. It stopped so abruptly that nothing seemed funny. It was like the quiet that had not been quiet. "But no matter how awful life was, I would never want to give up. I would always want to keep living. Just waiting for that moment when it might get better. You need to remember that, Marge. You must never give up again." She touched her belly. "We are not the things that happened to us. We can be what we like."

Sometimes Enid still surprised Margery—the way she could look into the air and come out with a piece of wisdom, as if an invisible sign had just lowered in front of her and she was reading it aloud. Points of sunlight landed all around them and danced on the water, and the women moved their hands, making the light dance even more. There were dragonflies the size of birds.

"Promise me one thing."

"What, Enid?"

"If I lose this baby, don't tell me it's for the best. You'll want to because you're my best friend. You won't want me to feel pain because it'll hurt you, too. You know that, Marge?"

Margery reached for Enid's hand. Her skin was cold and wrinkled. "I would never say that losing your baby was right. I know what your baby means to you."

Enid ducked her head underwater. When she came back up, her hair was so wet it was completely black. She looked like a seal.

"You know, we could go anywhere in the world. We could just keep searching, you and me. We could go anywhere we like."

"But how would we get my collection home? How would I present it to the Natural History Museum? Anyway, what about your baby?" Margery laughed. "You talk some nonsense, Enid."

High up, they heard the dog barking. Enid whistled but he didn't come down. Then they swaggered out of the bathing pool. The sun hit the water so sharply it was like walking into a blaze of light. They found their way to their clothes. "Look at me," said Enid. "Look how fat I am, Marge."

"Are you sure there's only one baby in there? How are you going to last until May?"

They dressed slowly. Their skin was wet and so were their clothes. Margery's hair felt heavy and cool on the back of her neck. Enid whistled again for Mr. Rawlings.

An hour later, they were still searching. Enid called and called, shouting his name more and more desperately, "Mr. *Rawlings*!" They went on all afternoon. They kept to the path, they went off it, they tried the places he knew. They clapped their hands and called until their throats were sore. It was already getting dark when they came to the edge of a ravine.

"Oh, no," said Margery. "No, no, no. Enid, no."

Fear ripped through her. Fast and reptilian. Enid stood at her side, working her tongue in her mouth as if she were checking it for water. They were motionless, gripped in each other's arms, starched eyes wide open, mouths dropped.

The dog had fallen twenty feet. He lay on the stones at the bottom of the ravine, like something tossed away.

39

Funeral Stones

Enid's loss resembled an endless forest in which she could find no landmark. She kept staring at nothing, bewildered, as tears ran down her face. Everything came back to the dog and made her cry, even things that had nothing to do with him. "He was such a good dog," she said all the time. "He was such a good dog. Why would he run off like that, Marge? I don't understand."

They buried Mr. Rawlings near the spot where she'd hidden the gun. Margery didn't ask why. It made sense to Enid, and that was all that mattered. If Enid had asked her to construct a mausoleum, complete with a statue, she would have done her best. Enid had not lost her baby, but she'd lost the nearest thing, and even though it was almost unbearable to watch, Margery knew she must allow Enid to grieve. She had climbed down the ravine, gripping hold of roots that came away in her hands even as she pulled at them, her feet shooting away from beneath her. She had lifted him, this solid weight, in her arms, and struggled to carry him back to Enid. He'd seemed so much heavier than she remembered. She'd never made any secret of the fact she disliked the dog, but his importance to Enid made Margery humble. They did not think of music as they buried him, but it rained—pearls spilling from the sky, then the giant leaves—and that was music of a kind.

Every day, Enid went back and sat by Mr. Rawlings's grave, her legs wide, fanning her face with her hand.

"He was lucky. He was a lucky dog. I'm frightened everything will go wrong now."

She had a belly like a whale. But still. She seemed to diminish, as if she'd lost something that wasn't just a dog but deep inside her. She became an even more concentrated version of herself, pared back to her essence, both fierce and starkly vulnerable. No matter how far they went—and they really didn't get very far anymore, certainly nowhere near the top of the mountain—she always wanted to come back and sit with the dog. She collected stones to take to him, and as she arranged them on his grave, she talked about him endlessly. She blamed herself for going into the bathing pool. She blamed herself for letting him out of her sight, then being too slow to catch up. And even though Margery had tried not to think about him, as they sat by the dog's grave and Enid wept, and talked and talked, and piled new stones on his grave, there was something untrammeled about her pain that reached inside Margery, too. It was the professor who came back to her. It was his loss she felt now.

History is not made up by events alone, but also by what lies between the lines. The friendship Margery shared with the professor lasted ten years. Not that he called it that, and neither did she. By leaving it nameless, it remained secret, and without obligation. She felt lucky. Lucky that this great and distinguished man had chosen her, of all people, to work at his side. She accompanied him to his lectures, having copied out his notes and put them in order, and she sat not at the front where people might notice but hidden in the middle. They went to tearooms, where he always introduced her to the waitress as his niece, reaching beneath the table for her knee, and a little higher. He gave her a present every Christmas and birthday, small things like a new notebook, but he could have given her an acorn and she would have been happy. She called him Peter, which was not his first name, but it was as if everything was a secret between them, and that gave her a feeling of being special, even if no one said it.

She was twenty-seven when her aunts died. They did it without fuss or, indeed, pain relief. They refused to rest. The bronchitis that killed them took one and then the other; in death, they went in a pair. Margery inherited everything, including the now almost-blind Barbara, who refused to wear glasses so that life was an infuriating blur and she was constantly bumping into it. She died a year later. Finally Margery was alone.

One afternoon she was in Professor Smith's office at the museum, pinning specimens, when she said, in a rush, "Professor, there is something I need to say. I now have the means to go to New Caledonia. I could fund our expedition." It was not a speech she had planned—or, rather, it was not a speech she had planned to make—but now that she was in it, she didn't dare stop. That she should not make a fool of herself or even hint at her true feelings had been such reliable guides until now, and it was like pushing herself into an unknown country where everything grew wild. She staggered on. "I'm in love with you, Professor. I love you with all my heart. I have loved you for years."

There was a pause during which she felt she would pass out with anticipation, and he turned wax pale. He confessed the truth. The truth took less than a minute. Afterward, he asked her forgiveness and wept, and said he did not know how he would live the rest of his life, but at least she was young, and there would be plenty more opportunities for her. His distress seemed to take up all the emotion in the room, so that what was left was a small, strange neutrality that made her say things she didn't mean and also without emotion. She suggested that perhaps it would be better if she did not come to the museum again, simply voicing the worst scenario so that they could build back from there. Instead he thanked her for being so sensible. He had always known she was a strong young lady.

And that was it. It was over. Ten years of her life had been snatched away, and yet he was actually wiping his eyes and opening the door. She put on her coat, her hat; she picked up her handbag, feeling that she had somehow done this to herself, wondering how it could be reversed before it was too late. Waiting for him to call her back. She left, her cheeks burning, her legs weak but still behaving like sensible legs, still moving, people glancing away as she passed—the cleaners, the pot washers—as if she had become a difficulty, an embarrassment, even a joke, that no one wished to see. The shame was crushing. She had no idea how a person could get over it.

The truth had been as plain as it had once been about her father and brothers. Any other woman would have spotted it a mile off. And even though she was ransacked inside, she still could not connect with what that really felt like. In every glass case of the museum, she saw the reflected and slightly red face of a stranger. A young woman who was not good enough for pot washing, let alone love, yet who'd stupidly dared to lift her head above the parapet and believe she might be. The impossibility of her life was apparent to her as it had never been before. Most women of her age were already pushing baby carriages.

Later, she trudged up the stairs to her flat. She got every photograph of herself that she could find and—meticulously, methodically—she cut her head from each one.

A week later, she took a teaching job. She exchanged her love for a career in domestic science. There would be no more searching for beetles. No more wild talk of New Caledonia. She threw out her insect net, her killing jars; she put her notes into a box. She never saw him again. She was a woman who'd had a period of excitement, who'd dared to dream of adventure and the unknown, but who had retreated instead and made no further disturbance. She had not killed her love. How could you kill something that wasn't there? She'd simply walked away.

● ● ●

They were sitting by the dog's grave. Enid was adding more stones. It wasn't a mausoleum yet, but if they hadn't been due to go home in a few weeks, it could easily have got there. Enid said, out of the blue, "He was married, wasn't he? He had kids. That's the reason Professor Smith broke your heart. That was the complication. The reason you gave up."

"Yes, Enid."

"Did he pay for your work?"

"Of course not."

"He didn't even pay you?"

"I believed we were above that."

"Oh, Marge. That man took you for one hell of a ride."

It came back to Margery as if she had never felt it before, the hurt and humiliation, the limitation, too, like being squeezed into a tin, when you heap your love somewhere so small and thin. Sensing there was nothing she could say to heal this wound, and honest enough not even to try, Enid laid her hand on Margery's. It was as neat as a shell.

"We never had much luck in love, you and me."

"No."

"Or maybe we just looked in the wrong places."

"Maybe."

"But we have each other now. We'll be okay."

Margery looked at her, and her eyes smarted with tears. "Yes, Enid. I think we will."

Enid lifted another stone. But she didn't add it to the pile she'd made. She passed it to Margery. And, without having to ask, Margery understood what she needed to do, and put it on top of the pile. Enid passed another, another, another. A blue one, a round flat one, a stone with a hole through it. Margery added them to the grave. She thought of nothing except balancing them carefully so they would not fall. And gradually Professor Smith was yet another thing there was no need to carry, not even in the darkest recesses of herself. There was no need to keep Professor Smith or any memory of him. The man was gone.

Enid hoisted herself up to get more stones. She said she wanted to find some real beauties to finish Mr. Rawlings's grave. Margery continued to arrange those they had. She even began to make a little ring of ochre-pink ones toward the top. Then suddenly Enid shouted as if she'd been hurt and Margery sprang to her feet.

Enid wasn't hurt—she was clutching her belly—but her face had lost all color. She stood pointing at a shallow hole in the soft red earth, freshly made, leaves pulled back, pine needles in a heap.

"The gun," mouthed Enid. "The gun. It's not here, Marge. Someone's taken Taylor's gun."

40

An Unexpected Development

Mrs. Pope had decided to do a little investigating of her own. It wasn't that she expected the women to be criminals. Not as such. She just wanted some rational explanation for the way she felt about them, the suspicion and unease she couldn't bring herself to admit might be misplaced.

So she was going to make a few innocent little inquiries. She had no idea where they would lead.

It had all started when she was emptying her husband's waste-paper basket: Maurice was getting careless. He dropped things into bins that staff should not see, and wives should not see, either—the man couldn't keep his hands to himself. What she hadn't expected to find were the torn-up scraps of a letter from the Natural History Museum woman. Intrigued, she put together the pieces like a jigsaw. The letter said something about needing his help to get a visa. Miss Benson had given the address of the board-inghouse where they were staying, and since it was only a short ride in the car, and since it was a lovely day, and since Mrs. Pope had nothing better to do, she decided to pay a visit.

Just in a friendly way.

The owner of the boardinghouse was one of those difficult

French women. She complained extensively about a dog the women had smuggled in. She went on and on about this dog. No, she had no forwarding address for Miss Benson, because if she did, she would send her a bill for the dog, though now that Mrs. Pope mentioned it, she remembered there'd been some kind of issue with her luggage.

"What kind of issue?"

"It never arrived."

"Do you mean they left Nouméa without it?"

The French woman shrugged. All she knew was that they'd gone in a jeep, very early in the morning.

"A jeep?" Mrs. Pope was aware of sounding too excited. Alarm bells were ringing inside her, like chimes. She said, "I suppose they bought the jeep for the journey?"

The woman shrugged again. All she knew was that she'd never seen them with a jeep before, and suddenly they had one. Mrs. Pope thanked her for being so helpful and promised that if she saw the women she would mention the complaints about the dog.

It took several calls to find the lost-property offices for the airline, but once she had the right one, there were no more hitches. She drove straight there. Yes, they had received two items of luggage belonging to the passenger Margery Benson.

So where were they now?

They were in the cupboard, waiting to go back to Britain.

Mrs. Pope moved her tongue precisely as if she were clipping out the words with scissors. "You mean that you have them here?"

Yes, yes, said the very helpful official. Would she like to take them?

Mrs. Pope said thank you, she would. She would like that very much. Splendid.

The official asked if she could see Mrs. Pope's paperwork. Mrs. Pope said she could not understand what difference her paperwork would make. She was simply trying to help a poor British woman who'd been left stranded on the island without her luggage.

The official said that if she did not have Mrs. Pope's paperwork, she could not let her take the luggage.

She said in her best French, "Seriously?"

The official looked right back at her and said, "Yes. Very seriously." As if she was actually accusing Mrs. Pope of deceit.

Mrs. Pope drove home and collected her paperwork, but by the time she got back, the office was closed. She watched the official, flipping the sign on the door from *Ouvert* to *Fermé*. She rapped on the glass. The official waved and pulled down the blind. It wasn't even midafternoon.

The office was closed for the rest of the weekend, though Mrs. Pope drove down twice while Maurice was at the golf club. She was in a foul mood, even at the concert that evening in aid of the local missionary school. It hurt to keep smiling.

She went back with her paperwork, first thing on Monday. It was a different official this time, and he said nothing about needing authorization. She waited as he went to a cupboard at the back to fetch the luggage, feeling a sudden prick of disdain that it should be so simple. He brought out a battered plastic suitcase, not even real leather, and an incredibly heavy Gladstone bag, both of which he placed at her feet.

Guilt clawed the back of her neck, but only briefly. She said she would make sure it was returned to Margery Benson. She got him to fetch a cart and load it into the back of her car. She whipped a few French banknotes from her purse—she was overtipping, but she felt less compromised now she'd paid.

Back at home, she broke the lock first on the suitcase, then the Gladstone bag. The suitcase was filled with old clothing. You couldn't even dump it on the women at the mission. It was the Gladstone bag that intrigued her.

One by one, she removed glass vials, a Kilner jar, plastic tubes. Bottles, which she opened and smelled. Collecting equipment. The sort of thing you would find in a chemistry block at a school . . .

She fingered the pearls of her necklace. She laughed. "Got you," she said. "Got you."

• • •

"You mean?" said Dolly Wiggs, at Friday craftwork. "That it was the two women who broke into the Catholic school?"

"Yes," said Mrs. Pope, all over again. They'd been through this a number of times.

"Margery Benson and her assistant?"

"Yes."

"And stole all those things?"

"Yes, Dolly."

"And then a jeep?"

"I can't believe we actually met them," said Coral Pepper. "So do you think they are spies, after all?"

"I don't know. I have written to the Natural History Museum, asking if they know about her. Of course, I did it in a clever way."

"Of course," chorused the women. Mrs. Pope would only do anything in a clever way.

"They just seemed so *nice*," said Dolly. "It's hard to imagine them stealing."

Coral Pepper looked on the verge of tears. "What should we do? Should we ring our husbands? Send the police to Poum?"

But Mrs. Pope had enjoyed her foray into detective work, and was not ready to hand it over to men. Now that the Three Kings party was over, she had nothing to look forward to until Valentine's Day, and Valentine's Day was not something she enjoyed. All the anonymous cards for Maurice, crowding his wastepaper bin. Besides, she wasn't sure men would pursue the case. Men, she found, often lacked a woman's drive.

"We need to wait until I've heard back from the Natural History Museum. Then we will know for certain."

At this point, the wives went off on a tangent. They began remembering other things that had gone missing over the past few weeks. Someone's frock had gone from her washing line. Coral Pepper had lost silver sugar tongs that had belonged to her mother. Daphne Ginger was sure she'd left a steak once on the kitchen counter, which wasn't there when she'd got back. Mrs. Pope felt the conversation skating toward thin ice. Some of these things had happened months ago, way before Margery Benson had arrived in Nouméa with her assistant. As much as she disliked them, it was unlikely the two women had gone round pinching frocks off washing lines, not to mention choice cuts of meat. Then Daphne went completely sideways and suggested Margery Benson might even be the murderess they had all been reading about in the British papers from home. Could she, in fact, be Nancy Collett, traveling under an alias, and hiding in New Caledonia? And was her blond assistant really the Woman With No Head? Shouldn't they should alert the French police immediately? Maybe even phone the editor of *The Times*?

Mrs. Pope clapped her hands. "Order!" she cried. "Order, ladies! It's about hard evidence! We just need to wait. *Something* will bring them back. And as soon as we know what they're up to, we can make our move."

41

The Connecting Line

He had them in his sights. He was always there, a little behind, not close enough for them to see, but following. He was waiting for the right moment. He reckoned a few more days, then he'd take charge. The blonde looked tired now. Really tired.

He couldn't understand why Miss Benson was blond as well. He didn't know why she was trying to confuse him when he had come all this way to lead her expedition.

The dog was an accident. He hadn't meant to kill it. But it knew he was there. It barked. Even though Miss Benson didn't notice Mundic, the dog still pricked up its ears. And when he'd found it alone, it wouldn't sit, even though he said to it, "Good doggy, sit, sit." It had gone for him with its teeth. It had torn his trousers. And when he tried to bat it off, it went for his hand as well. It wanted to kill him. So he grabbed it by the neck and he saw its teeth and he felt the flame, and the flame was in his chest, it was in his head, and his throat hurt, and suddenly he couldn't remember what was in his hands, he just knew he had to stop it. Afterward he laid it down, and said, "Good dog," but it didn't wake up. So he rolled the dog away, like the Japs rolled the bodies away, because he didn't want to see.

He kept following Miss Benson and the blonde every day. He had his haversack filled with his things, and sometimes he went all the way back to the little room and slept on a grass mat so he could get up the next day and go back and hunt for them. If the shantytown kids came up, wanting to sell him crap, he shouted at them to clear off.

He wrote in his notebook about the things he ate, like the tins from the shop with a picture of a fish on them, and he wrote about what he could see, and when he was thirsty he found water. But his legs were bad again with the beriberi, and even though he wrapped them in leaves, like he'd learned to do in Burma, he could feel the muscles wasting, and it made his chest hurt to keep breathing. When the sweats came, he wrapped himself in his yellow towel, and he said to himself he would not die, he would not die, he was a special boy, just like he'd said to himself in Burma, but there were sores in his mouth and it hurt to keep swallowing.

And worse things were beginning to happen, too. There was a Jap. Ever since the dog, a Jap was here. Mundic could see him. And the Jap had a stick, and he was watching Mundic, and following him. And the Jap thought Mundic didn't know, but Mundic did. So Mundic had to get away before the Jap came after him, but there were times he couldn't remember anymore why he was there. He was slicing his way through the undergrowth, he was ducking between lianas, and his heart was pumping fast, and his legs were mush, and he couldn't remember but he thought he had escaped from the POW camp and there were snakes in the forest. And he didn't know why he had tried to escape from the camp because he knew what happened to the prisoners who escaped. If the Jap found him, he would beat him. He would drag Mundic back to the camp and round up all the other prisoners and make them watch as he put the gun to Mundic's head. So he was trying to get away, but there were snakes, there were snakes everywhere he looked, coiled around trees, thick at his feet, and he sliced his knife at them, so hard the knife went spinning from his hands and disappeared. He just wanted to get back to the POW camp and be safe.

Then he'd remember. He was in New Caledonia. The Jap was not there. The Jap was a tree. Just a tree. There were no snakes. He wasn't a POW. He was free.

Mundic got out all the things he had taken so far. He laid them on the ground. The knife was gone, and so were the towel and the hat, but he had the map, his notebook, the battery, the soup label. He looked at the gun he had found close to where they buried the dog. He stared at each thing and tried to see what came first. He put them in a line, and it went map, label, notebook, battery, gun. But something was missing. There was another line before the one he could see in front of him. It had his mother on it, and the way he always got it wrong as a kid, and the POW camp, and men dying on their feet, and the time the Japs had punished the men who'd tried to escape and everyone had to watch, and then the journey home, and the mayor who didn't turn up, and the demob suit that was too big. And the things he couldn't see were so much bigger than the things he could.

He put everything back in his haversack, but he didn't know what to do with the things from the past. He had no idea where you were supposed to put things that existed only inside your head.

The trees stood tall. A basketwork of leaves. Then slowly they began to swing, up down, up down, until he threw up. And suddenly he wasn't sure anymore. He wasn't sure how much longer he could keep going.

42

Enid's Red Valise

"Marge, I wish you'd stop going on."

"Enid. I'm just trying to be practical because you are being bewilderingly vague. We are leaving in two weeks. We need to think ahead."

"I don't want to think ahead. I want to look for the beetle."

"But it's already February. You're having a baby in May. We have to make plans for when we get home."

Time, which had moved at different speeds throughout the expedition and taken different shapes, was now solid and clearly defined. Every day was one step closer to the end, and every day they did not find the gold beetle or the white orchid, it seemed more likely that Margery had been wrong; they were not there. It would have been so much easier if Enid had agreed to spend the final two weeks lying flat on her back on the veranda, or adding to her already substantial collection of knitted baby clothes, or even discussing the future, while Margery packed what they already had, and prepared for the journey home. But Enid wouldn't do any of those things. Since discovering the gun was gone, she was even more jittery. She was constantly stopping to check over her shoulder. "Do you think someone's following us, Marge? Do you think

he's here? The man from Wacol? Do you think he has the gun?"
And even though Margery reassured her—the gun had surely been
washed away during the cyclone, or even dug up by animals—Enid
stuck so closely to Margery it was difficult not to fall over her. If
they slept in the bungalow, Margery often woke and found Enid
wedged at her side. "Are you sure my baby's okay?" she'd say, over
and over again. She did not want to talk about the future. She did
not want to talk about going home. She did not want to do anything
except creep around next to Margery, holding up her enormous
belly with one hand and dragging an insect net with the other.

"Are you worried about money, Enid?"

Enid simply shrugged.

"Because I owe you. I need to pay you for your work. As soon as
we're home, I'll do that, Enid."

Enid kicked a stone.

"Or you can live with me. You can have a room in my flat. At
least until you're sorted out. Have you thought about a hospital?"

"Beg pardon?" Enid yawned.

"Where you can have the baby, Enid? You need to think about
these things."

"Marge, can you stop going on? It's giving me a headache. It's all
you talk about. What I want is to find the gold beetle. Why do you
have to keep spoiling things by talking about home?"

Every room in the bungalow was now filled with their collection
to date—at least a hundred and fifty specimens, some already
pinned, but most either stored in naphthalene or carefully wrapped
with lint. Margery was using everything they had left to keep them
in—all Enid's old bottles and jars, as well as washed-out tins. As for
sending things ahead, there was no need: there was actually nothing to send. In Nouméa, they would buy a few basics for the
journey—she couldn't stride about on deck dressed like a man, and
Enid would somehow need to cover up her pregnancy. If only Enid
would talk about these things.

Suddenly there was only a week left. At Enid's insistence, they
continued to search but caught little apart from more clown bee-

tles. Another day it rained so hard they came back and found the
boys from the shantytown sheltering beneath the bungalow. But
there was no chewing gum left to give them. Margery began to
store things in the jeep, ready to depart. She'd given up all hope of
getting a bus. She hadn't seen one in the entire time they'd been
living there.

February 13: two days before they were due to make the journey back to Nouméa. Margery was working late on the veranda, lit
by the hurricane lamp, when Enid appeared. She was so big she
almost filled the open doorway. Margery laughed. She didn't even
mean to. The laugh came out by itself. She'd thought Enid was
asleep.

"Enid?" she said. "Why are you dressed up like that?"

Enid was holding her red valise and her handbag. Not only that,
she had somehow squeezed herself into her old pink travel suit and
pom-pom sandals. She had even tried to pin her hair into a neat
style and finished with her tiny hat. "Enid? What are you doing?
It's not time to go yet."

Enid didn't laugh. She crossed the veranda slowly, her belly
sticking out through the skirt. The fabric was stretched to within an
inch of its life. Clearly she couldn't do up the zipper, though she'd
covered the gap with a scarf around her waist. She lowered herself
into the chair beside Margery's and sat motionless, staring carefully
at the black trees and stars as if committing them to memory.
Watching her, Margery suddenly felt a strange kind of ease and
freedom that seemed more acute because she sensed that, even
though she didn't know what it was, something was wrong, and her
peace was about to be shattered. "Enid?" she said. "What is it?"

Enid took off her hat. She set it on her lap. Then she said to her
hat: "I killed him, Marge. I killed Perce."

The truth cannot be understood all at once. It can only be done in
pieces, bit by bit. As Enid explained what happened, Margery
found she had to keep taking a break. But there wasn't much time.

The more she heard, the more she understood that something would have to be done quickly.

Enid was not Enid. She was called Nancy Collett. She had killed her husband before she left home. The British police were trying to find her; she had found that out on Christmas Day when she got her radio signal. She was not Enid Pretty. Enid was her alias.

"Okay. I see." Margery went down to the bottom of the dirt garden. She threw up in the dark. She came back. She sat down.

Enid wanted to go to the French police. She wanted to turn herself in. She spoke slowly, almost in a daze, as if she'd been hypnotized. The words seemed terribly ordinary and yet the thing she was saying didn't, so that every sentence had a kind of solitary quality, like a group of castaways.

Enid said the British police wanted Margery, too. They thought she was Enid's accomplice. They thought she had been involved in the murder. Enid wanted to tell the truth.

Again, Margery needed a pause, but she couldn't leave Enid another time. She looked up. She gazed at the thousands of stars in the sky. She didn't know why, but she envied them. They seemed to run like water. She wished she liked smoking.

Enid said she wanted to tell Margery about Perce. He liked the lads. He liked them very much.

"Yes, you told me that before. I understood."

"He couldn't bear so many young boys dying in the war. He talked about it all the time. In the end he decided he had to help. He was too old for the front, but he signed up for the Home Guard. He was back after six months. Lost a leg during training. He'd been accidentally shot by one of the lads."

"I see."

"After that, I took a catering job at a bar. I catered for all sorts of things. If the cash was there, I did it. Now that Perce was injured, we needed the money."

"I see. Yes."

On the whole Margery understood what Enid was saying, but

sometimes the words didn't fit together. Enid was telling the whole story as simply as possible, yet Margery had to repeat the sentences in her head. It was as if she didn't have the brain room to take them all in. She felt she needed an extension.

Enid kept talking. Slowly and without lifting her eyes from the pink hat on her lap, but stroking it sometimes, she told Margery how Perce had been in constant agony. "He could feel the leg he had lost. It wasn't there, but it was like his foot was on fire. Sometimes he screamed at me to get a bucket of cold water. So I'd fetch the water, but then I'd have no idea what to do with it. He'd just point and point at the space where his leg wasn't, screaming that it was burning up.

"I managed the physical stuff for years—the picking him up and taking him to the lavatory, getting him to bed, giving him a bath. I could do that. I'm strong. But I couldn't make him happy. I couldn't make him forget the pain. I tried everything. I cooked his favorite meals, I massaged the other leg, I tried to think of things he could look forward to. But he was locked in the pain. He couldn't get away from it.

"Then Perce saw your advertisement. He said I should apply. He said he would live with his brother for five months, and I should have a break. He wanted me to put myself first for a while. We were both sad when I didn't get the job."

"Did you know you were pregnant?"

"Yes."

"But it wasn't your husband's baby?"

"Marge? This is difficult to say."

"You'd better say it, Enid."

"There were a few fellas. It could have been any of them. I don't know who the father was."

Margery had to reach out. Even though she was sitting, she had the sense the ground had gone on a slant and she was going to fall off. She gripped the broken railing of the veranda very tightly. It was talking about the baby, not the uncertainty about who the father was. Already she cared about this baby so much. She hadn't realized until now. Lit by the hurricane lamp, her hands had little brown spots on them. She hadn't noticed those, either. She was getting older.

The rest of the story Enid managed in fits and starts, though she still insisted on telling it to her hat. It seemed it was the only way she could say it, just as Margery could listen only if she kept looking aside. Enid had got back from work one night, and found Perce covered with blood in bed. He'd tried to cut his wrists but made a mess of it. Enid had wanted to get a doctor, but Perce wouldn't have it. He begged her to let him go. He couldn't take any more. If she really loved him, she would help him end it. "Please," he kept saying, "please." If she thought too hard, she knew she would have refused him, so she grabbed the pillows and pressed them over his face. He didn't even struggle. And then she realized what she was doing and pulled the pillows away, but it had happened so fast. She couldn't get the ache out of her arm. That was the thing that confused her most. She'd thought it had happened quickly, yet afterward she could barely move her arm, as if the effort she'd made was huge and the ghost of the weight would always be there.

Enid's shoulders slumped forward. She made a tiny sound like a doll that you turn upside down. "Muh muh muh." She reached for her handkerchief very slowly and held it to her nose and blew. Then she made a ball of the handkerchief and told the rest.

"I stayed at home. I brushed my hair and waited for the police to come and arrest me. I knew what I'd done was a crime, and I knew I had to pay for it. Somehow in my head I thought the police would know that, too. But they didn't come. I don't really know what happened after that. If I ate or slept, I can't remember.

"Then something else came. It wasn't the police. It was your letter. It was your last-minute invitation to New Caledonia, and it was like a special lucky sign. A sign from Perce that I had done the right thing and now he wanted me to get away from Britain, and be safe. So I closed all the curtains, I made his suits hang all nicely in the wardrobe, and I tidied the house before I packed everything I owned, ready to depart. I put on my best pink suit. I wrapped Perce's razor and put it out with the rubbish. But even as I left the house, a part of me was still waiting for the police to stop me."

Enid paused. She opened her handbag and passed Margery a scrap of newspaper. A British one. Margery read the headline. SPINSTER TEACHER IN DARK LOVE TRIANGLE. Presumably it was the paper she'd caught Enid reading outside the café. Beneath the headline was a pen drawing. A cartoon.

"Enid? Is that supposed to be me?"

"Yes, Marge."

"But, Enid, I have no head."

"You've become a bit of a joke."

"I have?"

"Yes."

"In Great Britain?"

"I'm sorry, Marge."

It was like looking at something underwater. At first she couldn't make sense of it. What she was staring at was a sketch of a large woman brandishing an ax but lacking a head. The artist had, however, given her big legs. And maybe to make up for the lack of head, he had also given her feet the size of planks. Briefly the sketch came back to her from the school. That terrible sketch, all those months ago, with the mad bird's nest hair and potato nose. She even remembered the British consulate wives laughing at her best frock. She felt hot and smothered with shame, yet also strangely calm. She said quietly, "A joke. Of course I am. A joke." Then her hands began to tremble, and it was hard to stop them. She handed back the article, and Enid tore it to smaller and smaller pieces that fell to the ground.

"Marge? Has a pregnant woman ever been hanged?"

"I don't know."

"Would they let me have the baby first?"

"I don't know."

"Who would look after my baby when I was dead?"

"I don't know."

"It took two goes to kill Norman Skinner. They had to retie the noose and do it again."

It was too much. This was not the kind of conversation Margery had the vocabulary to enter. Nothing about her life so far had prepared her: her father had walked away, her mother had spent her life in a chair, her aunts had prayed, while Barbara had mainly bashed things. Margery was so out of her depth she didn't even know what to call Enid anymore. Surely not Nancy: Enid was the most Enidy person she'd ever met. And yet despite all her inadequacies and shortcomings, she didn't want to fail Enid. She wanted to be woman enough to meet her. She didn't want to be that awful cartoon sketch.

Enid reached for her red valise. Slipping her other hand down her bra, she pulled out a key and undid the lock. She rested one hand on the chair so that she could struggle down to her knees, and pushed open the lid. She swiveled the case round so that Margery could see. At first, Margery thought it must be a mistake. Once again, she had to bite on the impulse to laugh. "Pillows? We've come all this way, and all you've been hiding are two pillows?"

Enid gave a gasp as if she'd run too fast and was about to fall. She lifted the pillows, and crushed them in her arms, keening, pushing her face into them, one cheek, then the other. "I don't know what I was thinking. I just thought everything would be all right, so long as I kept the pillows safe. Oh, God, Marge. I'm so sorry. Oh, God, what have I done? I wanted to tell you. I wanted to tell you so many times. But I couldn't, Marge. It was too terrible."

Crouched on the floor, she looked tiny. She was the size of a house but so frail now that a whisper of wind might take her away. As Enid cried and dug her face into the pillows, looking for comfort that was not there, Margery stepped forward and helped Enid to her feet, then took her solidly in her arms. She remained braced and poised while Enid howled and shook and cried so hard she seemed made of bone and liquid. Margery placed her feet squarely and did not let go. Her shoulder was sodden, so was her neck. Once Enid even roared and pummeled her with her fists, then fell limp again and sobbed. As Margery held tight, she did something she had not done for a long time. She noticed the smell of Enid. She breathed it in. But no matter how hard she tried, it didn't seem the same. It wasn't big and bold and offensive anymore; it was a new kind of smell that was so lonely and frightened she could hardly bear it. She kept taking it in, trying to find something in the smell that would take her back to the way things had been before Enid had admitted the truth about Perce.

But it wasn't there. Everything was different.

Margery persuaded Enid not to go to the French police. She helped her to undress and wash her face, then put her to bed. Enid asked what they should do, and Margery said she didn't know yet, but she was going to work it out. Afterward she stayed on the veranda, watching the trees in the dark, whitened by the moon, which hung high and so full it looked like a cutout. It struck her again: a life was such a short thing. All those things people carried, and struggled to carry, yet one day they would disappear, and so would the suffering inside them, and all that would be left was this. The trees, the moon, the dark. The stars were a mesh of holes, so many you could have sewn them together and made a blanket. She thought of the museum. Her beetle collection. The day her father had walked away. And she put those stories together, just as she'd tried to link the stars, and it occurred to her that where she was now was not the ending she'd written in her mind. And even though the not knowing inside her would mean nothing one day, for now it meant everything, and she must do something.

Throughout her life, she had treated grief like a powerful engine that she could avoid if she got out of its way. But this time was different. Deep inside, she'd sensed for a long time that Enid was running from something terrible. She had sensed it in every way except with her brain. And now that she knew, it seemed obvious.

Suddenly there was nothing she remembered that didn't hold a clue. Even the first time she saw Enid, smoking nervously across the concourse at Fenchurch Street station. Her story was so full of wild bad luck it was hard to believe it had happened, yet Margery did. She believed every word Enid had told her.

Morning came, and it was small and blue. The moon turned from silver to chalk. Margery knocked on Enid's door and crept inside. Enid was asleep beneath her mosquito net with her mouth wide open, like an animal that had been chased down a hole. Light lay across the room in strips like bamboo and the only sound from outside was the gentle flapping of palm fronds.

Margery knelt at Enid's side. She whispered, "Enid?"

"Yes, Marge?"

"What do I call you? Do I call you Nancy?"

Enid kept her eyes closed. She seemed to want to remain as close to sleep as she could. She barely even opened her mouth. "No. Call me Enid. I'm Enid now." Her voice was low.

"Is there anything else I don't know? Because you have to tell me. If I am going to help you, I have to know everything."

"I've told you everything. Are you going to turn me in?"

"No."

"What will you do?"

"Stay with you."

"Are you angry?"

She couldn't even answer that.

"Do you think my baby is still okay?"

"Yes, Enid."

"What about the ship? It leaves in a less than a week."

"I won't take it."

"But what will happen to your collection? How will you get it to the museum?"

"I don't know, Enid. I don't know yet. Get more sleep. You look pale. I'm going to buy food. We need to eat, Enid. Then I can work out what to do next."

* * *

The sun was high already. It was good to be on her feet. It was good to have a task. The dirt track was soft and red beneath her boots. Either side, the treetops were bright green clumps, and the sharp smell of pine was in the air. Beyond the trees stood the mountain, its two prongs piercing the great blue of the sky. She had no idea how they would keep going. She had no idea where they would hide, or how she would get her collection home. She didn't know what they were going to do for money. They couldn't even sell their tickets for the RMS *Orion*. The boys from the shantytown ran out to say hello, but seeing her alone—and, more significantly, not in the jeep—they politely turned away.

The gold beetle was nothing anymore. Her ambition was nothing. Her only thoughts were of Enid. Last night her mind had felt slow to keep up, but now it was filled with scattered thoughts, like a hundred birds in a tree. If only she could talk it through with someone.

In the end she spoke to her shadow. Given the present circumstances, it was the best she could come up with. It hung behind. A bit sulky.

"No one knows where Enid is right now. That's good. But the police are searching for her. That's not good. She stole the collecting equipment and the jeep. That's not good, either.

"It's not safe to go back to Nouméa. But she's going to have a baby in May. There's also the problem of the visa. And Enid doesn't have a passport. Even if we could leave the island, where would we go next?" Lie low for the time being. It was the best she could think of. Stay on at the Last Place until she had a better plan. No one knew where they were. And hadn't Mrs. Peter Wiggs said it at the British consul party? People got lost in the far north. The best thing they could do for now was absolutely nothing—the very thing she had once been so good at. Before she knew it, the dirt track had ended and she was in the middle of Poum, such as it was. She passed some goats and some old men and made her way to the shop, where she bought eggs, fruit, yams, and salt for Enid. She hunted the shelves, but there was no sign of a British newspaper.

Outside, Margery caught sight of her reflection in the shop window. She paused. It was the first time she'd seen what she looked like in weeks, and she barely knew herself. Just as Enid had seemed smaller on the veranda, Margery seemed to have grown again. And not in terms of weight or width—she'd lost both those. Despite the bandages on her calves, the muscles in her legs appeared firm and strong. Enid was right. She had good legs. They had carried her up and down the mountain, and she loved them. Her shoulders were sturdy and capable. They had borne her haversack every day without complaining. She had the look of someone she'd known about but never met. And then it occurred to her that the person she looked like was Margery Benson. She removed her helmet for a better inspection. She took in her big yellow hair—thank you, Enid—she stared at her bright eyes, her solid jaw, her dark, round cheeks.

She was not the face she'd seen reflected all those years ago in the glass cases of the Natural History Museum. Neither was she a woman with no head. But she was possibly a woman who had not held it very high until now. And she liked it. She liked how strong it was, how intelligent, how kind. She even liked her yellow hair. She wetted her palm and smoothed it around her ears. This head was not the kind of head that gave up, or failed her friend.

Margery made her way along the dirt track back to the bungalow. She would do the unthinkable. She would sell her entire collection of beetles. She would not present it to the Natural History Museum. It contained rare species; she knew that. There were private collectors who would pay good money and not be fastidious about the paperwork. She would pin every specimen and label them, and get the whole collection in perfect order. She would write to the Royal Entomological Society about a buyer. Within a month, she would have enough money to get Enid away from the island. She would find a way to put her flat on the market. So, even though she had believed a few hours ago that she was staring catastrophe in the face, she found there was still this small place in which to hope. Far away a bird whooped, as if its insides were being scraped out with a spoon. She slowed to listen.

Her blood stopped. Everything inside her stopped. It wasn't a bird. And it wasn't whooping. It was Enid. Enid was screaming.

Margery dropped the eggs. The salt. The yams. She ran.

NOUVELLE CALÉDONIE

HUNTED!

43

Victoria, You Are Getting
Carried Away

Mrs. Pope was in full flow at Friday craftwork. The wives were surrounded by cut-out felt Easter bunny pieces that they were assembling for the orphanage. There were separate ears and tails, as well as little gray rabbit bodies, but no one had touched them. They had barely touched their coffee, either. "You mean," said Daphne Ginger, "she is not who she said she was?"

"That is exactly what I mean."

"How do you know, Mrs. Pope?"

The expectation in the room was as sharp as lights. It was like stepping onto a stage. Mrs. Pope took her cue.

In brief, there had been another significant development. She had heard from the Natural History Museum. Or, more specifically, the Natural History Museum had heard from her. Frustrated with waiting for a reply—and frustrated also by her Valentine's Day party, which had been a disaster: barely anyone had come, let alone bothered with fancy dress; worse, Maurice was openly flirting all night and had even disappeared for a while down in the garden— Mrs. Pope had taken matters into her own hands. She had made use of her British consulate connections and requested a long-distance trunk call to London.

No one from the Entomology Department of the Natural History Museum had heard of Margery Benson. No one had sent her on an expedition. There were no women working in the department. As for New Caledonia, they weren't entirely sure where it was.

The wives collectively gasped.

"You mean," said Daphne Ginger at last, "that they are not real?"

"Of course they are real, Daphne. They are here."

"Are they spies, after all?"

"No."

"Are they Communists?"

"I doubt they have one political bone between them."

The British wives continued to stare at Mrs. Pope with open mouths, like helpless chicks waiting to be fed. "What are they, Mrs. Pope?"

Mrs. Pope put down her sewing. She drew her head tall. She paused, she paused, she paused. Then she delivered her line: "They are Nancy Collett and Woman With No Head."

The wives sat, stunned. Even more stunned than before. Mrs. Pope took advantage of their shock to produce a dossier of newspaper clippings. She had got hold of every British journal she could find; fortunately everything was delivered to the consulate, even the lower-class rags. She swept aside the craftwork from the table, and where there had been needles and thread and pieces of cut-out felt, she now laid out her articles, side by side. A picture of Nancy Collett getting married; another with her husband at a chimps' tea party; a third in a hat with cherries. The women peered closer.

"It's terribly difficult to tell who it is," said Coral Pepper. "There isn't really a close-up of her face. Mostly she's hidden by other things."

"And who is that other one? The cartoon?" asked Daphne.

"That is Miss Benson."

"But she has no head."

"It's an artist's impression."

Mrs. Pope thumbed through her newspaper cuttings, searching for the only one that actually revealed Miss Benson's full name. The wives picked it up and read, and passed it round, then the other articles, one by one. They took in the headlines carefully, the details of the crime, the witness accounts, the stories from Nancy Collett's lovers.

WHERE IS NANCY COLLETT?

THIS WOMAN MUST HANG.

BRITAIN'S MOST WANTED CRIMINAL.

What should they do? Go to the French police? Phone the British government? Write to the king?

Mrs. Pope said, "These women must be arrested. They must be taken back to Britain. They must be tried. They killed a war hero. We simply cannot sit here and allow them to get away with it." The women nodded.

Then a girlish voice said: "Victoria."

A sudden hush. You could have cut through it with craft scissors. No one ever called Mrs. Pope by her actual name. Not even Maurice used it—though presumably he didn't call her Mrs. Pope in bed. But if anyone had that thought, they ran away from it. It wasn't something anyone wanted to dwell on.

The voice came again. A little bolder. "Victoria, you are getting carried away."

Mrs. Pope turned. "Mrs. Wiggs? Are you questioning my judgment?"

Dolly had flared the red of a tulip. Even her neck was red; so were the lobes of her ears. "Victoria. I'm sorry. But when Daphne suggested this a few weeks ago, you warned us all to be sensible."

"That's right, Mrs. Pope," murmured Daphne, terribly quietly. "You did say that."

"We need to stop, Victoria, before we make complete fools of ourselves. Remember the knitted rockets? You need to let this go before we become a laughingstock. What have those women done to any of us? They're just looking for beetles."

At the mention of the knitted rockets, a further silence fell over the women. This one was more like British snow—the kind that doesn't settle, just creates a thin, slippery mess. Suddenly Daphne Ginger and Coral Pepper realized it was time to go. They had matters to attend to at home. Within half an hour all the wives had remembered things that required their attention. They were picking up their summer coats and hats and handbags.

"But we have to do something," said Mrs. Pope. "We can't let those women get away with it. . . ."

Too late. Not even Dolly stayed. Friday craftwork was over and no one had touched their Easter rabbits. She had been thwarted and made a fool of, and she was furious. She would show them all, not just the wives but Margery Benson and Nancy Collett. She would show them all she was not to be slighted.

Mrs. Pope took the car straight to the British consulate. Maurice was in a meeting about an extension to the golf club. She had to wait for over an hour. Afterward he said he could not see how two British women wanted for murder could have made their way as far as New Caledonia. For a start, they wouldn't have got past customs. He asked if she had remembered that the Dutch minister was coming for canapés and drinks at six.

At the door, she paused. "Will you be dining at home?"

"Not tonight."

"Shall I wait up?"

"I wouldn't."

"Of course," she said. "Of course."

Mrs. Pope drove to the French police station. It was packed. Not just people, but their dogs and baskets, even a pig.

At last it was Mrs. Pope's turn. A police officer beckoned her forward. She explained very clearly in French what must be done. The British citizens wanted for the break-in at the Catholic school had escaped to Poum. She knew who they were. They must be brought back immediately. They must be handed over to the British government. They were the murderers Nancy Collett and her accomplice. She had to say it several times. The French policeman had no idea what Mrs. Pope was talking about.

"They are wanted in Great Britain." Mrs. Pope produced her dossier. She took out her press cuttings. They trembled in her hands like paper flags. "This is a matter of extreme urgency."

The police official tried to make sense of Mrs. Pope's newspaper cuttings. He was obviously having difficulty.

She repeated in French, "You are looking for a large woman with big brown hair, aged fifty plus. The other is small with bleached hair. Very thin. There might also be a man with them. I'm not sure." She added that the large woman had no dress sense, but he didn't seem to think that made any difference. He didn't even open his notebook.

She pulled out her last stop. She said, "Don't you realize? They have no visas. These women are in New Caledonia illegally, without visas. My husband is the British consul and he could not help them."

At last the police official shrugged. He said, *"Bien sûr."* He would send a car up to Poum.

44

Who Knew There Was So
Much Blood?

It took two whole days. Enid screamed blue murder. She swore in languages as yet unknown to man. She refused to be seen by a doctor. Not that Margery could have found one. They were in a bungalow at the foot of a mountain. Even the boys from the shantytown made themselves scarce. Enid insisted that since Margery had brought her here, the least she could do was deliver her child.

"But it is not due." That had been Margery's first reaction on flying into the bungalow and discovering that Enid was not—as she had feared—being held at gunpoint by some stranger they had never met, but standing in a pool of water. It was even running down her legs. "Enid," she had warned. "Enid, you said your baby would not come until May. You promised me. No more lies. We said that—"

Enid had begun to puff like a bulldog. She'd yelled as if Margery was still halfway down the track. "Maybe I got my dates wrong. I told you I was hazy. Anyway, I didn't want to worry you—"

"Worry me? How could you possibly worry me any more than this?"

Enid growled. She actually growled.

"Enid, I have no idea what I'm doing. And I'm terrible with

blood. You know that. Stop this right now. You can't have your baby here. We need to get you to the hospital in Nouméa. You need to be safe."

In reply, Enid had screamed in yet another foreign language. Then she'd made knuckles of her fists and said, "You may have forgotten this, Marge, but we are wanted for murder. Not to mention petty theft. Checking in at a hospital may not be such a good plan. And, anyway, how would we get there? Hitch a lift? My waters have broken. My baby is coming. This is the safest place I could be. So do not pass out on me, Marge. I swear I'll kill you if you pass out. We need clean towels, clean blankets, hot water, clean knives. . . ."

Hour after hour. It went on and on. Margery barely closed her eyes. Sometimes Enid roared and crawled on her hands and knees, her face scorched, insisting this was it, get ready, Marge, I'm having a baby, but then the pains would come to nothing. Instead she would sit very quietly with her back to the wall, or even curl up and sleep. Other times she paced up and down the veranda, moaning and gripping her back. She circled the front room round and round—Margery had to move a chair to mark the weak spot in the middle of the floor, she was so terrified Enid would crash through it. In Poum, she had made the decision to start work immediately on her collection. Instead she wrapped a huge cloth round her waist and another round her head, turban-style, and within no time, she was fetching pans of water from the creek, and trying to light a fire outside to warm them; she was searching for towels and washing them, hanging them on the line, flapping them to get them to dry more quickly. She even cleaned the bungalow.

Everything she did was bewildered and complicated. She brought Enid water, she rubbed Enid's temples, she held her hand, she cleared up the mess when Enid couldn't relieve herself in time. She fetched all the blankets she could find. She sterilized anything that was even vaguely sharp. She just hoped that, when the moment came, Enid would deliver her baby quickly and without requiring any real assistance. Margery didn't know how long it would take, or what it would involve. The only person in her life who had ever given birth was her mother and, of course, she'd said absolutely nothing on the subject. In fact, now that Margery thought about it, the idea astonished her. That her mother had given birth, and not once but five times. It seemed so unlikely.

Meanwhile, Enid screamed, she cried, she raged, she bucked, she whimpered, she sweated, she crawled, she crouched. Her belly was hanging so low, it was hard to believe the whole lot wouldn't slide out in seconds—though how exactly it would all fit, Margery had no idea. She couldn't remember a time she had felt more useless. She was folding the mosquito nets and scrubbing corners, cleaning things just to appear busy. One moment it was broad daylight, the next she had to light the hurricane lamp.

"Branston pickle, hot baths, autumn leaves, toast with marmalade . . ."

Another thing that happened to Enid: after twelve hours of labor, she was so exhausted she became morose. In between pains, she began to list all the things she missed from home. She wouldn't stop. She sat with her feet in a bucket, reeling them off, like an outrageous shopping list. Light rain, green grass, pigeons. Cricket, fish and chips, Weetabix, Vim, Robin starch, Sylvan Flakes for home washing, Rowntree's Cocoa, Quaker Puffed Wheat, Shippam's fish paste, Bird's Custard Powder. Even smog. She actually said she missed British smog.

Fake coal fireplaces where the coals glowed red and smelled of nothing. Yes, she missed those. Daffodils, white bread. She was in tears now. She couldn't believe she was never going to see them again. Salad cream, paper bags, traffic lights, proper queues, ration books. Rain hats, bus conductors, the *Radio Times*. "The Festival of Britain," she bawled. Her nose ran with snot. "I will never get to see the Festival of Britain!" Yet again the hours had hurtled past. Outside, dawn light was already filtering between trees.

Margery knelt beside her. She was so exhausted that the air was swimming, and yet at the same time, her body felt like a plank. She wiped Enid's face with a cloth, she rubbed her feet, she even made the mistake of holding Enid's hand: a new pain came and Enid might as well have run over Margery's arm with the jeep. Then Enid relaxed. She remembered again that she missed home. She resumed her crying.

"I'm a burden. It's all my fault. If it wasn't for me, you'd have found the gold beetle. And you'd be going back to Britain. You'd have all those things to go back to. You'd have been better off if I'd stayed in Brisbane with Taylor. I told you to leave me behind."

"It's not true, Enid." Margery bathed Enid's head with cold water. Enid wriggled down, much like an enormous caterpillar, and lay with her head in Margery's lap. Margery stroked her hair. It was half black now, only the ends still bleached. Margery watched Enid's great belly twitch and buck and harden.

"Talk to me, Marge. Tell me what you miss about home. Do you miss snow? Biscuits? Buckingham Palace?"

"No, Enid. I don't. I don't miss any of those things."

"You're saying that to make me feel better. You're being nice because I'm having a baby."

"I'm not, Enid. I don't miss them."

And it was true. She wasn't being kind. As she continued to stroke Enid's hair, she tried to summon up pictures of home. She thought of the serrated edges of her aunts' grapefruit spoons—on which she'd almost sawed off the end of her tongue so many times. She thought of the cagelike elevator to her flat, which was never in use because people always forgot to close the gate properly. She even pictured her front door. A lamp in her bedroom with a tasseled shade. And those things stayed exactly where she pictured them, back in London, happy to be there, not requiring Margery to miss them in any significant way, or even use them again. She settled Enid on a blanket and got up to stretch her legs. From the veranda, she watched the flaming sun beyond the trees, she smelled the sweet air, she heard the orchestra of birds and insects, and far away the ocean; she saw the red flowers like two hands in prayer, the vast kauri trees, and realized that the strangeness around her now felt like home. Without her even realizing it, this had been home for some time. She had traveled to the other side of the world, but the distance she'd covered inside herself was immeasurable.

And, after all, what did it mean? Home? Suppose it was not the place you came from, but a thing you carried with you, like a suitcase. And you could lose your suitcase, she knew that now. You could open another person's luggage, and put on their clothes, and though you might feel different at first, out of your depth, something inside you was the same, and even a little more true to itself, a little more free.

Then finally it happened. After forty-eight hours, Enid's baby came.

Margery had just been to fetch more water from the creek. It had taken longer than normal because there were so many tiny eels; they kept swimming into her pans and she had to keep fishing them out. By the time she got back to the bungalow, Enid was on the floor, wiggling like an overturned beetle. She screamed and went rigid, as if she'd been lashed from the inside. Next moment, she was on her hands and knees.

"Oh, God," she roared. "This is it, Marge. This is really it." Margery's head began to swing, like a lamp in the wind. Somehow, she had got used to Enid's labor. She had got so used to it, she had forgotten it would end in actual childbirth. "Enid," she said. "You're going to have to talk me through this."

But Enid's face twisted as a fresh wave of pain hit her. The tiny hairs of her eyebrows locked together. For absolutely no reason, she began to sob again. Her cries were desperate and childlike. "I can't do it. I can't do it."

"What do you mean, Enid?"

"I've changed my mind. Marge, I don't want to have a baby. I want to go home." She curled into a weak little ball.

Right, Margery said to herself. You have crossed to the other side of the world. You have climbed a mountain. You have slept in hammocks. You can do this, too. She pushed up her sleeves. She readjusted her turban. For a glorious moment, she felt like Barbara.

She parked herself squarely in front of Enid. She said, "Enid, stop this right now. You are having a baby. You wanted this, remember? You have wanted this for so long. So no more crying. Where is your *gumption*? Get that baby out."

"Yes, Marge." Enid hung her head and strained, as if she were relieving the most awful constipation.

"Big breaths."

"Yes, Marge. Big breaths! Whoof. Whoof. Whoof. Is it coming?" While it was true that Margery's mother had never talked to her about childbirth, it was also true that she knew about beetle reproduction. She knew that insect eggs came out of the opposite side of the head, and that, as lovely as Enid's face was, she was staring at the wrong end to be of any practical help.

"I'm going to take a look, Enid. Is that all right?"

"No, Marge. I think I've made a mess."

Margery moved to Enid's rear quarters. Her mind clouded. Enid was right. The mess was terrible, the stink unholy. But she must not faint. She must not fail Enid. A dark glistening head was stationed between Enid's legs. Enid screamed and screamed and screamed as more of it slid out. "Don't black out on me, Marge!"

Too late. Waves of nausea were filling her. Everything was appearing in multiples: where there had been one head, she was now seeing three or four. Margery was lifting, she was drifting, she was about to fly . . .

"Get down!" cried Enid. "Catch it!"

"With what, Enid?"

"Your hands! Your hands!"

Margery got to her knees just as a shoulder appeared. It was like reaching for something terrible down a hole. Then Enid gave the roar of a bear and out squirted the whole bloody, wrinkled baby in one go. Legs, arms, torso, even feet. Everything. Right into the cup of Margery's hands, like a skinned rabbit.

"Is she alive?"

"Yes, Enid. She's alive."

"Show me!"

Nothing for it but to clasp this miracle—this slippery, bloody, fat-covered thing—in her arms and pass it to Enid between her legs. Enid sobbed. "Oh, my baby! Oh, my baby!" She rolled onto her back, and as her eyes alighted on its face, she gasped with joy as if she'd been struck by a thunderbolt. "Quick! Warm water! Blankets!"

Margery brought clean warm water. She brought blankets. But something was terribly wrong. Something was attached to the baby. A blue belt. Margery had no idea how to mention it.

"It's the cord. You have to cut it," said Enid, suddenly super-casual. "Get the knife. Sterilize it."

"Cut it? Are you sure, Enid?"

Enid instructed Margery to fetch string and make two ties in the cord—one near the baby, one near her—and cut in between. The knife went through the rubbery gristle with an ease that appalled her, though Margery could barely look. Enid made no sound whatsoever. She didn't even seem to notice. She was too busy inspecting her baby's fingers, her toes, her ears and mouth, wiping her with a cloth, rubbing her to keep her warm.

At last it was over. Margery felt as if she'd been run over by a herd of buffalo. She would willingly climb up and down mountains for the rest of her life rather than deliver another human baby. But just as she reached for the floor to lie down—a chair seemed a complete waste of time—Enid screamed again, and announced she was ready to push.

Again.

Another child? More screams. More panting. Margery crawled to inspect Enid's business end. It gave a belch, then spat out a lump of her liver.

"The afterbirth," groaned Enid. "You must get rid of it."

Margery fetched a pot and took it out of the bungalow and as far into the garden as possible, trying her best not to have anything to do with it, though the mosquitoes had got wind of the awful thing and were following her in clouds. By the time Margery returned to the bungalow, Enid had wiped the blood and fatty substance from the baby's face and was smiling as if she had just birthed an angel.

"Marge! You didn't faint! You did it! You gave me my baby!" Euphoric, she fitted the child to her melon-sized bosom, and in what seemed like no time, the baby lifted her mouth, latched on to the nipple, and began to feed. And there it was. The love. Margery watched and tears sprang from her eyes, and she wiped them away, but more came.

Enid said softly, "Is your hip hurting?"

"My hip's fine. I haven't even felt it."

"You should get some rest."

"Yes, Enid. Maybe I will now."

Margery staggered out to the veranda. Yet again it was dark. Her clothes looked like a butcher's.

How many trillions of millions of times had this scene been played? For every human life there was this. The elemental battle to take the first breath, and survive. Finally Margery sat on the veranda, ready to pass out, yet so keyed up she had no idea how she would ever sleep again. Her thoughts felt cosmological in size. Enid had done it. She had fulfilled her vocation. She was now a mother. And how wrong Margery had been. There was nothing small about it, and nothing ordinary, either. What a monumental vocation it was. Everything led to this: no responsibility in life could be greater. It seemed only right now to sit and contemplate the stars. They reeled and pulsed above her. A kaleidoscope of lights.

Margery counted on her fingers, trying to find the date. Trying to learn the day that Enid's baby had come into the world: February 16. The day they should have left New Caledonia to begin a completely different journey home.

"Well, I never," she said to the silence. "Fuckadoodledoo."

And when her eyes began to close, the person who came to her mind was not her father. It was her mother, sitting patient and solid in her chair at the window. Maybe not so much wasting her life as doing her best, as far as she knew how, to wedge herself between Margery and the outside world, and offer protection. Mad though it was, she wished she could have thanked her.

A car's headlights made their way slowly past the shantytown, and out toward the bungalow. But Margery did not see them. She was fast asleep.

45

Snakes

The beriberi was back, and he was sick. Very sick. He spent more time asleep than awake. If he tried to eat, he threw up. It hurt to move and it hurt to breathe. He had been ill for weeks.

He didn't like to be still. If he was still, the memories came back. He had to be doing something to stop them all the time. He counted the leaves on a tree. He counted every stone at his feet, or how many steps he took before he needed to be ill again. Because if he did not have his mind on numbers this inhuman fear came over him, and he did not know where he was, and he did not know what he was doing anymore.

Then he would see Miss Benson. He would remember he was here to lead her expedition. He would look at his notebook and he didn't know what day it was. He only knew there had been Christmas, and after Christmas he had waited for his passport, and then he had made his way here, and he had a room to go to, but he couldn't find it. And he would look at the dates in his notebook and it said leaving Brisbane on February 18, and that must be soon, but he didn't know why so many things kept getting in the way. The police who put him in a cell.

The British consul. The blonde. A dog. There had been a dog that tried to kill him. And a gun. He had a gun. He couldn't remember why he had stolen it. But it was the Japs that were the worst thing. They were everywhere.

And now he was running. He was running fast. He didn't know anymore if he was asleep or awake. He was pushing his feet through the red earth of the track toward the bungalow, but it was dark ahead and he couldn't make his feet work. They were going to fall off. His legs were falling off because of the beriberi. And the lights of the Jap tanks were getting closer. He could feel them on his back. If he didn't get away, they would catch him and take him back to the camp, but there were snakes. There were snakes everywhere he looked.

He remembered them in Burma, coiled beneath the huts, slipping out of view, the whip of a long skin, like rope. Back then he'd found a way to bear everything. The dysentery and the lack of food and the fellows dying of cholera and the trudging for miles, and he could tell himself that the bodies weren't dead, they were just lying in the sun, and he could say to himself he had the flame inside him, he was his mother's special boy, he was not like the others, he was better than them, he would not get lost out there, he would not die, but what he couldn't get away from was the snakes. There had been lads who'd chop off their heads and eat them, but he'd rather starve in a hole than see snakes.

And then there had been the chaps who'd tried to escape and been brought back, and he remembered how they were left outside the barbed wire but no one was allowed to help because they must be punished. And all night Mundic had heard them screaming. And he'd tried not to listen, he tried not to feel, but someone kept shouting, "Snakes! Snakes!" And in the morning the bodies were black and half eaten. Even though he knew the snakes couldn't do that to a human body, the idea was pinned through his head and it was all he could think about.

And now Miss Benson had done something terrible. He had gone to the bungalow to have it out with her once and for all, and he had waited outside and he had heard the blonde screaming, and it had gone on for hours. Then he had seen Miss Benson come out of the veranda and she was covered with blood. And it was so terrible he had begun to run. He had begun to run back to Poum and he was almost there, he was running, he was running and his head was swinging, and then the car had appeared in front of him and he had no choice anymore but to fall to his feet and surrender.

The car stopped. A Jap pulled him up and put his flashlight in Mundic's eyes, and Mundic cowered, waiting for the first strike, but it wasn't a Jap. It was a policeman.

He said something Mundic didn't understand.

Mundic didn't know what to do. He showed the guy his passport and his visa, and he crawled to his knees and begged for his life. He said, "Mercy, mercy," like they said in New Caledonia.

The policeman looked at Mundic's passport. He studied the pages. He said, *"Oui, Monsieur,"* and he didn't kick him; he helped him to his feet. He picked up Mundic's haversack and helped him put it back on his shoulders. *"Anglais?"* he said. "Breeteesh?"

Mundic nodded to say he was. The fellow offered him a cigarette, then struck a match and lit it for him.

He said, *"Les dames? Les dames anglaises?"*

Mundic hadn't a clue what he was talking about. He shook his head to show he wasn't trying to escape. He said, *"Non."*

"Elles sont ici?"

"Non." His heart was going like the clappers.

"Il y a une maison?"

"Non."

"Personne ici?"

"Non."

The policeman shone his flashlight into the dark. He passed it over the track and the trees. Nothing moved. He nodded. He said, *"Vous avez raison. Rien ici. Merci, Monsieur. Bonsoir."* He gave Mundic the packet of cigarettes to keep and then, just as he was about to walk away, something stopped him and he held out his hand. He said softly, *"Monsieur, vous êtes malade, non? Vous venez avec moi? Vous êtes très malade."*

Mundic turned on his heels and staggered into the dark.

46

Tiny Thing of Wonder

Safe. She must keep Enid and the baby safe. So long as they were safe, she would be able to live the rest of her life in peace. But so many things seemed to cloud her mind. Enid insisted she was well, but she was as pale as milk; she even had that bluish hue to her skin, and she was still bleeding. Margery needed to get her collection in order quickly, and sell it. She needed to raise enough money to get them off the island. But most bewildering of all was the baby. The baby had tipped Margery's life upside down.

Enid's love for her child was so big and fierce, she couldn't stop giving her names. She went through them like clothes, trying them on for size, then flinging them off. Nothing was right. Nothing offered the protection Enid wanted her baby to have, and she changed her mind by the hour. Hope. Greer, after Greer Garson, *Mrs. Miniver* being her favorite film. Betty, which had been her mother's name. Little Wren, because she was so tiny. Things more biblical: Kezia, Rebecca, Mary. A brief flirtation with French names, like Cécile. In the end, she settled on Gloria. As for her surname, she wanted Benson. She wanted a proper name, not a bogus one, like Pretty. She wanted her daughter to have a name she could be proud of.

"But, Enid," said Margery, "that is my name."

"Yes, Marge. I know. I want to name her after you."

"But why?" Since the birth of Gloria, everything seemed to bewilder Margery and reduce her to tears, as if she were suddenly living with her vital organs exhibited on the outside. "I am not her father," she said, blowing her nose.

"I am going to call her Gloria Benson, because I know you will always look after her."

And already Margery knew this to be true. In fact, the words were small-fry. They didn't even skim the surface of what Margery felt about this baby. This puking, bawling, yellow-shitting tiny thing of wonder. She had entered Margery's life with the force of a missile and taken up residence in a place Margery hadn't even known was there, let alone vacant. Despite her size—she was smaller than a doll, and her bones stuck out like beads inside all of Enid's knitted baby clothes—she was clearly her mother's daughter, and a survivor, even in the middle of absolutely nowhere. Margery had not enjoyed more than an hour of solid sleep since she'd been born. Gloria screamed and arched her tiny back until she had Enid's nipple; then, sated, fell asleep, yellow milk caked around her mouth and spilling down her tiny chin. Enid set up camp in the middle of the main room, surrounded by blankets and mosquito nets, like a giant nest, with pots of hot and cold water, and whatever Margery could produce to feed her; Enid's hunger was a monster. So Margery belted up and down, ripping up cloths to make new diapers, boiling everything that was soiled or bloody or covered with baby vomit, providing fresh rags for Enid, yet stopped by her every time she got anywhere vaguely near the door to come back, come and see what's she doing, Marge. Look, look. I think she's smiling.

Margery gazed at the baby's shut eyes with their regal lashes, and her good intention of a nose. Fingers that even came with their own miniature nails. The wild mop of her hair.

"She has your hair, Marge."

"That cannot be true, Enid." And yet. Her hair was thick and curly. It was marvelous hair.

The first time she heard Gloria burp, she almost exploded with joy. How could such smallness contain so much perfection? Margery's feelings for Enid were pale and ordinary beside this primordial expansion of her heart. It was so vast and painful, she couldn't see where it ended—she could barely step away from Gloria without rushing back to check she was still breathing in and out. How shallow Margery's existence had been until now, how naïve and small and ignorant. Suddenly she worried about things she hadn't even noticed before. A rain cloud. A spider. For Gloria's sake, she wanted to live in a clean, fresh country where there was no illness, no dirt, and people were only kind.

But there was work to be done. Her collection must be correctly pinned and labeled, her notes must be finished, before she could even try to sell it. When Enid and the baby slept, she took herself to her study. She shut the door, not to keep them away but to keep herself inside. She forced her eyes to focus. A specimen must be taken out of alcohol and dried and then it must be pinned while it was still soft. But the pinning was an exact process. The first pin must be guided through the right side of the upper half, taking care that the height of the beetle on the pin was correct: half an inch. The antennae must be carefully positioned, the legs displayed, without flattening them or losing even the tiniest hair, the elytra coaxed open to display the papery wings beneath. And there was not much time. There was so little time. She needed to get Enid and the baby to safety before anyone came searching. So long as they stayed north, they would be fine.

"Enid?"

"Hm?"

"Enid, are you all right?"

"I think I have a headache, Marge. That's all."

Five days after Gloria's birth, Enid became ill. She made light of it. She even pretended she was tired. But as she crossed the veranda, she went very slowly, almost creeping, clinging on to things with one hand as she passed, and there were dark circles beneath her eyes. Out of the blue, she asked if her mother was coming for tea.

"Your mother?" said Margery. "Your mother's not here, Enid. We are in New Caledonia. Your mother died when you were small."

Enid paused, the baby cradled now in both arms, like someone about to step into a busy street, who pulls back at the last minute. "What am I saying?" She laughed.

But it got worse. Later she appeared wearing two blankets when it was now broad daylight and boiling hot, even in the shade. Her skin was covered with goosebumps. She couldn't face food. Didn't want to drink. All she wanted was sleep. She dropped off even while she was feeding Gloria. Then she began to shake.

"What is it?" said Margery. "What's wrong?"

"I'm cold," she said. "I'm so cold."

Margery grabbed every item of clothing they owned between them, and piled them on top of Enid, even the old pink dressing gown. It made no difference: Enid was still freezing. She lay bundled up, shaking so hard her teeth rattled. And there was a smell, too. Margery didn't like to say it, but there was a smell coming from Enid and she knew it wasn't right.

A terrible thought dawned on her. It was so awful she didn't even want to give it words, but she had to.

"Enid? You did have vaccinations. Didn't you? Before you came away?"

Even as she got to the end of the question, she knew the answer. There'd been far too little time for Enid to have vaccinations. Besides, she had been sitting at home with a dead body, waiting for the police to appear. She didn't even own a passport. Vaccinations would have been the last thing on her mind.

"Enid, is the bleeding worse?"

"I'm fine, Marge."

"No, Enid, we have to get you to a doctor."

"We can't go to a doctor. They'll arrest me. It's nothing, Marge. I want to stay here with you and Gloria."

Enid continued to refuse to accept she was ill. "I've just had too much sun," she kept saying. "I'll be fine." But since the birth, she'd been nowhere near the sun. She slept all day, waking only to feed Gloria. She complained of a headache that was like a pole being pushed through her head, and then she tried to get up and doubled over, grabbing her belly.

"What is it now, Enid?"

"Nothing, Marge."

"Are you in pain? Where does it hurt?"

"I'm fine, Marge. I just need to sleep."

Margery tucked Gloria safely into Enid's arms and lumbered down the steps to the dirt track. She needed air. She needed perspective. She couldn't tell if she should be afraid. Or, rather, she wasn't ready to be afraid. She felt they'd already had their fair share of fear, as if bad luck was something that came in reasonable portions, when people were prepared. A bit for you, a bit for me.

She walked in the shade of the palm trees, the day clicking with insects, the thick smell of the forest. A bird flew ahead, like a blue doll, cutting its path through the air. To her right rose the rumpled flanks of the mountain, warmed and reddened by sun, the forest covering it in pleats and folds. Then something made her freeze.

Someone called her name. "Miss Benson?"

She stopped. Dead still. She felt a flash of fear, an actual physical jolt. A man had called her name. She knew it. She scanned the wall of trees on either side, the undergrowth. No one. And yet she knew a man was close. She heard a smaller sound: a snap, a shuffling of leaves. Breathing. She listened so hard, the silence was like something solid. Not even the shantytown boys were around. "Hello?" she called. Her voice was small. Almost defying anyone to hear it and reply.

A breeze took up and rattled the leaves. All around her the trees whispered and shifted. Her body turned to rubber. Before anyone could appear, she turned. She fled to the bungalow, dragging herself up the steps, pushing open the flap of a door.

The moment would have continued to unsettle her, but by the time she got back, Enid was even worse. She was still on the mattress, and still covered with everything they owned between them, still shaking. Margery touched her forehead: hot as a furnace and soaking wet. And her mouth. Her mouth was so blue she looked as if she'd eaten the nib of a fountain pen.

Margery fetched more firewood, boiled more water. She was frantic at the idea of something happening to Enid. She hated the sky for staying so clear, as if nothing was the matter. Hated the birds, calling indifferently. But, most of all, she hated herself for bringing Enid here in the first place, for not getting her to a hospital to have her baby, for not even fetching proper help. She had no idea how she'd bear the rest of her life if Enid did not survive. Yet she still seemed to be stuck in the present.

She tried to lift Enid, but Enid screamed that it hurt too much, and begged to be left where she was. She lay another hour on the mattress, while Margery hunkered beside her, batting off flies with her hand. She felt like a radio that had lost its frequency. She still had a vague notion that if she delayed long enough, things might get better of their own accord. But as the sun went down, Enid began to hallucinate. She was sweating heavily one moment, cold as stone the next. And the smell was even worse.

"I had so many babies, didn't I?" Her eyes were wide and frightened.

"No, Enid. But you have Gloria."

"I loved them all."

"You need to feed Gloria, Enid."

"Tell me their names."

"Their names?"

"I think one was called—what was she called? I think she was called Table."

"Enid?" said Margery. Less of a question, more a command. "Don't be so stupid. You never called a baby Table. Stop doing this, Enid."

Enid's eyelids fluttered up and down, but behind them, her eyes were blank, like a shop that is closed for the night.

And then the truth occurred to Margery, so fast it was like becoming another version of herself. Just because Enid didn't want to leave the bungalow, and didn't want to see a doctor, didn't mean she was right. Enid hadn't a clue. Margery experienced a plummeting feeling inside. What had she been doing all this time? Waiting for Enid to get better? She had only made things worse. She'd been wrong to believe she could be a true friend to Enid. She was just as afraid and useless and dithering as she had been all those months ago when she'd limped through the school, unable to find a door that even opened. She bundled Enid up, ignoring her cries and whimpers, and bore her to the jeep, where she laid her on the back seat. She rushed back for Gloria, and placed her beside Enid in a box that could act as a makeshift cradle. She went and threw a few things in the red valise. Blankets. They also needed blankets. She couldn't find any. She couldn't remember what she was looking for. Blankets. She was looking for blankets. And water. Enid needed water. She remembered the blankets. But what else? In her panic, her mind had become full of holes. Water. But if she put water in a pan, it would spill. She was running out of the bungalow, then straight back in. Nothing made sense. Food. Enid needed food. It was not safe to take her to a hospital but she needed a doctor and a clean bed, and she needed them immediately. Suddenly she had no idea why she was worrying about blankets and food and water when Enid might be dying. She dropped the blankets, the pan of water, the food. She hurtled down the steps with Enid's valise. She flung open the passenger door and dived in, ready to depart.

What was she thinking? There was no driver.

Margery's mind locked again. She needed to find a driver. She needed to drive to get a driver. . . . Absurd. Also, she had never driven a car in her life. Until meeting Enid, she hadn't even traveled in one.

Enid groaned.

"Margery Benson," Margery said out loud. "You have delivered a baby. Now where is your gumption? Drive a car."

She hoisted herself into the unfamiliar space behind the steering wheel. She tried to recall what she had seen Enid do. She twisted the key. The engine roared. She yanked at the handbrake, she flattened her foot on a pedal. The jeep leaped backward into a coconut stump. But Enid did not cry out. She did not even attempt to escape. Briefly she sat up. She said something about putting your foot down gradually, not all at once. She also said something about putting the jeep into first gear.

"Headlamps," she murmured. Then she fell asleep again. Margery flicked every switch she could find. Windshield wipers, hot air, even a radio—who knew the jeep had a radio?—came to life. At last, headlamps. The track shone ahead. A tunnel of light between trees. She eased her foot more slowly on the pedal, crunched the gear stick, and finally the jeep rolled forward. She pressed harder. The jeep was straining as if held back by a giant rubber band. She fumbled for the handbrake. Yanked it. The jeep clunked, it stuttered, it stalled. She tried the key again, the pedal again, the engine flared, she wrenched the car toward the track and picked up more speed. Faster, faster. Too fast. She was hitting stones, she was flying into branches, she could not understand how to stay in a straight line. When a drunk staggered out of the dark, she shrieked and swerved the car just in time, crunching the side of the jeep against rock, but she did not stop, she would not stop, she kept going.

They traveled all night. She drove like a madwoman, praying out loud that every French policeman in New Caledonia was in bed, while also keeping the dial on the speedometer in the red. She no longer felt fear. Fear had penetrated right through her and out the other side. When Gloria began to cry, Margery cut the engine. She threw herself out of the driver's seat. She scooped Enid in one arm, Gloria in the other, and did her best to attach the baby's mouth to Enid's bosom, like fixing a bivalve to an old pipe. After that, she continued, hurling the jeep over gravel roads, dirt tracks, bouncing through holes, steering hard to avoid a fallen tree, a herd of goats, with the radio playing at full volume, and also the heat. She was hungry, she was boiling hot, her legs were on fire. Dawn came. A sky so orange, the trees blazed; and there was the ocean to her right, full of flames. Then at last they reached the solid, elegant buildings of Nouméa. The Place des Cocotiers. The market. The port.

Enid sat up. Briefly wiped the hair out of her face. Murmured, "Where are we, Marge? What are we doing?"

"I've thought it through. Don't argue with me. We have no choice. I have to save your life. I would never forgive myself if something happened to you."

Bougainvillea hung like purple lamps. The air was sweet and warm. Sunrise flared against windows.

Margery pulled up outside the British consulate.

47

Beetles and Eyes

He staggered toward the bungalow. He went flailing through the dawn light, swiping at leaves that were not there, stamping his boots to ward off snakes. He had been asleep again and he had woken, and it had struck him like a lightbulb going on. He had to get to the bungalow. He had to lead the expedition. That was why he was here. He had saved her life, and now she needed him to lead the expedition. He had no idea what he'd been doing all this time. He'd been sleeping and dreaming, and thinking people were chasing him. He even thought she'd tried to knock him over with the jeep. But that was just something in his head. There were no Japs. No snakes. This was not Burma. He was a free man.

He reached the end of the dirt track. The sun was rising over the mountain, and everything was gold. He could see the washing line at the side of the bungalow, and there were little squares of cloth hanging up like handkerchiefs. He made his way to the steps that led to the veranda, hauling himself upward with his hands, but his legs trembled with the effort, and once or twice his feet slipped, and halfway there was a rough sound of sawing coming out of his chest that he realized must be his breathing. He must get to her.

He must get to her before he got sick again and forgot what he was doing.

He knocked at the door and peered in at the window. He called, "It's me! Boo! Rise and shine." He guessed she must still be asleep, so he sat outside the door for a while and he rocked in her chair, like he'd seen her doing. And when the bad thoughts came, he gripped his hands into fists and told himself it would be okay now: he was here and so was she. Together they would finish the expedition. By now the sun was full on him and he was beginning to sweat.

And suddenly he realized what must have happened. He'd seen the blood on her, she needed his help—she was lying inside the bungalow, waiting for him to save her. And he staggered out of the chair so fast it fell over, and then he swung his foot hard and kicked open the door.

A terrible stillness. There was a mattress on the floor, piled with towels and blankets; there were pails of water. He called her name but even as he went from one room to the next, and he held out the gun, in case something sprang out, he knew she was not there. He saw the room where she slept; he saw piles of clothes, a makeshift kitchen with a sink. In her study, he found trays everywhere, stacked high, and he lifted them, and in each one there were beetles, like jewels, pinned, with their wings open. There was notebook after notebook, with neat writing and careful diagrams. There were even papers pinned on the walls, and boxes and boxes of little pots and jars, hundreds of tiny things wrapped in bandages, like cocoons. He unwrapped them, one after another, throwing off the bandages, like wrappers. He was aware of feeling cold and trembly, and his face being wet, and it was tears. He was crying—he was crying so hard he didn't know how to stop.

She had gone. She had gone without him. She knew he was leading her expedition, but once again she had given him the slip. He hadn't dreamed the jeep, after all. He didn't know why she kept doing that. It hurt him so much. They were together. He had saved her life. And suddenly the flame was inside him and it was so big he roared with it and lashed out, kicking the blankets, punching walls, throwing old tins, pushing over pots of water; he was back in the camp, and the Japs were waiting for him. Somewhere far away he thought he heard the sounds of pain. The green of the trees seemed to steal all the air so that even inside the bungalow everything had a strange glow.

He picked up the first tray, and he lifted it over his head, ready to smash it. But the sounds of pain were not inside him anymore. They were beating on the roof and hammering at the doors and they were yelling at the windows. The trees were laughing, and the wind was laughing, and even the hundreds of beetles in the trays. Ha-ha-ha. He looked from one corner of the room to the next, terrified, confused. There were beetles flying at him, there were eyes. The shantytown boys were everywhere—they were peering in at the windows, they were crowding at the door, they were swarming around him, hanging upside down, doing cartwheels and somersaults, pulling at his clothes and poking him with sticks, shouting and pointing at him, as if he were a joke, yelling, shoving, and dragging him away from the study and toward the door. Some were even picking up the mess he'd made, and he did not know the words, he did not know what they were saying, but it sounded like *Ree-tard. Ree-tard.*

He shoved one beetle into his pocket, put his hands to his ears, and ran.

48

Sanctuary

It was over. The terror was over. Enid was alive.

A private doctor had operated immediately, removing what was left of the infected placenta. No questions were asked. Enid cried briefly but she had no strength. Gloria did the serious bawling. It was Margery's limp that seemed to worry the doctor the most. When he saw the state of her legs, he was appalled. She needed penicillin immediately and a poultice. After that, he prescribed rest.

"Yes, Doctor," said Dolly Wiggs. "Thank you, Doctor."

What had made Margery change her mind at the last minute and drive away from the British consulate? Something had seemed to plummet through her. The sudden knowledge that the British consul was the last person who would help her, even if she explained, as she intended, Enid's whole story. She had caught sight of Mrs. Pope on the freshly cut grass, with her hair already coiffed, and dressed in a crisp housecoat; she had seen Mrs. Pope shouting at a gardener, a man so old he stooped to stand; she had seen Mrs. Pope wagging her fingers right up close to this man's nose; she had seen Mrs. Pope glance suddenly toward the jeep and lift her hand to her eyes, trying to block out the early-morning sun. And Margery had realized in that moment that this woman was far more dangerous than Enid's illness. To ask her husband's help was the worst idea Margery had come up with so far. So, instead of getting out of the jeep, she had dug through her handbag. She had pulled out the slip of paper—*Mr. and Mrs. Peter Wiggs*—that Dolly had given her all those weeks ago at the consulate party. Margery had urged Enid to lie low in the back seat and hold tight to Gloria. Then she had whacked her foot down on the accelerator, revving off at full speed, checking in her rearview mirror that Mrs. Pope was not on her trail, slowing only when they were safely round the corner to ask complete strangers for help, pointing at Dolly's address, trying her best to understand the directions that came back at her in French.

Dolly Wiggs had answered the door straightaway. She had gasped. "Miss Benson? You two look like wild women!" Nevertheless she had helped Margery carry Enid inside the house, saying nothing about the red dust that ended up on the multiple frills of her skirt.

"She's had a baby," Margery had said. "She needs medicine. A doctor. You are my last chance, Mrs. Wiggs. No one knows we're here. Please help."

Dolly had paid the doctor, and now she was sheltering the women in a summerhouse at the end of the garden. It was perfectly safe. Peter was up at the mine and wouldn't be home for weeks. Dolly prepared the hideaway with two beds and a flask of tea, along with china cups. It was those that moved Margery most, not the fresh bed linen and towels, or the neat curtains with ties, but the delicacy of the cups. It had been a long time since they had drunk from anything but tin mugs, or the jerrican, and even though china cups had seemed pointless to her once, she saw how beautiful they were, how important. Inside her hand, with its broken nails, those cups looked small and sanctified.

Dolly fetched spare clothes that smelled of summer, though she wasn't sure whether to supply Margery with frocks or her husband's trousers, and in the end provided a freshly laundered selection of both. She was constantly bringing plates of food down to the summerhouse, sprigged with flowers, and she was clearly smitten by Gloria. She even produced a suitcase of unused baby clothes, folded between tissue.

"You, too?" said Enid.

"Yes." Dolly nodded but she didn't cry. "May I hold Gloria?"

Dolly could spend hours happily easing Gloria's tiny legs and tiny feet into cotton baby nighties, and white dresses with smocking, polka-dot romper suits, little pink cardigans with felt flowers sewn on them. She made up bottles of formula so that she could feed Gloria while Enid slept, and she taught Margery how to do the same. Margery and Enid were free to wander the garden and wash whenever they chose. There were baths filled with bubbles. Thick towels heated on a rail. Dressing gowns. Slippers.

Nevertheless, the mountain pulled Margery. From Dolly's garden, she often stared at the great knuckles of rock that stretched away, scarlet by day, blue at dusk, with the evening star shining above. She would picture herself standing at the two-pronged peak that she knew was like two chimneys; she would imagine the tiny rooftops of Poum in the distance, the shantytown, the expanse of blue ocean; behind her, the forested slopes and jagged peaks, and far away the tiny beaten track that she and Enid had made, snaking between the foothills.

When clouds took shape, and with them a current of hot air so that the atmosphere felt ready to burst, and the sky held a tacky glare, she knew a cyclone was on its way. Sure enough, it came within hours, a wheeling pillar driving up from the coast, blowing up so much dust it coated everything in red. Palm trees bent at a slant, thrashing against the sky, giant birds were tossed like scraps of paper. Then the clouds opened and the rain came in a waterfall. She watched it bounding down the sides of the nearest peaks and knew there would be flooding all over the island and trees down. She thought of the Last Place, and worried it had not survived. She thought of her collection and hoped against hope it was still in one piece. Even though she'd abandoned the beetle, in the last two nights she'd dreamed about it, as if, now that she had given up, it had decided to come and find her instead.

It rained for three more days. A torrential rain that came down perpendicularly, and fired off every surface. The whole garden shuddered under the weight of it and began to change color, tree trunks slicked to gray, leaves shiny and black. Out in the bay, the ocean churned. And then it was over. Once again, the sky was blue, the water calm, the mountains so clear she could make out the many folds and colors. Tiny insects spiraled through the light. She took up her position outside, staring upward.

"It isn't over, you know," said Enid. She was cradling Gloria. Margery had not even been aware that Enid had followed her into the garden. "You can't give up. You promised you wouldn't."

"But that was before. Everything's different now."

"We'll go back to the Last Place and keep looking."

"It is very definitely over, Enid. Tomorrow Dolly is going to put out feelers for someone who might buy my collection. I just hope it's still in one piece after the cyclone. Then we need to find a way of getting off the island. We can't stay here. We have Gloria to think of."

"You're behaving as if you can turn your back on your vocation. But it's not like that, Marge. It won't let you off so lightly. You're deep in this. You're in it up to your eyebrows. And you don't seem to realize. It isn't like me. Your vocation is not your friend. It's not a consolation for someone you lost once, or even a way of passing the time. It doesn't care whether you're happy or sad. You must not betray it, Marge. And Gloria will not thank you, you know. It will be a terrible thing for her to bear if she learns one day that you gave up on your vocation simply for her. You saved my life, Marge. I will not let you kill yours."

Enid was crying. She could not say any more. But Margery looked at her and knew she was right. As impossible as it seemed, finding the beetle was still her vocation, and that wasn't even a question of choice. It was a terrible thing, it was a beautiful thing, and she had no idea anymore if she had chosen it or it had chosen her. Either way, it was in her makeup. It was a part of her in the same way her blood was a part of her, and so were her hands.

But that was by the by. Within a few hours, they would be in the jeep for the last time. Hurtling back north.

Dolly was buying provisions in the market. The cyclone had cleared the air, and it was the bluest kind of morning. She took pleasure in finding the best guavas and chokos, the sweetest pineapples. Three of everything. It took her a moment to notice that a shadow had grown behind her.

"You've been quiet, Dolly," said Mrs. Pope. "You didn't come to Friday craftwork. You didn't even telephone or send a note. We were all worried about you."

Dolly was at a loss. Something dangerous was passing between them, and she felt the need to do a little ironing, just to uncrease her mind. She stared at the watermelons in her basket. "Gosh!" she said. "Don't you love tropical fruit?"

"I thought Peter was still at the mine?"

"He is!"

"Are you alone?"

"Yes!"

"Since when did you buy three melons?" Mrs. Pope scanned the contents of Dolly's basket. "Or three croissants? Or three of anything?"

Dolly's face went blank. She had no idea what expression to put on.

"A funny thing," said Mrs. Pope. "I swear a jeep stopped outside the consulate villa the other day. Without a number plate."

"Oh, Mrs. Pope," said Dolly in a rush. "They have a baby now. They're lovely women when you get to know them. They're not evil. I swear it. On my children's lives. You don't know them. . . ."

Mrs. Pope straightened. "But, Dolly, dear, you have no children." She reached for her wrist, and squeezed hard. "Where are they, Dolly? I know you know."

Dolly burst into tears and told Mrs. Pope everything.

49

Mrs. Pope

Mrs. Pope hesitated as she picked up the phone. She had been made a fool of twice. Not just the embarrassment with the knitted rockets, but now the recent business with the French police. They had driven all the way to Poum and found the British man, just as she'd said, but his paperwork was exactly as it should have been. There were no dangerous women. They had asked at the café: no one had seen them in weeks. The head of the French police had complained to Maurice. He had suggested his wife should not be wasting police time.

Mrs. Pope took a deep breath. She dialed the operator. Prepared her best voice.

She had wanted to be an actress when she was young. People always said it: "What a little actress! She should be on the stage!"

And even though her parents resisted at first, she had persuaded them to let her try. She'd had a private teacher who taught her how to walk with a book on her head, how to tuck in her derrière. An elocution teacher taught her how to stand on a chair and recite Shakespeare—she could still summon the lines—*"Make me a willow cabin at your gate"*—and if she did, she could feel the expectation. The certainty. The fierce thrill of being watched.

She felt it now.

"Number, please?" asked the operator in French.

But Mrs. Pope hesitated.

She was remembering the day she had auditioned for the Royal Academy of Dramatic Art. It was a memory she kept away from herself, but suddenly it was back. She remembered waiting outside the audition room, in her best frock, with other young women who looked more bohemian. She remembered walking with her straight spine into the audition room, wishing the panel a very good afternoon and clearly stating her name, asking for a chair and getting on top of it without bending her spine, and reciting *"Make me a willow cabin"* in her best frock and hat, with her white gloves, and in her best clear voice.

It had occurred to her she was shouting. It had occurred to her she should not be on a chair. It had occurred to her she could not remember what came next.

A delicious warm sensation down her legs.

The appalled politeness of the examiners.

The bohemian girls noticing the back of her frock as she fled. Putting their hands to their bohemian mouths to hide their bohemian laughter.

Her mother slapping her in the car because she couldn't stop crying in front of the chauffeur.

Her parents packed her off to all the parties. She was engaged within six months, and on her way to the South Pacific a year later. And her life, which should have been one of Shakespeare and touring and greasepaint, was a round of cocktail parties and staying thin, and sheer stockings even when the thermometer hit ninety-six. It was going to bed fully made up, not because you had a play to do but because your husband must never realize your eyes were on the puffy side, and you had new wrinkles spreading out like feathers. Her life was not about remembering Shakespeare's verse, but people's names, and being interested in nickel mines when she couldn't have given a damn. It was about keeping out of the sun for fear of freckles, and dressing up like Cupid in homemade wings, and never saying the wrong thing—how she wanted to swear—and not wolfing an entire plate of canapés even though her stomach was so starved and empty it was crunching inside her sodding Playtex girdle. It wasn't even that she disliked the two women. Not really. It was that they had found a way to be themselves.

"Number, please?" repeated the operator.

Mrs. Pope cleared her throat, and spoke in her best French.

"Good afternoon, Operator. Please will you put me through to the French police, and afterward the editor of *The Times* in London?"

50

No, I Am Not Traveling by Mule

She felt almost calm. They were back in the jeep, they barely had enough fuel to get halfway up the island, let alone to the far north, but they had money and she could do this. Enid sat in the passenger seat with Gloria in her arms, shrieking every time a bird so much as flew overhead. Margery drove north methodically, thinking of nothing except where she was going, just as she had driven south only a week earlier, though this time it was broad daylight. With no license plate, and no paperwork, she must take care to keep out of trouble.

Dolly Wiggs had come tearing toward the summerhouse, screaming at Margery to hurry because they would soon be at the villa. No time to grab anything except the basics. Diapers, formula milk, a wad of banknotes from Dolly, and baby clothes for Gloria. "Quick," she had shouted. "Quick!" She would hold off the police for as long as she could, and if they asked questions, she would send them in the wrong direction. In parting, Margery had taken Dolly in her arms and hugged her hard.

"I gave the game away!" Dolly sobbed. "I let you down!"

"You didn't, Dolly. You saved our lives. And I will pay you back, as soon as I've sold my collection."

The jeep spluttered and banged, but Margery kept her foot on the accelerator, scanning the rearview mirror for police cars, steadily making her way past the port and shantytowns toward the west coast road. They passed banana groves, abandoned trucks, goats, some boys on bikes—

"What is that?" screamed Enid.

Margery braked so hard that Enid flew forward in her seat and saved Gloria only by jamming her hand against the dashboard. Trees. Ahead, the west coast route was entirely blocked by trees. They lay, felled across the road, as vast as pillars. But even worse than the trees were the number of police cars parked in front of them. The officers stood around, laughing and smoking, while others batted a cricket ball. It was practically a police party.

"Oh, no! Oh, no! Oh, no!" yelped Enid.

Margery shifted into reverse but the gearbox got stuck, and the jeep jerked forward instead. She tried again: same thing. An officer noticed and began a slow swagger toward them. "I can't look!" yelped Enid. "I can't bear it!"

Margery said, in her calmest voice, "Enid, you really have to stop doing this. Can't you fall asleep?"

Enid tried. She slid down the seat with Gloria, and slapped her free hand over her eyes. "We'll never make it."

Margery swung the car to the right. No alternative but to cut across the island and use the east coast road. Briefly Enid unhid her eyes and had the presence of mind to check the Reverend Horace Blake's pocket guidebook. "He doesn't mention any problems with the east coast road," she said. "There are just some pictures of banana trees."

The landscape quickly transformed from lush green to a red and scarred terrain, cat-scratched by mining exploitation, the hills terraced into scores of concentric circles and rivulets. The road was bony with ridges; the tires struck potholes every ten minutes. Margery had to swivel the wheel sharply to avoid them. But there was little sign of life—it was more like a wasteland—and the road was now no more than a track, the mountains to their left looking bare and gouged, almost decapitated in parts.

"Is anyone following us, Enid?"

"No, Marge. It's all clear."

The track climbed. It twisted. It rose like a wall. Skin glued with sweat, Margery kept her nerve. The jeep forged on. Enid scanned the horizon, but there was still no one coming after them. Briefly the wind picked up, and the air clouded with dust, but Margery held firm to the steering wheel.

Then, just as she thought they were safe, the dust cleared, revealing a parked police car straight ahead. Blue light flashing. Enid tightened her grip round Gloria. "Oh, no, oh, no," she groaned. "This is it. We have no license plate. What will we do now?"

Margery slowed. It was too late to go back the way they'd come, and impossible to plough forward. The policeman stepped out of the car and motioned at her to stop. She did so, not as smoothly as she might have hoped but at least she hadn't run him over. He threw away a cigarette and then yanked at the waist of his trousers. A pair of handcuffs hung from his leather belt.

"Enid?" Margery whispered. "Can't you do something? Can't you open your top?"

Enid gasped, appalled. "I'm a *mother*. What do you take me for? You do it."

"Me?"

"Yes. You have plenty up there. You open your top. Or flash him your legs. Show him what you're made of."

"He'll think he's being assaulted by a music hall act. Have you looked at me recently?" She was staring straight at the police car. The policeman had gone back to check his cigarette was properly extinguished. There was something unexpectedly careful about the way he lifted his boot and twisted the toe on the ground. The truth hit her. "Enid? Opening my top will not work. And neither will flashing my legs. He's a woman."

"Wait. The policeman is a woman? How can that be?"

"I don't know. But it's a woman."

"No. I have never seen a policewoman. When did that happen? They don't have women policemen in New Caledonia."

"Well, maybe on the east coast they do. Or maybe she's the policeman's wife and the policeman is sick today so she's doing the rounds on his behalf. I don't know. We have no time to debate this fascinating subject. She's coming toward us, Enid." She tightened her fingers around the wheel to still the tremor in her hand.

The policeman/woman was now standing right beside the jeep. She was as broad as the uniform, with her black hair tied in a ponytail and two small curls hanging on either side of her face in loops. She gave a polite knock on the window.

"Bon *shoor*," said Margery, incredibly sweetly.

"*Ou allez-vous?*"

"She wants to know where we're going," said Enid.

"We can't tell her where we're going," said Margery. Followed by "Bon *shoor*," again to the policewoman, who was waiting patiently.

"*Passeports?*"

"She wants our passports."

"Yes, Enid. I know. I worked that one out."

"We don't have any."

"I am aware of that, too."

"You have no visa. Your visa has run out. What will we do? This is terrible."

"Enid, could you possibly stop talking and just smile?"

"*Passeports,*" repeated the policewoman. "*Papiers.*"

Margery pulled out her handbag and produced a wad of Dolly's cash. The policewoman looked briefly taken aback. Not only had they just met the only policeman in the world who was actually a woman, but she had principles. "*Non,*" she said. "*Merci, mais non.*"

"Marge?" hissed Enid. "What are you doing? You think you can bribe her?"

The policewoman cast her eyes over the inside of the jeep. Margery watched, barely daring to breathe, as the woman carefully took everything in: the steering wheel, her handbag, the Reverend

Horace Blake's pocket guidebook, a jerrican of water, the red valise, Enid, the baby. She nodded and then stepped back to examine the exterior. . . . The handcuffs at her waist gave a little clink clink.

"It's over now, it's over," said Enid through clenched teeth.

There was no arguing with her. In a matter of moments, the policewoman would see the jeep had no license plate. Then she would ask again for their papers. Margery's mind went blank. She couldn't move. She was conscious of a dull stinging somewhere in her body, an aching, a tremendous heaviness. All she wanted was to sleep. And then an idea came to her. Without even thinking about it, in fact before she could think about it, Margery knew what to do. She knew how to rescue the situation. As if it had shot straight from the sky, a useful everyday French phrase landed in her mind. She spoke in perfect French, complete with rolling *r*'s and buzzing *s*'s: "I am going to the next village to sell my grandmother's hens!"

The policewoman paused. She blinked. *"Comment?"*

Margery said it again.

The policewoman stared, she cocked her head, she stroked the two little looped curls on either side of her ears, then suddenly she grinned. And that was it. That, apparently, was all the situation required. That one terribly useful everyday French sentence. *"Ah, bien sûr! Bien sûr!"* She stepped aside, merrily waving them goodbye. Merrily Margery waved back. They were through.

After that the road was quiet. They stopped every now and then so that she could refill the jerrican with water from a fountain. She bought more petrol. They traveled without speaking, barely able to believe they had got away, and because it was better for their thirst if they kept their mouths closed. It was a strange journey, this new one, where the only question was what would happen next. Clearly they needed to get off the island as soon as possible. No more waiting to be done.

Margery took a corner, narrowly missing a man gesticulating at them wildly, then turned another corner and swerved to a complete halt. She was lucky to slam her foot on the brake in time.

"Oh, no, oh, no!" gasped Enid yet again.

The Reverend Horace Blake was prone to exaggeration. Moments of poetry. Margery could forgive him those. Besides, one of his useful everyday phrases had just saved their lives, or at the very least put the police temporarily off their trail. But what he'd failed to mention anywhere in his passage on "The Beautiful East Coast Road" was that it stopped south of Hienghene, on account of the river. And not a stream, not a brook: a great channel of foaming dirty water, thirty feet wide, gushing down the mountain, like sand from a chute, complete with whirlpools, vapors, and spume, and rising even as they watched. The noise was extraordinary. There was no bridge. No tunnel. There was just road. Raging wild river. Then, across on the other side, happy road again.

"I reckon I can do it," said Margery.

Enid screamed. "Have you lost your mind? I have a baby. There's only one way to cross this." She flung out her arm and pointed to the water's edge.

A collection of the world's most villainous-looking mules waited, overseen by a band of boys, whose collective age could not have been more than thirty. Barefoot, smeared with mud, their bare bellies distended above the elastic bands of their gym shorts, they were already waving at Margery and shouting, "Thees way! *Vite! Vite!* Thees way for tourists! We take *voiture*! You go by moool!"

"We are not going by mule," said Margery.

"Are you joking?"

"We can wait for the ferry."

"Margery, there is no ferry. Get on a mule."

"I can't."

"You can't?"

"I'm terrified of mules. I got bitten once. Enid, I cannot go on a mule. It will bite me."

"Margery, if you do not get on a mule, I will bite you."

Margery would not have done it to save her own life. Whether she would have done it for Enid was doubtful. But she gave in. For Gloria's sake, she gave in. She agreed to mount a mule.

• • •

The arrangement was that they would cross the river through the shallows, while the boys drove the jeep. According to the boys, they knew where the rapids lay, and the most dangerous currents. But she needed to hurry. *Vite!* The river was rising because of the cyclone, and if they did not leave straightaway, it would be too dangerous: they would have to wait at least a few days. But the money they were asking was extortionate. She offered half. They laughed and walked away. "Marge!" yelled Enid. "Just pay!"

The river rushed by, full of fast-moving driftwood, jetsam, leafy boughs, and several trees. In the end she gave the boys all but twenty francs.

A scrap of a child, no older than ten, leaped into the driving seat of the jeep and began to rev the engine. In moments he was zooming toward the water. The other boys hurried their animals closer.

Margery had been right to spend her adult life avoiding mules: they were not supposed to be ridden. Also, owing to her size, and possibly her attire, the boy in charge had allocated her one that looked like the kind of mule people didn't normally mount. The kind of mule that carried bags at the rear. It couldn't even be bothered to stand up.

The mule boy thwacked Margery's mule. This seemed foolish. The mule rose, one furious leg at a time, and stared at her, then drew the black skin from its gums to reveal a full working set of hideous yellow teeth. It was like a direct message. Mule to Margery. Actually, less a message, more an extremely nasty threat.

"Quick! Quick!" shouted Enid, whose sweet, docile mule had actually bent its legs—*bent its legs*—to enable her to take hold of the reins, and spring up. Within moments she was sitting astride her mule, holding Gloria.

Margery grabbed the part of the mule that looked least mule-ish: the leather saddle. As she lifted one leg and hauled herself up, the saddle promptly slid toward her, dumping her in the river. To add insult to injury, the mule splashed her.

"Ha-ha-ha!" laughed Mule Boy.

She had no choice but to pitch herself over its back, her head and arms on one side, her rear and legs the other. Mule Boy thwacked it again, and the mule pitched forward. It was everything she could do to stay on top. Hanging on by her arms, she hauled up her legs so that she was at least in a vertical position.

No one in their right mind would describe Margery as a natural horsewoman. And nothing about riding a mule struck her as something that should happen. She knew, as she clung to the mule's lower half, and it repeatedly smacked her over the head with its tail, that she would never, ever do this again. She wouldn't even pat one or offer it a cube of sugar. But at last they were heading into the water: the other side of the river was clearly ahead. And then, just as she thought things could not possibly get worse, her mule decided it was having such a lovely time with Margery, it would take her for a swim. It was no longer going straight ahead to the other side, it was doggy paddling, with Margery hanging on, in splashy circles. Already, Enid had dismounted on the other side, and waited with Gloria. The jeep was dripping water, but also parked on the other side.

It came to her suddenly that Barbara had once said, "Well, if you think I'm cross, you can think again. I simply won't notice you until you finish your greens."

Margery pretended she was indifferent. She said to the mule— which was probably not an English speaker but so what? She was desperate: "I don't care. You can swim as much as you like. I'm not bothered." She affected an attitude of bored indifference. She even whistled.

The mule gave up its swim and trotted calmly to the other side.

The sky was a lamp of stars by the time they got to Poum. Margery banged at the door of the café until the owner appeared at the window, sleepy-eyed and confused. It was his wife who came up with a plan. ("I didn't even know he *had* a wife," said Enid.) They knew a man with a fishing boat. In twenty-four hours, Margery would need to be ready at the bay: there was bad weather expected in the day but the fisherman would take them out under cover of night. There wouldn't be much room for luggage, but he would do it. He would help them leave New Caledonia.

By way of payment, Margery offered him the Reverend Horace Blake's pocket guidebook. It was all she had left.

"Ha-ha," howled his wife, pointing at the pictures. *"Comme c'est drôle!"*

They approached the bungalow slowly, too scared to look. But, once again, it had not failed them. Everything was almost exactly as they had left it. The door was closed, the roof intact. Inside, nothing had been smashed or flooded; if anything, the bungalow had been tidied. Discarded blankets and towels were now folded. Bowls that had contained water were dry and arranged in a line. The mattress Enid had used as a nest was now back in her room; her Baby Jesus painting hung at a straight angle on the wall; the chairs on the veranda were carefully positioned to admire the view. It was only really in Margery's study that she got the strangest sense of malice. Things had clearly been picked up and shoved back in different places—some specimens were not packed in lint in the boxes where she'd left them but unwrapped and scattered on the floor. A notebook was open, a tin of Spam discarded, a tray was even in a different place. Nothing had been destroyed as such but it had definitely been touched and prized apart. She counted the specimens, trying to work out if anything was missing—again, she had the strangest sense there was. But, then, the last time she had been in her study was a week ago, when Enid was so ill, and her thoughts had been a jungle. Immediately she began to repack specimens and order her papers. In twenty-four hours, they would be free.

"I have an idea," said Enid, that night. They were sitting side by side on the veranda. Gloria was asleep, and Enid had started flicking through one of Margery's old beetle books as if it were a travel guide. "Borneo," she said. "There's lots of nice beetles there. See?"

She held up the book. Upside down, but never mind. "We should go to Borneo. I reckon it's hot there. We could find a little hut. Change our names. I have a good name for you, Marge."

"Oh?"

"Trixie Parker."

"Are you serious? 'Trixie Parker' sounds like a showgirl."

"Well, you have the legs for it, Marge. I'm just telling you. You can be what you like. You're an amazing woman. I never thought you could pull this off. And you're funny, too. I think you're funny. I never had a friend like you."

"I never had a friend like you either, Enid."

"I'm sorry we never found your gold beetle. Maybe it's in Borneo."

"Why would it be in Borneo?"

"I don't know. I just have an idea."

They went quiet, watching the moon. A ragged cloud passed over it, silvery white. "We won't give up, Marge. We'll keep looking for beetles. There are some real beauties out there."

Suddenly Margery laughed. But this time it wasn't what Enid had said that made her feel light inside. She said, "Enid, I've just realized the date. It's my forty-seventh birthday. I'm forty-seven today."

Enid squeezed her hand. Remarkably painful, even for a new mother. "Next stop, Borneo. The cocktails are on me."

51

London, February 1951

There were no more headlines about Nancy Collett or the Woman With No Head. Their story didn't even make the back pages. An electric beginning, all the ingredients for a big trial, possibly a double hanging, then nothing. Not only had both women disappeared, but there was no progress in the case, except for some evidence that just made everything more complicated.

Namely: the brother of the deceased had come forward with a letter from Percival Collett in which he stated his intention to end his life by whatever means he could. It didn't exonerate his wife, but she couldn't be described as cold and calculating anymore. Even more compromising, there were rumors he was a homosexual. And since the botched hanging of Norman Skinner, many people had begun to question the notion of capital punishment. There had been protests outside prisons. Petitions. As for the Woman With No Head, also known as Margery Benson, it appeared she had simply been going on a big holiday.

Fortunately, plans for the Festival of Britain were now in full flow—a milestone between past and future, to enrich the present—and everyone wanted to read about that. The exhibitions, architecture, technology, the very best of British in science, industry, and the arts. People had suffered years of war: they had lost too much that they loved and been crushed by rationing. Now they wanted to think about the future, and they wanted hope. In London, the largest dome in the world, standing ninety-three feet tall, would hold exhibitions celebrating discovery not only in the New World, but also at sea and in outer space. A cigar-shaped tower, the Skylon, gave the impression of floating above the Earth. A new plush concert hall, the Royal Festival Hall, already stood on the South Bank. The Telekinema promised 3D film and large-scale television. And, for once, it wasn't just London: the festival was for everyone in Britain. It would be nationwide.

A country that had spent years in rationing, in gray and brown, was coming alive with the promise of color and new possibility. Barely anyone cared about Nancy Collett and her accomplice with no head.

So even though a new sighting of the two suspects came through to *The Times*, it was from some woman yelling down the phone from an obscure little island no one had heard of, let alone been to. The editor let it go. What was the point, he asked his deputy, in giving people the stories they no longer wanted?

Britain had moved on.

52

Living Jewels

Dawn came. The loveliest so far. The steps, the veranda, the dirt garden were all shuttered in gold. Out in the forest, an enormous tree she'd never even noticed suddenly burst into flower, with buds like candles. It was good to be here for the last time, and clear themselves out of the place that had become home. Like last rites, thought Margery, not that she'd ever observed any.

They would take the fishing boat and get off the island. Make their way to Australia. Change their names. Keep moving. She would sell her flat in London. Take work where she could. When she thought about the future, she saw herself, Enid, and the baby, nothing else.

No one could get to them via the west coast road, and Margery knew from the mule boys that the river would not be passable for at least a day or two. There was nothing to do but wait until midnight for the boat. Outside she buried a little pile of the worst of the rags, then carried the old chairs back to the garden. She left a few pots, a few pans in the kitchen, the very last tins of Spam, in case the boys from the shantytown needed them. In her study, she packed away her notes and journals. Wrapped her specimen trays in the blankets. She left Enid's rug where it was, to cover the weak spot in the floor, then washed diapers for Gloria. She made up bottles of Dolly's formula milk, in case Enid needed to sleep.

Mother and baby were lying on a blanket on the veranda. Enid was already dressed in her pink travel suit, ready to depart, with the red valise next to her packed with baby clothes. Margery was just at the top of the steps when Enid opened one eye. "You're going for a last look, aren't you?"

"No, Enid, I'm not. I'm hanging out diapers."

Enid laughed, pulled Gloria close, and began to feed her. "Don't be late for Borneo. There are two gin and limes out there, and they've got our names on."

Margery picked her way barefooted across the garden. It was already midafternoon, but the sky was one of those blue ones that looks as if it will stay that way forever. Margery kept her back to the mountain as she pegged the diapers on the line. She didn't want to see it, yet she could sense it. She could sense it as clearly as if it were tapping her on the shoulder.

Years later, she would still not be able to explain the wildness that suddenly came over her. The strange whipping up, like being yanked by the neck and hurled toward a cliff edge, the quickening of her breath, the goosebumps prickling her arms, and the feeling of lightness that followed, as if she were already free-falling. Possibly it wouldn't have come at all, if Enid hadn't planted the idea. It was as absolute and undeniable as the moment she'd picked up the lacrosse boots and walked out of her job all those months ago. Margery threw down the washing basket. She turned to the mountain fast, as if she might catch it moving.

The elephant grass lay flat but the path they'd once cleared was already overgrown. The new leaves were a lighter green, but the lianas had swung back into a closed curtain, the ferns were tall, and boulders blocked the way. High up, threads of mist sewed the two-pronged peak, and birds of prey drifted, smaller than feathers. Everything seemed so still. She ran forward. Hauled herself over the first rock.

It was easy. Without shoes, she felt nimble. And she knew which plants to hold on to, which to avoid. Creepers hung like braids, and she swished them to the side, bowing her head. Higher. A little higher. Plenty of time. She balanced on the balls of her feet.

Quickly, she reached the real thick of the forest. Her blood was pumping, her mouth dry as paste, the old weakness in her hip playing up again, her lower legs sore, but she could do it. She heard a caw, a twitch, a boom, the rustling of water. She pressed on. Three red parrots flew out. She pressed on. A trace of smoke. She hauled herself over another boulder. The bare soles of her feet tingled and felt good. Then, in the time it would take to turn and begin to climb back the way she had come, there was a smell of cold, and a mist dropped, billowing out of the sky, blotting out treetops, shooting at her, as if from an explosion. She was surrounded. Driven into a pool of white emptiness.

The mist would go: it had come fast. But she hugged her arms, suddenly chilled. Even sound had gone. All she had to do was turn round and go carefully back the way she'd come, but she couldn't see it—she couldn't see a thing.

And now she wasn't thinking, or planning; she was trying to feel her way back down, through this blindfold of mist. Branches nicked her skin, snagged her hair. She could barely breathe. Her bare feet were stumbling, slipping, twisting. Stung. She went on and on, scrambling clumsily, reaching for things that were not there, even crawling sometimes on her knees.

She was lost. Lost in a mist up a mountain, while Enid was down below in the bungalow, waiting. She kept going. Flailing. Pushing. Then her foot came down on something razor sharp. She could feel it open like a knife through a piece of fruit.

Exhausted, terrified, knowing she was defeated, but also not knowing what more to do, she stopped. She sat down. She had crossed the world to find her father's beetle and yet here she was, behaving like her mother, a woman who'd never done anything with her life except stay in a chair.

"Help me," she said. "Please. Help me." She didn't even know whom she was talking to. Whatever it was, it wasn't logical.

The mist didn't go immediately. She had to wait, and it felt like hours. And maybe it was only because she was staring at it now, instead of fighting, but bit by bit, she could detect a movement, a thinning out, a shifting, until a white ball of light emerged high above, like a blind eye, that she knew must be the sun. A stone revealed itself at her foot. A blurred red shape became a flower. The mist parted, rolling back, pouring away, and the world came to life once more. Trees. Stones. A crown of blue above. She was in some kind of glade.

At first she thought it had snowed. White flakes lay all round her. But they weren't snow; they were tiny frilled wax-white flowers on deep purple spikes, the blooms so small she could barely see the individual petals, with green leaves the size of her fingernail. The air smelled so sweet it was heavy.

No sooner had the word "orchid" formed itself in her mind than she saw a flash of gold. And not one. Many. Clasped like tiny gold jewels to the white flowers and the green leaves and the trees above and the vast fronds and rocks. Hundreds of thousands of gold beetles. The more she looked, the more she saw. They were popping out everywhere. And, for the first time, she had no killing jar. She didn't even have a net.

She would grab one. There were enough. She scanned the clearing. As if by magic, a specimen flew down and landed on her left wrist. She stared in wonder. Tiny gold head, thorax like a gold puffy skirt, tiny gold legs, long antennae like a gold tiara. It was the most dressed-up little extrovert she'd ever seen.

One swift movement of her right hand, she'd have it.

But before she could twitch so much as a muscle, the beetle opened its elytra and unfolded a second set. Even its delicate papery wings were gold. And for some reason it did not fly away. It opened and shut its wings in a kind of butterfly stroke—how lightly they performed the task of taking life forward. Then it closed everything compactly again, the soft wings folding and folding in their simple and yet infinitely complicated way beneath the hardened shell of the elytra. It crept closer to her knuckle. She couldn't

believe her luck. A suicidal beetle. It was practically turning itself in.

She looked at the tiny brilliant thing on the back of her hand.
She looked and looked. She could not feel its weight, yet its presence on her skin was like being seared.

Enid had been right. She had been right all along. Margery's
adventure was not about making her mark on the world: it was
about letting the world make its mark on her. That she and Enid
had survived, that she had found a beetle that until this moment
had lived in her imagination, that Enid had had a baby, that Margery had delivered this child, that she could still breathe in and out,
that the world was in one piece after so much devastation, all this
was a miracle. There was no need for her to kill the beetle or pin it
or name it after her father. It was enough to know she'd seen it
once, and would probably never see it again. She would leave the
discovery of the beetle for someone else.

And suddenly she felt as if she were spread over the whole island, and inside things, too. Never in her life had she felt so near
that porous line where her own body finished, and the earth began.
And blessed. She felt blessed.

Another beetle made a landing on her shoulder. Then one more,
alighting on her nose. Three on her right arm. Two on her elbows,
a whole batch on her foot. They were falling on her, like gold rain.
And Margery Benson, who had not picked up a toy since the day
her father had stepped out of the French windows, was up a mountain, on the other side of the world, reaching up her fingers, jigging
an arm, wobbling her arse. She had the strangest feeling she was
not alone, that her brothers were there, her aunts, her father, even
her mother and Barbara. They were all there, playing with a hundred thousand gold beetles, as if joy was the most serious thing—
and, what was more, a hundred thousand gold beetles were playing
with them. She felt more alive than the world itself.

It was getting dark by the time she scrambled down the end of the
path and crossed the garden to the bungalow. The rickety silhou-

ette of the Last Place was ahead, with its broken steps and veranda, lit up from inside by a hurricane lamp. Already she could make out Enid's profile at the window.

"Enid!" she yelled. "Enid!" She waved.

But as she got close, it was not Enid she could see at the window. It was someone else. A face she didn't know. Spotting her, he waved.

Margery scanned the gloom. In flashes, she saw the dirt track. The dusty garden. Diapers on the line. No sign of Enid. The baby. Her red valise. They'd gone.

53

Almost There

He was hunched by the window in the light of the hurricane lamp. All around him, moths flapped against the walls of the bungalow, throwing papery shadows. She had no idea who he was.

Enid was there, too. She sat in a chair in the corner with Gloria clutched tight to her shoulder. Bright pink. Black-and-yellow hair. Spine stiff. She looked terrified. Catching Margery's eye, she gave the smallest shake of her head. A vein in her neck seemed to quiver.

As Margery stepped forward, he straightened. "Hello," he said. He sounded nervous, unsure, and yet relieved. He looked desperately ill. His face was hollow and gray, the bones poking out of him. His clothes were rags; his skin blistered and slashed; his short hair matted. Barely human. Something hung from his back like a punctured balloon. She realized it was an old haversack.

Horror clawed her skin. Her first thought was to get Enid and the baby out of the bungalow, but she had underestimated him. She'd only glanced from Enid to the door when he pushed past, jerkily, blocking her path. He kept one hand in his pocket. She wondered if he was hurt.

"I thought you'd gone without me, Miss Benson."

It was like falling down a step that she hadn't seen, and trying to keep her balance. She felt hollowed. So he was British. He knew her name. Not only that, he knew she had been living here, and that she was planning to leave soon. She sensed it would be a good idea to address him by name, too, if only she knew what it was.

Panic made her stupid. She couldn't think. Her brain could only produce fleeting and useless images of men in the dining room on the RMS *Orion,* or the migrant camp at Wacol, men at the British consul's cocktail party, customs officers and policemen. But none was a match for this fragile one in front of her, who had now inched so close he could reach out and touch her hair. Sweat was running off him.

"Who are you?"

He blinked. Astonished. He gave a short laugh as if he didn't believe what she'd just said. "You don't remember me?"

"Did I teach your sister?"

"No."

"You work at the Natural History Museum?"

"Of course I don't." He gave a nervous laugh, like a child beginning to lose confidence.

This was worse than being stuck with Rumpelstiltskin. The guessing could go on for years. He said, "You didn't want me to lead your expedition. But you were wrong. I came, too."

With an almighty thud, she got there. She remembered where she'd met him. Lyons Corner House. The man who'd been a prisoner of war. But what was he doing here on the other side of the world? Shivering in the front room of a bungalow that barely anyone knew about? Her heart began to move like a train.

She said, "What do you want?"

"What do I want?" he repeated, as if he hadn't thought of this question before or, rather, as if he was no longer sure of the answer. "What do I want?" He wandered in a loose zigzag from the door, and back to the window. Watching him, she felt suffocated. "What do I want?"

"You look ill. Are you ill?"

He ignored her. "I was on the ship. I found you at the bottom of the stairs. I took you to the nurse. If it wasn't for me, you would never have got here. I have been following you all this time. I saved your life, Miss Benson. We're together now."

She barely moved yet she caught Enid's eye, and saw the terror there. Her mind was trying to shift back to the ship, but it was so hard to think of anything except the present. He glanced at Enid briefly, as if she was some kind of hindrance. And then Margery got it. Dimly she remembered the ship's sick bay, a man helping her to her feet, how she had curled into him briefly, wanting to stay asleep.

"I told you," said Enid, in a steady, quiet voice. "I told you someone was on our trail. I just thought it was me he was after. Not you."

"I have been with you all the time," he said. "But I'm sick. It's over now. It's time to finish this, once and for all."

She went white. She could feel it. Her breath emptied from her chest and her blood froze over. She had no idea how to move. Then, carefully using his free hand, he dug into his pocket and pulled something out. The hand opened, and at first it was hard to see because his palm was so dirty and cut, but there in the middle was her missing beetle. Its pin was gone and so was the label, its legs were not splayed but squashed, at least two were missing, the elytra gone, the antennae mangled. It was one of the most pitiful things she'd ever been given.

"You see?" he said.

"Yes. I see."

"I brought this back."

Her mouth dropped but the voice that spoke was not hers. It came from Enid: "Marge, be very careful." She had her hand cupped over Gloria's head, the way she did when it rained. "What's he got in his other pocket, Marge?"

Mundic ignored Enid. He just kept staring at Margery. His face continued to pour sweat.

"Mr. Mundic, you should go now," said Margery. "You should leave."

"I made notes, too. Like you said."

He leaned down and placed the squashed beetle with great care on the floor. Standing upright, he flapped impatiently through his pocket, still not using his right hand: that remained hidden.

"Don't go near him, Marge," called Enid. "Keep your distance."

He grunted, twisting his hand in his pocket, frustrated with the effort of trying to free whatever it was.

"Marge, I don't like this," said Enid.

At last he had it. He pulled out a notebook and thrust it forward. He held it toward her, stabbing the air.

"You want me to read this?"

She took it, but her hands had begun to shake. Inside, the pages were yellowed, many coming loose, and others marked with rust from the two thin metal staples holding it together. The writing was tiny, as if a child had been doing pretend writing. The words went up pages, down them, even at a diagonal slant. She couldn't make sense of a single one.

"Is it good work?" he said.

"Yes. Very."

"Read it out."

"What is it?" Enid's voice came again from the door, stripped and thin. "What's he given you?"

"I don't know."

It was the wrong thing to say. Mundic flipped. Too late, she remembered the balls of spittle flying from his mouth as he shouted at her in Lyons Corner House. "Read it!"

Mundic's right hand shot from his pocket and instinctively Margery ducked, while Enid screamed from the door.

He was pointing Taylor's gun straight at Margery. The barrel was no more than a foot from her chest.

Something fell right through her. She staggered backward and crashed into a hard edge with her shoulder that turned out to be the hurricane lamp. It swung, it dropped, it hit the floor. It struck hard but didn't go out, so now they appeared to be lit from the feet upward. She snatched a glance at the chair. Enid and the baby were gone.

Suddenly Margery felt a strap of tightness round her chest. Had she been shot? Was she hurt? She hadn't heard the gun, and if she'd been shot, surely she'd be bleeding, or on the floor, or in actual pain, but she wasn't, she was still standing, and Mundic was still pointing the gun at her. Never in her life had she been so unsure what would happen next.

When her voice came it sounded rusty. "Please, let's put down the gun. I will read your notes. If that's what you would like, I can do that. But please, please, put down the gun. It's not safe, Mr. Mundic."

He kept the gun pointed at her. He shifted the weight on his feet, as if he couldn't find his balance. He didn't seem to know what should happen next, either. If anything, he seemed to be waiting for her next move.

At this point something pink charged through the door. Enid was wielding a frying pan as if she were about to offer someone a cooked breakfast—but no: she raised the pan and smashed it over Mundic's head. The assault seemed not to concuss so much as baffle him. He dropped the gun. It went skittering toward the corner.

"You?" he said, delivering a punch to Enid's rib cage that sent her reeling. "Why are you always in my way?"

Gloria? Where was Gloria? Margery cast around, desperate.

"She's safe in the kitchen," gasped Enid.

Like a demented chef, Enid now produced more culinary items with which to bang Mundic. Sticks, spoons, a tin bowl: they came whizzing through the air with the force of missiles. Mundic ducked left, he ducked right; only a few hit home. Coconuts, tinned Spam, half a yam, her Miss Lovely Legs trophy, a shower of loose hair grips. She even grabbed her Baby Jesus painting and smashed it over his head, following this with a knee to the groin. Mundic screamed.

"Run, Marge! Get out!"

But before Margery could move, Mundic twisted round and grabbed Enid by the neck. With a roar, he hauled her off the floor. She kicked and jabbed at the air; it made no difference. Teeth bared, he kept hold of her throat so that she could do nothing but wriggle.

Margery lunged toward him. A white dart of pain shot through her hip and sent her sideways. She grabbed another tin of Spam, and hurled it at his head. It missed. He staggered with Enid toward the door and pitched her through it, so that she went flying over the veranda. He had just thrown her best friend out of the bungalow.

Margery had never been a violent woman but she had—with reason—been an angry one. Now she saw red. Everything—the bungalow, her hands, Mundic's face—was ablaze. The pain in her hip was unbearable, but she made a lurch forward, her legs so weak her feet were all over the place, and grabbed hold of Mundic's shoulders, shaking him hard until his face began to wobble. She did not see the next part coming—his fist. It launched from behind his back and whacked her so full in the mouth it bloomed like a hot stinging flower. Struggling to keep her balance, she caught Mundic in both arms.

An awkward embrace, but all Margery needed was purchase. While he blinked with confusion, and reached to touch her mouth, she leaned far backward and then returned, slamming her forehead smack into his nose. A terrible crack. A hot wetness splattered Margery's face. Blood everywhere.

Mundic howled. Margery howled. Stumbling, flailing, Mundic reeled. Stumbling, flailing, Margery reeled but remained upright. She had just headbutted Mundic.

He seemed stunned. So was Margery. Her head split with pain, and flashes of white lightning obscured her sight. She could barely see. Who knew that inflicting pain on another person could be so painful? Then a hand seized her by the shoulder. Before she knew it, he was clamped to her back, riding her as if she were a mule.

She yelled. Outraged. She swung, this way, that way, trying to throw him off, but his hand was smothering her face. Only just in time did she avoid the rug that hid the dangerous weak spot in the floor. She shunted him off with one jab from her elbow, and he deflated and fell from her to the ground, knees curled in tight.

She turned to run after Enid, but he reached to catch her foot and brought her down.

This time, the fist was inevitable and swung into Margery's belly, driving the breath out of her. Blood in her mouth, blood in her hair. Impossible to tell now which blood belonged to whom: it all seemed to be outside the bodies, instead of in them. And a smell, too, a terrible smell of vinegary wet meat.

Was she dying? She didn't know. There was a pulpy substance all around her that she assumed was bog, until she remembered she wasn't in one. Then, opening her eyes, she saw, in an unfocused way, the bloodied face of Mundic peering over her.

The gun was back in his hand. But he was no longer pointing it at her. He opened his mouth to cram it inside. His eyes bulged.

Fear turned back to rage. Margery was one bleeding mass of flesh, she was winded and ready to pass out, but she crawled to what she hoped were her knees and roared, "No. You will not. You will not do this to me. No." As she made a lunge to stop him, pain shot through her legs, like bolts of electricity, so that she crashed into Enid's eel bucket and it fell on its side. Water tipped everywhere.

Then: "Snakes!" he screamed. "You said there were no snakes!"

It must have been the rain that had brought them out. Two tiny eels were moving in scribbling loops across the floor. It was the light of the hurricane lamp they were after, but Mundic didn't know that. They had no wish to harm him. He didn't know that, either. He dropped the gun, his face caught open in a silent scream, and leaped backward, crashing into the hurricane lamp, so that he lost balance and tripped over the rug, falling into it.

Beneath him, the floor opened like a trapdoor. Lamp, rug, Spam, Mundic. Everything shot through the hole and disappeared.

It was dark but the moon was full. The land was lit like a photograph. Whitened palms, and where there were gaps, the whitened ocean. No sign of the mist, except a few threads snagged in the highest branches. The first stars had begun to flicker.

Enid was lying in the dust just beyond the steps. Her body wasn't curled over, or twisted. She didn't seem in pain. She lay in her pink travel suit with her eyes closed, as if she'd fallen asleep, a boulder as a pillow. On her feet the tiny sandals she loved with the pom-poms. Her skin was dark, a patch flaking on the end of her nose, her hair loose. If anything, she looked like a child.

With great difficulty, Margery dropped to her knees. Some-where in her mind she had known the moment she caught sight of Enid that she was too late. She'd known as she lumbered down the broken steps, as she dragged herself through the grass and red dust, even now as she felt for Enid's pulse. But she kept searching with the tips of her fingers, pressing Enid's wrists, loosening Enid's collar, pressing her throat, looking for the smallest flicker of life. She called Enid's name repeatedly. She told her to come back, come back, Enid, stop this right now. Throw any surprise you like at me, Enid, but not this one, please. I'm not ready. She even shook her—not very hard—but hard enough. Then, with her two hands, she pulled Enid's face toward hers, and yanked her fingers inside Enid's mouth, and pushed her own over Enid's. Live, Enid, damn you. You wanted life. *Live.* For as long as she kept searching for a trace of life, it was possible to hope it was there, waiting, just the tiniest flicker, and Margery would not give up, she would stop at nothing, she would find it. She had saved Enid's life before: she could do it again. Enid still smelled of Enid, after all. But her ef-forts to make her alive came to nothing. Whatever she had been, it was gone. Suddenly Margery felt so cold.

She took Enid's hand. She held tight. Fragments of pictures passed through her mind, small but uncannily distinct. She saw Enid totter across Fenchurch Street station, trying to carry four suitcases and wave with her foot. "Ta-da!" Here was Enid, throw-ing open the door of their cabin on the RMS *Orion,* with flowers, a whole mountain of flowers, borrowed from first class. She saw her wiggling through rainforest with her little dog until she hoicked her frock up to her knickers and ran free. Enid had rescued her from her stunted life and Margery loved her more than she could make sense of. She kissed the back of Enid's hand and pressed it to her face, and when her tears came, she didn't try to hold them back even though they hurt like great big stones. She just held Enid's hand and sobbed. In the darkness, one face, then another, then another moved closer. The boys from the shantytown. They bowed their heads.

This was not Margery's last day in the world: she had many more to come, though barely one would pass without some memory of Enid, however faint, either in a gesture that Gloria made, or the movement of light in the trees. The cold she felt now would lessen but never go away, because her friendship with Enid had been one scorching flame. If life must go on, then so must death, and, like life, it would be a continuing story.

In the meantime, Margery had a man with a broken neck to deal with, the imminent arrival of the French police, not to mention a fishing boat making its way to Poum. But for a moment she wanted nothing more from life than to hold this human hand.

A baby's cry echoed from the bungalow. It was time to feed Gloria.

THE NATURAL HISTORY
MUSEUM, LONDON

FREYA

54

The Golden Beetle of New
Caledonia, 1983

Several years after the disappearance of Margery Benson and Nancy Collett, an anonymous parcel was delivered to the Entomology Department at the Natural History Museum, postmarked Borneo. Inside was one leather-bound notebook, sixteen drawings of a beetle no one had ever seen before, and three pinned pairs of specimens, male and female. The diagrams were impeccable. The notes gave exact descriptions of the beetle's size and appearance, its habitat—a remote peat swamp forest in Borneo—as well as accounts of its mating patterns, diet, and the wormlike larvae the female buried in the roots of swamp trees. The beetle's presence in the ecosystem was vital: its larvae fed on bugs that were attacking the roots of the swamp trees. It was labeled *Sphaeriusidus enid-prettyi.*

In the next thirty years, more anonymous parcels were sent to the Entomology Department, not regularly but every once in a while, and from all over the world. They always contained a leather-bound notebook and sixteen anatomical drawings of a new beetle, as well as three pairs of perfectly preserved specimens. No one had any idea who was sending them, but they became a mystery that the department enjoyed. For a while a story went round that one

of the deceased curators had faked his own death and was actually
back in the field.

Thirty years after the first parcel came one more, addressed not
to the Entomology Department in general, but specifically to
Freya Bartlett, the only woman working there at the time. Freya
had heard about the strange packages that turned up occasionally
and, like everyone else, she was curious as to who might have sent
them. She didn't know why but she had a feeling they were the
work of another woman. Maybe it was just her fantasy. She was
lonely, that was the truth, really lonely. Her working hours were so
long she'd given up on the idea of having a family—she couldn't
even hold down a relationship—and when she went on an expedition, she was set apart from her male colleagues by problems they
didn't have to think about. Not only periods, or where to pee safely,
not even the endless jokes about her physical strength. But the
sense she was never really going to get what she wanted. More
than a few times a colleague had reached out a hand when she
didn't need help, and squeezed too hard. She'd been talked down
and talked over. She'd missed a couple of promotions she should
have got.

And yet, deep down, she knew she couldn't really blame anyone
else. Out of some strange mad desire not to upset the status quo,
she'd become complicit. She had laughed when she should have
been angry, or said nothing when she should have said a lot. She'd
belittled her own achievements, calling them small or unformed or
even lucky when they were none of those things. And it wasn't
simply opportunities at work she'd lost out on: she had—and,
again, this was her own choice—missed the weddings of her clos-
est friends, just as she'd missed their children's christenings. Only
a month ago her oldest friend had written, inviting her to Scotland
for her godson's birthday, "But I guess it will be difficult for you to
get away." And it was true. Some nights Freya worked so late, she
took her sleeping bag out of her locker and slept on the floor under
her desk. She actually kept a toothbrush there and a set of spare
clothes.

She felt the parcel. It was thin. Too thin to hold anything of interest. Postmarked New Caledonia. She opened it.

There was no leather-bound notebook. No sixteen drawings. No perfect specimens. Just an envelope. Inside the envelope, a black-and-white photograph.

It showed two women. An entomologist and her assistant. The entomologist stood right in the center, a pretty young woman with a big smile on her face, her hand stretched out to meet the camera. Her face was round, proud, happy, as if she'd found something really exciting that she wanted people to see. Her fair hair was loose and thick; she was dressed in a frock and boots, a pair of binoculars round her neck. Freya fetched a magnifying glass. The young woman had a beetle in her hand. Hard to say from a black-and-white photograph, but it was clearly brightly colored. Maybe even gold. Couldn't be a scarab or a carabid. It wasn't round enough. Surely not a soft-winged flower beetle. No one had ever found one of those. No wonder the woman looked happy.

Freya moved her magnifying glass to the assistant. She was much older. Too old, really, to be in the field. Tall, big-boned, but frail, dressed in a man's jacket and loose trousers. She stood at a sideways angle to the camera, gazing off to one side. There was something in her hair. A flower or something. At first Freya couldn't make it out and then she realized it was a pom-pom and laughed. The old woman must also have suffered some kind of accident: one leg looked stiff and she leaned on a cane. Freya touched the photograph, wanting to know more.

It was the closeness of the two women that got to her—and their different attitudes to the camera, the young woman looking straight at the lens, while the older one gazed to the side as if a third person in the distance held her eye. As if she no longer needed to demand the attention of the world because her love for the young woman was greater. Mother and daughter? Not quite. But Freya could feel their devotion, even in a black-and-white photograph.

She looked again at the beetle in the young woman's hand. Suddenly she couldn't tell any more if this woman was showing Freya what she'd found, or inviting her to come and see for herself. Turning the photograph, she found a caption.

The Golden Beetle of New Caledonia. 1983.

Freya drifted to her desk. Already it was midmorning. She riffled through papers, picking them up and putting them down, as if none of them were the things they should be. She checked the atlas for New Caledonia and found an island shaped like a rolling pin on the other side of the world. She made a coffee that she forgot to drink. She put her eye to the microscope and failed to see. She couldn't stop thinking of the two women. They seemed to inhabit every path she had not followed, every place she did not know, every friend she had not cared for. Freya felt a sudden tingling through her skin, a wildness in her breathing. A bolt of excitement.

Swiftly she found her passport, notebooks, boots, toothbrush, and a few vials, and rolled them into her sleeping bag. She didn't know if she was going to Scotland first, or New Caledonia. She didn't know how she was going to get there, or when. But the real failure as a woman was not even to try.

And she was going.

ACKNOWLEDGMENTS

When I set out to write a book about beetles and New Caledonia, I knew nothing about either of them. While this might have put some people off, it felt (to me) a very good place to begin.

Alongside endless online maps—old and new—blogs, vlogs, websites, and articles, the following were invaluable in my research: *Pocket Guide to New Caledonia* issued by the U.S. War and Navy Department; *New Caledonia Illustrated*, 1942; *Lonely Planet Guide to Vanuatu & New Caledonia*; *Who Stand Alone*, *Things Worth While*, and *Time Well Spent* by Evelyn Cheesman; *Unsuitable for Ladies: An Anthology of Women Travellers*, edited by Jane Robinson; *The Blessings of a Good Thick Skirt*; *Women Travellers and their World* by Mary Russell; *Collecting*, Muensterberger; *Beetles* by Richard Jones; *British Beetles by* Norman H. Joy; *Fabre's Book of Insects*; *The Book of Beetles* by Patrice Bouchard; *An Inordinate Fondness for Beetles* by Arthur V. Evans & Charles L. Bellamy; *Living Jewels* by Poul Beckmann; *Beetle* by Adam Dodd; *On the Track of Unknown Animals* by Bernard Huevelmans; *Ten Pound Poms* by A. James Hammerton and Alistair Thomson; *Singled Out* and *Perfect Wives* by Virginia Nicholson; *Stranger in the House* by Julie Summers; *Austerity Britain* by David Kynaston;

Prisoner of Japan by Sir Harold Atcherley; *Burma Railway Man* by Charles Steel.

Despite all the above, I could not have gotten very far without the kindness, patience, and expert wisdom of several entomologists who not only made time to speak to me, but explained—in words I could understand—their passion for beetles and how vital it is to learn what we have in the world before it is too late. Beulah Garner, senior curator at the Natural History Museum; Adam Hart, professor of science communication, University of Gloucester; Sally-Ann Spence, Oxford University Museum of Natural History and founder of Minibeast Mayhem; Simon Leather, professor of entomology at Harper Adams University: a million thank-yous.

Thank you to BBC Radio 4 where, years ago, I heard John Humphrys roasting a man about the madly brilliant world of cryptozoology and was so hooked I had to drive straight home and look it up. From there came my idea of an undiscovered gold beetle.

Thank you to my sister Amy who read many versions and made suggestions that not only turned things around but brought them to life; to my mum, and to my sister Emily, who loved Enid so much she still can't forgive me for the ending. Thank you to my friends Niamh Cusack and Sarah Edgehill, who also read scraps of early drafts (terrible things) and urged me to keep, keep going.

Thank you to a man I never knew—my husband's great uncle Mont—who made a trip from Tilbury to Brisbane on the R.M.S. *Orion* in the fifties and kindly wrote a very long letter about it.

Thank you to Lisa Marshall for her generous advice on obstetrics and home-birthing half way up a mountain, and to Professor Dame Sue Black for knowing the answers to everything a person could ask about head wounds, suffocation, the decomposition of a human body, and how it would smell in a 1950s house without heating.

Thank you to my agent and friend Clare Conville; thank you to Jake Smith-Bosanquet, Alexander Cochran, Kate Burton, and the entire wizzy team at Conville & Walsh. Thank you to Nick Marston, Camilla Young, Katy Battcock, and all at Curtis Brown. Thank you to Clio Seraphim and the amazing team at Penguin Random House U.S.: Avideh Bashirrad, Whitney Frick, Allyson Lord, and Katie Tull. Thank you to everyone at Transworld; to my editor and friend Susanna Wadeson, who has stood by me all these years and knew when exactly to wrench this book out of my hands; to Sharika Teelwah; to Katrina Whone, Kate Samano, Josh Benn, Hazel Orme, and all Doubleday editorial; to my friend Alison Barrow, every writer's dream publicist; to Bradley Rose; to Emma Burton in marketing; Alice Twomey in audio; to Tom Chicken, Deirdre O'Connell, Emily Harvey, Gary Harley, Hannah Welsh, and all the U.K. sales reps; to Bethan Moore, Natasha Photiou, and all the international sales team; to Catriona Hillerton in production; to Richard Ogle in the art department; to Larry Finlay and Bill Scott-Kerr. Thank you to Neil Gower for the exquisite UK jacket; to Kimberly Glyder for the equally exquisite U.S. jacket. ("Never judge a book by its cover"? Get out of here.) I owe each and every one of you a small gold beetle.

Thank you to the women in my life. I wrote this for you.

Thank you, Susan Kamil. We talked about jeweled beetles and friendship over lunch at Claridge's. I wish I could have shared this with you, too.

Thank you most of all to my husband, Paul, who patiently reads every page at least six hundred times and still manages to look interested. Who has learned that even when something doesn't work, it is best to start the sentence with "Yes, it's very good. . . ." Without you, I wouldn't keep writing.

MISS
BENSON'S
BEETLE

RACHEL JOYCE

Random
House
Book Club

Because
Stories Are
Better Shared

A READER'S GUIDE

IN FICTION, ANYTHING
IS POSSIBLE

An Interview with Margery Benson and Enid Pretty

Rachel Joyce: It's very kind of you both to speak to me today. I appreciate the distance you've had to travel—not just physically but also spiritually—in order to make this happen.

Margery Benson: It's a pleasure.

Enid Pretty: And anyway, it's nice to get a change of scene.

RJ: I think it's fair to say your friendship changed your lives—

EP: Oh no. That's it. I'm crying already—

RJ: —but what did you really think of one another when you first met?

MB: I am not spoiling anything by saying it wasn't the best circumstances in which to meet a person for the first time. I thought she was awful.

[*They laugh.*]

EP: Looking back, I was the last person Marge needed.

MB: You were the last person I *thought* I needed.

EP: I was on the run. I was in shock. But Marge saved my life, right from the start. And I had watched her for a while, you know, on the station concourse. My first thought was how is this going to work? But I am an optimist. I try to make the best of things.

RJ: For me, a turning point is where you see yourself in a shop window, Margery, and realize you like yourself. Until that point, it seems to me, you've avoided seeing who you really are.

EP: I love that moment. It makes me so proud of Marge.

MB: It takes a long time for some people to face their reflection and like what they see.

EP: Oh I agree. There's such pressure on women to look like something they're not. You know. To try and turn themselves into someone else.

RJ: Does that include dying your hair?

EP: Of course it doesn't. Dying your hair is fun.

RJ: So what were the turning points for you, Enid?

EP: A real low point for me was what happened on the RMS *Orion*. It felt like everything was over.

MB: I behaved so badly. I am still ashamed to think about that day.

EP: Yes, it hurt terribly that you abandoned me. But looking back, I don't see how you could have responded in any other way. You didn't know how to at that point.

MB: It was only in meeting you that I learned how.

EP: Same for me, Marge.

RJ: Any other moments that took you by surprise?

MB: Obviously finding out the truth about Enid's past was a big turning point, though deep down I think I'd known for a while that something terrible had happened. But there were other turning points that—even though they might seem smaller—had a deeper impact. Finding Enid at the camp in Waco and realizing that money was not enough was a big turning point. I realized I wanted to be the kind of woman who could be a friend to another woman. I also believed it was too late.

EP: It was the same for me. I realized I had to take a risk and follow you to New Caledonia. Relying on a man to get me through was not the answer. Or rather, it wasn't the answer I wanted for myself any more.

RJ: What advice would you give to a young woman today?

MB: Open your own bank account.

EP: Learn how to change a car tire.

RJ: Do you think your life has been shaped by men?

MB: It's true that we both had a hard beginning, but I wouldn't want to say that made us the women we are.

EP: That would take away our spirit.

MB: I fell in love with the professor at the point in my life when I had to accept I had lost my father. You could say I replaced one lie with another.

EP: We were expected to be less than we were, and to be happy about that. I realized when I met Marge that I wasn't.

RJ: What do you miss about New Caledonia?

EP: The freedom. Definitely.

MB: There's nothing like the first expedition you make. The sense of achievement when you do something you didn't realize you could do. Coffee has never tasted the same since.

RJ: What does friendship mean to you?

MB: My feelings about friendship changed during the course of knowing Enid. I realized that before meeting Enid, I spent a lot of my time trying to throw people off the scent. It was as if I had a mask on my face—and it's also true that I couldn't bear to *see* my face.

EP: So sad.

MB: I was always cutting my head out of photographs. But Enid was not the kind of woman who respects boundaries. That was a big lesson for me.

EP: And you have to be able to disagree.

MB: Also, surprises. Enid is the person I know best in the world, and she is certainly the person who knows me best. But she never does what I expect.

EP: All I am saying here is . . . mules. That's all I'm saying.

RJ: What about you, Enid?

EP: It's funny. I knew loads of people before I met Marge but I never met someone who was so solid.

MB: Solid! That's a good word for it! And I'm even more solid now.

EP: I needed to become more like Margery, and I guess Marge needed a touch more Enid.

MB: I still can't wear pink, though.

EP: You can't. No offense, Marge, but it isn't your color.

[*They laugh so much they have to hold hands.*]

MB: The thing about friendship is that you can't have that kind of love with every one you meet. A true friendship requires that you put in time. And you have to be prepared to go the whole journey.

RJ: Mrs. Pope said of you that you hadn't a political bone between you. Is that right?

EP: She *said* that . . . ?

MB: Everything is political. Everything you do, where you shop, what you buy, how you live your life. You are a member of the world, you have opinions.

EP: Even if you don't go round shouting them.

MB: Exactly. It's still political.

RJ: You use the word "vocation" a lot. What exactly do you mean by that?

EP: Oh that's a very good question.

MB: It wasn't a word I used before I met Enid but it is a very important word. Bigger than something like "follow your dreams." Dreams imply that the thing you want to do is out of your reach, and airy. Whimsical even. A woman's vocation is an expression of who she is. There is nothing whimsical about that.

EP: It's your calling. It's the thing that hits you like being punched in the heart.

MB: You have to learn to believe in yourself despite the evidence. I felt I had a little flame of belief inside me, not a big one, but a little pilot-light-sized flame of belief.

EP: Whatever it is that you need to do, you've got to look after that belief because, let's face it, no one else is going to do it for you. I mean you could have waited your whole life, Marge, if you were hoping for someone else to tell you to go and find that gold beetle.

MB: I almost did.

EP: Yeah but you didn't. You know what I think?

MB: No. What?

EP: I think your love of life kicked in. I think it just wouldn't let you go.

RJ: Do you think that need to be brave is essential for all women? Just women?

MB: It is essential for us all, but I think women have been behind. It takes tenacity and determination to bring about change, and I know many women who have that, but I also see women who allow it to get put away.

EP: You can't always blame that on other people. You have to take— what's the word?

MB: Responsibility?

EP [*laughing*]: Exactly!

RJ: Men don't come out of this adventure especially well. There's a view that they are just stereotypes of the worst kind of masculinity. Do you think that's a problem?

MB: Nineteen-fifty was a time of terrible low after two world wars. Both men and women had suffered, and in different ways. There were men, too, who had seen such terrible things they couldn't come back from them.

EP: The society we lived in felt so narrow, we had no choice but to escape.

MB: Besides, there are plenty of stories where men go off on adventures.

EP: Yes, if men are unhappy, they can read those!

RJ: What happened to Mundic? Do you know?

MB: I heard he died in hospital. But I also heard he became a missionary.

EP: Swings and roundabouts.

RJ: What do you feel about the end of the novel?

MB: It still breaks my heart.

EP: To be honest, I haven't read it.

MB: The quality of a life is defined not by its length, but by its depth, its actions, and achievements. It is defined by our ability to love. By these criteria, Enid did a very good job with the years she was given. And I was lucky. I was lucky to get the chance to love someone so much. Every year that she is not with me, her memory becomes simpler, and I hate that.

EP: I seriously must read the ending.

MB: Seriously. I don't think you should.

RJ: Can you tell us what happened to Gloria? Did Freya find her? Did she find the gold beetle?

EP: [*laughing*] You want us to tell you *everything*?

MB: Some things are just what they are, as well as being a sign of something more. I once found a dead blue bird. It was the most beautiful thing, and so delicate. I said to myself, "Do you think it's a sign? Or just a dead bird?" It was only years later it occurred to me it was both a sign *and* a dead bird. Sometimes we have to live in the mystery.

EP: Oh that's lovely.

THE PHOTOGRAPH THAT
INSPIRED A NOVEL

For a long time, I had a feeling I was being followed. I'd look up and see someone, out of the corner of my eye. Or I'd walk into a room and feel certain that even though it was empty, someone was actually there. It wasn't frightening. Once I sensed a large figure in trousers who seemed to be very interested in our drains. Another time it was a much smaller person, sitting in the driver's seat of my car. And then it began to dawn on me that it wasn't just one person but two, and not only that—they were women. One was large, one was small, and I don't know how but I sensed they had something to tell me.

After my father died, I had a phone call with a clairvoyant. I was deep in grief and I wanted to be given some reason to believe my father was still present, and still loving me. At one point she said, "What about the two women?"

I said, "What two women?"

She said, "I see two women."

But that wasn't what I wanted to hear, and instead I asked another miserable question about my father, and that was how we went on, me asking about him and her giving answers that seemed not at all what I needed. Truthfully, the whole clairvoyant thing just left me feeling even more bereft. But a few months later, I passed two women sitting on a bench. One was whittling a large stick and the other was eating sandwiches. I turned to look again; they weren't there.

Was the clairvoyant right? Were they real? And if so, could they be something to do with my past? As a child, I had an Aunty Edith who wasn't technically an aunt but one of my grandmother's many single friends. She was a short woman, though not in any ways small, her bosom heavy like a bolster, the folds of her body packed within buttons and hooks. I liked my Aunty Edith. She had a soft voice and she smelled of violets, both of which I found comforting; also, she loved me, and because her love was all she had to give, it seemed especially pure. Then there was my mother's Aunty Gwen, another adopted aunt. She was tiny and annoyed my grandfather—a singularly gentle man—because she never stopped talking and wore red lipstick that bled from the sides of her mouth. Aunty Edith and Aunty Gwen were spinsters who had lived through two world wars. They had lost fathers and uncles in the first one, and brothers and sweethearts in the second. There was definitely something about the two women on my trail that reminded me of my aunts. Something solid; something kind. More importantly, something individual. And yet when I tried to make sense of the two women by turning them into my aunts, I saw I was wrong. Unlike my aunts these two had a life that was independent of mine. They didn't belong to me in any way. If anything, it seemed to be the other way round.

Twelve years ago, we moved to the house where we live now and I wrote my first novel, *The Unlikely Pilgrimage of Harold Fry*. I knew almost as soon as we arrived that I was supposed to be here; that's the best way I can put it. There is an energy. The night before my book was published, every piece of electrical equipment in the house switched itself on. As my husband and I stumbled round in the dark, trying to turn off light switches and fire alarms, and radios that had sprung to life, we put it down to a power cut. Only afterwards I began to sense that it might be something—some*one*—else.

Not the two . . . ?

Finally, a breakthrough. I learned that two women had owned our home in the 1920s. They had been nurses during the First World War and, shaken by what they'd seen, had come here to care for victims of stress and trauma in a more spiritual way. Describing them as "maiden ladies," an elderly neighbor told me Miss Hudson was very tall, elegant, and pale, related to the wealthy Hudson Sunlight Soap family, while her companion was altogether smaller, very dark-haired and olive-skinned. However, he didn't seem to feel they were the type who would follow people. What he mostly remembered was that they dressed like nuns and had a vacuum cleaner.

It almost fit, and yet deep down the answer still didn't feel right. One of the women I had seen wore trousers. She was also very interested in our drainage. The other, the smaller, I had caught in the act if not of stealing my car, then at the very least of driving it. After that my life got taken over by other things and I began to lose a sense of the two women. It occurred to me they might have found someone else to follow. I began working on a new novel set in 1950 about a miraculous search for a gold beetle on the other side of the world.

The reasons why you choose to tell a certain story are not always clear. I like to compare the first stages of writing to finding a house in the woods that has no windows and no doors. You long to go inside, but you have no idea how, so all you can do is keep circling it, trying to find the tiniest crack. In those early months, or possibly year, nothing about my new book was clear to me—even my protagonist kept changing. One week, it was a man. The next it was a woman. Another day she would be large and broad-shouldered. A week later, she'd gone bleach-blonde and wiry. I feared I was in something that was way too big for me—no matter how many times I circled it, there seemed to be no way in—and from there I began to tell myself I wasn't a proper writer at all. I felt lost and exhausted. Then, bang in the middle of all this, a Canadian friend came to visit. I put my writing and research to one side. We talked books, we walked. I took her for a picnic by a pond—until we were politely told by an elderly man in rust trousers that we were sitting in his garden—and finally I drove her to Kelmscott Manor, the once country retreat of Pre-Raphaelite artist William Morris.

It was a cold spring day. We admired the rooms hung with Morris tapestries, the floors smelling of wax and creaking beneath our feet. We were about to leave when my eyes landed on a small black-and-white photograph.

The hairs stood on my neck. I felt a kind of rushing of blood and a simultaneous plummeting, as if my feet had missed a step.

It was them. It was the two women. I absolutely knew it. One was older and more frail, gazing off to the side; the other, the more dominant, stood in jodhpurs, tie and jacket, dressed like a man and broad-shouldered—a large woman with short curly black hair, staring straight at the camera. She looked exactly like the woman I passed once whittling a stick, and the woman I had seen beside our drains. To be honest she also looked like the kind of woman who would know how to short fuse our electricity.

I grabbed the friend I didn't know terribly well and hugged her. We bought a postcard of the photograph in the gift shop, and as we drove away, I knew that my book was about two women—not one—and that one of them was the leader, while the other her assistant. What's more, I knew that their extraordinary and against-the-odds friendship was the beating heart of my book. The whole story suddenly made sense—the house I had been circling all that time had windows and doors after all, as well as doorknobs and tiny handles. Not only that, I understood what those two women who'd been following me wanted.

Only it wasn't me they wanted. They were asking *me* to follow *them*.

So I turned the tables. I found out everything about them. May Morris—the older of the two—was the youngest daughter of William Morris. She had been married briefly, and unhappily, and by the age

of twenty-three, she was also the director of the embroidery department at her father's company. The woman at her side, Mary Lobb,
was officially her gardener, unofficially her live-in companion. (So I
was wrong. The woman who I'd believed was the one with power, was
actually lower in status. We make mistakes all the time.) Mary liked
the land, machinery, and horses. She also liked cider and sticking
things in scrapbooks. They stayed together for twenty-two years, and
they traveled, camping in Wales, Cornwall, and Iceland. Mary threatened May's publisher when he rejected a writing idea of May's, and
May paid for operations for Mary—who was overweight and drank
too much and smoked too much—as well as a pair of pink spectacles
when her eyesight failed. On her death, May left most of her effects
to Mary. Mary died five months later, stating in her will that she should
be driven not in a hearse but in a motor lorry. She bequeathed her
entire collection of scrapbooks to the National Museum of Wales.

Search for Mary Lobb on the internet and you will find images of
her sitting astride a wall, or lounging against a haystack. She is dressed
in men's clothes. She is often controlling some kind of heavy machinery, and if she isn't, she's cuddling a small fluffy dog. She is always
staring straight at the camera, and her face is strong, open, round. As
a young woman she made the headlines of a local newspaper: *"COR-
NISH WOMAN DRIVES STEAM ROLLER. Miss Lobb, of Trenault,
a lady of independent means, is to be seen every day driving a steam
roller on the main roads near Launceston."*

The more I found out about them, the more I learned about the
two women in my book. It was as if my characters had been empty
vessels and now I had so much detail, so much love for them. Margery
Benson and Enid Pretty would not be the kind of women who sat
around, waiting for life to happen. They would be brave, they would
be unafraid, they would be full of life. Together they would travel
across the world to New Caledonia, despite the fact they had one
passport between them. They would search for a tiny gold beetle that
everyone said was not there. They would drive a jeep—no, they would
steal a jeep—they would trek up mountains, sleep in hammocks, dress
as men if they felt like it, dye their hair, travel by donkey, survive a
cyclone as well as heatstroke and insect bites. In short, they would

undertake every possible adventure I could throw at them, and even though their relationship had started with Margery as leader and Enid as her assistant, the balance of power would constantly shift as they learned from one another. In overcoming difficulties, and in sidestepping convention, they would realize their best selves. And what was more, they required of me that I wrote about them without stopping to think about whether people would like it, or whether I was a *proper* writer. The adventure was mine as much as theirs, and they demanded that I kept writing, even when I thought I couldn't do it, or was too tired, or not up to the job. (Can you imagine Mary Lobb giving up on a job?) I kept the postcard of her and May Morris with me all the time, and I now have it framed above my desk.

I love the way those two women stand together. I look at them and I think, Well aren't you great? Look, I want to say to my daughters, look what women can do. Look what friendship can do. I love the way that Mary stands square to the camera, her legs apart, one hand in her pocket, wearing her jodhpurs and button-up jacket. I love her big dark curly hair, her unapologetic stance with the camera. I love the way May, thinner and older and looking more frail, gazes off to the side, wearing a thick striped skirt (has she taken up the hem?) and a long rope of beads and a patterned jumper. I love the fact they do not have to look at one another because their love is a given. I love the way that Mary holds her cigarette in a no-nonsense way like a pencil stub, while May holds hers as if it were a champagne glass.

But most of all, I love the way that standing beside Mary allows May to become a little more ethereal, a little more *May*, and the way that standing beside May makes Mary a little more solid. It is in measuring themselves against one another and acknowledging their differences that these two women discover who they truly are. And this is what I took to my novel in the end: The truest friendships are those that allow us to step out of the confines of what we once were, and to realize instead what we might be.

So, were Mary Lobb and May Morris the two women I sensed close to me all those years ago? It's a beautiful thought. And certainly, when I saw their photo, I felt I knew them. Was the clairvoyant right?

Were there actually two spirits who had a message for me? Or was the book I finally wrote just a very long time coming?

Ideas happen in many ways, and so do stories. The word "inspiration" is from the Latin *inspire*—to draw breath. What I believe happened when I first realized I was being followed was that somewhere inside me I knew I needed to write a book about female friendship; the love between women that extends beyond boundaries. Those women were with me all the time that I was bringing up my four children, reminding me that there would come a time when my children would leave home and begin their independent lives, and after that it would be time for me to be brave, to look deep into myself for my sense of self-worth, and not demand that from my children. Moreover, they told me that the relationships which would sustain me post-children were those I had forged long ago with other women. A book can require you to write it, without necessarily being so good as to inform you what it actually is.

The other day I got into my car and there were old sweet wrappers everywhere, not to mention dog hairs and cigarette ends. And I swear I could finally see them, full on and three-dimensional. I could see them squashed in the backseat of my car, smelling of violets and cigarettes, old wool and a touch of paraffin. Mary Lobb and May Morris, my aunts Gwen and Edith, Miss Kessler and Miss Hudson, Margery Benson and Enid Pretty.

Oh and what a glorious racket we made.

QUESTIONS AND TOPICS
FOR DISCUSSION

1. How do the various members of Margery's family—her father, her mother, her aunts, Barbara—inform who she is as a person? What values and beliefs do they give her, either good or bad?
2. How do Margery's core beliefs change throughout the novel?
3. When Margery stole the boots, what was your initial reaction? What do you think the boots represent to Margery throughout the novel?
4. How does Margery and Enid's relationship evolve over the course of the novel? How do they complement each other as characters? What do they learn from each other?
5. Why do you think Mr. Mundic fixated on Margery to the point that he followed her to New Caledonia? What does the journey mean to him? Are there any similarities Margery and Mundic share as characters?
6. How did you envision Margery's helmet, which had its own presence in most scenes of the book? What does it represent to you?
7. What characters did you find yourself identifying with? Are you more aligned with Margery or Enid in personality?
8. Do you think Freya will actually go to New Caledonia? What about Margery and Gloria's story do you think inspired her?
9. What does the golden beetle mean to Margery? Do you have a "golden beetle" in your own life? If so, what is it and what does it mean to you?
10. What did you think was going to be in the red valise? Were you surprised when it was finally opened?

ABOUT THE AUTHOR

RACHEL JOYCE is the author of the *Sunday Times* and international bestsellers *The Unlikely Pilgrimage of Harold Fry, Perfect, The Love Song of Miss Queenie Hennessy, The Music Shop,* and a collection of interlinked short stories, *A Snow Garden and Other Stories.* Her books have been translated into thirty-six languages, and two are in development for film. *The Unlikely Pilgrimage of Harold Fry* was short-listed for the Commonwealth Book Prize and long-listed for the Man Booker Prize. Joyce was awarded the Specsavers National Book Award for New Writer of the Year in December 2012 and was short-listed for the UK Author of the Year in 2014. She has also written more than twenty original afternoon plays and adaptations of the classics for BBC Radio 4, including all of the Brontë novels. She moved to writing after a long career as an actor, performing leading roles for the Royal Shakespeare Company, the National Theatre, and Cheek by Jowl. She lives with her family in Gloucestershire, England.

rachel-joyce.co.uk
Facebook.com/RachelJoyceAuthor
Instagram: @rachelcjoyce